Praise for Lee Martin

Such a Life

"[Martin's] prose is carefully controlled, which is a welcome counter to the flash, drama, and broad comedy that mark noisier (and more factually suspect) memoirs.... Martin is an expert memoirist willing to explore every remembered utterance for emotional weight."

—*Kirkus Reviews*

"Both frank and compassionate, Martin's tales will entertain memoir readers as well as fans of his novels."

—*Booklist*

"Indeed, though his latest may be just one iteration of many possible tellings of his life, Martin's honest and well-paced prose makes the repeated attempts feel fresh, and most of all, worth it."

—*Publishers Weekly*

"Martin has, over a series of books in various genres, detailed a galaxy of remembrances that have largely revolved around his relationship with his father. Their tempestuous relationship provides the heat and the light for this new collection—heat generated from their years of conflict, and a light that shines on everything Martin does and has become. While this light can be unsparing (Martin doesn't shy away from detailing his own foibles), it also provides clarity and under-standing—all we can hope for in an essay collection."

—*Minneapolis Star Tribune*

"In vivid and lyrical prose, [Martin] explores the relationship be-tween childhood and the adult self. What is the connection between a first kiss and the adult demands of marriage? Between that first sensual awakening to language and the language of responsibility and commitment? Childless himself, Martin's quest to unite his past and present forces him to confront the fundamental issues of mortality and meaning with the largeness of his big, easily broken, but irrepressible Midwestern heart."

—Sue William Silverman, author of *Fearless Confessions: A Writer's Guide to Memoir*

"Rich with empathy, wisdom, and wry humor, each essay in this remarkable book rewards the reader with exquisitely captured detail and brilliant characterization. In *Such a Life*, Pulitzer Prize finalist Lee Martin proves once again that he is the consummate storyteller, no matter where he puts his talents. An extraordinary, unforgettable book."

—Dinty W. Moore, author of *Between Panic and Desire*

"At one point in Lee Martin's contemplative memoir, the narrator muses: 'I shake my head over all the things we can't say, all the secrets we carry around, all of us swollen with worry.… I've had to write this [book] to claim the whole, weighty truth of myself.' Throughout his tale, Martin does indeed articulate weighty truths, but he does so with such clarity that he reflects this truth-seeking light back on the reader. We find ourselves shaking our heads, mulling over our own secrets, and looking to Martin to help us find the language to speak them."

—Brenda Miller, author of *Season of the Body* and *Blessing of the Animals*

Break the Skin

"I was worried for these characters as I'd worry for my own friends. The women want normal things—connection, stability—but get in their own way of finding peaceful lives. I love reading about characters in Illinois, a place not often depicted in fiction. This is a suspenseful, engaging book."

—Alice Elliott Dark, author of *Think of England* and *In the Gloaming*

"Young and lovesick, Lee Martin's low-rent heroines live the stuff of country music. Earnest and innocent, they get caught up in trailerpark romances and what Alice Hoffman called practical magic. *Break the Skin* is a gossipy, rollicking Witches of Wal-Mart."

—Stewart O'Nan, author of *Emily, Alone* and *The Speed Queen*

"Mr. Martin is a top-notch craftsman...what is most remarkable about *Break the Skin* is its restrained tone and the author's generosity toward his very needy characters. His sympathies for them rarely seem to wane, even when they are harboring criminals, conjuring hexes, or plotting murder."

—*The New York Times*

"South of Scandinavia, there are fewer icicles and serial killers, but no lack of sinister intrigue. Pulitzer Prize finalist Lee Martin's latest, *Break the Skin*, is a Lucinda Williams ballad of a small-town love affair—a teenage dropout, a nameless stranger—gone horribly wrong."

—Vogue.com

"Small town, big secrets; we're in Lee Martin territory. Martin...gets the claustrophobia of small-town life just right. With their oh-what-might-have-been voices, these women win our hearts."

—*The Cleveland Plain Dealer*

"Disaffected teenager Laney has no one in the world but the older Delilah, whom she clings to like a raft. Then the police start asking Laney questions that link her to the sadder-but-wiser Miss Baby, who thinks she's finally found true love with a gentle man who can't remember his own name, and the story of a wrenching crime emerges. Martin has a following—he's won a passel of awards (e.g., Mary McCarthy Prize in Short Fiction), and *The Bright Forever* was a Pulitzer finalist—so maybe *Break the Skin* will break him out."

—*The Library Journal*

"Martin, whose kidnap novel *The Bright Forever* (2005) was a finalist for the 2006 Pulitzer Prize in fiction, expertly applies shades of James Cain–like noir to a modern story that might have been inspired by one of the Lucinda Williams songs on this book's soundtrack. Black magic, daughters cursed by the loss or absence of their fathers, post traumatic stress syndrome, small-town secrecy and lies, pre-teen voyeurism: Welcome to life 'on the other side of right thinking.' An intoxicating small-town thriller that quickly gets under your skin."

—*Kirkus Reviews*

"Carrying an almost archetypal resonance, this well-crafted tale of romantic desperation feels as sad and inevitable as an old murder ballad and should have an appeal beyond readers of serious fiction."

—*The Library Journal*

"What we really want from our summer reading is a chance to escape ourselves, to disappear for a while into the lives of other people. *Break the Skin* allows us to do that, while delivering a fast, suspenseful read."

—*Seattle Post-Intelligencer*

"The simple poetry of his language and the generous empathy Lee Martin has toward characters he refuses to judge make *Break the Skin* a deeply moving and cautionary tale for us all, wherever we come from and whoever we are."

—*The Anniston Star* (AL)

"There's murder and mayhem for the reader who hungers for that, but the reason this novel succeeds as entertainment is that the author treads lightly with the plot and constructs his characters—even the secondary players—with subtle feeling.... You will be moved by Lee Martin's writing. My guess is that you'll want to see what else he's written and read him again."

—*The Advocate* (Baton Rouge, LA)

River of Heaven

"Graceful, evocative."

—*Chicago Sun-Times*

"One, part domestic novel, one part confession, and one part thriller.... This novel is about the toll living takes on our skin and our soul."

—*Cleveland Plain Dealer*

"If you don't know Lee Martin, you should.... [*River of Heaven*] is a page-turner, both tender and tough, with real insight into how people live and breathe and love and worry."

—*Lincoln Journal Star*

"Intricately plotted...Martin is an able storyteller who doesn't need to resort to flashy verbal tricks to establish his credibility as a writer of literary fiction. In *River of Heaven*, he's created an accomplished and deeply satisfying work."

—*Bookpage*

"Martin crafts eloquent sentences."

—*Publishers Weekly*

"Lee Martin's portrait of Sam Brady, a man in fear of his life and crippled by it, lingers painfully and persuasively."

—Amy Bloom, author of *Away*

"Sam Brady, sixty-five, has kept a secret for half a century. 'We can't tell,' his brother decides for him, and Sam doesn't, but the cost of his silence has been profound. Few writers could unfold Sam's history with the grace and compassion of Lee Martin. *River of Heaven* is an unusual novel, wise and humane, a story of cowardice and courage and the tortuous passage between them."

—Kathryn Harrison

"In *River of Heaven*, Lee Martin has created that rare thing: a literary page-turner. This is a story about the corrosive power of a childhood secret, and the way our lives are shaped as much by what we withhold as what we reveal. An elegantly structured, powerful and original novel, full of heart."

—Dani Shapiro, author of *Black & White*

From Our House

"Martin has written a memoir to read slowly and savor.... Over the course of the memoir, Martin shows how he and his father learn to overcome their shame and control their rage. The honest and straightforward description of their relationship and their obvious affection for each other completely involve the reader. Highly recommended."

—*Library Journal*

"Martin's memoir evokes the secrecy of family violence and the isolation of growing up in a rural community.... This is a touching and honest portrayal of family life, violence, disappointment, and coming of age."

—*Booklist*

"A lyrical, finely wrought memoir of grief, pain, and joy."

—*Chicago Tribune*

"Wise and healing."

—*Publishers Weekly*

"A moving memoir that portrays the complexities that exist in many American families—equal parts frustration, anger, yearning, and tenacious familial love."

—*USA Today*

"A story of great pain, told with great dignity and remarkable forbearance.... Moves toward an ending filled with the presence of grace."

—Charles Baxter

The Bright Forever

Pulitzer Prize Finalist for Fiction, Book Sense Pick

"Well-crafted, a cleanly written, artful...page-turner."

—*San Francisco Chronicle*

"A deeply traditional novel, 'literary' in the old-fashioned sense.... Its overall tone is as soft and giving as one of Mom's old blankets."

—*Washington Post*

"[Martin] does a good, clean job of keeping the reader in suspense, which is the lifeblood of the literary thriller he has set out to write... Martin has real talent."

—*Chicago Tribune*

"Compelling...*The Bright Forever* is both harrowing and deeply felt.... The multiple life stories are seamlessly interwoven...the suspensefulness never dips.... [Brings] to mind Alice Sebold's talent for writing in a literary voice without airs."

—*New York Daily News*

"His prose is spare, his description efficient. Sometimes just a word can transport readers back to small-town America in the 1970s.... *The Bright Forever* is a modern morality play without preaching or scolding, told by characters who are neither wholly evil nor wholly innocent."

—*Columbus Dispatch*

"A harrowing novel filled with lonely misfits desperate for love, or at least tenderness."

—*The Oregonian*

"Remarkably beautiful, eloquent on the subject of love, on the beauty of purple martins…. Much of the power of Martin's novel comes from the uneasy sympathy he creates with his characters, who are all too recognizable, in their foibles and desires, as ourselves."

—*Raleigh News & Observer*

"Mesmerizing."

—*Evansville Courier and Press*

"[A] vividly nuanced portrayal of a small town in the heat of a troubled summer."

—*Newsweek* (International Edition)

"Captivating…Martin has created an exquisite page-turner…. *The Bright Forever* is a masterpiece in its own right. Readers will be entranced by the story from the get-go, and held until the end by a string of unnerving suspense and quiet disbelief."

—*Kings Features*

"Martin shifts back and forth in time, skillfully dropping clues, countering readers' expectations, and building tension. Combining elements of family fiction, psychological thriller, and small-town nostalgia, this book is written in lyrical prose that will engage readers of all types."

—*Library Journal*

"Rich details and raw emotion mix as Martin, in engaging the human desire to excavate the truth, underscores its complex, elusive nature."

—*Publishers Weekly*

"Gripping…mesmerizing…Martin's novel is hard to put down."

—*Booklist*

"Lee Martin's *The Bright Forever* goes deep into the mystery of being alive on this earth. Written in the clearest prose, working back and forth over its complex story, and told in the dark, desperate, vivid voices of its various speakers, it holds you spellbound to the end, to its final, sad revelations."

—Kent Haruf, author of *Eventide* and *Plainsong*

"I read Lee Martin's *The Bright Forever* in one sitting. I couldn't put it down. Part *Mystic River*, part *Winesburg, Ohio*, this harrowing and beautiful book is one of the most powerful novels I've read in years, and heralds the breakout of a remarkable talent."

—Bret Lott, author of *Jewel* and *A Song I Knew by Heart*

"Like *Winesburg, Ohio*, *The Bright Forever* captures, in alternating voices, the individual acts of desperation that lead to a community's sorrow. And, like Sherwood Anderson, Lee Martin is not happy to let guilt reside singularly or simply. This is a morally complex quilt, a page-turner that also insists on the reader's participation in moral contemplation."

—Antonya Nelson, author of *Female Trouble* and *Talking in Bed*

"With what consummate skill Lee Martin conjures up a small town in the grip of tragedy and how deftly he explores the way in which a casual remark, a brief kiss, a white lie can have the most terrible consequences. *The Bright Forever* is a remarkable and almost unbearably suspenseful novel."

—Margot Livesey, author of *Banishing Verona* and *Eva Moves the Furniture*

"*The Bright Forever* is ravishing.… Lee Martin's characters, dear readers, are us—riven and bedeviled, our souls gone grainy and rank, our hearts busted and beating heavily for love. We have Lee Martin to thank for having the moral courage—yes, an old-fashioned but rare virtue—to tell it to us plain."

—Lee K. Abbott, author of *Living After Midnight*

"*The Bright Forever* will get under your skin with its exquisite psychology and fine-tuned suspense. Lee Martin has created a world of aching beauty and terrible loss."

—Jean Thompson, author *City Boy* and *Wide Blue Yonder*

Turning Bones

"[A] lyrical, imaginative work.... [T]his ambitious work weaves together many strong, intriguing people, brought together by a skillful writer for a family reunion across time."

—*Publishers Weekly*

"Like the celebrants in Madagascar who practice the 'turning of bones' ritual—dancing with their ancestors' corpses—Lee Martin unearths his ancestors' stories and places them alongside his own, creating a dance of power and grace. *Turning Bones* is a skillful blending of lyrical prose, painstaking research, and well-wrought fiction that calls up the dead and wakes us, the living, into a freshly imagined world."

—Rebecca McClanahan, author of *The Riddle Song* and *Other Rememberings*

"A beautiful intertwining of memoir and personal historical fiction. In a thoughtful, contemplative way, Martin works like his own private detective to make sense of his family and his place in the larger world."

—Mary Swander, author of *Out of This World: A Journey of Healing*

"A moving family history and cultural excavation."

—*The Virginia Quarterly Review*

"Lee Martin animates his family tree with a variety and vibrancy of stunning prose engines. Rarely are story and history so effortlessly and enjoyably entwined. Rarer still is this hybrid fruit of the said intersection. *Turning Bones* is a miraculous and many-splendored invention."

—Michael Martone, author of *The Blue Guide to Indiana*

"*Turning Bones* epitomizes creative nonfiction at its best, fusing the deep, seasonal rhythms of lyric poetry and a believable story which, like a great novel, brings wisdom and tears."

—Jonathan Holden, author of *Guns and Boyhood in America: A Memoir of Growing Up in the 50s*

"Martin brings his forebears to life with affection and empathy, brilliantly interweaving their stories with his own, and leaving us with a greater appreciation that our lives are but a series of intersecting tales, ones that, with luck, we add to and continue to tell."

—Kathleen Finneran, author of *The Tender Land: A Family Love Story*

"*Turning Bones* is part memoir, part epic, and part historical fiction. Lee Martin weaves creative technique, research, and personal essay together beautifully, shedding light on history and teaching the reader something new about not only America's maturation, but about modern life as well.... It's a book like this that makes you realize you've come from somewhere real and tangible, and that those places and people are a part of you and will be a part of many generations to come."

—J. Albin Larson, *Mid-American Review*

"Through white space, Martin guides readers through his tale of his family's past, as well as his own, in a captivating tale of love, heartbreak, and redemption."

—*Ashlee Clark, Ohioana Quarterly*

Quakertown

"A consistently impressive and often dazzling new novel. Lee Martin has written one of the best books of the year."

—*The Washington Post*

"Exceptional. Martin has done just about everything right. His writing is both lyrical and precise. His plotting is razor-sharp, unpredictable, and calculated for maximum suspense. His characters are vividly alive. Quakertown is an important addition to the literature of black America, and to that of Texas in the twentieth century."

—*Fort Worth Star Telegram*

"[Martin] can take your breath away."

—*Chicago Tribune*

"Lee Martin's brilliant first novel...*Quakertown* deserves a wide audience."

—*Portland Oregonian*

The Least You Need to Know

*Winner of the 1995 Mary McCarthy Prize in Short Fiction,
selected by Amy Bloom*

"Together, the pieces make for a hauntingly coherent first collection, often about pitiful family scenarios in which loyalties are tested, lies offered and exposed, and in which ironies abound.... Bleak, Midwestern landscapes well serve many of these stark and solid narratives."

—*Kirkus Reviews*

"Most of the stories in this debut collection revolve around the relationship between teenage sons and their fathers in the Midwest of the 1950s and '60s. Although Lee Martin favors endings in which the young protagonist's world is shattered by a selfish paternal act, he manages to infuse each of these similar situations with its own particular twist.... What (his characters) learn...is just how easily a life can come apart."

—*The New York Times Book Review*

"These are beautifully written stories of violence, fathers and sons, and the large and small improvisations that make up American life. Lee Martin's is a very impressive first collection."

—Lorrie Moore, author of *A Gate at the Stairs*

"Martin's work resists the pull of shiny look-at-me prose.... Martin wants to tell the story. He wants us to know everyone and give them a chance, to understand what is happening, even as we are shaking our heads at how appalling, how lame, how stupid, how vulnerable we all are."

—From the Foreword by Amy Bloom

Late One Night

Late One Night

a novel

Lee Martin

DZANC
BOOKS

DZANC BOOKS

5220 Dexter Ann Arbor Rd.
Ann Arbor, MI 48103
www.dzancbooks.org

Library of Congress Cataloging-in-Publication Data

Names: Martin, Lee, 1955- author.
Title: Late one night : a novel / by Lee Martin.
Description: Ann Arbor, MI : Dzanc Books, [2016]
Identifiers: LCCN 2015040872 | ISBN 9781938103490 (hardback)
Subjects: | BISAC: FICTION / Literary. | FICTION / Thrillers. | FICTION / Crime. | GSAFD: Suspense fiction.
Classification: LCC PS3563.A724927 L38 2016 | DDC 813/.54--dc23

First US edition: May 2016
ISBN: 978-1-938103-49-0
Book design by Michelle Dotter

Printed in the United States of America

10   9   8   7   6   5   4   3   2   1

For Cathy

Silently, one by one, in the infinite meadows of heaven,
Blossomed the lovely stars, the forget-me-nots of the angels.

—Henry Wadsworth Longfellow

1

Ronnie swore it was talk and nothing more. Jesus. Just the hasty words of folks eager to blame someone. They'd wanted answers ever since the news first broke and then traveled across the southern part of Illinois and as far north as Chicago, where the AP wire service picked it up and sent it all over the country. News from a house trailer along a blacktop road ten miles east of Goldengate in the dark of a winter's night. News the like you'd never want to hear if you could help it.

"You really think I could do something like that?" Ronnie said to the sheriff, Ray Biggs. "You think I'm that kind?"

Biggs was a tall man with dark hair that came to a widow's peak. He squinted his eyes, the worry crease above the bridge of his nose furrowing into his brow. "Motive and opportunity." He slapped his hand down on the table twice, the heavy gold band of his Masonic ring making a sharp clacking noise. "Doesn't take a blind man to see you had both."

Ronnie watched out the window as snow fell on the courthouse lawn. Half rain, with just enough snow mixed in to add to the cover already on the ground. Through the bare limbs of the giant oaks, he looked down onto State Street. Lights were on in the windows of the J.C. Penney store, and the Mi Casita Mexican restaurant, and the Reasoner Insurance Agency. A man came out of Penney's, a blue scarf wrapped around his face, his shoulders hunched up against the frigid air. He leaned into the wind as he hurried down the sidewalk. Ronnie wished he could be that man, making his way through the cold, making his way home to his family.

"You better start talking." Biggs leaned back in his chair. "You better tell me something I'll believe."

"So it's a story you want?" Ronnie kept staring out the window, thinking how pretty that snow was on the grass and the boughs of the evergreen trees on the courthouse lawn.

"A true story," Biggs said. "A story so real it'll save you. A story as real as that."

2

Della and the kids—the oldest fourteen, the youngest still a baby—lived in a trailer just south of the Bethlehem corner. Lived there by themselves because late in September, Ronnie moved out and took up living in town with his girlfriend, Brandi Tate. For a while, it was the talk all around Goldengate and out the blacktop to the farms and the shotgun houses and the trailer homes. All that autumn and up through Thanksgiving, folks spoke of it at Read's IGA, Inyart's Sundries, Johnstone's Hardware, the First National Bank, the Real McCoy Café: Ronnie Black had walked out on Della and all those kids.

It was ten thirty on a bitterly cold night in January when Missy Wade, Della's neighbor, looked out her bedroom window and could hardly believe what she saw.

The trailer was on fire.

Missy and her husband, Pat, lived a hundred yards to the west of Della, a barren cornfield between them. It was mostly open land out there. The flat fields stretched back to thin bands of woodland. That night, there was snow cover on the fields and the temperature had gone down below zero. Across the road from Della's, a pole light lit up Shooter Rowe's barnyard and the square, low-roofed ranch house where he lived with his son. Missy saw them running toward the trailer: Shooter and Wesley, the simpleminded boy everyone called Captain.

Pat was already asleep, and Missy shook him hard. The phone was in her hand, and she was calling 911.

"Wake up," she said. "Pat, wake up. Della's trailer's on fire."

Pat was up in a snap, throwing on the Carhartt overalls he'd left draped over a chair, pushing his feet into boots, grabbing a coat, and then running out into the cold night, running up the blacktop, his heart beating hard, the frigid air stinging his nostrils and pushing an ache into his throat and chest.

Shooter was already at the trailer. The front door stood open, and his bulk nearly filled it, his broad back and shoulders, his height, the mane of his long silver hair. When Pat got there, he saw that Della was handing out one of the twins. The little girl was in a white sleep shirt, and Shooter held her and turned to Pat with the most helpless look on his face, as if he wasn't sure what to do with this bare-legged, barefoot girl.

Captain stepped up. He was nearly as tall as his father, a sixteen-year-old boy whose body was growing into manhood. Without a word, he took the girl from Shooter and handed her to the oldest girl, Angel, who was in sweatpants and a T-shirt. Hannah, the next in line, was there too, a wild look in her eyes, her face red from the heat of the fire.

Pat counted in his head—three kids safe and four more still inside.

The air stank of burning plastic and fiberglass insulation and melting vinyl. It all popped and crackled. The roof was starting to go.

"Oh, good Lord," Shooter said.

He started to go into the trailer, but then Della was back. This time she had Sarah, the one born a few years after Hannah. Della handed Sarah out to Shooter, and he gave her to Pat. She clung to his neck, and he could smell the smoke on her, could feel the heat from her body.

Off in the distance, the sirens from the first fire trucks grew louder.

"You better get out of there," Shooter yelled.

Della shook her head. "I'm going back for Emily." So the first twin had been Emma. Pat would tell Missy later that Della was calm. She wasn't panicked at all. "I'm going to get Emily and Gracie and Junior," she said. "I'm going to get them all out."

3

Earlier that evening she'd scooped the hot ashes from the Franklin stove into a cardboard box. She was burning wood in the stove because the wall furnace had been cutting out. She couldn't have that, not with the baby, Junior, sick with the croup.

Her parents dropped by around suppertime, carrying in hot dogs and buns and bags of potato chips, and after they ate, her father, Wayne, gave the furnace a check. Slowed by age, he still did a few home repairs and small jobs here and there, but nothing to count for anything. Wayne Best used to be able to go longer than the day itself, folks said, but now he had tremors in his fingers and sometimes dizzy spells that knocked him flat. He was a lean man who kept his white hair cut in a flattop. He had a white moustache that his wife, Lois, kept neatly trimmed.

"Your pilot light's out," he told Della.

He relit it, the match flame wavering in his unsteady hand, and after a while he said everything seemed to be working fine.

"Maybe you should gather up the kids and come spend the night at our place," Lois said. "Just to be on the safe side. Weather on the radio said we might get down to ten below."

"Daddy's got the furnace running." Della was too tired to think about all it would take to get the kids bundled up, and pajamas and things gathered, and then over to her parents' house. "I'll keep the Franklin stove burning just in case."

Wayne helped Lois on with her coat. She was a heavy woman with a knee that needed to be replaced. A round-faced woman with deep lines around her eyes and on her forehead from her tendency to worry things to death. She took Wayne's arm and they started for the door.

"Better pull your car into the garage." Wayne opened the door and the cold air came rushing in around Della's legs. "Save your battery."

The garage sat at the end of the short lane that ran alongside the trailer. Since Ronnie had left her back in the fall, she'd never had a thought of putting her car in the garage, which had always been for the Firebird he'd restored. It was easier now for her to leave her Ford in the lane.

"I will, Daddy," she said. "Be careful on those steps. They're icy."

The wind was up now, out of the north, sweeping across the flat land. Lois and Wayne leaned into that wind. Wayne opened the passenger-side door and helped Lois up. He tucked the hem of her long coat into the truck and then closed the door. He turned back to the trailer and gave Della a wave. She waved back. Then she stood there in the cold as Wayne got behind the wheel, backed out onto the blacktop, and set out for home.

After they were gone, Della asked Angel to carry the box of hot ashes out to the compost pile when she went to feed the goats the girls kept for their 4-H project. Five Nubian goats—two nannies with long floppy ears, two kids stubbing around on their short legs, and the billy with his horns curved back over his head.

"It's Hannah's turn to feed," Angel said. She was fourteen and strongheaded, a girl with light blue eyes that went icy when she cut them at someone who'd rubbed her the wrong way. Her blond hair fell across her forehead, and she swept it back with a jerk of her arm.

"I just went out for more wood," said Hannah. How rare it was for her to put up a fuss. She was twelve, the dependable one, the obedient one—a Sunday's child, bonnie and blithe and good and gay. Her hair was in a neatly wrapped braid.

"Mom?" said Angel. Della just stared at her until finally Angel said, "Whatever."

But then *American Idol* came on TV, and the girls settled in. Even Della watched. She liked the reality shows like *Idol* and *Dancing with the Stars*. Everyone always looked so glamorous, and for at least a while, she could ignore the mess of her own life.

The twins, Emma and Emily, were six, just old enough to be excited when their older sisters were. Sarah, the forgetful one, was nine, and Gracie, a pistol and a scold, was three. Junior was just barely a year. Della's family. Hunkered down in their trailer on a cold winter night.

After the show was over, the phone rang, and it was Lois calling to see whether Della had put her car in the garage. "Your daddy wants to know."

"Tell him I've taken care of it," Della said, and then, after she was off the phone, she put on a coat and went out to make good on her word.

What little was left of the evening whirled by in a tangle of voices, the music of her children rising and then gradually falling as they got ready for bed, slipped between the covers, and drifted off to sleep.

Della was so tired. She was flat worn out. So tired that when she took one last trip through the living room, switching off lights, and saw the cardboard box of ashes still by the Franklin stove, she couldn't bring herself to wake up Angel and tell her to finish her chore. Nor did Della feel like getting her coat back on to haul the ashes out to the compost. She opened up the back door and set the box outside on the wooden stoop. The wind was still up, and she shivered as she closed the door.

Just then, the phone rang. She didn't recognize the number on the caller ID, so she let it ring and ring. She was too worn out to talk to someone anyway. What a day it had been—all the houses she'd cleaned, and a run-in with Ronnie to boot.

She put another log in the Franklin stove.

"Who was on the phone?" Angel called to her as she passed by in the hallway.

"Wrong number."

She went into her bedroom, where she checked on the baby and then lay down and quickly fell asleep, not giving that call a second thought.

In town, Ronnie hung up the payphone at the Casey's convenience store and got in his Firebird. He had a five-gallon can of gasoline on the seat beside him, and he knew the way out the blacktop, knew it by heart.

4

Della, nor anyone else for that matter, had any way of knowing that a few weeks before the fire, Shooter had forced himself to go through more of his wife's things, a task he'd been doing a little at a time since she died back in the spring. All that was left were a few boxes still in her closet, just a few cardboard boxes that held who knew what and then it'd all be over, nothing more to do but take care of Captain. And that was turning into a full-time job and then some.

Shooter sat on the floor outside the closet and opened the first of the three boxes that he'd eyed throughout the summer and autumn and into December, putting off the moment when he'd open them, trying to make his chore last as long as he could, dreading the time when it'd be done and the ache of Merlene's absence would settle around him with a completeness he feared would bring him to his knees.

The box was full of photographs, some of them as old as Merlene's girlhood. Little girl with her hair in braids and a calico cat squirming in her arms. Teenage girl in her high school graduation gown, a pair of white pumps on her feet. Pictures of her and Shooter when they were young and just starting out. Merlene was such a tiny thing next to his bulk.

In one picture, she stood in their kitchen archway, turned sideways so the swell of her stomach showed. She was pregnant with

Captain, and looking at that picture Shooter felt his throat close, overcome as he was with what it'd felt like to be that young couple expecting their first baby, thrilled and in love. Then he'd come, Wesley, and Shooter hadn't known what to do with him, had been afraid to hold him, had little by little slipped away from him and Merlene, and now here he was, the one left to do right by their son.

The second box had mementos in it: Captain's storybooks from when he was a kid, drawings he'd done, cards he'd made for Merlene on Mother's Day. Some of Merlene's favorite books were there, too, like *The Diary of Anne Frank*. Shooter leafed through its pages, and to his surprise a snapshot fell out. A shot of Ronnie sitting inside Shooter's house, sitting backwards astraddle a ladder back chair, his hands folded on the top slat, his chin resting on top of them, his eyes closed.

At ease.

The words popped into Shooter's head. It was plain that Ronnie was content to be where he was. At peace. It came to Shooter, then, that Merlene had taken that picture—he couldn't remember ever having seen it—and had kept it back so she could look at it any time she chose.

"He's trouble," she said about Ronnie once. Shooter had never forgotten it. "But he's got a sweetness about him. Sweet like a little boy."

Shooter scoffed at that. Ronnie was just mean and tricky enough to do some damage if the punching and gouging got going. He had a tattoo on the back of his neck, BAD MOON. Shooter knew enough of his history—orphaned young and farmed out to one foster home after another—to make him believe it was true; he'd been born under a bad moon on the rise.

Now, looking at that picture, Shooter wondered for a moment whether Merlene had been more smitten with Ronnie than Shooter had ever known. Something about that photo nestled there with all those family pictures—when in the world would Merlene have taken it, sometime when she and Ronnie were alone in the house?—pricked at Shooter and led him to imagine things he'd be ashamed to admit.

Just his mind running away with him, he thought. Just nonsense. Nothing more than that. Merlene had thought the world of him. She'd never have done anything to be ashamed of, and particularly not with the likes of Ronnie.

Then Shooter opened a blue stationery box. He remembered buying it for Merlene one year for Christmas. Oh, how she loved that stationery, each sheet embossed with her monogram. "Now, that's fancy," she said when she opened it, and she held up a single sheet and traced her finger over the M, and the R, and the E. Merlene Elizabeth Rowe. "My, my, my," she said. "It's fit for a queen."

A few sheets still remained, three to be exact. Shooter plucked them from the box and held them to his nose. He swore he could still smell a faint scent of Merlene's perfume, White Shoulders, but then he thought it was just his imagination. When he went to put the sheets back in the box, he noticed a piece of gray cardboard, cut to fit, snugged into the corners. He ran his finger over it and felt the outline of something in the shape of a rectangle. He pried at the corner of the cardboard with his fingernail and finally got it so he could pull it free.

Underneath that piece of cardboard was an envelope, nothing written on the outside of it, no stamp or postmark, just a plain white envelope. Inside was a greeting card with two blue flowers on the cover. Forget-me-nots, Shooter knew, because it was Merlene's favorite flower.

Apparently someone else had known that, too.

Shooter opened the card and read the printed verse:

Just wanted to let you know
That I am thinking about you!

Below it, Ronnie had written a personal message:

M., we both know Captain is a gift,
a forget-me-not of the angels, like you always say.
Some people just can't see that. Shame on them.
Don't let Shooter get you down—♥, R

That exclamation point, that heart. The fact that she'd saved the card and secreted it away. That snapshot. What was Shooter to make of all that except that in her heart of hearts she'd wished for a different sort of husband, had harbored a crush on Ronnie, had told him things meant to stay inside their house.

Shooter tore the card in half and then tore it again. He kept tearing at it, realizing, finally, that he was making grunting, animal sounds, keening cries coming from a place deep inside him where he felt betrayed.

It was then, though he wouldn't be aware of it until later, that he began to build an idea—it would come into focus a little at a time—that he would find a way to hurt Ronnie, a way to make him wish he'd never given Merlene that card, never said those things, never opened the door to this rage in Shooter, a rage he wasn't sure he could stop, even though he was afraid of where it might take him.

5

The trouble between Ronnie and Della came to a head one evening in early September when she showed up at a Kiwanis Club pancake supper with her long blond hair hacked off and ragged, tufts of it sticking out from her head and hanks hanging down along her slender neck. Lord God. It was a sight. Like someone had taken a knife blade to her hair and sawed and hacked until the job was done. That's right. Della Black. Walked into the grade school cafeteria as big as day.

"How you like my new hairdo?" she asked of no one in particular.

Just stood there in the middle of the cafeteria, blue jeans too big on her skinny hips, a chambray work shirt, sleeves rolled to her elbows. She turned this way and that like a fashion model. Even put a hand to her head and gave a hank of hair a little fluff.

No one said a word. Everyone was sitting at the cafeteria tables, where only moments before they'd been talking about crop prices, and Lord couldn't we use some rain, and hell, yes, it was hot. Too hot for September. That was for damned sure. It was just now coming on dusk, and the cafeteria lights were on. Della stood there in that fluorescent light, and everyone shut up so for a while there was only the sound of pancakes on the griddle in the kitchen and the cash drawer on the register going shut.

Then a single low voice—a woman's voice—said, "It's got something to do with Ronnie. I'll wager you that."

The woman was Laverne Ott, who had taught Della in grade school. Now Laverne was a caseworker for Children's Protective Services. She knew trouble when she saw it.

She came down the center aisle and put her hand to Della's face. Washed out and not a lick of makeup. "Oh, honey," she said, "where are your kids? They're not with Ronnie, are they?"

Della shook her head. "They're with my mom and dad." She raised her hand to her head. Her fingers were trembling. She touched her hair, patting the tufts. "Stylish," she said. "Don't you think?"

Laverne leaned in close and whispered, "Did Ronnie do this to you?"

"Why Miss Ott," Della said, "why in the world would you think that?"

Laverne thought it for the same reason so many others were thinking it. Ronnie Black had a temper, and he'd used it in the past to cause misery for Della. Lord knows, he'd had his brushes with the law—accusations of stolen gasoline from farmers' tanks, domestic disturbances in the middle of the night, bar fights—but nothing that ever landed him in a jail or a courtroom. He was that kind of man, troubled in the heart and full of fight. Pissed off at his life because he couldn't manage to hold down a job, and there were all those kids—yes, seven of them—and folks had witnessed more than one tussle and throwdown between Della and Ronnie out in public.

He'd left her stranded in Goldengate one night when they got in a snort and holler because she wanted to buy a doll baby for their littlest girl and he said there wasn't money enough for something extra like that. Right there in Inyart's Sundries, Della told him there'd be more money if he could do a better job of providing it.

"The way I see it," she said, "it's my money anyway since I made it from cleaning houses. I'll spend it however I please."

All right then, he told her. She could just walk home if that's the way she wanted it. And with that he stormed out of the store.

She was a few miles up the blacktop in the gathering dark when Missy saw her and stopped to give her a ride. Della had been friends with Missy and Pat ever since grade school and thought so much of them that she'd made them godparents of all her kids. Missy had always been such a dainty girl, with her dark hair and her brown eyes, and though she'd grown to be a beautiful woman, the years had put enough vinegar in her to make her say exactly what she thought.

"I don't know why you put up with that man," she said to Della once she'd heard the story of the fight. "I really don't."

Della turned away from Missy, and her voice, when she finally spoke, was the soft voice of a woman who was embarrassed but determined to speak the truth. "Well, we're a family. That's what we are. I know it might not seem like it all the time, but we're who we have and that counts for something, doesn't it?"

"I guess it's up to you to decide if it counts enough," Missy said.

Said Della, "I've been married so long. I wouldn't know myself without Ronnie."

6

In his heart Ronnie often felt all scraped out and empty over the way his life with Della was—too much want, too much lack, too much desire running up against the no-way-in-hell of it all. The truth was he'd loved Della once and loved her hard and still could from time to time when there came a snatch of breath in the suffocation of trying to provide for her and all those kids. Sure, she'd told everyone that it was him who'd wanted to keep trying until they had a boy, but Ronnie would tell them, if they'd ever listen, that it was Della who kept wanting to get pregnant. "I just love 'em to death," she kept saying. "Ronnie, I love having a baby in the house."

"We can't go on like this," he told her in the summer when he was having trouble finding construction work—the work was there, but he'd proven himself too unreliable in the past for contractors to take a chance on him—and it was getting harder and harder to feed everyone. "We just can't, Della. We've got to stop. You've got to get back on the pill. We just can't be having any more babies. Do you understand?"

She nodded her head, but he made her say it.

"Do you, Della?"

"You're right," she said. "We need to do better looking after the ones we've got."

So Ronnie thought they had an understanding. Each morning he got up and went looking for work. The air was cool and there was dew on the grass and the birds were singing, and the day seemed full of promise. He'd find work, he told himself. Today would be the day. He'd find steady work, and he'd be a man who could make a good life for his family. He'd be the man he'd meant to be all along.

He knew what the neighbors surely thought of him each time Della locked him out of the trailer and they heard him banging on the door, heard him cussing on the step, heard him getting all teary-eyed and saying, "Aw, now come on, baby. Don't be like this."

Pat and Missy and Shooter and Captain knew too much about him, but not even they knew what happened before Della walked into that Kiwanis Club pancake supper. They didn't know that earlier that day, while she was in town cleaning houses, Ronnie hauled an old chair out the back door, setting it up against the trailer in the tall grass that he never quite got around to weed-eating. The chair's upholstery, a corduroy brown, had split open in a number of places and the foam stuffing stuck through. One of the legs had come off and disappeared. Just an old chair gone to ruin and no good to anyone. He thought maybe he'd carry it back to the burn barrel and light it up, but while hunting for a fresh box of Diamond matches inside the trailer, he found Della's birth control pill case in a drawer of the bathroom vanity.

Ordinarily, he wouldn't have thought a thing about that white case, but in light of the conversation he'd had with her he considered opening it just to make sure that she'd been keeping good to her word. But, no, that wouldn't be right. That wouldn't be trusting her. He closed the drawer and went on about his business, forgetting about that old chair and his plan to burn it.

He was alone in the trailer. The kids were with Della's folks while she worked in other people's houses.

His own house put him to shame—the tables heaped high with toys and clothes, the counters littered with unwashed plates and saucers, the sink full of pots and pans, and there on the sill of the window above that sink, a bud vase with a single silk rose in it, a hurtful reminder of a more orderly life.

As a boy he'd lived in enough foster homes that were cluttered and dirty and now he couldn't stand the reminder. He forgot about that old chair and instead started to clean. He did the dishes. He wiped down the counters. He picked up toys and carted them into the kids' rooms and put them where they were supposed to be. He vacuumed. He dusted. He folded laundry and put it away. All the while he was working, he remembered how nice Della had made the place in the beginning before there were all the kids. He remembered how they'd started out, full of hope, drunk on love. Recalling all that made him feel a misery born from the fact that so much had changed.

He went into the bathroom to clean there and he opened that vanity drawer again and took out the case that held Della's birth control pills. He stared at it a long time before he worked up the nerve to open it.

"My, oh my, oh my," Della said when she came home and saw how Ronnie had cleaned. "Mercy, what a surprise."

He was sitting on the kitchen counter, twirling a matchstick between his fingers. He'd finally found a box in the pocket of a flannel shirt hanging in his closet. He was swinging his legs and drumming the heels of his boots against the cabinet.

"Don't do that," Della said. "You'll leave scuff marks." He kept swinging his legs. He wouldn't look at her. "Ronnie, I said don't."

She walked over to him and pressed her hands down on his knees to make him stop.

That's when he grabbed her hair, wound the long blond hair up in his fist and jerked her head over close to his face. She smelled like

bleach and furniture polish. She grimaced and he watched the lines
fan out from the corners of her eyes.

"You think I'm a fool," he said.

"That hurts, Ronnie." She tried to tug away from him, but he
held fast. "I mean it."

He let go of her hair and shoved her away. "We had a deal, Della."

"I don't know what you're talking about."

"Those pills."

She looked away from him. She bit her lower lip.

He said, "Jesus, you haven't been taking a one."

She put her hands on her hips. She stomped her foot on the floor
so hard he felt a little vibration come up through the cabinet and into
the backs of his thighs.

"You think you can just snoop into my things any time you
want?" she said. "Some things are private."

He stopped swinging his legs. "We had a deal," he said again,
his tone even and measured. "Leastwise, that's what I thought we
had. Looks like you were just playing me." He took a matchstick and
pressed the head into the strike strip along the side of the box. He
held it there with the tip of his forefinger on his left hand. He curled
the forefinger of his right hand back against his thumb and held it
up to the middle of the matchstick as if he were going to flick it away
from him. It was a little trick he knew, one he used to pass the time
on occasion, just flicking that match out so it was lit when it took
to the air.

"How many kids do you want?" he asked.

"Don't you do it, Ronnie." She lifted her arm and pointed her
finger at him. "I mean it. Don't you light that match."

When it finally happened—when that lit match twirled out into
the air and landed on the floor at Della's feet—he couldn't say for
sure that he'd done it on purpose or whether the finger on his right

hand had uncoiled with no thought on his part. He only knew that once it was done he felt he had to do it again to keep himself from doing something worse. He was certain that Della had purposely lied about taking her pills because she wanted to have so many babies he'd never be able to leave her, wanted to fence him in so he'd never get out.

The thought of her deceit enraged him. Sure, he knew he'd been the one to deceive her first, but when she'd agreed to start taking her pills again, he'd told himself he'd stay. He'd forget this business with Brandi, and he'd stay and be a father to his children and a husband to Della. They'd start fresh.

That was out the window now. "How many do you want?" he said, and now he was vaguely aware, as she was, that he was talking about something other than babies. He flicked another lit match at her, and another, and then another. She put her hands up around her face because the matches were coming dangerously close to her now. He flicked another, and it hit her hand and she gave a yelp and jumped to the side. "How many, Della?"

The last match went tumbling over her head.

"That's enough, Ronnie." She was crying now. "No more."

The misery in her voice caught him by the throat and squeezed. He jumped down from the counter and went to her. He put his arms around her shoulders, raised one hand to pet her hair.

That's when he felt the heat. The last match had lodged in Della's hair and started to burn. The stink was all around them now.

"Oh, good Lord," she said, swatting at her head. "Look what you've done."

He got the fire out by beating at it with his hand. He felt the burn on his fingers.

She jumped back, holding her hands to her head. "Don't touch me. Not now. Not after what you just did."

"What *I* just did?" He balled his hands up into fists. "Damn it, Della, you made a promise to me."

"Promises, promises," she said. "I've seen the way you look at that Brandi Tate." For a good while he didn't speak, and that was enough to tell Della that she'd struck a nerve, that what she'd never thought was possible now just might be, that there was something going on between Ronnie and Brandi. "Oh, no," she said. "No."

He took her by the shoulders and gave her a shake. "Can't you see I'm trying?" he said.

"You're not trying enough. That's plain."

"Neither are you," he said.

"I'll never forgive you for that, Ronnie. Never. Do you understand?"

"Understand?" He gave her a little smirk and then a cut of his eyes that sent a chill through her. "Oh, I think I understand everything just fine," he said, and then he walked out.

"He looked like he could have killed me," Della said to Missy when she told the story of the matches. "Honestly. Like I wasn't nothing to him at all."

She had to take the scissors to her hair, to cut out that little burned patch. If she did it just right, she thought, she wouldn't have to cut much at all. But looking at herself in the mirror and thinking about how worn down she looked—nothing like Brandi Tate at all—she grabbed a large bunch of hair and sawed away at it until it was cut. She kept going, her hands trembling. Cutting and cutting. Sometimes so close that she nicked her white scalp. She left some of the hair long. She made herself as ugly as she could, as ugly as Ronnie must have thought she was. Good thing the kids were with her folks so she could have time alone to do this thing.

And once it was done, she got into her old gray Ford, the one with the passenger door caved in and the tailpipe hanging loose, and she drove into Goldengate. She walked into that pancake supper. She said as big as she could, "How you like my new hairdo?" And she let all those people think what they were going to think, the same thing that Laverne swore was true—Ronnie had done her wrong, had treated her no better than he would an old mangy dog, and then set her out to find her way.

At the time all this was happening, Ronnie was driving out to the river, to an old fishing camp, and with him was Brandi Tate. She was listening to his story.

"The woman's crazy," he told her. The next day, he'd start to hear the talk around town about what he was supposed to have done to Della's hair, and he'd know he'd made the right decision to stay at Brandi's that night and not go home, not to go back to Della who was telling such a lie on him, not to go back to a woman who would hack at her hair that way and then let people believe he'd been the one to do it.

"Sugar," Brandi said, "you've got to get out of that mess."

And Ronnie stayed with her, stayed as autumn stretched on to the first frost, and then the killing frost, and then the dark, damp days of November.

7

By Thanksgiving, Della's hair was growing back. Even though she'd gone to the Looking Glass Salon to have it shaped up, there was still a bald spot on the side of her head that was hard to cover. Her mother caught sight of it when Della brought the kids over for dinner.

"Mercy," she said. "I don't know how you can stand to show your face around town, what with Ronnie shacked up with that girl."

Della gave a little wave of her hand. She was trying to be tough-minded about it all. "Oh, these are modern times," she told her mother. "People don't think a thing about something like this."

But she heard the talk, felt the eyes on her as November turned into December and she went about her business cleaning houses for those who hired her. She took the kids to the Bethlehem Christian Church for Sunday School and to 4-H meetings at the fairgrounds. She kept her gaze steady, met everyone with a smile, looked them in the eye and said it was good to see them and that she hoped they'd have a Merry Christmas.

Then one morning Missy and Laverne Ott stopped by the trailer with a Christmas box from the church: a twenty-pound turkey, a ten-pound bag of potatoes, a head of cabbage, cans of Ocean Spray jellied cranberry sauce, Green Giant sweet peas, Bush's baked beans, a tray of dinner rolls, a box of Carnation powdered milk, frozen pie crusts and pumpkin filling, tangerines, ribbon candy, chocolate bars, peanuts in the shell.

Della looked through the box while Laverne and Missy went back to Missy's van to tote in gifts for all the kids: new winter coats, boots, mittens, and wrapped packages, one for each, seven in all.

"We could have stopped at five and had a basketball team," Della used to tell folks, "but we decided to keep rolling the dice and hit that lucky number seven."

She was thirty years old, and she'd been pregnant most of her life since she gave herself up to Ronnie at sixteen. She had six girls. Angel, Hannah, Sarah, the twins Emily and Emma, and then Gracie. In order, from age fourteen to three. All of them were fair-skinned like their mother, small-boned and blue-eyed, with fine hair the color of straw. Her girls. She'd taught them to love Jesus and to know what it was to work. They were good girls—even Angel, who had streaks of Ronnie's spit and vinegar. Della tried to be patient with her. Angel was fourteen, Della reminded herself, remembering that when she was that age Ronnie had started taking note of her. Fourteen and beginning to feel the charms she held for boys. Fourteen and sure of too many things. Whatever mistakes she'd made with Ronnie along the way, at least she had these beautiful children now, her treasures. Ronnie could run off to Brandi Tate and Della couldn't stop him, but her babies were hers, the joy of her life, and no one could take them from her.

She'd wished and wished for a boy, and finally just before last Christmas, he came along, Ronnie Jr. Ronnie was in heaven. He loved on that baby boy more than he'd ever loved on anyone in his life. You'd thought, folks said later, it would've been enough to keep him from Brandi Tate.

"You've got a brood," Laverne said as she brought the last of the Christmas gifts into the trailer. "I swear, Della. You really do."

Her glasses were steamed up from coming in out of the cold, and when she took them off, there was a hard set to her face. She'd never married, and now on the other side of sixty, she found herself alone. A broad-shouldered woman with big hands, the fingernails clipped straight across. She wore no makeup, nothing to give her thin lips any color or shape, nothing to enhance her pale gray eyes. Her only indulgence was her hair, which Della knew she darkened with Clairol Nice 'N Easy—Light Caramel Brown—Della had seen the empty box in Laverne's trash when she cleaned her house. Laverne kept her hair long and wore it in a braid that came down to the middle of her back. She took a handkerchief from her coat pocket and wiped her glasses. She put them back on and studied Della, who knew that she was well-acquainted with situations like hers—a woman left with all these kids—and even worse.

Della would think later that Laverne hadn't meant for what she said about her brood to sound like a judgment, but at the time Della heard it that way, just a smidge of resentment from having to be out in such vicious cold, toting boxes to a woman whose husband had left her to care for all those kids.

Missy patted Della on the arm. "We just want to make sure you and the kids have something for Christmas," she said. She knew that Ronnie had tried to bring presents, but Della turned them away because the money that bought them came from Brandi Tate. "You know I love them all to pieces," Missy said. "I always have."

Della tried her best not to be envious of Missy, but, gracious, just look at that new house Pat had built for her—a two-story house with dormer windows and gingerbread trim and fretwork on the wraparound porch. Della cleaned that house each week, and though she tried to stay a Christian woman, she couldn't quite press down the bad feeling that rose in her when she saw the already tidy house with hardly a speck of dirt that needed cleaning—nothing really that required Della's attention, but she dusted the furniture that already gleamed, wiped down the bathrooms where silk flowers in dainty vases sat on the counters and the towels were folded neatly over the rods, ran the vacuum over carpets that looked like no one had walked on them.

Della did all that because Missy paid her for her services, and she tried not to resent too much the fact that Missy could afford that charity. Della tried not to get all out of shape because the girls loved Missy so much. She always made such a fuss over them, bringing them little doodads, having them up to the house to roast marshmallows or color Easter eggs or trim the Christmas tree. It was enough to make Della think sometimes that the girls would be better off with someone like Missy for a mama, someone who could give them every little thing that they wanted and keep them loved and happy and safe. "You wouldn't want the mess of them for always," Della told her once, and Missy said, "Oh, Della, I'd give the world for just one baby to brighten my days."

"Well, it's just too much," Della said now, looking at the kitchen counters piled up with the groceries and the packages. "I don't know what to say."

Laverne had a jingle bell brooch pinned to the lapel of her coat, and it made a merry noise every time she moved. "Della, this is from the church. It's from the heart, honey. It's nothing more than what we want you to have."

"We know it's not been easy," said Missy. She had such black hair—such shiny, thick black hair falling over her collar—and Della had always envied it. How pretty Missy was with her red lipstick and her eyes so bright, her liner and shadow applied just so, her lashes stiff with mascara. The suede glove she was wearing was so soft on Della's arm. "We have to look out for one another. I know you'd do the same for me, if you could."

That was enough to set Della's teeth on edge. She turned away from Missy for a moment, fussing with some of the grocery sacks on the counter until she could compose her face.

"I take care of my kids," she finally said. She turned back to Missy and Laverne. She hoped her smile didn't show the strain she felt—how badly she wanted to tell both of them to take back everything they'd brought, but she couldn't. "There's not a thing in the world I wouldn't do for them."

"Della," Laverne said. "We know that's the Lord's truth, but there's no shame in accepting a little help now and then, especially the way that Ronnie's up and done. Everyone says it's a pity. We all feel sorry for you, honey."

That was enough to make up Della's mind. The way that Laverne and Missy made it plain that she was now gossip, someone people talked about, maybe felt badly for, maybe sat in judgment of, all because she was letting this mess with Ronnie and Brandi string along, all on the chance that one day he might come home. She'd forgive him everything. Forgive him for that episode with the matches, forgive him for falling for Brandi, and she'd ask him to forgive her for not taking her birth control pills and for the way she let the lie spread that he'd chopped off her hair.

They'd been kids together, Della and Ronnie. They'd been friends before they loved each other, and even now she felt a little crinkle in her heart, a heave and a flutter because she'd known him first and best. All of her adult life, she'd known him. Nothing would ever change that.

"Don't you remember who I am?" she asked him the night he came for his things.

He couldn't look at her. He stood at the trailer door, the last of his clothes on hangers hugged to his chest, and he bit his lip.

It was like she went rushing back through the years, trying to gather everything in: the way he sang in a low murmur beside her in church and she felt the vibration of his voice and she thought no matter what troubles they had there they were, together and safe; the lopsided birthday cake he baked for her one year; the way he said, "Della, oh Della" whenever he felt overwhelmed with whatever it was that kept them together so long; even all the times he'd done something stupid, like he was still sixteen, and then he'd come to her looking all hangdog, and she'd forgive him. She would have even forgiven him that night when he was about to leave if he'd only said he was sorry. She would have put her arms around him. She would have told him to stay. But when she asked him if he knew her and he finally looked at her with a stare that was flat and empty, like he wasn't looking at anyone who mattered to him, she knew that they were in more trouble than she'd first thought. "I have to go," he said, and then he did.

On Christmas Day, she asked her daddy for the loan of enough money to hire a lawyer. She asked him when the girls were out feeding the goats and her mama was napping in the reclining chair.

"I wouldn't ask if I had some other way," she said. "Daddy, I know this isn't how we'd want it."

It was all she could do to face him on account of she knew how badly she'd disappointed him when she was sixteen and pregnant. He'd stood by her, though. When everyone else was telling her to give the baby up for adoption and forget about Ronnie Black, her daddy said, "You do what you feel in your heart. Whatever that is, I'll be there to help you when I can."

"I can't hardly stand the way Ronnie's done you," he said.

"You coming down with a cold, Daddy?"

He cleared the hoarseness from his throat. "Come see your mama tomorrow. She can drive you in to the bank."

———

It was just after New Year's when she finally filed for divorce. She left the attorney's office in Phillipsport, intending to drive to her mama's to pick up Gracie and Ronnie Jr.—Angel and Hannah and Sarah and the twins were in school—but at the last minute she decided to drive to Goldengate. Her nerve surprised her, but she wanted to look Ronnie in the eye and tell him what she'd done.

She found Brandi's house on Locust Street, a one-story frame house with white clapboards and a porch, wide red ribbon wrapped around the posts, Christmas lights still hanging from the eaves. A house not much better than the trailer Ronnie had left out in the country. But it was quiet there, he'd told her back in October when he moved out, and maybe that's what he needed, he said, a little quiet.

He came to the door when Della knocked, and for a moment she almost lost her voice. Then she told him what she'd come to say.

"I'm looking you right in the eye, and I'm telling you, Ronnie. I'm not going to let this go on."

She told him she'd thought and thought on the matter, and if he was going to keep on with Brandi, then she didn't have much choice. She had to do what was right for her and the kids.

"You understand, don't you? I can't let you keep making a fool of me. I'm going to have to cut you loose and put an end to the two of us. I've been to see a lawyer."

The wind was blowing hard and there was Ronnie in jeans, but with no shirt and barefoot. He was standing in the doorway to Brandi's house, his bare chest white and hairless, goose pimples dotting his arms.

"Della? What about the kids? Those are our kids."

"Come back." She leaned in and whispered it. She was surprised at how little it took to make her want him. She could tell the lawyer she'd changed her mind. Her forehead rested just an instant on Ronnie's bare chest. She could feel how cold his skin was. "I mean it, Ronnie. Come back, and we'll be a family."

"Maybe," he said. "Maybe that could be true. Maybe you mean it this time about not having any more babies, and maybe you're sorry that you lied about me cutting your hair."

"I was just mad," she said.

He looked at her for a long while. "I need some time to think about it. You'd give me that if I asked you, wouldn't you?"

"I wouldn't give you forever."

He reached out and took her hand, held it just a little while the way he had when they first started out one night at a football game at the high school. "I'm not a good enough man for you."

Somewhere in the house, Brandi was calling for him. Della hadn't known she was there.

"Ronnie? Baby? You still out there talking?"

Already he was easing the door closed. "I'm letting the cold in," he said. "I'm sorry, Della."

Something about hearing Brandi call him baby and then seeing how he wanted to get back inside and pick up whatever the two of them had been doing made Della's mind up for good. "You're right." She'd let the divorce papers do what they were meant to do. Let Ronnie have what he wanted. Let him have Brandi Tate. "You're no kind of man," Della told him, an ache in her throat as she fought against the tears that were threatening to come. "No kind of man at all."

"Della," he said.

He reached out for her, but it was too late. She'd already turned to go, and she didn't look back. Not once. She'd said what she'd come to say and now it was done.

8

Ronnie drove out to the trailer to see her the day he got the papers, one of those gray winter days in southeastern Illinois when the sun, if it ever tries to come out, is just a watery light for a speck or two before it goes back behind the clouds. Corn stubble dusted with snow in the fallow fields. Bare branches of woodlands black against the sky. Smoke curling up from chimneys at farmhouses along the blacktop. Wind scattering snakes of powdery snow across the road.

Shooter told Missy later he saw Ronnie's car—that old Pontiac Firebird he'd bought on auction at a salvage yard and rebuilt and painted cherry red—sitting in the gravel lane alongside the trailer that afternoon.

"Captain spotted his car," Shooter said, "and he told me to come look."

Captain's head was filled with motors and cars. A good thing something was up there, folks said. Maybe he could make a mechanic someday. He hadn't come out of the oven right, they said, but Laverne Ott, who'd had him in school just before she retired, didn't care for that sort of talk, nor did she have patience for the other words—"special," "challenged," "developmentally disabled," and especially not the harsher ones like "dummy," "moron," "retard." To her, Captain was Captain. Child of God. A boy who was who he was. She asked no more of him and no less. Each night she said a prayer that he would find a place in the world, that people would be kind to him, that he would know love.

"You know he was always nuts about that Firebird," Shooter told Missy. "He stood at the front window and said, 'Sugar tits!' Forgive me for talking like that, but you remember how Ronnie always said that when something tickled his fancy. I guess Captain picked it up from him. I've tried to break him of it, but no luck. 'Ronnie's back,' he said. He wanted to go over there, but I told him, no, leave those folks alone. He put up a fuss. That's been his way ever since his mother died. Now he's getting more bullheaded every day. Just wants to do what he wants to do. I told him whatever was going on over there at the trailer wasn't any of our concern, and that was that."

Shooter tried to keep to himself, to live a quiet life on the other side of his wife's death. But on occasion, when he caught someone making fun of Captain, his temper got the best of him. He'd been known to use his fists, and on occasion to level his twelve-gauge. He'd gotten his nickname from that fact: high school kids come to toilet paper his trees and soap his windows, hunters trespassing on his posted land, meth cooks snooping around his anhydrous tanks? The word was out: *Look out for Carl Rowe; he's a shooter.*

"You can't be threatening people with guns," Biggs told him when such matters came to his attention.

"I'm not asking for trouble," Shooter said, "but I'm going to protect my property, and I'm sure as hell going to look out for my son."

So, yes, Shooter told Missy, he and Captain were watching out the window that winter day when Ronnie pulled his Firebird into the lane and got out.

Della heard the car door slam. She went to the trailer's front door, where she fingered the edge of a curtain panel and saw Ronnie looking her way. He had on a flannel shirt and an orange insulated vest. He took a breath and let it out, his steam hanging a moment in the frigid air.

She let the curtain fall back and waited.

He was taking in the sight of that trailer, remembering when he and Della had first moved there. The two of them, alone for a few months before Angel came, and then all the babies after her. Could he say for sure that he no longer loved Della? The divorce papers had made that a hard question to answer, hitting him, as they did, with the knowledge that what he'd thought he wanted might not be what he wanted at all. He'd come to Della's to talk it over with her.

In a snap, she heard his boots on the steps to the double-wide. Then his fist pounding on the door. She took a breath and opened it.

He started right in. What did she mean by having those papers served on him? What gave her the right to do something like that? To determine that they were done when he hadn't decided that at all?

"Jesus, Della. I just need some time to figure out what I want."

"Time's up, Ronnie. I'm telling you the same thing those papers are telling you. You walked out. You made a fool of me, and I'm not going to let that happen anymore."

"I want to see the kids."

"Ronnie, you know it's still school time."

"I want to see Gracie and Junior."

"Junior's asleep."

Gracie poked her head around Della's leg. Gracie with her chubby cheeks and her big gray eyes and her blond hair pinned up on her head with a pink clip in the shape of a star.

"Daddy, the goats been eating too much."

The girls kept them in a pen out behind the trailer. These cold days, the goats huddled up in the low-roofed shed inside the pen.

"That right, sweetheart?" Ronnie reached down and cupped his hand at the back of her head. "Maybe they're just hungry in this cold weather."

It was a gesture Della had seen him make so many times over the years she wouldn't even know how to count them. That hand cradling a head, holding it up when the kids were just babies, petting them when they got older the way he was now with Gracie. His hands were beautiful, but she'd never told him that because it wasn't the sort of thing a man like Ronnie would want to hear. It was true, though. His hands were long and narrow with thin fingers, and when he spread them like he had now, palming Gracie's head, the tendons stood up on the back of his hand, and there was something strong and delicate all at the same time about the way he touched his children. When Della looked at his hand, it was hard for her to believe that she was looking at the hand that had touched Brandi Tate in all sorts of ways she didn't want to imagine.

Gracie grabbed onto his other hand with both of her little ones. "Come inside, Daddy. Come on. I'm getting cold."

So Della let Gracie pull him into the trailer, and she shut the door.

It felt strange to have him there after so much time. Strange and familiar all at once. The sound of his footsteps—a whisking shuffle she'd know even if a million years went by before she heard it again. "That boy never picks up his feet," her mama told her shortly after they were married. "Not even at the church during the wedding march. Did you notice that? He was dragging his feet like he was on his way to get hung. Oh, Lord, I hope this hasn't been a mistake."

"You getting on okay?" He looked around the trailer, and she knew he was taking note of the pile of laundry on the couch in the living room, waiting to be folded, and the scatter of crayons and coloring books on the breakfast table, and the mess of CDs Angel and Hannah had left by the boom box on the kitchen counter. Maybe he was looking for something that would make him come back. Maybe all she had to do was admit she needed his help. "Della, you got more than your hands full."

"We're doing just fine," she said.

He looked down the hallway. The double-wide had three bedrooms. She and Junior and Gracie slept in one of them. Angel and Hannah in another. The last one was for the twins. A bath and a half. Fifteen hundred square feet. A double-wide Fleetwood trailer with underpinning set on a piece of ground Della's parents owned along the blacktop. It'd been her home for fourteen years, and even if it was a little worse for wear these days, it was still hers.

"See you got a fire going." Ronnie nodded toward the Franklin stove in the corner of the living room where Della had just put on a new split of wood. "Guess you need it in this weather."

"The furnace has been acting up. Daddy thought he had it fixed, but it keeps cutting out. Sometimes I don't even notice it until I wake up in the middle of the night, froze to death."

"The blower?"

Della shrugged her shoulders. "Something about the pilot light, I think."

"Want me to see what I can do with it?"

"Daddy's coming over today to take another look. If he can't fix it, I expect we'll all go over to their house to sleep tonight."

That was enough—that mention of Wayne Best possibly appearing at any moment—to put Ronnie into action. He went down the hallway, and Della followed him, Gracie skipping along between them.

Junior was asleep in his crib. "I don't want you waking him," Della said in a whisper. "He's got the croup and I just now got him to sleep."

"Does he need a doctor?"

"If he does, I'll see to it."

"He sounds like one of the goats," Gracie said, whispering in imitation of Della. "I heard him last night."

Ronnie was whispering, too. "I didn't mean to suggest you couldn't take care of him, Della."

"It's all right. I'm just tired. Haven't been sleeping much." She put her hand on Gracie's back. "Why don't you go out and color Daddy a picture?"

"I'll draw you something nice, Daddy."

"All right, baby. You do that."

Alone, Della and Ronnie watched Junior sleeping the way they'd stood together at cribs over the years looking down on their children.

"Guess it's my fault you haven't had your sleep," he said.

"Guess it is," she told him. "You and seven kids."

She watched him looking down on Junior whose jaw was slack, a little bubble of spit at his lips. The room smelled of the Vicks Vapo-Rub she'd used on his chest, and it was, at least to her way of thinking, a good smell. A scent she always associated with her own mother and how she'd cared for Della when she was a little girl. That heady smell of camphor and eucalyptus that said Mom was there and she knew exactly what to do.

"I hate this, Della. I really do. I hate the way it's turned out. All this burden on you and now these divorce papers. It's got me shook. I can tell you that."

Junior squirmed a little in his sleep, his arm flying over across his chest, and Della held her breath, hoping he wouldn't wake.

She and Ronnie were talking in such small voices now they had to stand close to each other to hear.

"You want to do something about it? You want to come home and give up this nonsense with Brandi Tate?"

For a long time, he didn't say a word. Then she heard a little choke of breath, and his shaky voice said, "I can't do that."

It came to her, then, something she should have known. "She's pregnant, isn't she?"

He wouldn't admit it. He couldn't face her and own up to it, but she felt sure she'd hit on the truth. She knew it in the way he looked at Junior, the way he reached into the crib and dabbed the little spit bubble with his finger. She could tell it from the way he wouldn't look at her, the way he got all shy, the way he said, "Della, I—" and then couldn't go on. She knew he wasn't completely done with babies.

"You better get a lawyer," she told him, and he said, "All right, then, if you're saying it's over, then by God let it be over. I can make it so you'll wish you never started this."

"I didn't start it. So don't you come in here threatening me."

"Oh, I'm not threatening. It's long past that now."

"What in the world does that mean?"

"You'll find out, Della. You can count on that."

9

The Firebird's tires squealed and laid black marks on the pavement when Ronnie left Della's.

"He sure took out of there a-hellin'," Shooter said to Captain. They were outside rounding up one of Della's goats. The pen she had behind the trailer had a wood fence, and there was always a plank or two busted out and those goats would get free and wander across the road and Shooter would have to get them back in the pen. He'd take over a hammer and some nails and patch things up enough to hold them until the next time he'd find a goat or two in his garden, chomping up anything they could get to. It didn't set right with him. None of it. Ever since Ronnie had left Della for Brandi Tate, the place had gone to hell.

Shooter had tried his best to do right by Della, helping her out with this and that when she needed it, trying to be someone that she and her kids could count on, but as the weeks went on it began to wear on him and he started to see Della as someone who was incompetent. She was a problem he couldn't solve, and Lord knew he had enough worries of his own as Captain got older and more headstrong.

The Firebird shot up the blacktop, tires squealing and smoking, and Captain and Shooter listened to Ronnie let that engine out for a good long ways.

"Sugar tits," Captain said.

"Don't talk like that, Wesley." Shooter hated to see that hangdog look on Captain's face, that look that said he knew he'd done wrong, but he just couldn't help himself. "Come on, Captain," Shooter said. He only called him Wesley when he wanted to be stern. "Let's get after that goat."

Missy met Ronnie's Firebird on the blacktop outside Goldengate. She was waiting behind the school bus that'd just put out its stop sign when Ronnie went roaring past, no regard for that bus at all.

On the bus, Angel saw the Firebird shoot by and she said to Hannah, who was sitting beside her, "There goes Dad."

Hannah came up on her knees and squirmed around in her seat to look on down the blacktop. Her braid swung out and hit Angel in the face.

Some of the other kids on the bus had seen the Firebird, too. Angel grabbed Hannah by the arm and pulled her down.

"He's been to see Mom," Hannah said. "Do you think—"

"No, I don't think," Angel said. "Not with him driving like that."

"Hey, Angel," a boy called from the back of the bus. It was Tommy Stout, a boy Angel secretly liked. "There goes your dad," he said, in a voice that wasn't mean, but it called attention to what Angel had spent months trying to forget. Her dad had walked out and was living with someone else. "Looks like he's in a hurry," Tommy said, and Angel closed her eyes.

Missy used her cell phone to call Pat on his job site. "It's a wonder no one got killed," she told him. "I'm sitting here right behind the bus, and I'm shaking. I'm watching one of the Thacker girls cross the road, and I'm thinking about what might have happened. That Ronnie Black is out of control."

Pat was a quiet man, and, when he spoke, he said his words slowly, as if he'd given them a good deal of thought and wanted to make sure he got them right. "He was just out here looking for work." Pat's construction company was building a house near Goldengate. "He said Della had papers served on him, and that girl he's living with—that Brandi Tate?—well, she's got a baby coming. He seemed pretty shook up."

"Don't make excuses for him. He's only getting what he's had coming."

"I was just giving you the facts." Pat's voice shrank and got that little bit of hurt in it that always startled Missy whenever she heard it. "I didn't mean to stand up for him."

"I know. I'm sorry. I didn't mean to jump on you. I'm just so mad at Ronnie for doing Della the way he is."

On up the road, Della threw on an old John Deere jacket that Ronnie left when he moved out, the first thing she grabbed from the coat pegs by the front door, not even noticing what it was until she was out in the cold. The buses would be coming soon—first Angel and Hannah's, and then Sarah and the twins'—and she wanted to be there waiting for them, the way she managed to be every day no matter that she felt like her life had blown to pieces. She wanted her girls to know that nothing was going to change. They were going to get along as a family for a good long time.

Shooter had a rope around the neck of the billy goat, Methuselah, who was always butting his way through the rotten fence. Captain was walking alongside. When he saw Della, he gave her a big wave. His face lit up, the way it always did whenever he saw her. He swept the shaggy blond bangs away from his eyes.

"Della, we got your goat," he said, and even though she was embarrassed about the stray goat, she felt a warm glow inside because to Captain it meant nothing that this was the umpteenth time that he and his father had to round up one of her goats. It was something he was glad to do, and he didn't have it in him to pass judgment on her or anyone else for that matter. She was the same Della to him that she'd always been and this business with Ronnie—even though she knew Captain missed having him around—didn't matter at all.

Shooter, though, was a different story. She knew that Shooter thought she should keep a better grip on things. "Damn it, Della," he said to her once. "You've got to get things under control."

She'd done her best to keep those goats inside their pen, but Methuselah was always breaking through the boards.

"Well, Della, looks like I've caught another one," Shooter said, and though he said it with a smile, she knew that deep down he was tired of chasing goats. "I'll put him back in the pen and see what I can do to patch it."

"I'm sorry," she said, and he gave a little wave of his hand as if to say he didn't want to hear her apology.

At least he didn't say anything about the way Ronnie had driven out of there like a crazy man. At least Shooter left that alone.

"You're going have to come up with a better arrangement for your animals," he said. "Come spring, I'm not going to have them eating up my garden. I mean it, Della. You're going to have to find some way of making sure they stay where they're supposed to be." Then, as he led Methuselah around back of the trailer, he said something she wasn't sure he meant for her to hear, but maybe he did. Maybe this was his way of saying he was tired of the whole damn deal. "Some people," he said. "Captain, best thing would be to put a match to that fence and start over."

Something about the way Shooter said *some people* struck Della wrong, and though she was generally a good-natured person, she snapped. She knew it was the bad feeling inside her after her run-in with Ronnie that made her so angry with Shooter. In fact, she was more embarrassed than anything, ashamed to be the woman who caused so much trouble. She followed Shooter and Captain behind the trailer.

"You don't have to do anything to that fence," she said. "In fact, you don't need to do anything for me ever again."

Shooter turned to look at her, and the wind bit at his face. The sharp tone of her voice caught him by surprise and made him get his back up even more.

"Damn it, Della. I'm trying to do the best I can for you, and you talk to me that way?"

"I know what you told Missy." She took a step toward him. "I know you wish I wasn't your neighbor."

For a few moments, he didn't know what she was talking about. What had he said to Missy? Then it came to him. Just a wisecrack. That was all. Just something he said and didn't think for a minute that it'd ever get back to Della, and even if it did, wouldn't she know he'd only been joking? *You know, I'd like those people a lot better if they lived somewhere else.* That's what he'd said to Missy one day when he'd rounded up those stray goats and patched that fence again.

"Hell, Della. That was just a joke. I didn't mean any harm."

"You know what they say," she told him. "In every ounce of jest there's a pound of truth. If I'm so much trouble to you, just leave me alone."

She whipped around and stomped off toward the road.

"That woman needs to learn to be more grateful," Shooter finally said to Captain. "Come on. Let's patch that fence while we've still got good light."

10

It was a little after ten thirty that night when Brandi heard the fire-house siren. The television news had gone off, and she'd come to bed. She was sitting up with the lamp on, reading a book called *Getting Ready for Baby*. She had a whole stack of books like that on her night table: *The Calm Baby Cookbook, What to Expect When You're Expecting, Pregnancy Without Pounds*.

"Fire," she said, not looking up from her book, and Ronnie, who was on his side, the blankets pulled over his shoulder, didn't say a word.

He'd gone out for a drive earlier—no, he didn't want company, he'd told her—and he'd come back, got into the shower, and then slipped into bed. It wasn't uncommon for him to go driving when he got antsy—just getting the kinks out, he always said—and Brandi didn't make a fuss about it. She knew it wasn't easy for him, all this mess with Della, particularly now that she'd filed for divorce. But Brandi, with no family nearby, had long ago grown tired of being alone. She'd come to count on Ronnie.

Just that morning, she'd run out of gas when she was so close to work that her boss, Mr. Samms, was able to push her Mustang into the parking lot at the Wabash Savings and Loan. She'd called the house, and Ronnie had gotten out of bed and carried five gallons to Phillipsport and poured it into her tank. If he wanted to get out for a bit in the evening and be alone with his thoughts, as he had tonight, who was she to say anything about it?

She was wearing a low-cut black chemise that came down over her hips and a pair of black bikini panties. A little pooch had already come to her stomach. It wouldn't be long, she'd told Ronnie, before she wouldn't be able to wear anything sexy to bed, or at least not that he'd want to see her in, so he'd better get an eyeful while he still could. She'd brushed out her hair, and it fell in waves over her bare shoulders, the tips snaking across the tops of her breasts.

For just an instant, she looked over the tops of the round rimless glasses she wore for reading. She looked toward the window and then quickly went back to her book.

Ronnie knew everyone thought he'd left Della because he was chasing tail and it ended up being his own that got caught in the door, but that wasn't true. More than anything, he'd ended up with Brandi because she'd given him what he needed most: a peace in the heart he'd been hard-pressed to find on his own. She just had this calm way about her. She never got flustered, never flew off into a panic, never felt sorry for herself. He convinced himself that life with her was going to be easy. He believed it right up to the point when he drove out the blacktop with that five-gallon can of gas. Now he heard the firehouse siren and a chill went through him. He'd come back from the trailer, and Brandi had asked him where he'd gone.

"Nowhere in particular," he'd told her. "Like I said. Just driving around."

Now he was thinking about how he'd driven that last quarter mile to the trailer with his headlights off so no one would see the Firebird making its way so slow and easy through the cold night.

Even now in the warmth of Brandi's bed he was trembling, chilled to the bone. He knew it would be a long time, if ever, before he'd be able to talk about that night and what had happened out there at the trailer. So for the time, he tried to hold himself suspended in that last quarter mile, the Firebird gliding along in the dark. He could see the trailer ahead of him, not a speck of light anywhere. He was almost there—just a little bit farther—almost to that place he'd known so long as home.

"Bite-ass cold night to have to fight a fire," he finally said to Brandi. He listened to the trucks' sirens start up and then grow faint. "Somewhere out in the country it sounds like."

"Yes, it does," said Brandi, in a faraway voice.

He lay there shivering until, finally, he fell into a fitful sleep.

Then someone was knocking on the front door of the house, knocking in a way that brought Ronnie up from sleep with a start, his heart pounding in his chest.

Brandi was up and slipping into her old chenille bathrobe, the yellow one with red hearts on it. A big one across the back had pink letters in the center that said BE MINE. She took her time. She pushed her bare feet into her house shoes. They were sock monkey house shoes, ones with the face from that kids' doll across the toes: black buttons for eyes, red-and-white mouth. Just a silly thing to make the winter a little brighter, she'd told Ronnie. Normally, when he saw her wearing them, he got a light-in-the-heart feeling, but tonight, still groggy from sleep, he was trying to figure out why she was taking time to put them on. She even picked up a brush from the dresser and ran it through her hair.

"Guess someone wants to talk to us," she said. Then she went to find who'd come knocking in the middle of the night.

Ronnie tried to get his wits about him. He got out of bed and started toward the knocking. Then he realized he was only wearing his boxer shorts, and he stopped to fumble around for his jeans. His foot kept getting caught in one of the legs, and finally he stumbled backwards and sat down hard on the bed.

That's where he was when Brandi came back and said to him in a voice so soft he had to take a second to make sure he'd heard her right, "Ronnie, you better come out here."

She helped him pull on his jeans, and while he fastened them, she brought him a flannel shirt from the closet. She held it for him and he put his arms through the sleeves. Then, with a gentle nudge against his shoulders, she turned him around so she could do up the buttons.

Her fingers were trembling, and it took her a good while with each button. He watched those fingers, and he knew something was wrong—so wrong that even she didn't know how to handle it.

Pat Wade was in the living room. He'd come because he'd asked to be the one to carry the news. He'd told Ray Biggs that he'd gone to school with Ronnie, had known him all his life, and he wanted to be the one to tell him. Better for this kind of thing to come from someone familiar rather than someone in a uniform who was merely doing his duty. Besides, Pat had been at the trailer long before Biggs arrived. He'd taken Sarah when Shooter handed her to him, and he knew he'd never forget the way she put her arms around his neck and clung to him, the way her body quivered, and the little whimpering noises she made in the cold night.

"Where's my daddy?" she said. "I want my daddy."

Biggs would never be able to tell Ronnie something like that, something to make him understand that no matter the choices he'd recently made he still had a family to see to, and he'd have to make sure he did right by them. Pat had taken it upon himself to be the one to try to hold him up and ease him along, knowing that if, God forbid, he ever found himself in his shoes, he might very well say the hell with it all.

He'd never been in Brandi Tate's house, never had any reason to be there until that night. Even in a nothing town like Goldengate, which wasn't more than the three blocks of Main Street, the B & O Railroad tracks crossing the heart of it, and streets named after trees and presidents running at right angles—a town of a thousand people living in small frame houses like this one on Locust—you could go your whole life and not think that some of those people would ever matter to you at all. Then a night like this would come to prove you wrong.

Pat felt ill at ease standing in Brandi's living room surrounded by the signs of her and Ronnie living together in what Missy had always called their "love shack." Ronnie's work boots on the floor by the couch, a pair of his gray wool socks lying across the toes. An empty plastic bottle of Mountain Dew was on the coffee table, along with an issue of *Gearhead Magazine* he'd apparently been looking at earlier in the evening, before what Pat had now come to tell him had happened.

"Who is it out there?" he heard Ronnie ask from the bedroom down the hall.

"It's Pat Wade," Brandi said.

"Pat Wade? This time of night. Maybe he wants me to come to work tomorrow."

"No, sugar. He's not come about a job."

The soothing tone of her voice caught Pat by the throat, and he choked down the ache it left. He'd never really thought of her in any way at all before. Or if he had, he'd only seen her through Missy's eyes. *Home wrecker, concubine, tramp.* A girl not yet thirty—maybe no more than twenty-five—who'd worked her charms on Ronnie and stolen him away from Della and the kids. *Temptress, Jezebel, harlot.* Missy always stopped just short of the harsher words—*slut, bitch, whore*—but Pat knew they were right below the surface of everything she said.

Here was her voice, soft and low, and a little shaky with what she knew that Ronnie didn't. Here on the coffee table was a necklace she must have unfastened from around her neck sometime while she was sitting on the couch with Ronnie. Just a simple silver necklace with a heart on the end of it. Maybe she'd had the television on. Maybe she'd asked if he wanted a Mountain Dew. Maybe they'd just been a couple like that, spending an ordinary night at home the way Pat and Missy had done before she looked out the window and saw Della's trailer on fire.

As he stood in Brandi's living room, waiting, he felt whatever ember of moral judgment Missy might have wanted him to stoke go cold. He could only think of Brandi as one more person whose life was going to change forever because of what had gone on out the blacktop.

The first thing that registered with Ronnie when he came out to the living room was the odor that Pat had carried into the house: a sharp scent that reminded Ronnie of the smell around the burn barrel at one of his foster homes, where they let him set fire to the trash for the time he lived there. Cold and smoke and something like burnt plastic and melted tin.

"Ronnie, there's been trouble." Pat had on an orange sock hat and he took it off and twisted it around in his hands. "That's why I'm here." He could barely bring himself to look at Ronnie. He looked down at that sock hat instead as if it were the most fascinating thing.

Ronnie was used to Pat's easygoing ways, and he'd always liked having him as a neighbor. Pat even tossed some work his way when he could. He always did Ronnie square even when Ronnie knew he didn't deserve his favor. He never felt like Pat sat in judgment of him—he wished he could say the same thing about Missy—but instead just took him for what he was. Pat never got ruffled or took a sideways route toward anything troubling that stood before him, but now he looked like he was having a hard time getting his bearings.

He looked worn out: coppery whisker stubble on his face, creases in his forehead as he bunched up his brow, slump of his shoulders as if he carried so much weight he could hardly stand. He was a lanky man with big hands beat to hell from hammers and crowbars and roof shingles and concrete. He had a long, narrow face and big old hound dog eyes. Eyebrows so white it seemed like they'd been permanently coated with plaster dust. A bald spot on top of his head.

"Sugar, listen to him." Brandi slipped her arm around Ronnie's and held on. "I'm right here," she said, and she squeezed his bicep with a fierce grip that made fire shoot up his arm.

Pat didn't know any other way to deliver the news but to say it straight out.

"Ronnie, there's been a fire," he said. "The trailer's gone, not much left but the gas furnace and the hot water heater."

"They were having trouble with that furnace," Ronnie said. "Della's dad was supposed to fix it."

"I don't know anything about that," said Pat. Then he gathered himself for the next thing he had to say. "Missy saw the flames from our place, and she called 911. By the time I got up there, Shooter Rowe and Captain were already doing what they could."

Ronnie said, "Thank God Della and the kids weren't there. Good thing they went to her folks' tonight."

Pat let him have that one moment of comfort, that brief time of believing that no one had been inside the trailer. Then he started in again. He took it slow. He let Ronnie have time to take in each thing he was saying. "They were there," he said. "Della was in the trailer, and she was seeing to the kids. She was handing Emma to Shooter when I got there. Angel and Hannah were already out. Then Sarah. Then—"

"They were there?" He couldn't believe it. He'd called from the payphone at Casey's, and no one had answered. Della's car hadn't been in the lane the way it always was. He'd gone out there to burn the trailer—that's how mad he'd been because Della had filed papers on him—but he hadn't intended anything like this. "She got them all out, right? Della? She got all the kids out?"

Just then, a clock on the wall marked the hour—one o'clock—with birdsong. A robin's happy call: *Cheerup.*

Brandi explained that the clock had a light sensor to keep it from sounding when the room was dark. She pointed up. "Ceiling light," she said, to make it clear why the clock had sounded.

Pat knew he couldn't take any of the pain from Ronnie. All he could do was say the rest.

"Della went back for Emily and Gracie and Junior. By that time, the fire was too hot, the smoke was thick." The orange sock hat slipped from his hands, and he had to bend over and pick it up from the floor. "I couldn't go in there, Ronnie." His voice was nearly a whisper now. "The roof and walls were already starting to go. If I could've done something. If I'd been there sooner."

Ronnie felt, then, like he was somewhere far, far away from where he really was, and, when he finally spoke, it was like he was listening to someone he didn't know—someone who was a stranger to him.

"Not one of them?" he asked Pat. "Not Della or Emily or Gracie? Not Junior?"

When Pat didn't answer right away, he turned to Brandi. She reached out and laid her hand to Ronnie's cheek. "No, sugar. Not a one."

Then Pat found his voice again, and he said the hardest thing of all. "The roof and the walls. They just went before Della could get the others." He remembered how the heat had forced him and Shooter and Captain and the four saved girls out into the road, where they could do nothing but watch the trailer collapse and listen to the sirens on the fire trucks as they came out the blacktop from town.

"They're gone, Ronnie. Della and the baby and Emily and Gracie. They're all gone."

It was said now—everything—and Pat waited for whatever would come next.

Ronnie got a hard look to his face. That gaunt face with the sharp cheekbones and the watery blue eyes and the little knob of a chin that wasn't much of a chin at all. He looked the way he had the first day he'd come to Bethlehem School, a new kid. He was no more than seven or eight, then, and yet he looked like an old man fretting something to death.

He took a few steps across the room, and for a moment Pat was afraid he was coming to do him harm with his fists, enraged because Pat had stood as witness to the fire. Then Ronnie stopped, and he said with a no-nonsense tone, "Where are my girls?"

"They're at my house," Pat said. "Missy's seeing to them."

Ronnie turned to Brandi. "I've got to go there. I've got to be with them."

She nodded. "I'll get dressed."

"Brandi." He stopped her as she started toward the bedroom. He reached out a hand. "Baby?"

She came to him and she threw her arms around his neck and pressed him to her, saying, "Sugar. Oh, sugar."

They stood there, rocking back and forth a little, and Pat, watching, didn't know what to do with this tenderness between them on such a night. "I guess sometimes, the hurt's so big," he'd say to Missy later, "nothing matters except getting over it."

He'd tell her about the way Brandi held onto Ronnie and told him she'd do whatever she needed her to do. "If you want me to stay here," she said, "I will. I'll be right here waiting for you to come back."

"I expect that'd be best," he said.

He knew she was offering to stand by him, the way she would if she were his wife.

That word was strange to him now. It flamed inside his head and got all twisted up with what he felt for Brandi and the child she carried—his child—and the life he'd shared with Della until he'd decided to walk out of it. He'd had this wife and seven children, and now three of them were dead, and Della too, and it made no sense— it nearly brought him to his knees—that they were gone and he was alive.

11

Shooter Rowe, if push came to shove, would admit that deep down there were times when he wished to be free of Captain, when he wished for a different sort of son.

It was the kind of truth a man comes up against late at night when he's alone with his thoughts, and he has no choice but to face facts. When he has to say, okay, this is who I am. The fact was, ever since he and Merlene knew something was wrong with Captain, that he wasn't ever going to be the sort who could stand on his own two feet and take responsibility for his steps through the world, sure or uncertain, Shooter tried to stay clear of him, wasn't a good father at all. But then Merlene took sick and died, and now here he was, trying his best.

Captain was incapable of understanding when he'd done something to deserve a stern word or a lick with Shooter's belt. It was so much easier to call Ronnie on his missteps. When he did something stupid, Shooter told him he'd fucked up, and Ronnie said, "Shooter, you're right. If I'd had you as a daddy, I would've turned out to be a better man."

Shooter wasn't sure about that—he was no kind of father—but he knew that to Ronnie he must have seemed exactly the man he needed to keep him on the straight and narrow.

Ronnie had never known his own father. Then his mother died when he was a toddler, and he grew up in a series of foster homes, each one of them leaving him with a little more meanness inside, a little more hurt, a little more ache for comfort and love. Finally, when he was fifteen, he lied about his age and got that tattoo on his neck. BAD MOON. Let the world know it; he was burning a short fuse.

So there they were, Ronnie and Shooter, each of them all mixed up, needing each other in ways they couldn't completely understand, ways that were complicated by the love and envy they both felt, and Shooter didn't know how he'd say any of this if he had to.

"You just fucked up big time," Shooter told Ronnie after he walked out on Della.

It was a night when Ronnie had come for the last of his things and Shooter caught him as he was about to toss a pile of clothes into the backseat of the Firebird. It was after dark, a quarter moon in the sky, the air with the chill that said winter was waiting, the chirr of crickets in the fencerows, the smell of wood smoke coming from the trailer.

"I mean it, Ronnie," Shooter said. "You're not thinking about how many lives you're affecting."

For the first time, Ronnie didn't take kindly to Shooter's assessment—his criticism—nor did he admit that there was any truth to it.

"Shooter," he said. "What do you know about what it is to love someone anyway?"

For a good while, Shooter didn't say a word. He knew what Ronnie didn't have the nerve to say. That Merlene had talked to him in a way that another man's wife shouldn't, that she and Ronnie had come to some closeness of their hearts.

Shooter said, "You and Merlene—"

Then he stopped, unable to say more, unwilling to admit that he'd found the photograph of Ronnie that she'd saved and the card she'd hidden away. He was afraid of what Ronnie might say about the two of them.

"She was a good woman," Ronnie finally said. "She deserved better than you."

Shooter was determined not to show how deeply he was cut. He'd had all those years with Merlene, a woman who—yes, Ronnie was right—didn't deserve the way he disappointed her too many times. For a while, he'd even blamed her for the way Captain was, told her she hadn't done something right when she was pregnant, but that didn't mean he didn't love her or that he didn't miss her now every minute of every day. It didn't mean he wasn't trying his best with Captain. It didn't mean he had to tolerate the way Ronnie was treating Della, even though there'd been a time in his life when he might have treated Merlene the same way.

"You're going to have a hard row," he finally said to Ronnie.

"Maybe so," said Ronnie. "But it'll be my row and not yours. You stick to your problems and I'll stick to mine."

"I suppose you think I'll take care of Della and your kids?"

Ronnie shook his head. "I can't think of them right now."

"You can stop." Shooter grabbed his arm. "You can go back in that trailer and you and Della can work things out."

Shooter wanted it to be so because he wanted to believe in the power of love. He wanted to believe that there were men who would always stay true, who would swallow whatever discontent they felt, all for the sake of the woman who had given birth to their children and for those children themselves. He wanted Ronnie and Della and their kids to be all right, to be a family, so he could believe there was still a chance for him and Captain.

"It's too late for that," Ronnie said, but still he gave a glance back at the trailer, and Shooter felt for just an instant, one little sliver of time, that maybe, just maybe, Ronnie would grab this chance and everything would work out for the best.

It was that instant that Shooter would try to live within as much as possible in the days to come. He'd still be trying to cozy up to it the night of the fire, and beyond that to the night when he'd stand over his burn barrel, trembling, asking God to forgive him for what he'd done, to understand that sometimes things happened you couldn't dream of and once they were over, all that was left was to go on through your days, pretending you were innocent. He'd long for that brief moment when everything that was about to happen wouldn't, when people's lives would still be happy and full of hope, when every mistake would be redeemed.

"Take your hand off me," Ronnie finally said, but Shooter wrenched his arm up behind Ronnie's back.

"You're a stupid man," Shooter said. "A selfish, stupid man." Ronnie tried to twist free, but Shooter held on, pushing him into the Firebird, folding him over the hood. He leaned down and put his mouth up close to Ronnie's ear. "I could yank this arm out of the socket. Quick as you please. Surely you know that."

Ronnie whispered through clenched teeth, "Do it and I'll make it so they lock you away."

That's when Shooter let him go. Ronnie stood up, rubbing his shoulder. He didn't say another word, just got into his Firebird and headed up the blacktop to Goldengate, where Brandi was waiting for him.

Shooter turned toward his own house, his hands clenched into fists. Later, he'd wish he'd been paying more attention to what mattered and what didn't. What was that photograph, that card, in relation to the fact that Merlene was dead? That night, though, he felt his anger flame again as he recalled when Ronnie and Della first moved into the trailer and Merlene stood at the window, watching them unload furniture from Wayne Best's pickup truck.

"Look at them," she said. "Just kids." Her voice shrank to a whisper. "Just starting out." She let the curtain panels fall back into place and smoothed them with the back of her hand. "They've got their whole lives," she said. He'd never forgotten the sad look on her face when she finally turned to look at him.   He'd never forgotten what she said next. "Remember what that was like?"

12

Ronnie and Captain hit it off from the get-go. One summer night, when Merlene asked Ronnie and Della over for ice cream and cake, he let the toddler hold on to his finger, and they walked around the yard in the twilight. Ronnie pointed to the fireflies flashing on and off, and he got a good, warm feeling in his chest when Captain pointed too and babbled and giggled with delight.

"That's right, Wesley," Ronnie said. He caught a firefly in his hand. He crouched down and held his fist open a crack, just enough for Captain to see the glow pulsing. His little mouth opened wide with wonder. "The world's a mysterious place," Ronnie said, and then he opened his hand and let the firefly go.

Captain kept touching Ronnie's hand, kept patting his palm with his little fingers. It seemed so long ago now, those days before Merlene gave Wesley the nickname Captain, those days before anyone knew about what would come to be called his "intellectual disability." On that long-ago night, he was a little boy amazed, and Ronnie, as the years went on, was glad that he'd been there as witness. He was still a boy himself, but married to Della and about to become a father.

"Oh, you'll do fine," Merlene told Della as they sat at the picnic table with Shooter and watched Ronnie. He and the boy who would become Captain were shadows in the dusk. A whippoorwill was calling somewhere back in the woods. The night air was pleasant, just cool enough on the skin, and it carried with it the sweet smell of cut hay curing in the pasture. Merlene and Della and Shooter could hear Ronnie's soothing, patient voice.

"You'll both do fine," Merlene said to Della. "Just look at how good Ronnie is with Wesley."

Shooter dropped his spoon into his empty ice cream bowl. "I'm sure Merlene is right," he said, "and if anything goes wrong, we're just right across the road."

From that night on, Captain adored Ronnie. Even as Captain got older and became more difficult, Ronnie was always the one he'd listen to, much to Shooter's dismay. Where he was sharp with Captain, Ronnie was patient; where he was stingy with his praise, Ronnie was generous.

"He thinks the sun rises and sets with you," Shooter said one day before Ronnie left for good, said it in a way that made it plain to Ronnie that he resented the fact. Shooter laughed, a nervous chuckle. "I swear he spends more time at your place than he does at home. Just like he's another one of your kids. I should pay you a little something for support."

They were alone in Ronnie's lane, Shooter already having sent Captain back across the road, despite his protests. Ronnie was adjusting the carburetor on his Firebird and Captain wanted to be there to watch, to fetch him a wrench if the need arose.

"It's all right." Ronnie stood back from the Firebird and wiped his hands on a red shop rag. He didn't mind humoring Captain, and that's what he thought he was doing, letting him hang around the way he did. Sure, he could be a pain sometimes, but nothing Ronnie couldn't stand. "He's not so much of a handful like you think."

Ronnie could tell from the way Shooter narrowed his eyes and set his jaw that he'd touched a nerve.

"I love my son." He took a step toward Ronnie and then stopped. "I want you to know that."

Ronnie kept quiet, unable to bring himself to say, *yes, I know it.* He didn't say a word, and after a time, Shooter said in a fierce voice, "Sometimes it's not easy."

"You know you're the whole world to him," Ronnie said.

Shooter snorted. "I can hardly believe that."

"It's true. He's like any boy. He wants his father to be proud of him."

Shooter looked down at his feet. When he raised his head, his brow was bunched like he was wincing in pain. "He tell you as much?"

Ronnie sensed a border he couldn't see, one that separated him from Shooter and Captain, one that he wasn't supposed to cross. "I don't even know who my daddy is," Ronnie said.

Shooter put his hands on the fender of the Firebird and leaned in close. Ronnie took a step back. He'd seen looks like the one Shooter was giving him now on the faces of his foster fathers just before they exploded with anger—lashed out with a belt, a switch, or, as he got older, a fist. They weren't all like that, but there were enough of them who were to keep him on his toes.

"I guess you're like so many of the others," Shooter said. "The ones who think they know exactly what's what when it comes to raising a boy like Captain. I do my best, Ronnie. I told Merlene I'd do everything I could for him. I'd make sure he stayed out of trouble. I wouldn't ever leave him to someone else's care. I promised that to Merlene when she was dying, and I don't intend to go back on my word. I do the best I can, but that boy's stubborn and headstrong." Shooter laughed. "I guess in that way, he's a lot like you."

"You too," Ronnie said.

"Then God help us."

So there was that between the two of them, that tension of father and son and the bullheaded refusal to admit how close they really were. Then there was Captain, who was eager for someone to show him how to best be a man in the world. None of them knew that the fire was coming, and once it was done, they would be forever bound. Bound by their stupidity and their love. Bound by the story of what happened one night to a woman and three of her children. Bound by the story of the four who survived.

"God help us," Shooter said to Ronnie that day in his lane. "God help us all."

13

Emma clung to Missy's hand and wouldn't let go. The girls were in Missy's house, and Emma kept asking where everyone else was—her mama and Gracie and Junior—and when Emily would be coming. The twins had been inseparable, and now Emma was lost without her.

"There was a fire," Emma said.

Missy stroked her head, the fine blond hair gritty with ash.

"Yes, there was." Missy was at a loss for what else to say. All her adult life, she'd longed for children. She'd secretly resented Della's ability to have so many when Missy and Pat hadn't been able to have a single one. Now here she was in charge of these four, and helpless. "It was a big fire," she said to Emma.

Sarah was crying. Her white pajamas were smudged with soot. Pat had carried her in and set her down, and she hadn't moved a speck. At first, she'd been quiet, a blank look on her face. Then the tears came. She didn't make a sound, but her cheeks, blanched white from the cold, were soon wet.

"They're not coming back," she said. "They're in Heaven, aren't they?"

Angel had her arms crossed over her chest, an angry set to her jaw. "They're dead." Her voice was too loud. "That's what they are. Dead."

Sarah cried harder and ran to Missy. Emma was crying, too, and Missy got down on her knees and let both girls lean into her. She wrapped them up in her arms, and she did the only thing she could for the time being. She let them cry.

Hannah wanted to go back outside and look for their goats. "I saw Methuselah run away." She was at the bay window, her hands pressed against the glass. "He ran into the woods."

"Why do you care about those goats?" Angel said. "You wouldn't even feed them tonight."

Hannah whirled around from the window. Her long hair, tangled with crusts of ice, whipped at her face. "You were supposed to take out that box of ashes, but did you? No."

"Girls." Missy interrupted. "Let's get you all into some fresh things."

Angel took a step toward Hannah, her hands balled into fists. Then she stopped. "Yes, ma'am," she said, and for now that was that.

Then it was a flurry of hot showers and the untangling and combing of hair. Missy found two pairs of her old pajamas for Angel and Hannah, and a couple of Pat's T-shirts that were long enough to be sleep dresses for Sarah and Emma. The things they'd been wearing reeked of smoke. Missy threw everything into the washer.

The girls huddled together in the living room. Angel and Hannah were on the couch, and Sarah and Emma were between them. Missy wondered how their lives would ever be whole again.

Then the front door opened, and Pat and Ronnie came inside. The smoke from the fire was still on Pat's Carhartts, and though Missy knew he couldn't help it, she wished he hadn't brought that smell back into their house.

Missy gave Ronnie a nod, and he came the rest of the way to the couch. He took his hands out of his pockets and he got down on his knees, wedged himself in as best he could between the couch and the coffee table in front of it. His hip knocked against the table, and Missy went over and scooted it out some so he could settle in there.

He cleared his throat once—tried to find his voice—but no words came and the silence went on, such an agonizing quiet, filled with everything that he couldn't bring himself to say.

Finally, Sarah hopped down from the couch. Missy had pulled her hair back into a ponytail, and she'd given her a navy blue T-shirt of Pat's that said CARPENTERS LOCAL 624 in white letters. The dark navy made Sarah's pale skin so white in the lamplight. She threw her arms around Ronnie's neck, and for a time that was all there was, just this little girl hanging onto her father in the middle of a cold winter night.

Then Angel said, "You think we're all going to forgive you easy as that? You got another think coming. I can tell you that for sure."

She stomped over to the window, arms folded over her chest. The old flannel pajamas of Missy's that she wore were lilac-colored and they had little penguins on them, pink scarves around their necks, their pink scarves furling out as if lifted by a wind, and they had the words "be cool" on them in lowercase letters because even the words were too cool to be capitalized. Missy couldn't bear the sight of Angel, her back to everyone, her foot stubbing at the baseboard under the window. While Sarah kept hugging Ronnie's neck and Emma said, "Daddy's here," and Hannah drew her knees up to her chin and closed her eyes, Missy walked over to Angel, and she reached out and put her hand on her back and rubbed slow circles to let her know there could still be tenderness in the world, even after the fire and all it had taken from her.

Then someone knocked on the front door, and Missy shaded her eyes and peered out the window. Wayne Best's truck sat in the driveway behind Ronnie's Firebird and Pat's truck.

Ronnie gathered Sarah into his arms and got up off his knees. He covered her up with his arms, holding her tight, as if he wanted to hide her away, close to his heart, where no one would be able to find her if they came looking.

It surprised Missy to feel what she did for Ronnie in that moment. She didn't want him to have those girls, but now the sight of him overwhelmed her. How much she'd give to have a child she could hold that way, hold as if her very life depended on that heartbeat thumping close to hers. Then she felt the old resentment blaze up—what right did he have to these girls after he'd walked out on them?—and she said, "It's Wayne and Lois." Said it in a way that made it clear Ronnie had something to be afraid of, and then she went to the door, leaving him to brace himself for what was going to happen next.

Lois came in first. She had on her nightgown, a white flannel that fell over the tops of her snow boots. She'd thrown on a black quilted coat, and the gown, printed with dainty lavender flowers, hung down below the coat's hem. Her hair was set in pin curls, and she hadn't taken time to put in her dentures. Her cheeks were all caved in, as if her face had collapsed from grief.

"Oh, mercy," Lois said. "Mercy, mercy." She stood just inside the front door, her arms folded over her stomach, shaking her head back and forth. Finally, she unfolded her arms and reached them in the direction of where Ronnie was holding Sarah, and Hannah and Emma were sitting on the couch. "Mamaw's here," she said.

Wayne had already started toward Ronnie, and by the time Missy noticed, Pat had made a move to stop him. Wayne was holding a tire iron. His face was red from cold and temper. His untied boot laces slapped and snapped across the leather as he stomped across the room.

"Wayne, I've got Sarah here," Ronnie said. "Don't do anything stupid."

"Come here, sweetheart," Lois said, and Sarah got down from her father's arms and went to her.

Pat wedged himself in front of Wayne and started talking. "I know you're torn up," he said. "You've got every right to be. But there's no reason for that tire iron. You don't want the girls seeing anything like that."

Wayne was chest to chest with Pat, his stare leveled at Ronnie as if Pat weren't even there.

"Don't you be talking to me about stupid, Ronnie." Wayne lifted his arm and pointed over Pat's shoulder with the business end of that tire iron. It wobbled in his unsteady hand. "I mean it. You don't have a right to any words tonight, far as I can tell."

"These are my girls," Ronnie said.

"If you think I'm going to let you walk out of here with those girls—" Wayne lunged at Ronnie, but Pat got his hands up into his armpits and held him back. "You're the stupid man, Ronnie," Wayne said. "You've been no good near most all your life."

Angel still stood in front of the window. Lois sat down on the couch. She put one arm around Hannah and one around Emma. Sarah sat on her lap. Wayne still had his arm in the air, his hand around the shaft of that tire iron. He looked at it, and then his shoulders slumped and his arm dropped to his side.

"I'm not here to make trouble," he said, his voice now heavy with shame. "Lord knows we've got enough of that."

"I just want to take my girls now," Ronnie said. "That's what I want to do."

"Take them where? To that whore's house?"

"Wayne, I won't have you talk like that. Not in front of my children."

"By god," Wayne said.

Then, before Pat could stop him, he got close enough to Ronnie to cold-cock him with that tire iron. A blow to the head, and Ronnie went down, face first.

"Wayne, my god, you've killed him," Lois said.

Pat kneeled beside Ronnie and gently rolled him over onto his back. He patted his cheeks a little, seeing if he could get him to come to, but Ronnie was out.

"Is he—" Missy couldn't bring herself to ask if he was still breathing.

When she paused, Pat filled the silence. He said, "Call for an ambulance."

14

Shooter finally got Captain settled down after the fire—got him to bed after the boy had paced the house, his face wet with tears, muttering from time to time. Now, he'd near about dropped off to sleep, and Shooter was sitting in the living room with the lights off, staring into the darkness, unable to get a handle on what had happened that night and what might be required of him now.

Then the ambulance came down the blacktop, siren shrieking, red lights spinning.

Captain was up in a snap, tugging on his jeans and throwing an orange University of Illinois sweatshirt over his head.

"We got to go." He stuffed his feet into his boots and wrapped the laces around the tops, tied them into loose bows. "C'mon," he said. "Get your coat. Maybe they're bringing them back."

Out the window, Shooter saw the ambulance pull into Pat and Missy's driveway. He saw Ronnie's Firebird there, and Wayne Best's pickup. He saw a fire truck across the road, a crew still spraying down the smoldering ashes and the debris from the trailer fire.

"Bringing who back?" Shooter asked Captain. "What are you talking about?"

"Della and her kids. Maybe they took them to the hospital and made them all right."

Shooter took him by the arm. "Now listen to me, son. You know what happened tonight."

"No." Captain shook loose, and before Shooter could stop him, he was out the door and running up the road, no thought of a coat.

Missy saw him first. The EMTs had left the front door open when they brought the gurney into the house, and she felt the cold air sweep over her. She turned toward the door just as Captain stepped inside.

Ronnie was still out cold, and the EMTs were loading him onto the gurney. Missy knew that one of them, the taller one with the black hair and the black moustache, was a boy from Goldengate, but she couldn't recall his first name. His partner was a stocky boy with a little bow to his legs. He had a pierced ear, the left one, where he wore a silver stud. Missy knew they'd already had a tough night—they'd been the ones who'd had to drive away with the bodies of Della and her kids. A man knocked in the head was nothing next to what they'd had to do at that trailer fire. Della and her babies. Missy's throat closed up with the thought.

No one else took notice of Captain. Pat was trying to calm down Wayne, who was beside himself with worry that he'd done exactly what Lois had said—killed Ronnie—and Pat was trying to tell him that no one knew yet how badly Ronnie was hurt. Hannah and Sarah and Emma had gotten up from the couch and gone to stand with Angel, as if to say the only thing they knew on this night when they'd lost their mother, two of their sisters, and their baby brother—and now their father lay unmoving on the floor—was that they had one another and didn't mean to let go. Even Angel and Hannah's little spat over the goats was forgotten. Lois, for whatever reason—maybe just to give her something to do with her hands—was busy taking the bobby pins out of her curls.

"Wesley, what are you doing here?" Missy asked Captain. "This isn't any of your business. Now, go on back home."

He shook his head. "What happened to Ronnie?"

"He fell down. He hit his head." Missy didn't figure she had any obligation to explain what had really happened. Not to Wesley Rowe. What was he doing out anyway, and here it was after two o'clock. Good heavens, what a night. She felt a headache coming on, a dull throb just above her eyes. "Wesley." She used a stern tone. "Wesley, do I have to call your daddy?"

Now there was another siren screaming outside, and red lights swirling, and she saw the sheriff's car pulled off the side of the blacktop. The siren died away, but those lights kept spinning, and she could barely look at them. Her eyes were so tired, and the pain from her headache was starting to pulse behind them.

Shooter Rowe came up the driveway just ahead of Ray Biggs. Shooter stepped into the house, and Missy saw the sadness in his eyes. His nose was red from the cold. He had hands roughed up like bricks—big hands with stubby fingers and swollen knuckles, the skin nicked and scarred and crosshatched with wrinkles. He rubbed a hand over his face, pulling his thumb and forefinger down his cheeks, stretching the loose skin beneath his eyes and making the sadness in them even more pronounced.

"Captain," he said in a low voice, and Missy heard the weariness in it. How many times over the years had he been in a similar position, having to rescue Wesley from some moment of awkwardness. "Son," he said, "we need to get out of the way here."

The EMTs had Ronnie covered with a blanket and belted to the gurney. They were headed toward the door, the tall boy pushing the gurney while his stocky, bowlegged partner walked alongside, using one hand to help steer.

Missy stepped out of the way. Shooter took Captain by the arm and pulled him back against the wall. The stocky boy took the end of the gurney with both hands and eased it through the front door, down the two small steps, and out onto the driveway. There, Ray Biggs had a few words with the EMTs.

"Not another one dead, is there?"

"He's good and concussed," the bowlegged EMT said. "But he'll come around."

"Jesus," said Biggs. "What a night."

Inside the house, Shooter was apologizing to Missy for Captain's interruption. "He heard that ambulance and he got confused." Shooter paused and cast an eye toward the girls still huddled together by the window. They'd turned to look outside at the EMTs loading their father into the ambulance. "He got it in his head that Della and the kids didn't really die," he whispered.

"He was right there tonight," Missy said. "He saw what was what."

"Yes, he saw. Just like we all saw." Missy could tell from the edge in Shooter's voice that she'd been too harsh with what she'd said. "Sometimes I can't explain him."

"No," she said, "I don't suppose you can."

Shooter heard the mix of pity and judgment in Missy's voice, but he wasn't interested at that moment in saying anything more about what it was like to have a boy like Captain. He didn't think it was the time to get his back up, not in the midst of so much sadness. It was time for sleep, if sleep would ever come that night. It was time to lie down and give thanks for their blessings. It wasn't easy having a son like Captain, but he was a good-hearted boy. He might not always know the right way to act, but he'd learned what it was to love folks, had learned that from Merlene. No one would ever be able to accuse him of not knowing that.

"Come on," Shooter told him. "It's time for us to go back home."

Captain was looking across the room at the girls. "Who's going to take care of them now that Ronnie's hurt?"

"I'll take care of my girls," Lois said. She came to Captain and she touched him on his arm. "Don't you worry about that, honey." Shooter appreciated the kindness in her voice. She was petting Captain the way Merlene would have done, soothing him. "You go on with your daddy now. You be a good boy."

Shooter put his hand on Captain's back and tried to guide him toward the door. He wouldn't budge. He was a stocky boy with thick legs, and he dug in and anchored himself. He looked down at the floor and then raised his head and studied Lois a good while. Shooter knew it was sinking in now, the truth of the matter.

"Della's not coming back?" Captain said.

"No, honey." There was a catch in Lois's voice, and Shooter knew it was sinking in for her too. "None of them are coming back."

Captain walked across the room to the girls. "I'm sorry," he said, and Missy heard the quiver in his voice. "I'm sorry," he said again, and he was still saying it when Shooter finally eased him toward the door and out into the cold.

The ambulance went back up the blacktop, headed toward the hospital in Phillipsport, and Ray Biggs came into the house. Missy closed the door behind him.

"Folks," Biggs said, "I'm afraid I'm going to have to ask some questions."

"I hit him," said Wayne. "I hit him with that there." He pointed to the tire iron that Pat had laid on the coffee table. "I meant to hit him and I did it. Now go ahead and do whatever it is you have to."

"Wayne, I'm not sure I have to do anything tonight." Biggs spoke in an even tone. "Lord knows you folks have got enough to deal with. What say we let this ride until we know what's what?" He went to where Wayne was standing by the coffee table. "Now, Wayne, I'm not going to lie to you. Could be you're in for some trouble over this. The ambulance boys say they think Ronnie's going to come to. Mind you, they're not doctors, but let's say they're right. Let's say Ronnie comes around. He could still press charges, Wayne. I'd have to arrest you for assault and battery. You understand that, don't you?"

"I said I did it." Wayne nodded toward Pat. "He'll tell you the same. I'm not going to try to lie about it."

"I'm counting on you not to try to run either." Biggs narrowed his eyes and studied Wayne. "Do I have your word on that?"

"Good God." Wayne could barely rein in his disgust. "Don't you know I've got these girls to see to. You really think I'd run?"

Biggs said it to him plain. "All I know is you hit Ronnie with that tire iron."

Wayne wanted to explain that he really wasn't that kind of man at all. It was just that he'd been carrying this heat toward Ronnie for a good while, and it'd finally got out of his control when he found out Della and the babies were dead. He blamed Ronnie for that, but, if he had to tell the truth, he blamed himself too. He should have insisted that Della and the kids come to their house that night. He should have been a better father. He should have made Della agree. He never should have let her marry Ronnie, but if he hadn't there wouldn't be these four here—Angel and Hannah and Sarah and Emma. He wouldn't have the joy of them, and now he'd let them down by pulling that stunt with the tire iron. Maybe he'd been that kind of man all along, and he just hadn't known it.

"I won't run," he said. "Time comes you want to take me in, you'll know where to find me. Now, I just want to take my grandkids home."

He took a few steps toward them, but then the room started to spin around, and he had to stop.

"Wayne?" Lois said.

"I'm dizzy." He managed to get to the nearest chair, an over-stuffed recliner, and he dropped down into it. "Everything's whirling all merry-go-round on me."

"He's been having these dizzy spells." Lois went over to where he was sitting, and she put her hand on his head. "Haven't you, Wayne?"

"They come and go," he said.

"Have you seen a doctor?" Biggs asked him.

"Doctors cost money," Wayne said.

"It's been a burden," said Lois. "Seeing to him."

For a while no one spoke. Then Biggs said to Lois, "You sure you want to take on these girls right now?"

"They're my grandbabies," Lois said, and her voice broke. "Lord, I feel like I'm a million years old."

"I can call Laverne Ott. She can get the girls into a foster care. Might make it easier on you, Lois." Biggs was talking in a gentle voice now. "Wayne, you hear what I'm saying?"

Missy couldn't bear the thought of that. Those girls shuttled off somewhere, put into a stranger's house right after losing their mother and their sisters and their baby brother. That wouldn't do. It wouldn't do at all. She caught Pat's eye, and she hoped her look of disapproval would tell him what she was afraid to say with words. For just a while at least, couldn't they take care of the girls? He nodded at her, as if he knew exactly what she was thinking, and she felt a rush of love for him, this man who was dependable, someone she could count on, a different sort of man from Ronnie Black.

Pat said to Biggs, "Is that really the best idea?"

"Well now, Pat. We've got to find a place for them. Ronnie's sure in no shape."

"We'll take them." Missy hoped she hadn't spoken too quickly or with too much urgency in her voice. She tried to stay calm, tried to make it clear that this was a kindness she was offering, and that if

Biggs said he couldn't allow that, she wouldn't feel her heart come apart as she feared it might. "They can stay here with Pat and me. We're their godparents, after all. We've looked after them plenty before."

"Oh, honey, are you sure you want to take on all that?" Lois said.

"I've given them showers," said Missy. "I've combed their hair and got them into clean things."

Should she try to do more for them? Do the things—she could hardly bring herself to say the word—that a mother would do? She wasn't sure. In fact, the prospect scared her to death, but she really didn't see any other choice, and she knew she wanted to try.

"Biggs?" Pat said.

"I guess it depends on what Wayne and Lois think of the idea."

Wayne said it was up to her. "I've caused enough trouble the way it is."

Lois nodded toward the girls, who were still in a bunch by the window. "Maybe we ought to ask them what they think."

Angel spoke for all of them. "I don't want to go back out in the cold. It's fine with me to stay right here."

She was afraid to be with her father because of how much she needed him now. It scared her to death to know that he was the one she'd have to count on and the one she would more than likely have to tell at some point that a few minutes before the trailer was on fire, she woke up and, through the slit between the panels of her window curtains, she saw sparks outside. At first, still not fully awake, she thought she was seeing lightning bugs because she'd been having a dream about summer, toward twilight, and a road snaking back into the woods, and suddenly Captain was there, and she was mad at him over something; she was yelling at him, and he kept asking her why, and then he was running and she was running after him, deeper and deeper into the dark woods.

As she watched the shower of lights, she began to understand that she was seeing sparks. She sat up in bed and parted the curtain panels. She saw the cardboard box of ashes, the one her mother had told her to take out to the compost, but she hadn't. Someone had set it outside. Who cared? Not Angel, not then, not until the trailer was on fire, and she felt certain that it was her fault. If she'd only taken the box of ashes to the compost and emptied it there, everyone would be alive. She didn't want to be around her father. She didn't want to tell him that, nor did she want to tell him what else she'd done. She'd gone back to bed, let herself drift into sleep once more, not thinking another thing about that box of ashes, not until her mother shook her awake and said, "We're on fire. Angel, help me."

She wished she could stand in Missy's living room now, knowing that she'd done just what her mother asked, but it wasn't the truth, not at all. She and Hannah had run out into the cold night. She'd left her mother inside the trailer to try to save the others.

How in the world would she ever tell her father, or anyone else, any of that, and how would she tell him that as she fell asleep that second time, she heard a man's voice outside, or at least thought she did. *Sugar tits,* she thought she heard, the way she'd heard her father—and then Captain—say too many times to count, but now she wasn't sure she'd heard anything at all. Maybe it was just the wind, the same wind that was tossing the sparks from the box of ashes into the air. A shower of sparks that Angel could no longer see, asleep as she was and back in the dream from which she'd awakened, back in the woods calling for Captain, not knowing where he'd gone, only knowing she had to find him.

15

So that's how the girls came to be with Missy and Pat, and that's where they were the next afternoon, a Saturday, when Ronnie got out of the hospital, his mind fairly made up that he was going to press charges against Wayne.

"The man attacked me," he said to Brandi. Pat Wade had called last night to tell her what had happened between Wayne and Ronnie, and she'd been at the hospital ever since. "He clubbed me right there in front of my girls. I've been thinking on it, and I'm not sure I can let him get away with that." Ronnie zipped up his jacket. "Where are they anyway? Who's got them? Wayne and Lois?"

Brandi shook her head. "Wayne's taken sick. It's Missy and Pat who's seeing to the girls."

"I like Pat okay. He's always been square with me. Missy, on the other hand—well, I know she wants to hold my feet to the fire—"

His voice trailed off, the word "fire" hanging in the air.

"Sugar," Brandi said, "what did you mean last night when Pat first told you the trailer had burned? You said it was a good thing that Della and the kids were spending the night with her folks. Why did you think that?"

Ronnie stuffed his hands into his jacket pockets. He looked down at his feet. Finally, he raised his head and looked at Brandi. "I was out there yesterday afternoon after I got served those papers, and she said if the furnace acted up, she'd take the kids to her folks for the night."

"But why did you think she'd had to do that?"

"I called out there last night when I was driving around. I stopped at Casey's and used the payphone. No one answered, so I thought—"

His voice got shaky then, and he stopped trying to talk. He bit at his lip.

"Oh," Brandi said. "I didn't know you'd done that."

"I just wanted to make sure they were all right."

"It's okay. It doesn't make me mad. There's been a world of hurt. Maybe it's time now to just let things be."

Ronnie turned away from her and stared out the window. From the third floor, he could look out over the parking lot to State Street and the Wabash Savings and Loan where Brandi worked. The time and temperature sign in front of the Savings and Loan said it was fourteen degrees, a fact that he found hard to fathom since from where he stood, the afternoon sun bright and warm on his face, it was easy to imagine the cold gone forever. It was one of those January days that broke clear after a stretch of gray skies, and if not for the puffs of exhaust from the cars and trucks moving along State Street, and the trees with their bare branches, and a woman getting out of her car in the parking lot, her hands held over her ears, he'd be able to pretend it was summer. He'd be able to picture himself in the porch swing at Brandi's house—*their* house—his hand on her stomach, waiting for the baby to kick. His baby. That life coming. He'd have that blessing. But the truth was—and he knew this that day in the hospital—every step thereafter would be weighted down with the fact of the fire.

"I don't know." He turned back to Brandi. "I want to do what's right. People probably wouldn't believe it to hear me say that, but it's true. People like Missy. People like Lois and Wayne. They've got their minds made up about me."

"Sugar, you've got to think about what you want on down the road." She went to him and slipped her arms around his waist. "Maybe now's not the time to make waves."

The two of them hadn't talked about that, hadn't said a word about how the life they'd been planning would now jostle up against the hard facts of the fire. All fall and winter, Ronnie had been busy imagining his new life with Brandi and the baby. Not that he thought he'd make a clean break from Della and the kids—not that he even wanted to. Maybe he'd have the kids a few at a time. An afternoon here, a weekend there, maybe even a week during the summer or at the holidays, before they went back to their trailer along the blacktop.

But things were different now. Della was gone, and the girls who'd survived the fire were waiting to see where they'd land.

Ronnie said, "They're my girls." He studied Brandi's face, tried to figure out how what he was about to say would affect her. Then, all of a sudden, he knew, and with the knowing came a great peace. She was looking at him, and he could tell that he could say what was in his heart and she'd accept it without question. "I want them to come live with us."

Brandi nodded. "All right, then." She kissed his cheek. "You ready?"

"I'm ready," he said.

She took his hand. "Let's go home, and let's not come back here until it's time for the baby to be born. Deal?"

"Deal," he said, and he knew, then, he wouldn't file charges against Wayne. He'd keep things nice and easy. He'd go get his girls, and Brandi would be right there beside him, no matter what people thought about that. They were a couple, and those girls were his children, and together he and Brandi would give them a good home.

That's the story he told himself as the two of them stepped out of the hospital into the cold, into a sun so bright it hurt his eyes, and he had to squint so he could see where he was going.

The visitation would be on Tuesday evening. In the days since the fire, folks from Goldengate had driven out the blacktop to get a look at the trailer. Car after car. Rubberneckers, Shooter Rowe called them, when a reporter from the television station up in Terre Haute came on Saturday and started asking questions. "Goddamn rubberneckers," Shooter said. "Busybodies who can't keep their eyes on their own business." The charred mess was nothing anyone would recognize as ever having been a home. Just a pile of smoldering debris, soggy from the pumper's dousing, only the hunks of the furnace and the hot water heater still standing to make any sign at all that a woman and her seven kids had lain down on their beds there the night before and gone to sleep. "Put that in your story," Shooter told the reporter. "People no better than turkey buzzards feeding off the dead. They've got no business out here."

They kept coming, people who'd known Della and her kids and people who hadn't. They came to lay flowers, teddy bears, and cards at what was left of the front step of the trailer. Someone tied four helium-filled balloons—red, yellow, blue, and green—to a low branch of the cedar tree at the corner of the goat shed. The heat from the fire had scorched the needles from the cedar and the branches were bare, the bark blistered and peeling in places. People came to bring the flowers and teddy bears and cards and balloons because they wanted to do something. A fire truck was still there, a hose run through the field to the pond where they'd had to chop through the ice to get water once the tanker ran dry. The Red Cross workers who'd been there most of the night had gone, leaving behind a litter of crushed coffee cups on the frozen ground.

Shooter knew that some people came because they'd been acquainted with Della and her kids from church, or school activities, or 4-H. He knew they came because they didn't know what else to do. He tried to make allowances for the ones like Laverne Ott. He saw her car pulled off the side of the blacktop in front of what was left of the trailer, and he let her sit there a good long while, left her to her grief until finally he started to worry. He came outside and crossed the blacktop. He tapped on her window and she pushed the button to power it down. Her glasses were crooked on her face.

"Oh, Carl," she said, using his given name. "My god."

"I know, Laverne," he said. "It just tears my heart."

"What it must have been like here last night."

He could have told her about the blaze and the sounds—the roar of the flames, the breaking of glass, the crackling of the vinyl and plastic, the popping of aerosol cans exploding. He could have told her about the cries he heard from the children and how there came a time when they stopped, and how that was the worst sound of all: the absence of anything human. He wouldn't tell her how the volunteer firefighters found Della holding the baby, with Gracie and Emily huddled up close to her. He wouldn't say that there'd been so little of them left that the coroner's deputies brought them all out in the same body bag. He'd spare Laverne Ott all that.

"It's nothing I want to talk about," he said. "Not ever."

He wouldn't tell her that around nine o'clock the night of the fire, Captain got all worked up over Della's goats, worried that the patch job Shooter had done on the pen wouldn't hold.

"It's not our job to see to those goats," Shooter told him, but Captain wouldn't leave it alone. If they didn't look out for Della, who would?

"We've got ourselves to look out for," Shooter had said, and he meant it. There he was alone with Captain to see to, and wasn't that enough without having to see to another man's wife and kids? Was it any wonder that Shooter got his back up each time those goats got out? A man should keep himself to his duty—if he's any kind of man at all.

"It's Ronnie's job," Shooter told Captain. "It's his place, but he's not man enough to know it. Don't you ever be like him, Wesley. I swear. He's not worth a damn."

That was the worst thing he could have said—and Shooter knew that as soon as the words were out of the mouth.

"Don't you talk about Ronnie like that." Captain balled his hands up into fists. "I mean it. Don't."

Shooter latched onto his arm. "Someday you'll know what I'm saying is true. It's just too much for you to understand now."

Captain broke free. "I'm not stupid."

"I'm not saying you are."

"You think I'm a retard." Captain turned and stomped into his room. He slammed the door, and Shooter heard the lock click, and then Captain's voice, more distant from the other side of the locked door. "You think I don't listen."

Shooter tried to tell him that wasn't true. He told him, as he always did, that he was a special gift from God. A boy with a good heart. "But damn it, Wesley. Sometimes you've got to know that goodness only carries you so far in the world. There are people—and Ronnie is one of them—who don't mind stomping on someone just to get what he wants. You need to know there are people like him."

Captain wouldn't say a word, and finally Shooter gave up. He brooded awhile in his reclining chair. Then he turned on the television and tried to get interested in an old John Wayne movie. After a time he dozed off and when he woke up it was ten o'clock and the movie was over.

He got to stewing then, recalling how Della had spoken so sharply to him that afternoon. Who did she think she was? The more he thought about it, the angrier he got. He'd been trying to do nothing but a good turn for her ever since Ronnie left, and then for her to snap at him like that. By god, he didn't regret for a second what he'd told Missy. He *would* like Della and her mob much better if only they lived somewhere else.

He wouldn't tell Laverne Ott any of that because now, in the light of day, that trailer collapsed and charred, it seemed like too shameful a thing to say.

"They need us now, Carl," Laverne said to him from her car. "Those girls and, yes, Ronnie too. All of us. It's going to take all of us."

He wanted to tell her he'd patched that goat pen. He'd done what he could. He wanted to tell her Captain's heart was full of love for Della and those girls. He wanted everyone to know that, to know there might not be any explaining when it came to why Captain did the things he did, but always he was a boy full of love. He didn't want anyone to forget that. He wanted to say all this, but it was too late. Laverne was gone, and there were other cars coming down the blacktop, slowing to a stop—gawkers—and he went back into his house where they couldn't see him or have the chance to ask him any questions.

Very few people—not even Shooter—knew everything that was happening in the days between the fire and the visitation for Della and Gracie and Emily and Junior. Sure, word had gotten around that Wayne Best had used that tire iron on Ronnie and put him in the hospital, and people knew that the girls were staying with Pat and Missy, at least until that mess between Ronnie and Wayne could be sorted out. Readers of *The Goldengate Weekly Press* learned that Angel, Hannah, Sarah, and Emma needed clothes and school supplies and toiletry items. Folks wrote down the correct sizes of shirts and pants and shoes and went shopping at the Walmart in Phillipsport.

They picked up packs of pencils and pens. They bought crayons and notebooks, tubes of toothpaste and toothbrushes, deodorants and shampoos. Some folks tossed in little extras like bubblegum or candy. They picked out baby dolls for Sarah and Emma, music CDs for Angel and Hannah, the sorts of things that normal kids their age would like because it was important for them to remember what it was to be a kid, particularly now that the fire threatened to rush them away from their childhoods.

The Bethlehem Christian Church accepted the donations, and in town the Goldengate First National Bank did the same. Missy started a fund at the bank to help with the girls' care, and people donated what cash they could manage. They didn't know that Missy had opened the fund on the condition that she be the account holder and the only one to make decisions about it. She didn't want to take the chance that Ronnie might get his hands on the money. She couldn't bear the thought of him and Brandi taking it and doing only God would know what.

Decisions like that got made behind doors closed to most of the folks of Goldengate and Phillips County. There was so much they didn't know and wouldn't find out until the visitation and the funeral and the days that would come.

They didn't know that Ronnie, once he was out of the hospital, drove out to Pat and Missy's, and Missy met him in the driveway holding her cardigan sweater closed by wrapping her arms across her chest.

"I won't have you upsetting them," she said.

"Missy, those are my girls, and I've come to take them."

Brandi was sitting behind the wheel of her Mustang, staring straight ahead, as if she weren't there at all.

"I guess she's agreed to that." Missy nodded her head toward Brandi. "Your girlfriend? She ready to be a mama four times over just like that?"

"She's got a good heart, Missy. I know you don't believe that, but it's the truth."

Missy stepped up close to him and kept her voice low. "Ronnie, there's no need to stir anything up right now. I've got your girls settled in here. The visitation's on Tuesday, and there's still this matter of what you're going to do about Wayne. Let things settle down, Ronnie. For those girls' sake, let them have some stability now."

"Their place is with me. I can take care of them."

"Can you, Ronnie?" Missy let a silence settle between them. The engine in Brandi's Mustang ticked as it cooled. A crow cawed as it circled overhead. Up the road at Shooter Rowe's, the engine of an ATV revved. "I mean," Missy finally said, "it's not like they've been used to having you around. They were making do without you for a good long while."

She knew as she said it that it was a mean thing to say. She could see the pain of it in Ronnie's pinched face, his downcast eyes, but she wasn't sorry. She'd told the truth, and where was the harm in that? She felt that already the fire had changed her, was giving her the chance to know her own heart in ways she'd never known it.

"I'd like to see them, Missy." Ronnie wouldn't look at her, and she knew what it was costing him to keep his temper reined in, to have to ask her for the favor of seeing his own daughters. "Is it all right if I just say hello?"

At that moment, Brandi put down the passenger-side window on her car and said, "Ronnie, what's the holdup? I'm getting cold."

"Guess you'll have to make it a quick hello." Missy nodded her head toward the house to let Ronnie know he should follow her. "Wouldn't want your girlfriend to get frostbite."

Ronnie hesitated, waiting for Missy to say it would be all right for Brandi to come inside with him. When it became clear that no such invitation was coming, he looked back at Brandi and gave her a shrug of his shoulders. Then he turned and went up the driveway with Missy.

Hannah met him at the door. She threw her arms around his neck, and the feel of her slight body was enough to bring him close to tears. She was so slender—all arms and legs—barely any weight to her at all.

"Daddy," she said in a whisper.

"Baby," he said.

Missy let them have that moment, and Ronnie was grateful. He held onto Hannah, as she clung to him with such a fierce grip his neck began to hurt, but he wouldn't for the life of him tell her to let go.

Few people would ever hear about this moment when he was so thankful for Hannah, and for Angel, even though he knew she still hated him, and for Sarah and Emma, who both watched shyly from the archway that led to the kitchen, keeping their distance as if they somehow knew that this moment between Hannah and their father was something special and held themselves back so it could last a little longer.

Finally, he eased Hannah away from him, and he saw Sarah and Emma. Sarah had a sucker in her mouth. Emma was holding onto a blond-haired doll wearing a bright blue and red plaid dress.

"Girls," he said to them, "is Missy taking good care of you?"

At first there was only silence, as if the girls were trying to figure out the right answer. Finally, Sarah said, "Yeppers," which was the silly way she had of saying yes, and for just an instant Emma giggled.

Ronnie didn't know what to do with that sound of joy rising up from so much sadness. He could tell Missy didn't know what to do with it either. He heard her intake of breath. Her eyes opened wide. He felt just as startled. He let the moment rest there, afraid to say anything, afraid to make a move, knowing that soon the moment would vanish—light as smoke—and they would come back to the facts of the matter. He would tell Hannah and Sarah and Emma that he'd see them in a few days. He'd say to tell Angel that he loved her.

"I love you all," he said. Then he nodded to Missy to let her know that he'd back off for now. He wouldn't rush things. He'd let her have her way, at least for the time. Then he went back outside and told Brandi he'd see her back in town.

He glanced at his Firebird, which he supposed Pat had had to move so he could get his truck out that morning.

"I'll get my car," Ronnie said. "Maybe I'll make a stop at Lois and Wayne's."

"You letting Missy keep the girls?"

"For now," he said. "Just for now."

Wayne wouldn't let Ronnie come inside. He stepped onto the porch of the box house set back a lane off County Road 550, and he said to Ronnie, "I guess I didn't kill you."

"I hear you've been sickly."

"Got the head spins from time to time."

Ronnie nodded. "I'm not going to press charges. That's what I came to say."

Wayne nodded. Then he said, "Lois and I have to be somewhere in a few minutes, so I don't have time to talk. At some point, though, we're going to have to come to a decision about the girls."

"What's there to talk about? They're mine to see to."

"Can you make a home for them, Ronnie? Can you make sure they get enough to eat, clothes to wear?"

"I get work here and there, just about like you, I expect." Ronnie narrowed his eyes. "And there's Brandi. She makes decent money at the Savings and Loan. I'll ask Pat for steady work once things pick up in the spring."

"I don't want to hear that woman's name. I mean it, Ronnie. Not ever. And I don't want to see her at the visitation or the funeral. You understand?"

"Is it the funeral home?" Ronnie said. It came to him with a force that made him feel weak in his legs that Wayne and Lois and maybe even Missy would make decisions about the funeral without asking his help. "Is that where you're going in town?"

"I don't have to report to you, Ronnie. It's not your concern."

So not even Ronnie knew until the night of the visitation that there would be only one casket. That was the first thing that everyone noticed when they walked into the Phillipsport High School gymnasium, that single casket, closed, at the far end near the free throw line. Missy and Lois and Wayne had decided the gym would be the best place to accommodate all the people who were sure to come, and now the rows of folding chairs on the floor were filling up, and people were scooting closer together to make room on the bleachers rising on both sides. All these people coming out on a cold night to pay their respects. People from all over Phillips County. Many of them hadn't known Della or Ronnie or any of their families, but they felt that they should be in attendance because there were those poor girls—the four of them standing near the casket with Wayne and Lois Best—and it was going to take a passel of folks to shepherd them now.

Some people, though they wouldn't admit it, were there because they'd heard the stories about Ronnie and Brandi, and they couldn't squelch their curiosity. Would she be there? Would they arrive together? The story of Wayne taking that tire iron to Ronnie had made the rounds, and as people chatted in low tones that night in the gymnasium, more than one person admitted that they had an inclination to do the same. A man like Ronnie Black. Of course, he'd be there for the sake of his children, but, mercy, it's a wonder he can even show his face.

He'd been there all along. He'd come before Wayne and Lois, before Missy and his girls, before Laverne Ott and Shooter Rowe and Captain, and all the people who'd followed, filling the gym with their footsteps, the scents of their perfumes and aftershaves, the smell of the cold outside that they carried in on their clothes. He'd come alone, and the only person there was Dean Henry, the funeral director.

"I guess Wayne and Lois made all the arrangements," Ronnie said.

Dean was a short man who was all-over bald. He'd just finished arranging the casket spray of yellow lilies, white carnations, and red roses. He stepped back a moment and took in the casket and the standing floral sprays on their tripods and the baskets and vases sitting on the floor. The air was sweet with rose attar, the perfume of lilies, the spicy scent of snapdragons, and the aroma of gladioli.

"That's right." Dean took off his metal-rimmed glasses, and Ronnie noticed the creases the stems had pressed into skin above his ears. "And Missy Wade. She made sure the casket was taken care of."

"Out of her pocket?"

"I really can't say."

Ronnie knew there was a fund at the First National to help with the girls. He'd read about it in the *Weekly Press*, but no one had said anything to him about it. No one had told him how to access the money because, so he assumed, no one thought he was capable of managing it. No one trusted him to make the right decisions. He'd lost three of his babies, and up to this point no one had given him a chance to do anything a father would have done.

"One casket," he said to Dean.

Dean put his glasses back on. "No need for others," he said in his gentle funeral director's voice. He patted Ronnie on the shoulder as he turned to give him a moment alone at the casket. "You take your time."

Ronnie stood there trying to recall what it was like when Della meant the world to him. He couldn't say that he'd stopped loving her, only that he'd reached a point where it was easier to be away from her than it was to be with her, disappointing her too much of the time. Then there'd been Brandi, and one thing had led to another until he was in too deep and there was no getting back to the man he'd been and the life he'd had. A life that was achingly real to him now and yet beyond his reach.

He recalled the smallest things. The way he taught Emily to swallow air and make herself burp; the months when Gracie had an imaginary dog she called Pitty-Pat Popsicle Pooch; the way they'd all sing "Walking on Sunshine"—even Della—and Junior would bob his head and pound his sippy cup on his highchair tray like a drummer caught in the rapture.

Just things like that. Just the stuff of being a family.

Finally, he slipped out through a rear door that opened onto the alley. It was dark, and snow had started to fall. A few feet up the alley two men leaned against the wall of the school, one of them smoking a cigarette, the cherry bright when he puffed. Ronnie noted something familiar in the set of his narrow shoulders and the way he stood with his chin thrust out in front of him. He knew it was Milt Timlin, the fire chief from Goldengate.

"Something odd about that fire," Milt said. "I was out there all night and most of the next morning. I can't put my finger on what it is, but something doesn't set right with me."

And the other one said, "It went up in a hurry. I can tell you that. Missy said, 'Della's trailer's on fire,' and by the time I got there—"

Ronnie knew then that the other man was Pat Wade.

"And Shooter Rowe was already there?"

"Him and his boy."

"No one else?"

"Just them."

For a while neither man said anything, and Ronnie could hear the sound of traffic on the street that ran along the school. He could hear car doors slamming shut and the hushed tones of people talking as they made their way inside.

Then Pat said, "You don't think someone set it?"

"I guess the State Fire Marshal will determine that," Milt said, "but I can tell you that blaze sure burned hot in a certain place."

That's when Ronnie coughed so the men would spy him there and stop their talking. "Pat, is that you?" he called down the alley.

"It's me," Pat said. "Sure is snowing, isn't it?"

Ronnie took a few steps and then stopped when he realized the snow was coming up over his loafers and the cuffs of his dress pants.

"You think I set that fire?" he asked.

Milt said something to Pat in a low voice, and then Ronnie thought he heard Pat say his name.

Then Pat's voice came louder. "Ah, Ronnie, we were just talking. We didn't say anything like that. Why in the world would anyone think you'd—"

Ronnie stopped him before he could say more. "I used to think you were head and shoulders above the rest of us, Pat." His voice was louder and it echoed down the alley in the snowy night. He said, "I really did. I used to think you were a good man."

He turned to go back into the gymnasium. He could barely catch his breath. The last thing he wanted was for anyone to know he'd been at the trailer that night. That was his secret, and his alone, and would be as long as he could keep it.

At the end of the alley he turned back to Pat. "I won't let you keep my girls." He was shouting now, and he didn't care who heard him. "You can count on that. Understand? You better tell Missy. You tell her exactly what I said."

16

Since her last miscarriage back in September, Missy and Pat hadn't talked much at all, just the words necessary between two people who shared a house. But one evening toward the end of October, he came home and she was gone. He waited and waited, and the more time he spent in the quiet house, the more he began to relax, relieved of the tension he usually felt from occupying the same space with someone to whom he couldn't say the things that mattered most to him. He'd tried to talk to Missy about getting pregnant again, but she'd made it clear that she didn't want to have that conversation. So they moved through their days, speaking of things like utility bills and the weather and, of course, Ronnie and the fact that he'd left Della, a story that Missy took a special interest in, all too glad to let the anger she felt over the circumstances of her own life find a target with Ronnie Black. She finally came home that night in October, and even now Pat could recall the sinking feeling inside him when she started to speak and he felt a part of their life together coming to an end.

"I've been driving," she said. "Thinking. Just driving around." Her voice was even and calm, no hint of exaggeration or dramatics, and he knew that what she was about to tell him would be something he'd never be able to change. "I'm done," she said. "That was the last time."

"Missy?"

"I'm done with babies," she said, and that was that.

Until the fire. "We could make a good home for the girls," she said to Pat as they were trying to fall asleep after the visitation. "Couldn't we? Oh, I'm sure we could, but whenever I think about it I get scared to death. Me? A mother? Maybe I'm being silly thinking about having the girls for good."

"Custody?" Pat said. "Is that what's on your mind?"

"I don't know. Pat, do you think—"

Her voice trailed off, and he put his arm around her in the dark. "You'd be a fine mother," he said, not having the heart to tell her that Ronnie had said he'd fight for his girls.

Pat woke the next morning and found himself alone in bed, the sunlight on his face. He smelled bacon frying in the kitchen. He'd had a miserable sleep, disturbed as he was by what Ronnie had said to him in the alley. One thought kept coming back: Why did Ronnie, eavesdropping from the alley, ask him if he thought he had something to do with that trailer going up? Why would a man ask that—jump to that conclusion—if he didn't have something to hide?

Missy had the girls up and helping her get breakfast on the table. They were still in their pajamas and nightshirts. They padded around the kitchen in their socks, barely making a sound. Pat stood in the doorway, watching them as they moved about the kitchen on this, the morning of the funeral. He listened to the whisk of their feet over the tile floor, watched as they turned their willowy bodies to keep from bumping one another as they moved about the kitchen. Angel used a fork to spear bacon strips from the frying pan. She dipped her wrist to shake the grease off the bacon and then lay each strip down on a plate covered with a paper towel. When the plate was full, she raised it high, arching her arm to avoid Hannah who was at the toaster, plucking out slices of bread with two fingers. Sarah poured juice into glasses, and when she carried them two by two to the table, she held them with care, taking tiny steps around Emma, who was dipping in and out between the chairs, arranging silverware just so beside each plate.

Missy was at the stove cooking eggs, and when she turned and saw Pat in the doorway, she smiled. "Well, girls, look who's finally here," she said in a teasing voice. "Mr. Sleepy Head."

He stepped into the kitchen, and Emma, who'd finished with the silverware, wandered over and leaned into him, laying her head against his leg. He let his hand trail through her hair, smoothing out the sleep tangles with his fingers.

"You were snoring," she said. "You were snoring like a big old bear."

"That's what I am," Pat said. "A big old sleepy bear. And you know what they say about sleepy bears, don't you?"

"No, what?"

"Don't wake them up."

He tickled her ribs until she laughed, and he thought, yet again—how many times over the past few days had he thought it?— that given the chance, he'd make a good father. He'd know how to protect his children.

They sat around the breakfast table, and they all joined hands and closed their eyes while Pat prayed that God would watch over them and keep them safe.

After breakfast, when Pat and Missy were in their bedroom dressing for the funeral, she came to him and helped him with his necktie. She made sure the knot was neat, and then she let her hand lay flat against his chest and she said, "You're so good with them."

"He's going to take them," Pat said in a whisper.

Through the closed bedroom door, he could hear the muffled voices of the girls who were dressed and waiting. Just the faintest sound of their voices and their footsteps as if they were already ghosts that had come to visit but only for a while.

"He's their father," she said in a tight voice.

"For better or worse."

Missy had a hard look in her eyes now. Just like that she was the bitter woman and he was the wary man they'd both been since the miscarriage in October.

"That's just like you," she said. "You've never had enough fight. Never."

"But what can we do?"

She didn't answer. She turned and marched out of the bedroom, leaving him stunned by how quickly she could change into that woman. All he could do was say what he'd just told her. The fact was Ronnie was those girls' father, and he had his rights to them. Not a thing anyone could do about that. Not a single thing.

"Nothing," Pat whispered. "Nothing at all."

And there wasn't. He knew it all through the funeral service as he and Missy sat next to each other, holding hands. They sat in the second row of mourners. The first row was reserved for the girls and for Wayne and Lois.

Across the center aisle in the front row sat Ronnie with Brandi beside him. He wore a dark gray suit, obviously new. The collar of his white shirt was too loose around his slender neck. He wasn't a man accustomed to wearing a suit and a necktie, but he didn't fidget or squirm. He sat still with his chin lifted and his narrow shoulders pushed back, and he stared straight ahead, knowing, Pat was sure, that so many eyes in the school gymnasium were on him and Brandi. She had on a black dress that under any other circumstances would have been considered modest, but because she was *that* woman, more than one person was quick to call the uneven cut of the hem too showy and the scoop neckline too revealing.

Pat understood that Wayne and Lois and the girls would always be set apart in Goldengate. What remained to be seen was how the story of Ronnie and Brandi would finally settle against this other story of four girls trying to make their way through the rest of their lives, of Ronnie and the girls trying to remember what it was to be a family because that was what Pat was certain would happen now. Ronnie would get his girls, and Pat and Missy would once again be alone in their house. It shamed Pat that he couldn't separate that sadness from the grief he felt over the deaths, but there it was, all mixed in together, and it stayed with him through the service and on to the Bethlehem Church Cemetery where the gravediggers had heated the frozen ground before they dug, and into the church itself where Laverne Ott and the others had carried a dinner into the basement to feed the family. Before they ate, the pastor, Harold Quick, who owned the Real McCoy Café in Goldengate, asked a blessing on everyone gathered there, and he asked God to hold Ronnie and his daughters in His loving hands, now and forever. Amen.

Missy felt herself go hard inside where she knew her Christian heart should be soft and forgiving. She just couldn't manage it, not after she'd spent the last days caring for those girls—cooking for them, helping pick out shirts and pants and dresses from the donated clothing, helping little Emma with her bath, combing tangles from her hair, tucking her and Sarah in at night and kissing them on their foreheads. Even Hannah and Angel—even tough, brittle Angel—allowed the same, lifted their heads a bit from their pillows to meet her lips and then sank back and closed their eyes and went to sleep.

Pat had been right. Ronnie would have those girls and there'd be nothing she could do about it. She could only say yes, which she did when Ronnie came to her as the dinner was winding down and the church basement was empty except for the family and those closest to them.

"I'd like to come by and get the girls' things," Ronnie said. "You've been a help, Missy, but it's time my daughters were with me."

Over Ronnie's shoulder, she saw Wayne and Lois giving each of the girls a hug. Wayne had on his coat, and so did Lois.

"What about Wayne and Lois?" Missy nodded her head in their direction, and Ronnie turned his head to look at them. "Have you worked it out with then?"

"They can't keep me from my girls." Ronnie turned back to Missy. "There's no call for anyone to keep me from them." He let that sink in. "So I'll be by for their things. All right?"

And Missy said the only thing she could. She said, "All right, let's put together some clothes for them." She'd pick and choose from the donations that were there at the church. "They've got things at our house, too. If you give me a couple of hours, I'll get it all ready."

But there was one problem: Angel didn't want to go. "I won't," she said in the van on the drive from the church to Pat and Missy's. She sat in the backseat, directly behind Missy. Hannah and Sarah were back there, too. Emma was on Hannah's lap. "He can't make me," Angel said. "I'm going to stay with you."

Angel's desire to stay took Missy by the heart and wouldn't let her go. She looked out over the fields, covered now with snow, and the rest of winter stretched ahead of her with its short light, the dark falling early, and the long, long nights. She wanted nothing more than the chatter of those girls to fill her house, but she knew it was out of her hands. She'd done what she could, and now it was her duty to let them go, no matter how much she disapproved of Ronnie.

"He's your father," she said.

It seemed like a long time before Angel spoke again. "Guess you don't want us," she said, and Missy tried hard to keep from saying what she really wished she could say: that she wanted Angel and her sisters more than anything. She wouldn't say it because she was trying her best to do the proper thing, to give in to law and nature. Ronnie was their father. He may have walked away from his family, but it was his place now to raise these girls. If that's what he wanted, there was nothing anyone could do to stop him. "I thought you loved us," Angel said.

"I do. More than you'll ever know."

"Then let me stay."

"Oh, sweetie. I can't."

So Missy packed up a box for each of the girls: shampoos and soaps and toothbrushes and toothpastes; deodorants and perfumes and toys and CDs; pencils and pens and notebooks and paste and crayons; pajamas and underwear and hair scrunchies and house shoes. It amazed her how much they'd claimed from the donations in so few days. She packed everything up, her steps leaden, her arms weary, her hands seeming to belong to someone else.

Much later, when the girls were gone, and she was washing the dishes from her and Pat's supper, she tried to convince herself that it had been simple: she packed up the boxes, and Ronnie came, and the girls told her goodbye. She knew she was lying to herself. Watching them go had been the hardest thing she'd had to do, harder in some ways than the miscarriages, hard to watch the faces of those girls at the windows of Ronnie's Firebird, waving goodbye, goodbye, all except Angel, who slumped in the front seat, staring straight ahead.

Missy was playing all of that again in her head when she heard the knock at the front door and Pat's low voice talking to whoever it was who had come to see them.

She dried her hands on the dishtowel and went into the living room to see who it was.

Shooter Rowe and Pat stood just inside the front door. Shooter had a fierce look on his face as if he'd thought hard about something and had just then come to a decision.

"Missy," he said when he saw her, "I hate to bother you, but there's something I got to tell you about Ronnie Black."

17

Missy barely slept that night, turning over and over in her head what Shooter had come to say and what Pat had finally told her. Milt Timlin thought there was something fishy about the way Della's trailer had burned.

That wasn't any surprise to him, Shooter said, not given what he'd seen the night of the fire.

"I saw Ronnie's Firebird pulled off to the side of the blacktop a little ways up the road, pointed toward town."

"You mean he was there?" Missy said.

Shooter nodded. "I saw him come from behind the trailer. He was toting something. I can't say what it was, but he put it in that Firebird, and then he started up the blacktop, not fast like he usually does, but real slow like he didn't want anyone to take note of him."

"Like he had something to hide," Missy said.

She was still thinking on it the next morning when she set out for town. She meant to go to the bank to speak with the president, Faye Griggs, about the fund she'd set up for the girls. Missy wanted to make sure that Ronnie wouldn't be able to withdraw that money. She was the account holder, and she didn't intend to step aside. This seemed important to her, especially in light of Shooter's story. If the authorities came for Ronnie, would he try to get what was in that account and then run?

"Good folks gave that money," she said. "Faye, it'd just kill me if it went for something other than what it's meant for. Can we make it so I can divvy it out as I see fit to help with the girls' care?"

They were sitting in Faye's office, Faye behind her desk and Missy in a chair in front of it. Faye leaned forward to close the space between them, and she spoke in a low, confidential voice. "You know, the world is full of folks who mean well. All sorts of people trying to do the right thing. What is it they say about the road to Hell? Paved with good intentions?"

Faye had worked at the bank as long as Missy could remember. Her hair had gone gray in all the time she'd worked there, and the skin had gone loose under her chin. She'd been at the bank so long she knew about everything there was to know about the business of the folks who lived in and around Goldengate. She'd notarized their wills, handled their quit claim deeds on land sales, set up annuities for their retirements, sold them certificates of deposit, taken note of the balances in their savings accounts. She was known from time to time to let something slip about how well-off someone was or what had caused someone to have to make a significant withdrawal. She knew about sons and daughters who needed bail money. She knew who had disinherited whom. She knew about people with accounts they were keeping secret from a husband or a wife. She was sometimes—to put it plainly—a gossip. Over the years, she'd come to believe—at least Missy imagined this was true—that since she was the guardian of so many people's business, she had a right to say whatever she wanted. "Sometimes it's hard, isn't it?" she said now to Missy. "I mean, it's tough knowing the right thing to do."

The smell of eucalyptus coming from a candle burning on one of Faye's filing cabinets was too strong for Missy's preference. She coughed a little. "Are you saying it's not right for me to watch over that money?" She'd lain awake long into the night thinking about what Shooter had said about Ronnie. She and Pat talked about it there in the dark of their room, wondering, again, whether they should carry Shooter's information to Ray Biggs, fearing, finally, that such a move might be risky. If Ronnie was capable of burning that trailer, then what might he do to them if he found out they'd talked to the sheriff? "Shooter will do the right thing," Pat said, and Missy agreed, but she didn't feel absolved of the burden of carrying what she knew. Still, it was a bit of a relief to have to do nothing, to wait for Shooter to come forward. She and Pat came to the conclusion that she passed on now to Faye. "There's no telling what he might do. Ronnie Black. You remember how he chopped up Della's hair back in the fall?"

"Night of the pancake supper. Oh, I know Ronnie Black." Faye tipped her head and looked at Missy over the top of her glasses. "Not exactly a model citizen, is he?"

"No, ma'am, not by a long shot."

Missy and Faye glanced at each other and then looked away, both of them aware that they were talking in less than flattering terms about a man who only a few days before had lost three of his children. Missy could hear the tellers chatting with customers at the counter outside Faye's office. A telephone was ringing. Someone was counting out money—"That's twenty, forty, sixty, eighty, a hundred."

"Well, it's just a fact," Faye finally said. "That's what it is. Don't worry, Missy. No one can get at that money except you."

"Thank you, Faye. That puts my mind at ease."

Missy stood up, and Faye came out from around her desk. "You're a good soul." She took Missy by the hand and squeezed. "Sometimes, though, you just have to trust folks to live their own lives."

"I wouldn't say that Ronnie's been any good at that up to now."

"No, sweetie, I guess not. But maybe he'll do better. Second chances, you know."

"We could hope," Missy said. "I guess."

When she came out of Faye's office, she heard a voice—too loud, too angry—and without looking, she knew it belonged to Ronnie.

"How in the world am I supposed to take care of my kids?"

Missy turned and saw him leaning forward across the counter, the teller on the other side, a round-shouldered girl with limp brown hair, trying her best to keep her voice steady.

"You'll have to talk to Miss Griggs," the girl said.

"The hell with Miss Griggs." Ronnie slapped his palm down on the counter. All the tellers had stopped their own business, as had the other customers in the bank. Everyone was looking at Ronnie now. "There's money here for my girls, and now you're telling me I can't have it?"

"You're not the account holder."

"Well, if I'm not then who in the hell is?"

The girl's voice was shaking. "I'm really not at liberty. If you'd like to talk to Miss Griggs."

"I said the hell with Miss Griggs," Ronnie said, and he stormed out of the bank.

Missy heard someone call her name. From the far end of the bank, Laverne Ott was waving at her. Laverne's voice rang out clear and strong the way it had so many times in a classroom. "Missy," she said. "Missy Wade."

Faye Griggs came out of her office to see what the commotion was all about. The round-shouldered girl at the counter was crying. Another teller, a middle-aged woman with bright red fingernails, came to see what she could do to help her.

Some of the customers were talking about what had just happened. A number of them were people who were familiar to Missy. They were talking all at once, their voices rising over one another's.

Then Lucy Tutor's voice, high-pitched and nasal, fought free from the others, and she said, "It makes a body wonder." Lucy drove a school bus and she was by nature a suspicious sort.

"What's that?" asked Roe Carl, a cashier at the Read's IGA.

"If Ronnie doesn't have that money, then who does?"

That's when Faye whispered to Missy, "Don't worry. I won't tell. It's no one's business."

Laverne Ott was with them then, and she said to Missy, "I wish people weren't so hard on Ronnie."

"You know what I heard?" Faye said. "Milt Timlin thinks there's something suspicious about the whole thing."

"The fire?" Laverne said. "Oh, don't tell me that. Hasn't there been trouble enough?"

Faye didn't say a thing. A few moments went by, long enough for each of them to let their minds go where they wished they wouldn't.

Laverne turned toward Missy, such a scared, lost look on her face. She was recalling the night in September when Della came to the Kiwanis pancake supper with her hair cut ragged, and Laverne's first thought had been that Ronnie was to blame. "Missy?" she said now, the way she had all those years ago when Missy was just a girl in her class and Laverne expected her to give the correct answer. "Missy, surely there's no reason to suspect Ronnie of anything?"

Missy could have said, no, of course not, don't be silly. She could have said it would be ridiculous to think so. She could have put that thought right out of Faye and Laverne's heads. But she couldn't forget what Shooter had told her and Pat about Ronnie. It was such an incredible thought that she found herself talking to herself—at least she thought—and then she realized she'd said the words out loud.

"I can't believe Shooter saw him at the trailer."

"You mean earlier that day?" Faye asked. "I heard he was out there then."

Missy gave such a gentle answer, but later she'd know it was the worst thing she could have said. She'd wonder if her words had been born of envy and anger and the desire to have those girls. "I don't know."

She said it so softly, Laverne had to ask her to repeat herself. "Did you say you don't know?"

This time—one last chance to stop gossip before it began—she did the worst thing of all. She didn't say a word. She turned and walked out of that bank.

18

That night, Pat came home and said to Missy, "Do you think Shooter told the fire marshal what he knows?"

"Maybe, maybe not. You know how people like to talk."

Pat nodded. "You can bet they'll run with it now. Maybe it's only right. The truth has to come out one way or the other."

It was the dead of winter, and people spent the cold, snowy nights at home, too much time on their hands—enough time to allow for gossip. This neighbor called that one up and down the streets of Goldengate, out the blacktop to Bethlehem, and all through Phillipsport, and before the month was out, while everyone waited for the fire marshal's report, there was more than one person who believed that Ronnie Black had tried to kill his wife and kids.

What could be the reason?

Speculation was he wanted a clean break and a new life with Brandi Tate that wouldn't carry with it the burden of supporting his family.

Well, look what he had now: four of those kids to raise.

That is, if he didn't end up in prison.

The good will that some had built up for Ronnie at the funeral proved to be brittle. Now that the funeral was done and the grave covered over at the Bethlehem Church Cemetery, it was simple for some to believe that the man they'd first held responsible merely due to his absence from the family might turn out to be more villain than they'd first had cause to know.

He'd been there. At the trailer.

The night it burned?

That's right. Ronnie Black.

People started wondering what they might say if asked. If the sheriff, Biggs, came wanting to know something about Ronnie and the months leading up to that fire, what would they recall that might be of use? They thought on the matter over lunch at the Real McCoy Café, getting their hair set at the Looking Glass, picking up a gallon of milk at the IGA, working their shifts at the oil refinery in Phillipsport, drinking shots and beers at Fat Daddy's.

Tweezer Gray, who tended bar there, remembered one night close to Christmas when Ronnie stayed until last call, and then said to Tweezer, "You know how much this divorce is going to cost me? Plenty, I can tell you that. A wife and seven kids. Jesus, what was I thinking?"

Willie Wheeler, who lived next door to Brandi, said he saw Ronnie come out the door the afternoon of the fire and take up the street in his Firebird like there was no tomorrow. "He was steamed about something," Willie told anyone who'd listen. "I'll tell you that much for sure."

"He's got a temper," Alvin Higgins said. "I was uptown at the hardware store one day back in the fall—this must have been around the time he moved out on Della and took up living with Brandi—and he wanted to buy a snow blower on time, and Jingle Johnstone told him his credit was no good. 'I can give you fifty dollars right now,' Ronnie said, 'and twenty a week until I pay it off.' Jingle wasn't going for it. 'Nah, Ronnie,' he said. 'The word's out around town. You're a bad risk.' Well, that set Ronnie off. 'Goddamn you,' he said. 'Goddamn you and everyone else like you.' There was a box of two-inch flat washers on the counter. Ronnie picked it up and slung it down the aisle, scattered those washers all the way to kingdom come. Then he just walked out, pretty as you please. I heard he came back later and apologized to Jingle, said he was just going through too much and sometimes he felt like he was going to bust, but still, there's no call for an outburst like that."

Anna Spillman from over at the Real McCoy Café said Ronnie used to come in winter days when he hadn't been able to scare up work, and he'd sit in a booth way back in the corner like he didn't want anyone to see him. "He'd order coffee, and sometimes, if Pastor Quick wasn't around, I'd let Ronnie have a piece of pie on the house because I felt sorry for him. I knew what he'd done to Della, but it was hard for me to think bad of him. He looked like he didn't have a friend in the world, and one day I told him that. 'Della's out to get me,' he said. 'She's going to make sure I pay for a good long while. She better be careful. Paybacks are hell.' I thought he was just talking big, but now I'm not so sure, particularly after what I heard from Taylor Jack."

Taylor worked down the street at the Casey's convenience store, and he saw Ronnie at the pumps the morning of the fire, filling a five-gallon gas can. He'd come back that night and bought five gallons more. That was the most damaging story of all. Two cans of gas in the dead of winter. What would a man who hadn't been able to buy a snow blower, and who didn't own a generator that anyone knew of, need with that gas?

And there was everyone who'd seen Ronnie come up the blacktop the afternoon of the fire, gunning that Firebird, not even stopping for the school bus. The driver, Lucy Tutor, reported it to the principal. "Ronnie came up that blacktop just a-hellin'," Lucy said. "Like if he killed someone he wouldn't care." She'd picked up all the latest lingo from the kids. "Trust me, that boy needed to slow his roll."

————

That's what Ronnie was trying to do in those days after the funeral. He was trying to get his life back on an even keel. He had the girls, and he and Brandi were determined to make them a home, even if Angel wasn't sure she was ready to accept it. The other girls were coming along just fine. Hannah, true to her good nature, accepted Brandi right away, weaving her a friendship bracelet from green and orange threads. She put it around Brandi's wrist and fastened it by looping one end around the green button sewn to the other end.

"You're supposed to wish for something now," Hannah said.

"Like money?" Brandi asked. "Is that what I should wish for?"

Hannah shrugged. "Something you really, really want," she said. "Keep this bracelet on until the yarn wears out and it falls off your wrist. Then your wish will come true."

They were in the living room on the couch, and Ronnie was eavesdropping on them. He lay on the bed in his and Brandi's room and listened to the sounds of the house after supper was done and the girls were chattering. Sarah was learning her part for a class play. She was the voice of the bridge in *The Three Billy Goats Gruff.* She kept saying, "Trip, trap, trip, trap, trip, trap." And Ronnie thought it was wonderful to hear those words again and again, to know they came from his daughter. Even the angry bounce of a basketball in the bedroom that Angel shared with Hannah was a sound that pleased him. Emma passed by in the hallway, singing the "Itsy Bitsy Spider" song, only she was trying to sing the special verse that Della always sang to her, and she kept stumbling over the first line about a sweetie-weetie butterfly. Ronnie sang the verse in his head:

A sweetie-weetie butterfly
Flew around and 'round;
A strong wind came along and blew it to the ground.

Out came its Daddy and gave it a kiss and hug,
And the sweetie-weetie butterfly was as happy as a bug.

Ronnie couldn't say he was happy—no, not exactly that. It hadn't been smooth sailing. Angel was still sullen and hateful sometimes. "Patience," Brandi told him. "It hasn't been easy for her. It hasn't been easy for any of them."

Sarah woke some nights, screaming from nightmares about the fire. Hannah sometimes went quiet in the midst of playing a game or watching TV and tears filled her eyes. Nights, when Ronnie was tucking Emma into bed, she might claim she'd seen Emily somewhere in the house—Emily skipping rope in the living room, Emily hiding in the closet, Emily in the kitchen eating Oreos. Little bumps, Brandi told him. Little by little, they'd smooth out. Only Hannah—dependable, level-headed Hannah—seemed beyond ruin.

If he wasn't happy, then at least he was thankful. He had his girls, and Brandi had opened her heart to them. They were back in school, and each day brought them closer to retrieving at least some of the life he'd taken from them when he'd left Della back in the fall.

A few days after he'd gone to the bank and tried to withdraw some of the money from the account set up for his girls, Missy paid him a visit.

She had a check she'd written out for him. Three hundred dollars for him to spend on the girls however he saw fit.

It was midmorning and the girls were in school. Brandi was in Phillipsport at work at the Savings and Loan.

Ronnie had just got home from the Real McCoy Café, where he'd sat drinking coffee and talking to the waitress, Anna Spillman. He'd just kicked off his boots when he heard the knock on the door.

He stood in the open doorway, studying that check.

"Missy?" he said.

She looked down at his feet and then over to the side of the porch. "You should know I'm the one who holds that account at the bank." She had her head turned toward Willie Wheeler's house, a squat bungalow with brown asphalt shingle siding. The curtains were open at all the windows. She was having a hard time facing Ronnie. She wondered whether he'd heard the gossip and whether he could guess that she'd helped start it. She wanted to be done with her chore and on her way. "I'd like to see that money build up interest and be there for the girls when they get out of high school," she said. "They might need it to help with college, or just to start their own families. I don't know. I just don't want to spend it down just for the sake of spending it." She turned her head and looked him in the eye for the first time. "If they ever need anything between now and then, something you can't afford, you let me know. How's that?"

"Is that the way you've decided it should be?"

She gave him a stiff nod. "I won't let those girls want for anything. You can count on that."

Ronnie heard what wasn't being said: that she didn't trust him to do right with that money, and for an instant he was tempted to tear that check up and throw the pieces into her face. But when would he ever have his hands on three hundred dollars again? It was true that he could put it to good use for groceries and the like.

He opened the door wider. "You want to come in?"

Missy shook her head. "I've done what I came for."

"All right then." He folded that check up in his hand. "Angel's been crying for a new iPod, but I won't throw this away on that. It's hard enough to keep them all fed and in decent clothes. I'd say thank you, but something tells me it's not thanks you want. I figure you aim to hold me accountable until the day I die."

Then he stepped back into the house and closed the door.

———

At first, he was unaware of the talk swirling around the county—the talk of him being at the trailer the night it burned. He thought that was his secret. Even Brandi was in the dark, and, as for the girls, they were busy being kids, busy trying to get on with their lives.

Then Brandi came home from work one evening and told them she'd been hearing gossip.

"About me?" he asked. "About the fire?"

Brandi studied him awhile. "Then you've heard it too," she finally said. "It's just talk. That's what it is. Just crazy talk from stupid people."

"Still, I don't want the girls to hear it."

"We can only hope."

One day at school—this was at the end of January—Tommy Stout, who'd been on Lucy Tutor's bus the afternoon of the fire when Ronnie went tearing by in his Firebird, said to Angel in the hallway at lunchtime, "Jeez, did your dad try to kill you all?"

At first, Angel couldn't decide whether she'd heard him right. There was all the noise of the crowded hallway—lockers slamming, people talking, someone shouting, "Oh, baby!"—and she thought she must have misheard. Then it slowly came to her that Tommy had said exactly what she'd first thought, and she said to him, "Where'd you hear that?"

"My dad. He was talking about it at supper last night. It's all over the county. Folks say your dad was out behind your trailer right before it caught on fire. Shooter Rowe saw him."

She'd never cared for Mr. Rowe. He was too grumpy, and he'd taken her to task more than once on account of those goats, but he'd been there the night of the fire. He'd been there when they'd needed him.

"If my dad was out there, how come I didn't see him?"

"Maybe he didn't want you to see him. Maybe that's why."

"That's just stupid, Tommy." Angel swatted him on the arm with a notebook. "That's almost as stupid as you."

She thought about it all afternoon, the chance that her dad might have been so mad at her mom that he'd gone off the deep end and lit the trailer on fire. He had a temper. No doubt about that. Look what he'd done to her mom's hair. How could Angel ever forgive him for that? And there were times, even though they were few, when one of them misbehaved and he lost his temper. Angel tried to forget those times when he let his anger get the best of him. In those days leading up to him finally walking out, he'd filled the trailer with his loud voice and his sharp words, but when Angel thought of him now and the way he was back through the years, she preferred to remember him as gentle and kind, which he was sometimes. He had a game he played with her before she got too old for it. Each evening, before her mother tucked her into bed, her father held his closed hands in front of him and told her to tap one. To her surprise, each time she did, he opened that hand and there on his palm was something just for her: an Indian bead fossil found in the gravel, a bird's feather, a locust's shell. Always something from an animal or a plant, something that had once been alive. She saved everything in a Buster Brown shoebox. Her treasures. Each time she tapped her father's hand and he opened it to reveal what he'd been hiding, he opened his eyes wide in surprise and he said in a hushed voice, "You've done it again, Miss Angel of my heart. Amazing. You've won the prize."

It took her a while to figure out that he had something in both hands. It didn't matter which one she tapped. She'd always be the winner. When she knew that, she felt a little squiggle inside, and she knew that squiggle was love. Her father loved her enough to make sure she was never disappointed.

All through her afternoon classes, she thought about how close they'd once been. As she got older, he took her with him when he went into the woods each spring to look for morel mushrooms or in the summer to pick wild blackberries. He taught her how to swim in the pond at Grandpa Wayne's. He gave her piggyback rides, taught her the names of the shapes the stars made in the night sky, pointed out the calls that bobwhites made and whippoorwills and mourning doves. In the winter, he pulled her on her sled and helped her make snowmen. Together, they'd lie on their backs in the snow and move their arms and legs to make angels. "There you are," he'd say, pointing at the shape she'd left in the snow. "My angel."

She wanted all of that back, but she didn't know how to say as much. She'd lost it, the closeness they'd once shared, when something went wrong between him and her mother, and suddenly nothing was right in their family. Angel couldn't say what had gone wrong. She only knew that her father, who had always been so tender with her, suddenly had no patience. He snapped at Emma and Emily for being chatterboxes, told Sarah to shut up when she whined that all her friends had this and that and she didn't, yelled at Gracie to pick up the toys she often left wherever they fell. He even had a sharp word for Hannah from time to time—kind, good Hannah, who did nothing to deserve his anger. The brunt of his disapproval, though, fell upon Angel, who didn't make Hannah's good grades in school, and dressed, he told her once, in jeans that were too tight and tops that were too revealing. "I know what's on boys' minds," he said. "Especially if you go around looking like that."

It embarrassed her and made her mad to hear her father talk to her like that, her father who'd always spoken to her as if she hung the moon, as if she could never do anything to disappoint him. One night, when she came back from a football game, he said her skirt was too short, that she looked like a whore, and that hurt her more than anything, to hear him say that, as if she weren't his daughter at all but just some girl he'd seen on the street. She didn't know if she'd ever be able to forgive him for that, and when he finally walked out, she thought, *good riddance.*

The bus went from the high school in Phillipsport to Goldengate, where they let the students off at the junior high. Then the country kids got on other buses to take them home. Hannah and Angel had been those kids just a few weeks back, but now Hannah waited in front of the junior high for Angel to get off the bus, and then they walked to Brandi's house, where they were trying to be a family. In the old days, the days Hannah had come to think of as "Before the Fire," she'd waited for the high school bus from Phillipsport, and then they'd climbed onto Lucy Tutor's bus and made their way out the blacktop.

On this particular day, though, the high school bus came and let everyone off, and Hannah saw Angel walking toward the bus parked near the front of the line, the bus she and Angel used to ride. Lucy Tutor opened the pneumatic doors, and they hissed and squealed.

By this time, nearly four o'clock, the moon was already rising—Hannah could see it low in the sky just above the treetops along Locust Street—and the temperature was dropping. She could feel the cold's bite on her face and through the fingers of her woolen gloves. She stamped her feet, and her toes tingled inside her boots.

She called Angel's name, and Angel stopped in the middle of the sidewalk and turned back to see who had called out and why. Two boys wearing Phillipsport letterman jackets split apart to move past her. Hannah knew the boys were football players. She could see the gold helmets they'd won for good plays pinned to the red wool of the jackets. Beefy, bareheaded boys laughing about something before they got onto the bus.

"Go home," Angel told Hannah.

"Where are you going?" Hannah ran down the sidewalk to where she was standing. "We're supposed to go right home. You know Dad wants us to watch Sarah and Emma." He'd said as much that morning. He'd pick up Sarah and Emma at their school and drop them off at Brandi's for Hannah and Angel to take care of until Brandi got home from work. He had to drive over the river to Brick Chapel to see a man about a job. "We have to go," Hannah said, and she took Angel by the sleeve of her coat. "We have to go right now."

"You can babysit." Angel jerked her arm free from Hannah's grasp. "You're the one Dad really trusts anyway. Not me."

In the days since the fire, Hannah had delighted in the fact that she and Angel were growing closer. They'd put away their argument about who'd been supposed to feed the goats the night the trailer burned and who'd neglected that chore and who'd failed to carry out the ashes from the Franklin stove. That had just been sniping between two sisters who didn't know what else to do in the aftershock of their disaster. It didn't take long for them to find comfort in each other's company. Nights, Angel often whispered to Hannah, who was in the bed across from her in the room they shared, and said, "You okay?" Sometimes Hannah nodded her head and said, yes, she was, and sometimes she said she didn't think she'd be able to go to sleep because every time she closed her eyes, she saw the flames and smoke of that night. Angel got into bed with her then. She crawled in under the covers, and she let Hannah lie close to her and they held hands and finally drifted off to sleep.

Now Angel was turning her away.

"I'll go with you," Hannah said even though she knew she had to go to Brandi's. "Are you going to Missy's?"

"I'm just going," Angel said. "Never you mind where."

The sidewalk was almost empty now. Some of the buses had already pulled out. The last of the stragglers were getting onto Lucy Tutor's bus.

And with that, Angel was gone. Hannah took a few steps after her, but she knew it was all for show. She knew she'd go to Brandi's like she was supposed to and she'd take care of Sarah and Emma. The only thing she didn't know was what she'd tell her dad when he'd ask her, as she knew he would, *Where is she? Where's your sister?*

The only seat left on the bus was the one behind Lucy Tutor—the loser seat, the one for dweebs and 'tards. Angel didn't care. She let her book bag slide off her shoulder as she dropped down onto the seat.

"That you, Angel?" Lucy wore a pair of glasses she kept on a chain around her neck. She lifted the glasses to her face. She tipped back her head and crinkled up her nose. "Honey, you know you don't ride this bus anymore."

"Are you saying I can't?"

"You live in town now."

"I know where I live." Angel let her voice get all sweetie-sweet. She leaned forward and whispered to Lucy, "I've been invited."

"Invited," said Lucy. "Invited to what?"

"It's very important that I be there."

"Oh, I'm sure it is." Lucy let the glasses drop onto her chest. "Is it Missy Wade? Is that who you're going to see?"

Angel smiled, and there was something in that smile that was enough for Lucy. She said, "Missy sure does love on you girls."

Then she put the bus into gear and slowly pulled away from the curb.

What was left of the trailer after the fire was still there. The furnace and the hot water heater rose up from the ruin. Angel turned her head as the bus went by. She saw the head of a wire coat hanger poking up along the trailer's underskirting, a litter of baking pans rusting in the weather, scraps of this and that turned black with char. She remembered in flashes of light and sound the bits and pieces of that night once she understood that the trailer was on fire. Her mother shook her awake. She could smell smoke, could hear the crackle of flames. Her mother said that word, *Fire*. She told her to help get the others out. She was coughing, and she made sure Hannah was awake. Then she turned and went on down the hall. Something exploded, and Angel heard a whoosh of fire the way she did each time the furnace kicked on. That's when she got more scared than she'd ever been in her life. She grabbed Hannah's hand. "C'mon," she said. "Run!"

That was the moment that Angel thought about some nights now as she lay in bed with Hannah. Angel wanted to tell her what her mother had told her to do—save the others—but Angel couldn't bear the thought of confessing that. She couldn't bring herself to say that she'd been too scared to try to save the others. She couldn't say that. Hannah, she was sure, would have been braver.

Just maybe, Angel wished it true—what Tommy claimed Shooter Rowe said. If her father had something to do with the fire, she'd have reason enough to put aside how much she hated herself for running out of the trailer that night and leaving her sisters and brother and mother behind, how much she regretted not taking the ash box to the compost as she was told to do. If her father was guilty, then how could she be too?

She realized how quiet the bus had become. The kids who'd been chattering had fallen silent. They were all looking back at the trailer's heap of ruin. Angel thought of all the people who'd given her hugs once she returned to school after the funeral. Kids and teachers crying with her, telling her to know that they were there to help her through, encouraging her to be strong. They'd given her cards—some of them were about their prayers being with her; others featured doves, roses, oceans, sunsets. Someone stretched a banner above the stairwell leading to the second-floor classrooms: *We ♥ You, Angel!* Every time she went up the stairs, she saw it. For a while, people left things at her locker—teddy bears, flowers, and, of course, angel figurines—but after a while that stopped, and she was secretly glad because deep down she didn't believe she deserved any of this kindness.

She was embarrassed that the burnt debris was still there for all the kids on the bus to look at. It was a sign of everything that had gone wrong for her family.

The bus was slowing in front of Missy's house, and for a few seconds Angel didn't understand that Lucy was stopping on account of her.

"Here you are, honey," Lucy said. The doors of the bus opened with a hiss. "You have a good visit."

Tommy's voice rang out from the back of the bus. "Why we stopping here, Lucy? Missy doesn't have any kids."

Angel gathered up her book bag and hurried down the steps of the bus before Tommy could spot her. She stood off the side of the blacktop and watched the bus go on. She stood there until she could no longer see it. Then she turned back to the south, back toward where she and her sisters and brother and mother and father had once had a home.

Captain was at the mailbox in front of his house when the bus went by. He didn't ride that same bus home from school. He got out of school a little earlier in the afternoon and rode a different bus—the short bus, all the kids called it—the one meant for people like him.

Angel called out to him. "Captain." She waved her arm back and forth over her head. "Captain, wait."

He saw her, then. Angel. She was back. Angel, so blond and so fair. Angel, who'd always been good to him. Angel with the silky hair. If he got close enough, he could smell her shampoo and it smelled nice the way Christmas trees smelled nice. Angel, the girl he dreamed about sometimes. Just last night, in a dream, she took his hand and they walked together down a grassy lane into the shade of a deep woods. It was summer, but the trees blotted out the sun. Overhead, squirrels chattered and leaped from limb to limb. Ahead, a red-winged blackbird took flight. He saw it all in his dream, and when it was done and he was awake, he thought for a moment that it was true. It was summer and Angel still lived across the road, and they walked down that lane into the woods. Then little by little he realized that it was winter—he could hear the wind outside, could feel the chill of the house—and the trailer across the road had burned, and Angel lived in town now with Ronnie, and the dream he'd just had was nothing he could hold onto.

"I'm here." He waved his own arm above his head and answered Angel. "I'm right here."

Then he ran down the blacktop toward her, and he couldn't help himself. He threw his arms around her, knocking her book bag off her shoulder and into the snow.

Over the past few weeks, Angel had gotten used to people hugging her. It seemed like wherever she went—to church, 4-H, school, Read's IGA—there was always someone who wanted to wrap her up in their arms and rock her from side to side. *Honey, oh honey.* So when Captain pressed her to him, she didn't find it odd at all, nor unwelcome. He lifted her from the ground, and she clung to him, this tall, strong boy who had yet to realize how easily he could hurt someone. She knew his gentle spirit wouldn't allow it, not even a thought of lashing out at someone like Tommy Stout, who sometimes teased him. Not really in a mean way. All in good fun, Tommy and the others like him would insist. Little jokes about the Captain. Snapping off salutes in front of him. Calling out, *aye, aye.* And maybe there was nothing wrong with that—after all, Captain enjoyed playing the role, saluting in response. She used to wonder whether, deep down, Captain knew it was all a joke at his expense and a way of pointing out that he was different from the "normal" boys.

Angel pressed her face into Captain's chest. She breathed in the smells from his wool coat—wood smoke and dried weeds, gasoline and hot cooking grease, snow and gravel—and to her it was the smell of home.

"You're back," he said.

Then before she could ask where his father was, Captain set her on the ground, grabbed her hand, and started running back up the blacktop. "C'mon, c'mon," he said, and she had no choice but to go with him.

He ran across the road, and finally they were turning up the short lane to the trailer's ruins.

She saw a purple knit glove on the ground, one with a silver star on its back. That glove had belonged to Gracie. Just a little glove for her little hand. It was enough to sting Angel's eyes. Gracie, who'd always been crazy about stars. And Emily, who for months when she was four insisted that she was a fairy princess. And Junior, who'd been Angel's to hold so many times when her mother was cooking or washing or cleaning. Junior with his silly grin and his bobbing head that made him look a little drunk. Angel could still remember the weight of him in her arms.

"C'mon," Captain said again, and he tugged her along to the ruined trailer.

She hadn't planned on this. She didn't want to be there and to look at what was left after the fire, but Captain wouldn't let go of her hand. He wanted to show her what all could be seen in the charred mess.

He pointed out the few items that were distinguishable in the rubble: a frying pan; a toaster oven; a door knob; the warped frame of Junior's stroller; the silver-plated lid, blackened now, from the heart-shaped jewelry box her mother had kept on her dresser; a metal hoop earring from a pair their father had given Hannah on her last birthday; a Slinky the twins had loved to play with; a buckle from the OshKosh B'Gosh overalls Gracie often wore; a rhinestone hair barrette that had belonged to Sarah; a 4-H pin Angel had stuck into the bulletin board in her room. She remembered the green shamrock on the pin, a white "H" on each leaf—*Head, Heart, Hands, Health.*

Captain said, "I wanted to save it all for you, but my dad wouldn't let me." He got a very serious look on his face, and he nodded his head. "So I've been keeping watch."

There it was—what remained of a life lived in that trailer. It hit Angel hard, how little was left, and she had to turn away and look off across the barren fields, corn stubble poking up through the snow, and tell herself not to cry. They were standing along what had once been the backside of the trailer. Captain had led her around the perimeter, pointing out the items, and now they were stopped at where the living room had been.

Angel took a step, and she felt through the thin soles of her Converse tennis shoes—Brandi had told her to wear her snow boots that morning, but she'd refused—something hard. She looked down and saw a pocketknife. It was pressed into the snow, and Angel knew it might have stayed there until the spring thaw when the meltdown began if she hadn't stepped on it just right so the butt of the handle dug into the ball of her foot. If she'd been wearing her snow boots, she might not have felt it, this sharp pain that made her hop to the side and then look down at the knife.

She recognized it right away: a Case Hammerhead lockback knife with black and cream handles. She knew that if she were to pick it up and nick out the blade, she'd find a hammerhead shark engraved on it. She knew the knife belonged to her father. He kept the blade honed and the handles polished. When she was a little girl, she'd asked him over and over to show her the fish on the blade, and he'd always obliged, opening the knife, telling her to be careful, hold-

ing her finger and tracing it over the etching of the shark. He loved
that knife.

She said to Captain, "Is your dad home?"

"We've got your goats," Captain said. "C'mon."

This time he didn't grab her hand. He turned and started hurrying toward his house. Before following him, Angel stooped and
plucked the knife from the snow. She closed her hand around it and
stuck her fists into her jacket pockets.

"C'mon," Captain said again. He turned around and waved for
her to hurry, and she caught up to him in the road.

Shooter was in the barn behind the house. He had the goats penned in
the stable that had been empty since he gave up his cattle, sold the last
of the Red Angus and the Herefords. He and Captain had cared for the
goats since the night of the fire. Shooter showed Captain how to milk
the nannies, wrapping his forefinger and thumb around the base of the
teat to keep the milk from going back into the udder when he squeezed
with middle finger and ring finger and pinky, one after another, in a
smooth motion, the milk spurting out into the galvanized bucket.

"Just like that," Shooter said as he stood behind the stool where
Captain sat. "One, two, three." He laid his hand on Captain's back
and let his fingers tap out the rhythm. "Don't pull. Just squeeze. One,
two, three."

They milked the goats in the cold barn while dusk fell. The milk
made a pinging sound when it hit the side of the bucket. Shooter
broke open some bales of alfalfa hay, and the air was sweet with its
dust. It was all right there in the barn with the fading light and the
steady rhythm of the milk and the smell of the hay, and Shooter
touching Captain with assurance, letting him know that despite what
had happened with Della's trailer, there still could be the grace of
these small things.

"It's okay, isn't it?" Shooter said. "Just the two of us right here, right now. Yes sir, don't you worry. Everything's going to be all right."

Captain stopped milking for a moment, and he looked up at Shooter with eyes that seemed to be lost. Then Shooter patted him on the back. "One, two, three," he said again, and Captain smiled and went back to his work.

They'd kept the goats because Shooter told Wayne Best he would, until Wayne decided if he wanted them for his own.

"I don't mind," he said. "I've got room in my barn."

"Lois says she wouldn't be able to stand having those goats around," said Wayne. "They'd make her think of Gracie and Emily and Junior."

So it was decided that Shooter would keep the goats for a time. The days stretched on into weeks, and he wasn't even tempted to bring the subject up again. As much as Shooter had always cursed those goats and the way they always got out of Della's pen and ran wild, he took to them now, helping Captain with the milking and the feeding and the mucking out the stalls. For the first time, it felt like the two of them were sharing something that brought them closer.

They sampled some of the milk themselves and Shooter sold what was left to mothers with babies who couldn't tolerate cow's milk or to elderly folks who swore that goat's milk helped their digestion, eased their arthritis, lowered their cholesterol.

Shooter was just about ready to step outside the barn and call for Captain to come help him with the feeding when he heard the door creak open. The light from outside swept into the stall, and when Shooter turned to look he saw Captain and the girl, the oldest one, Angel.

"Honey," he said, "what are you doing way out here?"

She took a step forward, coming up around Captain, her feet tamping down on the packed dirt floor of the feedway. Shooter watched her through the gaps between the wood-slat stanchions above the manger. Just a slip of a thing, her face all lips and eyes. Her cheeks were red from the cold, and her hands were in the pockets of her coat.

Captain was behind her, and, excited, he said, "Dad, Dad. Look who it is."

Angel kept walking until she was level with Shooter. If he chose, he could reach through the stanchions and touch her just like he'd held out his arms to take Emma from Della on the night of the fire.

"Mr. Rowe, I've come to ask you—" She stopped then, looked down at her feet, lost whatever nerve she'd been able to muster. "What I mean is, I got to know. I came all this way. Surely you'll tell me the truth."

He couldn't bear to see her stumble around, especially since he feared he knew exactly what she'd come to ask him. Word had finally gotten around to finding her.

"Your daddy?" he said, and she nodded.

He looked around her to Captain, who was reaching through the stanchions to pet the head of one of the goats, the billy that Della and the girls had always called Methuselah. Captain was saying something to Methuselah in a low voice that Shooter couldn't make out. The other goats bleated as if they recognized Angel and were asking her where she'd been.

"Captain," Shooter said, "run on up to the house and fetch my cell phone off the charger. It's on the kitchen counter, right where I always keep it."

"I'll hurry," Captain said and started running down the feedway to the barn door.

"Slow down," Shooter called after him, and he stopped, his hand on the door. "Take it easy. Nothing's on fire."

As soon as he said it, he was sorry. That word, *fire*. Would that ever be a word that anyone could say in the presence of Angel or any of her sisters?

"Did you see him?" she asked once Captain was gone. "Did you see my dad at our trailer that night?"

"That's nothing for you to worry about, honey."

"I need to know."

Shooter kept his voice even. "Some things aren't meant for kids."

"Did he set the fire?" She wouldn't back down. "Is that what you're saying?"

"If you've got something you want to know, go ask your daddy. It's not for me to talk about."

"But you've been talking about it. Tommy Stout said—"

Shooter reached through the stanchions and placed his finger on her lips, silencing her. "I guess you've already got your answer, don't you?" He could see that Angel was scared. She bowed her head. He took his finger away from her lips. He touched the underside of her chin and nudged it up so she'd look at him. "Listen to me now. You came asking, so I'm giving you what you want. Yes, your daddy was out there that night."

Captain was back with Shooter's cell phone. He was panting, having run to and from the house even though his father had told him not to.

"It was on the counter," he said. "Just like you told me."

"Good job, Captain." Shooter took the phone from him and then handed it to Angel. "Call your daddy," he said. "Tell him where you are. Tell him I'm going to drive you home."

———

Ronnie was furious. He'd dropped off Sarah and Emma at Brandi's and found only Hannah there to take care of them.

"You were supposed to be here," he said over the phone. "But, no, you had something more important to do, something all about Angel. Where in the world are you, anyway? We've been worried sick."

So Hannah hadn't told him where she'd gone. If not for the fact that she was standing there in the barn with Mr. Rowe and Captain listening, she might have told her father what she really wanted to say—that he was supposed to have been home with them the night the trailer burned, but he'd left for something that was all about him. She wanted to tell him that she had his pocketknife, was squeezing her hand around the handle in her coat pocket at that very moment and feeling the nick where, if she took a mind to, she could pry up with her thumbnail and open the blade. She wanted to say she'd found it in the snow behind what had once been their home. She wanted to tell him what she knew he'd surely find out before long: Shooter Rowe had seen him come out from behind their trailer on the night of the fire.

But all she said was, "At Mr. Rowe's. I rode my old bus out the blacktop." The next part, though a little bit of a lie, was true in its own way. She just hadn't known it until now. "I wanted to be out here. I wanted to be close."

Ronnie's voice was a whisper when he finally answered. "To your mother?"

"Yes." She could barely speak because of the ache in her throat. She choked back the tears. "And to Gracie and Emily and Junior. To where we all lived. I just—I don't know."

"Okay," Ronnie said, and she could hear him forgiving her. "It's getting dark. I'll come get you."

She couldn't bear to think of the ride back into town, just her and her father in his Firebird.

"Mr. Rowe said he'd give me a ride."

He held out his hand, and Angel gave him the phone. "Ronnie?" he said. "It's Shooter. Don't worry. I'll take care of getting your girl back to you." He listened for a few moments. Then he said, "Nah, it's not. Not for me." The light was fading and Angel thought he winked at her then, but she wasn't sure. "Not a problem at all. I'll take care of her."

She sat between Mr. Rowe and Captain on the drive to town. Mr. Rowe drove an old stubby Ford Bronco the color of a yellow peach. It had a bench seat up front and that's where Angel sat while the heater blew hot air onto her feet and the gear box pressed into her knee even though she kept her legs angled to the side. The little black steering wheel seemed so small in Mr. Rowe's big hands. He jostled her with his shoulder whenever he made a turn.

Captain counted the cars that they met, the headlights coming out of the dark, folks on their way home. Not so long ago, Angel thought, one of those cars might have belonged to her mother, and she would have been with her.

It made her sad now to think of how stupid and blind she'd been to the love all around her. In the last months of her mother's life, she'd been a difficult girl and for that she was sorry.

Mr. Rowe had on the radio, and because it was that time of the evening when WPLP, the voice of Phillipsport and Southeastern Illinois, broadcast the local news, they listened to the reports of a proposed increase in city water bills, a Phillips County United Fund fish fry at the American Legion, and the kickoff of this year's Relay for Life at the Phillips County Memorial Hospital.

Then the announcer said, "The Illinois State Fire Marshal's Office—"

But at that point, Captain reached over and punched a button that took the radio to a pop music station. Lady Gaga was singing "Bad Romance."

Mr. Rowe jabbed a button and turned off the radio. "Who wants to listen to that junk?" he said. "Just a bunch of noise."

Ahead, Angel could see the lights of Goldengate, few as they were. Mr. Rowe steered the Bronco through the last curve before town, and then they were passing the lit-up houses on the outskirts near the Pine Manor Nursing Home and J.D. Parker's Body Shop. The Bronco slowed to the speed limit, and just before Main Street, the yellow sign at the Casey's convenience store came into view. Then they were driving by the Real McCoy Café and the IGA and the time and temperature clock at the First National Bank. They bumped over the railroad tracks, and Mr. Rowe turned the Bronco onto Locust past the school where not so long ago Angel had gotten onto Lucy Tutor's bus and set out to find out what she could. "You've always got your nose into something," her mother used to tell her. "Sometimes it's best not to know everything."

Her mother had been right. Angel knew that now as she saw Brandi's house lit up ahead of them at the end of Locust. You could know too much. You could know more than you could figure out what to do with.

Mr. Rowe eased the Bronco into the driveway. Angel could see her father at the living room window, peering out, his hand shading his eyes.

"I guess this is it," Mr. Rowe said. "I guess this is where you live. Open the door, Captain, and let her out."

Captain got out of the Bronco, and Angel started to slide across the bench seat.

That's when Mr. Rowe took her by the arm. He leaned toward her and he whispered in her ear. "You got what you came looking for, didn't you?"

At first, she didn't answer. "Didn't you?" he said again, and in a soft voice, she said, yes, yes she had.

Then he let her go.

Her father met her at the front door. He said, "We were scared. We were all scared. Hannah said she didn't know where you were."

Angel wanted to believe that Hannah had kept quiet because they were sisters looking out for each other, but then the thought came to her that maybe Hannah hadn't said anything out of spite, knowing that the less she said the more worried her father would be and then Angel would be in trouble.

The light was on in the kitchen, and through the archway Angel could see the table set for supper. Emma was pulling out a chair. Brandi carried a teapot to the table and poured a cup for herself. Angel knew it was ginger tea, which Brandi drank because her nose was always stuffy these days and the doctor said the tea would help. It wasn't uncommon, she'd said one night at supper, for a woman in her second trimester, as she was, to have a stuffy nose and headaches. She didn't mind. They'd go away eventually. The main thing was the baby was healthy. Brandi had just had her amniocentesis test, and everything, she was pleased to announce, was as good as gold.

Angel, though she'd never admit as much, was fascinated with Brandi's pregnancy. The way she'd always been enchanted each time her mother had gone through one. Angel was careful not to let on to Brandi that she took note of anything at all, but the truth was each step along the way—the belly's swell, the darker patches of skin on Brandi's face, the amnio—were little thrills in what had become a long winter of loss. "You want to feel my belly?" Brandi asked her that morning when they found themselves in the bathroom at the same time, Angel brushing her teeth and Brandi in her stretch pants and a bra putting on her deodorant. Angel forced herself to put a bored look on her face. "Please," she said. "My mother had six babies after me. It's no biggie."

Now Brandi turned and spotted her through the kitchen archway. She came to her and wrapped her up in a hug. "Sugar, we were so worried. I came home from work and your dad was here just out of his head. He didn't know what to do."

Angel hated the musky perfume that Brandi wore because she used too much of it. Pressed into its heavy, animal smell now, Angel couldn't bear it. Before she realized what she was doing, she pushed Brandi away.

It wasn't a particularly hard push, not the kind Angel would have given Hannah if she'd been angry with her. Bat-shit-crazy mad. Just a little shove to free herself from Brandi's hug, but it was enough to make Brandi stumble back a step. The edge of the coffee table hit her in the back of her knees. She tried to twist away from the table and lost her balance. Arms flailing, she fell so hard that Angel felt the floor shake.

Brandi lay on the floor on her side, her right arm slung across her swollen belly. Angel started to go to her. She felt horrible about what she'd caused. Then her father grabbed her by her shoulders. "Look what you did," he said. "My god."

"I didn't mean—"

"You pushed her." He spun her around so she was facing him. He gave her a shake and her head snapped back. "What are you, crazy? A woman with a baby and you push her?" His voice was getting louder. "Your mother was right. You're out of control. You're hateful."

He went to tend to Brandi. His shouting had brought Hannah in from the kitchen, and she was helping Brandi sit up and get her wind back.

"I'm all right," she said. "Just a little tumble. I'll be fine."

Angel tried to explain again. "I didn't—I just—she—"

The words wouldn't come, and finally she gave up and ran down the hallway to the bedroom she shared with Hannah. She slammed the door so hard that Brandi's high school graduation portrait fell from its nail in the hall. Angel heard the glass in the frame shatter, and all she could do was throw herself on her bed and put the pillow over her head, trying to shut out what her father had told her, that her mother had said she was out of control, a hateful girl. Bits and pieces from their last night together flashed in and out of view—she'd argued with her mother about taking out that box of ashes; Angel had stomped off to her room and she hadn't carried the ashes out like she was supposed to, and later, when the trailer was burning, she failed her mother again. *She thought I didn't love her.* Angel couldn't keep herself from believing that. *She thought I hated her, and then she died.*

Angel knew it was wrong, but she couldn't stop herself from hating her father for having told her what her mother had said. He should have kept it to himself. It was nothing she needed to hear. He said it to hurt her, and she couldn't forgive him. She wouldn't, not even if he said he was sorry a million times. A billion times. Not even then.

She heard the footsteps falling hard on the floor outside, and then her door came flying open. Her father stormed in. She knew it was him without having to look—those heavy steps, the whistle of air as he breathed through his nose, the bitter smell of coffee on his breath.

"Get that pillow off your head and look at me," he said. "You're going to clean up that broken glass, and you're going to apologize to Brandi. Do you hear me, Angel? I mean right now."

She wouldn't budge. She held tight to the pillow and said in a muffled voice, "Leave me alone."

Apologize? No. Not now. Not after what her father had said. She heard Brandi in the living room pleading for some calm— "Ronnie, no," she said. "Please, let's just eat our supper."

It was too late, Angel thought. In fact, it'd been too late for a long time, ever since her father walked out on her mother. They were playing at being a family now, but the family Angel knew was the one in the trailer out the blacktop. Sometimes she thought of them, that family, doing their best to love one another, not knowing what was coming at them from the future. She couldn't say they were happy, but she couldn't say they were unhappy either. They were doing the best they could, and she liked to think of them—the parts of her and Hannah and Sarah and Emma that they'd left back there—going along again with their mother and sisters and baby brother. That was their family, the ones who tried their best to love one another when their father made clear that he couldn't love them enough.

Now he grabbed the pillow, but she wouldn't let go of it. He tried to get a grip on her so he could lift her from the bed, but she squirmed away from him. She tried to curl into a ball, but he got an arm around her waist and another arm under her knees. She kicked her feet at him, and he said, "You stop that."

But she wouldn't stop, and finally he grabbed her by the arm and shook her. The pillow fell to the floor. She was screaming now. She was telling him to stop. She was saying, "No, no, no."

"It's time you took responsibility for your actions," he said. "Damn it, Angel. Everyone else is trying."

She jerked free from his grip. "Don't talk to me about responsibility." She went after him with her fists. He crossed his arms over his face and tried to move out of her way. She followed him across the room, hitting him again and again. She hit him on the bones of his hands and arms, hit him until her own hands were sore. "What were you doing out at the trailer?"

He was backed into the wall now. He lowered his arms and said, "When?"

"That night."

"I was there earlier in the day before you kids got home from school. I had to talk to your mother."

"That night," she said again. "Tell me."

"Angel, I wasn't anywhere but here."

"You're a liar."

"Angel."

She took the knife from her coat pocket, the Case Hammerhead. She held it up to his face. "Say this isn't yours." He wouldn't answer. She was crying now, practically pleading for him to explain that he was innocent. "Say you didn't drop it behind the trailer that night. Say you weren't there."

Her father reached out his hand, and she let him take the knife.

"You know it's mine," he said, and that was all he said, his eyes going hard before he turned and walked away, leaving Angel trembling with the thought of what might happen next.

19

Ronnie stormed out of Brandi's house and drove out the blacktop to Shooter Rowe's. The Case Hammerhead was in his pocket. He was thankful for the dark and the little bit of ground fog starting to gather and swirl in the low-lying areas. He didn't want to see the ruins of the trailer, nor to remember the night it burned. He pulled into Shooter's driveway and saw a shadow pass over the closed drapes at the living room window. The porch light was dark, but there were lights burning inside the house.

Ronnie got out of his Firebird and felt the cold and damp around his face. The air smelled of fuel oil, and he took note of the flicker of flames at the trash barrel behind Shooter's house.

It took a long time for the porch light to come on after Ronnie knocked on the door, and when that door opened and Shooter saw who was waiting on the steps, he didn't waste any time. He said, "I won't let you talk to him."

Ronnie knew Captain was inside the house. He could hear what sounded like dishes being washed in the sink.

"You heard the talk?" Ronnie asked. "About me? About the fire?"

Shooter started to close the door, but Ronnie shot his arm out straight and braced it with his hand. Shooter frowned. "Can't stop people from wanting a story," he said.

"What did you tell my girl tonight? Have you talked to Ray Biggs?"

Shooter pushed against the door, but Ronnie pushed back.

"Your footprints were in the snow behind the trailer," Shooter said. "You think Biggs hasn't made plaster casts of those prints? You think he's not on your trail?"

Ronnie stared at Shooter a good long while. His voice went hard. "Go on. Tell Biggs everything about that night. Let's see if you've got the nerve."

"You think I won't? You want the whole story to come out?" Shooter waited a while for Ronnie to answer, and when he didn't, Shooter said, "That's what I thought."

"Merlene was right about you, Shooter. You're a hard man. No wonder Captain never felt close to you. Merlene, too, for that matter. She—"

Shooter put his shoulder to the door and drove it shut, Ronnie no longer able to stop him.

The porch light went out, and Ronnie stood in the dark, his wrist aching from where he'd tried to keep the door from closing. He shouted at the house. He said, "My prints weren't the only ones there. You know that, Shooter. If you're going to tell it, tell it all."

No one in town knew about that visit Ronnie paid Shooter, nor did they know that Captain had a knife like Ronnie's. That he had a Case Hammerhead lockback because Ronnie had bought him one.

"Now you've got your own," Ronnie said the day he gave it to him.

It was an evening shortly after Ronnie had moved into town, a warm Saturday evening in late September, one of the last warm days before fall set in for good. It wouldn't be long before the farmers were cutting their corn and soybeans, not long before the hickory nuts fell from the trees, not long before the time changed and the dark set in early and the countryside smelled of wood fires.

Ronnie drove out the blacktop with his windows down. Captain's knife, along with a leather sheath, a pocket stone, and a bottle of honing oil in a gift tin that said *XX Tested, W. R. Case & Sons Cutlery Company* was lying on the passenger seat. Ronnie had paid over seventy dollars for the set, money he'd asked Brandi to give him. He wanted to do something special for Captain, he told her.

Ronnie explained that he'd always let Captain keep him company when he was working on his car. "He's sorta an orphan now, just like I always was. I know how he feels. Captain always admired my pocketknife. I'd like to give him one as a gift. Just something to give him a boost. It's a nice thing I can do for him, and if you could spare the money—"

Brandi laughed. "Why in the world can I never say no to you?"

"Guess it's just my boyish charm," Ronnie said.

"Or could be I'm just stupid." Brandi swatted him on the shoulder and then gave him a wink. "Ever think it might be that? Maybe you're just taking advantage of me."

Ronnie got serious then. "Let's get my kids something, too. Would that be all right? Something for Christmas?"

"Yes, sugar, we can do that. We won't let them go without."

So that knife for Captain. Ronnie found him outside mowing the grass. He waited until Captain looked up and saw him. Then he waved him over. Captain cut off the mower and came across the yard. Ronnie picked the gift tin up from the seat, and Captain opened the door and got inside.

"We going for a ride?" he wanted to know. "Ronnie, where you been?"

"I don't live out here anymore." Ronnie glanced over at the trailer. Della's car wasn't there, and he guessed she'd taken the kids over to Lois and Wayne's for supper. "I live in town now."

Captain scrunched up his face. He rubbed at his nose with the heel of his palm. "Why is that?" he finally said. "You get lost or something?"

"Yeah, maybe that's it," Ronnie said. "Maybe I'm just lost."

"Nah, you're not lost. You're right here with me. Right, Ronnie? You're where you're supposed to be."

Ronnie hated to disappoint him, and he knew Captain would have a hard time understanding if he tried to explain. "You got that match trick down pat yet?"

Captain shook his head. "I can't do it like you can."

Ronnie had tried to teach him that trick with the matchstick, but Captain could never coordinate his fingers right to get the match to light as he flicked it across the box's strike strip.

"Keep practicing. I had to practice a lot. Don't worry. You'll get it." He tossed the gift tin over onto Captain's lap. "Here ya go. A little present."

"For me?"

"Open it," Ronnie said.

Captain took the lid off the tin. "It's like yours." He picked up the knife and opened the blade. "It's a Case Hammerhead. It's what I've wanted."

"Now it's official," Ronnie said. "We're brothers."

"Forever?"

"You got it, buddy. You and me. Forever."

When Shooter found the gift tin minus the knife itself hidden behind the dresser in Captain's bedroom—Shooter had been bringing clean laundry into the room to put in the dresser drawers, and he'd noticed that the dresser had been pulled out from the wall and not put back level—he knew exactly where it'd come from, and he didn't like it, not one bit.

He got on the phone and called Brandi Tate's house. Ronnie answered, and Shooter said, "Looks like you'd ask me before giving Captain something like that?"

Captain was outside burning trash in the old oil drum they used for that purpose. It was the one chore that Shooter didn't have to fuss at Captain to make sure he did it. Captain liked to light the trash and then stand over the flames, letting the heat warm him. He carried a small box of Diamond matches with him, the same kind that Ronnie used to burn his own trash. Sometimes at the barrel, Captain practiced Ronnie's trick with the match, but he still couldn't get it right.

Shooter watched out the kitchen window as Captain stood over the burn barrel, the flames rising above it.

"You hear me, Ronnie?" Shooter said. "I don't appreciate what you did. If my boy gets into any kind of trouble with that knife, I'll hold you to blame."

"Hold on now, Shooter. It was something Captain always wanted, and I was glad to get it for him."

"Did you ever think that maybe he's not steady enough to have a knife as sharp as that? Who knows what might happen." Shooter paused to let that sink in. "That's your problem, Ronnie. You never think anything all the way out."

And with that he hung up.

When Captain came into the kitchen, Shooter said to him, "You get a little present today? That why Ronnie came by to see you?"

Captain took the Case Hammerhead out of his jeans pocket, and he held it out on his palm, his head bowed, reaching the knife out to Shooter, expecting him to take it.

The gesture caught Shooter by the heart. How quick Captain was to surrender the knife. How easily he offered to give it up. So that was the sort of life Shooter had made for him, one he'd never intended to create but obviously had: a furtive life of secret pleasures, ones Captain feared his father would eventually take from him.

Shooter couldn't bear to ask for the knife.

"You be careful with it, understand?" he said. "That blade's razor sharp."

Captain pulled out the blade and studied it. Finally, he looked up at his father and his face was a face of delight. "Sugar tits," he said.

Shooter shook his head. "That Ronnie Black. He's nothing but a bad influence." Shooter could tell that Captain wasn't listening. When did he ever listen? He was folding the blade back into the knife and then taking it out again. Over and over. "You don't want to turn out like him. You got that, Wesley?"

Captain nodded his head. Then he walked on past Shooter, heading for his bedroom, still fascinated with that knife, not hearing, Shooter knew, a single word he said.

The night of the fire, he asked Captain for that knife, told him to hand it over pronto.

"Just look how quick trouble can come," Shooter said. "Why ask for it? Can't you see now how we all need to be careful?"

But Captain swore again and again, and so fiercely, that he'd lost the knife. Shooter, as uneasy as it made him, finally had no choice but to believe he was telling the truth. Of course, by that time Shooter was desperate to believe as much, eager to convince himself that trouble could come and somehow folks could get through it and make it to the other side.

"I promised your mother I'd take care of you," he said, and in an unexpected show of emotion, he threw his arms around Captain and gave him a clumsy hug. "That's what I aim to do. I'm going to look after you."

He was thinking of how Della had gone back into the fire that one last time, confident that she'd save Emily and Gracie and Junior. *I'm going to get them all out,* she said. And then, before anyone could stop her, she was gone.

20

The day after Angel confronted Ronnie, and he claimed his knife, Wayne and Lois were in Read's IGA, unloading their cart at the checkout. They heard a woman's voice two lanes over from theirs.

"It was on the radio last night and again this morning." The woman was Anna Spillman, who'd come down the street from the Real McCoy to buy five heads of lettuce. Here it was, almost the noon hour, and Pastor Quick had miscalculated how much they'd need for combination salads and sandwiches. And now she was talking to Roe Carl, who was working the register at that lane. "It just breaks my heart," Anna said, "to know someone set that trailer on fire and Della and her kids inside."

Roe shook her head and clucked her tongue. She had a pencil sticking out of her nest of gray curls, and she pulled it out and wagged it at Anna. "You just don't know," she said. "You never know about people. Now you can take that to the bank."

"I keep hoping it wasn't Ronnie," Anna said. "Even after all the trouble he caused Della, I still think he's got a good soul."

Lois was reaching into the cart for the last bag of Brach's candy—this one was Spice Drops—that she liked to keep on hand for the grandkids. Even Wayne was partial to them: Kentucky Mints, Root Beer Barrels, Star Brites. Not that she could afford them, what with Wayne having more trouble with the vertigo now. He was still having dizzy spells, which forced him to turn down jobs. The doctor said with vertigo, you could never tell. It might go away. It might hang on for a spell. Still, Lois wanted those candies. She loved their brightly colored packages and the way the Lemon Drops and Orange Slices glistened with sugar, the banana smell of the Circus Peanuts, the buttery toffee of the Maple Nut Goodies. Something to make her feel a little bit hopeful during these dark days.

But now this—what Anna Spillman had said. Lois couldn't help but speak up. "They had a bad furnace." Her voice was loud, as if she knew that if she didn't shout she'd never get out what she wanted to say. Roe snapped her head up to see where that voice had come from. Anna turned on her heel to look. "That furnace," Lois said again. "Della was burning wood. It was bitter cold and the baby had the croup. Something must have gone wrong with that furnace or with the Franklin stove."

She looked to Wayne then, and he could see the pain and fear in her eyes. He felt the store start to tilt a little and he tried hard to keep it from spinning all the way around. He focused on a spot directly in front of him, the sheepish look on Anna Spillman's face.

"It's just talk about that fire being set." He'd heard the rumors about the blaze being suspicious, and a man from the State Fire Marshal's office had been to talk to him, asking questions about the condition of the furnace and whether he knew of any accelerants stored inside or outside the trailer. Wayne knew folks were talking about Ronnie. At first he wanted it to be true so he'd have someone to call to account instead of blaming himself for not making Della and the kids leave the trailer and bunk up at his and Lois's house that night. Then he started to think it was better the other way, better if the fire was something no one could have helped. An accident flung down from the heavens. He wanted to believe that Della and the kids had been chosen because for some reason or another that wasn't for him to know, God needed them and this was his way of calling them home. Why he had to make them suffer so, Wayne couldn't figure out. He preferred to think of them made whole again and at rest in the hereafter. He'd leave the mysteries to someone else to fret over. "All that talk about Ronnie," he said, "it doesn't amount to anything."

"Wayne, you're probably right," Roe Carl said. "Hello, Lois. I didn't see you folks come in."

Lois held up the last package of Brach's and said, "I came to get candy."

"You didn't have WPLP on this morning?" Anna said. "The local news?"

"We don't listen to the radio anymore." Lois threw the package of Brach's onto the conveyor belt. "Ring me up," she said to the girl at the register, a skinny-minnie of a thing with lipstick the color of black cherries.

"The fire marshal's come to a conclusion," Anna said. "Oh, Lois, I'm just sick over all of this."

Wayne said, "You mean it was set? The fire? They know that for sure?"

He'd been by the place in the days after, and he'd seen the deputies from the fire marshal's office combing through the debris. They brought a dog with them, the kind trained to sniff for accelerants—gasoline, kerosene, turpentine, that sort of thing. The deputies got down on their knees and dug around in the ruins. They took samples to send to the lab in Springfield. "Multiple points of origin." Anna said the words carefully, recalling them from the radio news. "That's what they're saying."

Just minutes before, she'd heard the sheriff talking with the fire chief in the Real McCoy using the same words: *multiple points of origin.* She'd lingered, clearing the table behind theirs, catching as much of the story as she could. The dog had sniffed out gasoline. The fire had started in more than one place. There were trail marks, more than one burn-through in the flooring, spalled concrete. There was crazed glass, finely cracked; collapsed springs in the furniture and the bedding; alligator blisters on the charred wood—all signs that the fire burned fast and hot. "It was set all right," Milt Timlin said, and Biggs said, "The question now is who did it."

"So it's for sure?" Wayne said to Anna. The store was spinning fast now, and he couldn't take it anymore.

"Lois!" Anna called out in a frantic voice.

The skinny-minnie girl let out a squeak and said, "Oh, what should I do?"

Lois turned her head to look for Wayne, but he was on the floor, tumbled down so fast she couldn't have caught him if she'd tried.

At that moment, Roe Carl saw the sheriff's car drive past, heading south on Main Street, and she watched it go for the briefest instant before she picked up the phone and called 911.

Ronnie was on the porch of Brandi's house when he saw the sheriff's car coming at him down Locust Street. He'd spent the morning alone—Brandi at work and the kids at school—trying to figure out what he could and couldn't tell Angel about that pocketknife and how it came to be behind the trailer. Yes, he'd gone back there the night of the fire, but he didn't yet know how to tell that story in a way that would make any sense, because he still didn't understand why he'd done what he had—didn't like to think about it, truth be told. Didn't like to think about Shooter either and what story he might be spinning.

Here toward noon, Ronnie had finally decided to give up all that thinking and to drive over to Brick Chapel about that job the way he was supposed to have done the day before, but Angel hadn't come home, and he'd been too worried about her to do anything but get on the telephone and call anyone he could think of who might have seen her—even Missy Wade, as much as it galled him. He'd driven the streets looking for Angel. Then he gave up and went back to Brandi's, and that's when Shooter called.

Ronnie would have to find a way to explain all that to the man in Brick Chapel, and then hope he understood and still had that job. It was a good job at a garment factory, working in the warehouse running a forklift, moving bolts of material, loading and unloading trucks. A job with health benefits and profit sharing and a week's paid vacation every year. A steady job worth driving sixty miles there and back every day. He could work at it for years and years to come and make a life for his girls. Now that he had them, even with Brandi's check, things were going to be tight, especially with the new baby on the way. He'd made up his mind that he wasn't going to ask Missy for any of the money in the bank, not unless he absolutely had to. He wasn't going to give her the satisfaction of playing Good Samaritan to his need. He'd rather that money turned to dust in the bank and Missy would have to explain to all the good folks who made donations why she'd never let Ronnie use it for his girls.

That's what was on his mind when he stepped out onto the porch and saw the sheriff's car. He watched it come, hoping it might turn left onto Jones Street and move on out of his day, but he could already see that the car was slowing. It came to a stop along the curb just to the left of Brandi's drive, and Ronnie didn't wait. He went out to see what Biggs might want, fearing that he knew exactly why the sheriff was there.

"I told you I wasn't filing charges against Wayne," he said to Biggs, who had put his window down. Ronnie laid both hands on top of the car and leaned down. The two-way radio crackled, the heater fan blew out warm air. Biggs had an aroma made up of leather and fried foods and some sort of pine-scented aftershave.

"I'm not here about that." He reached over and squelched the two-way. "I need to talk to you about the fire."

"Now? I'm on my way to see about a job."

"I don't think we should wait. Haven't you heard?"

"It's over at Brick Chapel. A good job at the garment factory."

"Ronnie, the fire marshal's report came in. We need to talk."

Biggs wanted him to get in the car and ride over to the courthouse in Phillipsport with him.

"Like I'm some damned criminal?" Ronnie said. "Let people see me like that? Bad enough I got to stand out here talking to you and all the neighbors peeking out windows."

"I'm not out to make things hard for you. Lord knows you've had trouble enough." Biggs rubbed his hand over his mouth, considering. "Get in your car, then, and drive on over to the courthouse. I'll be behind you."

Next door, Willie Wheeler had come out to spread some salt on his walk, even though that walk was clear and there was no new snow in the forecast. Ronnie knew he just wanted to see if he could eavesdrop. A car came down Locust, Alvin Higgins in his old green Ford pickup with a tool case across the bed. He slowed down and took a good long look.

"All right," Ronnie finally said. "But I can tell you I haven't done a thing wrong."

By the time the ambulance got to the IGA, Wayne was sitting on a folding chair that Roe Carl had found for him. The medics checked him over, took all his vitals, asked him whether he thought he should go to the hospital.

He told them, no, he just got dizzy sometimes. "It's the vertigo," he said. "That's all. Tell them, Lois."

"He gets the spins," said Lois. "Been happening for a while now." She was stroking Wayne's head. "You feel better?"

"I feel all right." He met the eyes of the two medics. He cursed the vertigo and how it turned him into a fall-down dizzy old man. "I'm sorry for all the upset," he said, and that was that, so he thought. Just a little scare on a Thursday morning, that, thank goodness, came to nothing.

Ronnie eased his Firebird into a parking spot on the south side of the courthouse and watched Biggs pull his patrol car up the inclined drive reserved for the sheriff. Biggs got out and waited for Ronnie to come up the courthouse steps. It was twelve o'clock and the fire whistle was blowing to mark the noon hour the same way it'd done every weekday as long as Ronnie could remember. He knew Brandi would be leaving the Savings and Loan to slip out for lunch and maybe a little window shopping if she had time. She was starting to look at things for the baby. It would be a few weeks before the ultrasound would tell them whether they were having a boy or a girl. "It'll be a surprise no matter when we find out," Brandi told him when they were debating whether to have the ultrasound done, "so isn't it better to find out in advance so we can be prepared?" But she was starting to look at things for both genders. One night, she'd come home from work all excited about a *Willie Nelson Born for Trouble* onesie. The next night, she'd be laughing about a pink *Baby Boop* and then get all teary-eyed over a *Mommy's Little Girl*. Since it was her first, she was excited about everything, and because of that, Ronnie was thrilled too, even if he couldn't always bring himself to show it. "Aren't you excited?" Brandi asked him one night, and he said, sure, without a doubt, but she had to keep in mind that he'd just lost three of his children, and surely she didn't expect him to ever get over that. It was no good to even try.

So he found himself moving through his days like he was in a dream, which is how he felt now as he came up the steps to where

Biggs waited, and he knew there were people passing by watching him—the office girls from the Reasoner Insurance Agency on the east side of the square, the opticians from LensCrafters, some mechanics from Albright Chevrolet, even a few high school kids who'd walked uptown to grab lunch at the new Mi Casita Mexican place. Lord, what if Angel was one of them? What if she saw him there with Biggs, about to enter the courthouse? After that ugly run-in with her last night, he didn't need something else to try to explain.

"I know I don't have to talk to you," he said to Biggs. "Not unless I've got a lawyer with me. I know that much."

Biggs opened the heavy glass door to the courthouse and motioned for Ronnie to step inside. "This is just a friendly talk. There are things I need to tell you."

"You couldn't have told me back in Goldengate? You had to drag me over here?"

"It's better done here," Biggs said. "Just in case our little talk goes somewhere interesting."

Ronnie hesitated. He had things he wouldn't tell Biggs, not if he could help it. He had things he'd rather keep to himself forever.

"You've got no call to throw me in jail," he said, "if that's what you've got in mind."

Someone in a car going by called his name. He thought it came from a red GMC Sierra pickup crammed full of high school boys going by on Fifteenth Street.

"Ronnie," one of the boys said out the open window. He had red hair and freckles, an unlit cigarette dangling from his mouth. "Hey, Ronnie. You got a light?"

The truck went on by, the boys' hoots and whoops fading.

"Some people," Biggs said. "If I could only arrest someone for being stupid or mean in the heart, I surely would enjoy it."

"Let's do this," Ronnie said, impatient.

He stepped into the courthouse and then followed Biggs into the sheriff's office, where a deputy, a man with neatly combed white hair and sad eyes, was sitting behind a desk. Biggs nodded to him, and then he took Ronnie into his office and closed the door.

"So what's the fire marshal say?" Ronnie wasn't going to wait for Biggs to work his way up to giving him the news—not give him a chance to hem and haw and see if Ronnie would squirm. He'd just ask him straight out. "Must have found something out of the ordinary?"

He hadn't even sat down yet, didn't know that he felt like it, didn't want to give Biggs the notion that he meant to stay long.

Biggs unzipped his trooper jacket. He took it off and hung it on a coat rack in the corner. An American flag stood in the other corner, and Ronnie saw the plaques on the wall and the framed picture of the president, a man Ronnie hadn't voted for but no one he wished any particular bad fortune. One wall held a large map of Phillips County, and Ronnie knew if he were to trace his finger along the right roads, he'd eventually end up down the blacktop out of Goldengate to where he once had a home with Della and their kids.

"You think there'd be a reason for the fire marshal to find something worth us talking about?" Biggs walked around behind his desk and peered at a computer screen for a moment. He put his closed fists on the desk and braced himself with his knuckles. The office smelled of the limestone walls, damp and moldy—that and the cherry-scented air freshener that Biggs was using to try to make things more pleasant. He had a row of photographs lined up on a wide ledge that ran beneath the wall of windows behind his desk. Ronnie could see the pictures were of him and his family: a blond-haired woman with her arm around Biggs, a boy in Marine dress blues, Biggs with what must have been a grandson riding on his shoulders. "Ronnie, is there anything I ought to know?"

The pictures of Biggs's family had Ronnie all out of sorts. Here was a man who had everything right where he wanted it. A man with a wife and kids and grandkids, and here was Ronnie, a man fighting to keep his family together.

"I thought you already knew everything." He sat down then, sat right down on the chair across from Biggs's desk and let the sheriff look down on him. He sat down because he felt a trembling in his legs, and he feared if he didn't sit he'd fall over. "Didn't you say you had things to tell me?"

Biggs eased himself down onto his own chair. He rested his forearms on his desk and put his hands together, his thick fingers laced. "All I know is what the fire marshal's office told me." He looked at Ronnie for a long time, and Ronnie made sure to hold his gaze steady and not to glance away. "That fire didn't start all by itself," Biggs finally said. "It had help."

"Someone set it?" Ronnie said. "Someone put that trailer to burn with my kids inside?"

"With your kids and your wife."

"Who'd do that?" Ronnie jumped up from his chair. "Find out who it was and I'll kill the bastard."

"No one's going to be doing any killing," Biggs said. "Not if I can help it." He leaned back in his chair and put his hands behind his head. "Ronnie," he said, "where were you the night of the fire?"

"I was home," Ronnie said. "At Brandi's. I was with Brandi." He pointed his finger at Biggs. "Surely you don't think I'd do something like that. Try to kill my whole family?"

Biggs got up and walked around the desk. He stood with his face just inches from Ronnie's own. "I truly hope that's not the case, but someone set that fire, and now it's my job to find out who. I'm going to have to start talking to folks."

"You do that," Ronnie said. "You talk to everyone you can find who can tell you something."

"I may be back to talk to you."

"What can I tell you that I haven't already?" Ronnie shrugged his shoulders. "Like I said, I was with Brandi."

"I just want you to know that I'm going to be pushing this hard," Biggs said. "I've got a family of my own, and what someone did to yours makes my blood boil. It's the saddest damn thing that's ever happened around here. You get me?"

"You think it doesn't do the same thing to me?" Ronnie's voice shook and tears came to his eyes. "I may have left Della, but I had fourteen years with her, and we had all those kids. And now three of them are dead. I was their father. You remember that."

Outside the courthouse, a cold wind had come up out of the north and the temperature had dropped. By the time Ronnie got to his Firebird he was wishing for his gloves. He fumbled with his keys and they dropped to the street. He stooped to pick them up. Finally, he got the car unlocked and he slid in behind the wheel.

Anyone driving by just then would have seen a man pounding his fist on the dashboard, and if they didn't know he was Ronnie Black—and if they didn't know about what had happened at that trailer—they might have thought him a crazy man. Still others, just moments later, might have seen the Firebird backing out of its parking place and not thought anything about Ronnie and what he might be up to until they got home that evening and read about the fire marshal's report in the *Phillipsport Messenger*. Then they might recall seeing the Firebird on the courthouse square, and they might think about how slowly he drove, taking a left onto Fifteenth to the stoplight at State. Maybe they sat behind him there in their own cars. Maybe they saw him start to turn left when the light went to green— left to Goldengate—and then change his mind and turn right instead with a squeal of tires and a roar of engine like he didn't care who might be in his way.

Brandi came home from work and found the girls alone. "Where's your dad?" she asked Hannah.

"Don't know," Hannah said.

She was playing a game of Operation with Sarah. The two of them were on their knees on the living room rug, the large oval braided rug Brandi bought last fall to celebrate Ronnie's moving in. "This has just been a house," she told him. "Now it's going to be a home." When she found out she was pregnant, she counted back and thought that night must have been the night they made the baby. First part of October, the nights starting to cool and soon the leaves would turn and there'd be the lovely part of autumn that she'd always treasured. The leaves, and pumpkins on people's porches, and scarecrows on straw bales in front yards, and corn shocks woven around the gaslights. Indian summer days—a last time of warm sun and golden light before the turn toward winter.

"Don't know?" Brandi tossed her car keys onto the marble top of the old washstand that she kept just inside the front door. The house was full of things she'd inherited from her grandmother—a pie safe with punched tin panels, a Hoosier cabinet, a library table, a Morris chair, an apothecary dresser, a sleigh bed, a cedar chest. "I like old things," she'd told Ronnie. "They've got character." And he said, "Must be why you like me."

"Why in the world wouldn't you know?" she said now to Hannah. "Didn't he say where he was going?"

"Haven't seen him," Hannah mumbled. She was concentrating hard on removing the Adam's apple with the tweezers. "Don't know where he is."

The tweezers touched the side of the throat as she was lifting out the Adam's apple, and the buzzer went off and the red bulb of the patient's nose lit up.

"You lose your turn." Sarah clapped her hands together. Her bangs needed cutting. She kept brushing them out of her eyes. "Doesn't she, Brandi? Doesn't she lose her turn?"

"Where's your hair barrettes?" Brandi asked her.

Sarah chewed on her bottom lip and twisted up her mouth as she thought. "I don't know," she finally said.

Brandi put her hands on her hips and gave Sarah a disapproving look. "Did you lose them again? Oh, Sarah."

Secretly, Brandi was pleased. This silly, forgetful girl needed her to keep track of her hair barrettes, to comb the tangles from her hair, to cut her bangs, to remind her to brush her teeth before she went to bed. And there was Emma who liked it when Brandi read stories to her. And dear, dependable Hannah, who had woven her that friendship bracelet. It was Hannah who'd made room in her heart for Brandi first, and then the other girls had followed suit. All but Angel. She was the stubborn one, but Brandi was determined to win her over.

Last night, after the ugly scene with Ronnie, Brandi had a talk with Angel, just the two of them, in the privacy of Brandi and Ronnie's bedroom. Brandi sat on the bed with Angel, and she put her arm around her. Angel let her hold her like that, rocking her a little, stroking her hair.

"Your daddy loves you, and I love you," she said. "We're just waiting for you to love us back."

Angel said, "You're not my mother," and Brandi admitted that she wasn't. "No, I'm not, and I know this is all complicated for you. You're at that age when you're trying to figure out things about love, and I know your daddy and I haven't made that any easier for you, but trust me, Angel, I love you like you were my own. In truth, you are my own now. You and all your sisters. We don't have any choice." Angel levered herself away from Brandi's embrace. She got up and walked across the room to the door. Before she opened it, she turned back and said, "Maybe we do. At least I do. Maybe you don't know everything." Brandi asked her what that was supposed to mean, but Angel wouldn't answer. She just opened the door and left the room.

Brandi had spent a good part of her day mulling that over and had eventually dismissed it as Angel's way of saying how hurt she was, how much she was suffering, how confused she was. A girl who'd lost her mother and not willing just yet to let the world be kind to her. Brandi could forgive her that and try to be patient and persistent with her love.

"Where's Angel and Emma?" she asked Hannah.

Hannah was in her gawky stage now, all skinny arms and spindly legs, but Brandi could see she'd grow into a beautiful woman. That lustrous skin, those blue eyes.

"Angel's in our room," Hannah said, "and Emma's in her closet talking to Emily."

Poor Emma. She was having such a hard time being a twin on her own.

"Well, at least someone knows something around here." Brandi gave the girls a smile to let them know she wasn't angry with them. "Did your father pick you and Emma up at school?" she asked Sarah.

Sarah glanced at Hannah, and Brandi took note of how Hannah's eyes opened wide, as if someone were trying to pull something from her and she wasn't willing to let it go.

"We came home from school," Sarah finally said.

"Sarah," said Brandi. "Don't lie to me."

"They walked home from school." Hannah spoke up for her. "They were here when I got home."

"And your father nowhere to be seen and no way for me to call him." He refused to carry a cell phone. Hadn't had one all his life and didn't see any reason to start now, even though Brandi tried to convince him he might wish he'd changed his tune someday. "Maybe Angel knows something," she said, and went down the hallway.

Angel was lying on her bed listening to a new iPod. Her old one, of course, was gone in the fire. She'd begged her father for a new one, but he'd said no.

"Where'd you get that?" Brandi asked her.

Angel took her earbuds out and propped herself up on her elbows. "I didn't steal it, if that's what you think."

"I didn't say you stole it. I asked you where you got it."

Angel rubbed her thumb over the smooth face of the iPod. "It was a present."

"From a boy?" Brandi was aware of her voice rising in alarm, but she couldn't help herself. She knew what a boy would be after with an expensive gift like that, and it wouldn't be just friendship. "Was it that Tommy Stout?"

"No, not from a boy." Angel made fun of Brandi's anxiety, making her voice squeak with mock fear. "I'm not looking for a boyfriend." Her voice went flat and she gave Brandi a long stare. "I'm not on the prowl like you."

"That's enough, Angel. You don't know a thing about what brought your dad and me together."

Sure she'd locked eyes with him at Fat Daddy's one night back in the summer, had told him he looked good in those new jeans. Had said, "Della better keep an eye on you." She slow danced with him when the jukebox played Rascal Flatts' "Bless the Broken Road," and she sang all low and sexy in his ear, "Every long-lost dream led me to where you are." When the song was done, she said goodnight.

Then she just waited. It wasn't long before she'd hear a car coming slow down Locust, and when she'd look out her front window she'd see Ronnie in his Firebird, taking his time as he made the turn onto Jones Street. She came to know the sound of that Firebird. Five nights running, Ronnie came by. On the sixth night, she was waiting on her porch, and when she saw him coming, she went out to the curb and flagged him down. She leaned in through his open window. "Might as well come in," she said. "Don't you think?"

Angel didn't know how it could happen. You could be out there looking and not even know it until all of a sudden you were in the scene from your life that you'd been heading toward all along. Then, like that, it all made sense—every damned move you'd ever made, right or wrong. You were where you were supposed to be. Didn't make any difference that Ronnie was married. Didn't matter a snap that he had all those kids.

"I know one thing," Angel said. "You hurt my mom. You and my dad. Maybe you've got a way of not thinking about that, but I don't. I think about it every single day."

Brandi did too. She couldn't get it out of her head, the fact that she and Ronnie had ended up together and now Della was dead. At her darkest times, Brandi thought about how part of that was her fault. If she hadn't come up to Ronnie that night at Fat Daddy's. If she hadn't gone out to that Firebird that night at her house and told Ronnie to come in. If, if, if. A world of ifs, forever and ever. For that reason alone, Brandi was determined to love Angel and her sisters and to give them a good home. To make that one good thing she could do.

"That iPod." Brandi wouldn't admit to Angel how much what she'd said had shaken her. She made her voice go hard. "Who gave it to you?"

"Missy," Angel said. "She's taking us to 4-H tonight."

"Does your dad know about this?"

"Maybe you should ask him," Angel said. Then she stuffed the buds back into her ears, and gave Brandi the sweetest smile.

Soon it was evening, the dark coming on early. Out in the country, off a gravel road that snaked back a mile to the west of where the trailer had been, the pole light came on in Lois and Wayne's barn-yard.

They'd been resting, dozing in their reclining chairs, waking from time to time to watch out the picture window as the squir-rels and jays and quail came to feed on shelled corn tossed around the blue spruce. They'd kept the lights off, and now it was dark in the room and they talked back and forth in that quiet, just the two of them out there in the country.

"Have things stopped spinning for you?" Lois wanted to know, and Wayne told her he thought he felt some better and maybe could eat a little supper.

She made some grilled cheese sandwiches with sliced tomato, the way he liked them, and opened a can of tomato soup she'd brought home from the store. He said he could come in to the table to eat, but she told him there was no need. She'd set up TV trays, and they could eat in their chairs, maybe even put on the television. Not the news—they'd had enough of that—but maybe that *Wheel of Fortune* television show they liked to watch. They'd sit there and eat their sup-per and try to guess the puzzles on *Wheel*, and little by little—though they didn't say this—they'd try to get back to some normal way of living.

"It's a good thing we didn't try to take on the girls," Wayne said when Lois brought him his supper. "The way I am, and you having to take care of me, I don't know how we'd manage."

Lois turned on the TV and found the channel for *Wheel*. She and Wayne sat there, eating, watching the pretty woman turn over the letters of the puzzles, but they didn't try to guess like they usually did.

"It couldn't be true about Ronnie, could it?" Lois finally said. "He wouldn't have done anything like that, would he?"

"Turn it up." Wayne pointed to the TV. "I can't hear what they're saying."

Missy had been thinking about Angel all day and how maybe she shouldn't have given her that iPod—even Pat said it was bad business—but she'd wanted to do something nice for her, something to let her know she didn't hold any bad feelings over the way Angel had treated her after the funeral when the girls had packed up and left with Ronnie and Angel hadn't told her a word of goodbye, hadn't even waved at her as Ronnie drove away.

Out of all the girls, Angel was the one who most worried her. Angel, who seemed to have a turnip for a heart. Missy was determined to save her from her own anger, to keep reminding her that there were good people in the world who loved her.

"So you're going to give her an iPod?" Pat said to her that morning at breakfast. They were sitting at the table just after dawn when the light was watery and the radio was on. WPLP was giving the farm market reports from the Chicago Board of Trade before turning to the local news. "That's how you're going to teach her about goodness?"

"It's a start," she said. "It's just a way to love on her for a while. What's wrong with that?"

Pat didn't answer at first, but she could tell he thought she was overstepping her bounds and heading down a dangerous path.

"You control their money," he finally said. "Isn't that enough?"

Why did he have to say a thing like that, a thing that caught her by surprise and made her look at herself the way he saw her: a woman desperate with need? She couldn't deny it—didn't want to deny it, really. She wanted instead for the two of them to acknowledge what was lacking between them so they could let it draw them closer. She wanted to say, Don't you see how this is our chance?

Then the local news came on the radio, and the first story was about the trailer fire and how the State Fire Marshal had confirmed its suspicious nature. The investigation, the radio announcer said, was ongoing.

Missy recalled the day at the bank when Laverne had practically begged her to say that Ronnie couldn't possibly have had anything to do with the fire, and Missy had left enough space for that rumor to spread.

Now she only looked at Pat and said, "Oh, my. My word. Isn't that just the saddest thing? And after what Shooter told us about Ronnie."

Pat got up from the table and grabbed his coat and lunch box. He looked at Missy a good long while. "Do you think he really did it?"

"God help him," Missy said.

Pat nodded and then headed out the door.

She took her time washing the dishes, keeping an eye on the clock on the wall of the kitchen. The clock was round with a yellow sunflower painted on its center. Yellow numbers circled the sunflower just outside the reach of its petals. It would take thirty minutes to drive to the high school in Phillipsport, and Missy wanted to make sure that she got there in enough time to be waiting when the bus from Goldengate pulled to the curb.

At the school, she stood by her van, watching. When she saw Angel get off the bus, she called to her.

Angel stopped on the sidewalk, her backpack slung over her shoulder, while the students getting off the bus moved past her. They were laughing and shouting, their breath steaming in the cold air.

Missy waved at Angel, and her heart lifted when Angel finally raised her arm and waved back. Then she came down the sidewalk to where Missy was standing.

"I know you have to get to your first class," Missy said, "but I wanted you to have this."

Missy gave her the iPod, and Angel looked at it and looked at it and looked at it. When she finally raised her head, her lip was trembling.

"Thank you," she said in a soft voice.

"Your dad said you'd been wanting a new one."

Angel rolled her eyes. "He wouldn't let me have one."

Missy could have told her not to hold her father to account. She could have told her about the three-hundred-dollar check she wrote him and how he promised to make sure all the girls got something from it. But what she said was, "Sometimes dads just don't know, do they?"

"That's for sure," Angel said, and Missy thought she saw the trace of a smile.

"It's 4-H meeting tonight," Missy said. "You and your sisters want to go?"

"We don't have our goats anymore."

"Doesn't matter." Missy put her arm around Angel's shoulders and gave her a squeeze. "We'd all love to see you. What say I come by for you around 6:30?"

Angel nodded. "Okay," she said. Then the bell was ringing, and Missy told her to hurry so she wouldn't get in trouble.

By six o'clock that evening, Brandi had called everyone she could think of who might know where Ronnie was. He hadn't been in the Real McCoy Café or Casey's convenience store or the IGA. Shooter Rowe hadn't seen him, nor had Pat Wade.

"Tell Missy not to come and get the girls for 4-H," she told Pat. They hadn't had their supper, and Emma and Sarah were getting whiny. Emma was tugging at the leg of her slacks. Sarah was pressing the tweezers against the sides of the Operation game over and over so it made an annoying buzz. Angel and Hannah were back in their room.

"The girls?" he said, in a way that made it clear Missy hadn't said a word about it to him. "She's already gone," he said, and before Brandi could say anything else, he hung up.

She happened to think then to call next door to Willie Wheeler's.

"I saw Ronnie around noon," Willie said. "He was out to the curb talking to the sheriff. Then Ronnie got in his car, and Biggs, he followed up the street after him."

"Must have been something about the fire," Brandi said.

Some time passed before Willie said anything else, and when he did, Brandi wished she wasn't hearing what she was.

"Haven't you heard?" Brandi couldn't find her voice, afraid to ask what Willie was talking about. Finally, he went on. "It's about the fire all right. Fire marshal says it was set. It's all over the news."

The rumors about Ronnie that she'd so readily dismissed now took her by the throat. Arson, and now Ronnie was more in the middle of it than she'd ever dreamed.

She got off the phone and marched down the hall to Angel's room. She didn't bother to knock. She just pushed open the door.

Angel was standing behind Hannah, braiding her hair. "Is there anything to eat before we go?" Angel asked.

"You're not going with Missy," Brandi said. "I need you to get supper for your sisters and then look after them."

Angel took her hands out of Hannah's hair. "Why haven't *you* made supper by now?"

"I'm trying to find your daddy. Aren't you even worried?"

Angel just shrugged her shoulders.

Hannah said, "What's wrong? Is there something wrong?"

"No, there's nothing wrong. I just need to find him." She started to go. Then she turned back and said, "You're to stay here tonight. Do you understand me?"

Hannah said that she did. Brandi thought she might have seen
Angel nod her head, but she couldn't be sure. She guessed that was
the best she could do. Now she needed to find Ronnie.

He was in a bar in Brick Chapel—the Kozy Kiln—and had been
since three o'clock in the afternoon. He and Brandi had come there
once in the summer before he left Della and they were looking for
somewhere to be off by themselves. He drank a few beers while the
daylight faded and the streetlights came on and the headlights of cars
swept by the plate-glass window by the table where he sat.

The last of the afternoon shoppers hurried past, women with
scarves wrapped around their faces and snow boots on their feet.
They held shopping bags in their arms as if they were toting babies.
From time to time, one of the women laughed so loud that Ronnie
could hear it, a streak of a woman's bright voice that was his for just
a moment and then was gone.

The waitress came to see if he needed anything, said, "Darlin',
you've been in here a good while. Don't you have somewhere to go?"

She was a girl with yellow hair falling over her shoulders. A girl
with slender arms and long fingers. A girl with papery skin beneath
which Ronnie could see the faint blue trails of her veins. A girl who
put him in mind of Della when he'd first fallen head over heels for
her. Della the way she was before the kids and all those years, and
now he was starting over again, this time with Brandi, and he knew
he should be home with her and the girls, but he hadn't been able to
lift himself up and make the drive back to Goldengate.

"You don't know the half of it," he said to the girl.

Then he had to look away, had to turn his face to the window.
The girl was too beautiful in the way that Della had been, and if he
kept looking at her, he wouldn't be able to think of anything more
than the way he and Della had once promised themselves to each

other and how he'd broken his end of that promise and now she was dead.

"I hope things get better for you, darlin'," the girl said, and then he heard the heels of her shoes clicking over the floor and falling away to nothing.

He'd been to the garment factory to see about that job. The plant manager, a tall man with a big belly and a long, sad face, said, "Pardner, I had to get me someone in that warehouse." He hooked his thumbs into his waistband, on either side of an ornate silver belt buckle that featured an eagle and the Alamo and the words TEXAS TOUGH.

"My girl." Ronnie started in with an explanation. "She didn't come home. I didn't know what to do." He knew he was talking too fast. "Then today I started out, and, well, you probably know about the fire. My wife. Three of my kids. Well, mister, it's just been an unusual time for me. Otherwise, I'd of been here when I was supposed to. The truth is, mister, I need this job."

"I know about your trouble." The plant manager shook his head in sympathy. "Jesus, yes. But, Ronnie, I had trucks needed unloading, and I had to get another man in that warehouse."

Ronnie looked the man in the eye, gave him a chance to change his mind. They were in his crow's nest office, high above the factory floor where row after row of women had their backs curved over sewing machines. Even through the window glass, Ronnie could hear the angry buzz of all those machines.

"So that's the way it is?" he finally said.

"I'm afraid I don't have a damned thing to offer you now."

Ronnie hadn't gone home. He hadn't wanted to face Brandi and tell her he'd lost out on that job, and he didn't for the life of him know what he'd say to her about Biggs sticking his nose into things and where that might be heading. He'd driven around until he'd found the Kozy Kiln, and he thought he'd just hunker down there for a while. It wasn't until it was too late that he realized he'd forgotten all about picking up Sarah and Emma from school, and the fact of his neglect sent him into such a funk that he didn't know if he'd ever be able to face anyone ever again.

The phone was ringing behind the bar. Ronnie saw the waitress pick it up, and as she talked—he couldn't hear what she was saying—he noticed that she kept looking over to where he was sitting. She nodded her head. Soon she put the handset down on the bar and made her away across the room to his table.

"Darlin', are you Ronnie Black?"

"Who wants to know?"

She nodded over her shoulder to the phone lying on the bar. "You got people looking for you."

Missy pulled her van into Brandi's driveway and tooted the horn. She waited a few seconds and then saw little Emma at the front window, peeking out between the drapes. Missy waved, which seemed to startle her, because in a flash Emma was gone. Missy honked the horn again, and after a while Angel came out the front door and down the steps. Missy reached over and opened the passenger door for her.

"What's keeping your sisters?" she said.

"They're not coming." Angel got in and slammed the door. "Brandi's out looking for Dad."

"Who's looking after you all?"

"Hannah's in there with Sarah and Emma."

Missy looked out at the soft glow of light in the front room window. "So it's just you and me for 4-H tonight?"

Angel shook her head. "We're not supposed to. Brandi doesn't like it that you gave me that iPod."

"What did she say?

"She wanted to know if Dad knew about it. Then later she said I wasn't to go to 4-H."

Missy was disappointed, but more than that she was worried about the girls being alone. "Where's your dad?"

"No one knows. He didn't come home." Angel's coat was unzipped and she flicked at the zipper tab with her finger. Finally, she stopped fidgeting, and for the first time since she'd gotten into the van she looked fully at Missy and she said in a soft voice, "I think I know why. He's done something wrong."

Missy braced herself. Here it is, she thought. The hard thing. "Honey, you're going to hear some things about your father. Some horrible things."

Angel didn't hesitate. "I already know he was at the trailer that night."

Missy was doing her best not to poison Ronnie for Angel. "No one's guilty until it's proven," she said.

Angel was quiet for some time. She turned away from Missy and kept looking out the passenger-side window of the van. The heater fan blew out hot air. The digital clock pulsed to another minute.

Then Angel said, "I can prove it. I know what happened. I found his knife in the snow behind the trailer."

"His knife?" Missy reached over and took Angel's hand. "Honey, he could have dropped it there anytime."

Angel shook her head. "He was there that night. Mr. Rowe saw him."

"He told you that?" Missy's mind was racing. If that knife was proof of what Shooter claimed, that he'd seen Ronnie come out from behind the trailer that night, what else might there be waiting to be proven? She squeezed Angel's hand. "Honey, I'm right here. Don't be afraid."

"But what if he tries to hurt me? What if he tries to hurt all of us?"

Missy leaned over and gathered Angel up into her arms. "I won't let anyone hurt you." She rocked her back and forth. She said, "Shh, shh, honey. Nothing bad can happen. You're with me now."

She took Angel into the house and made sure the girls were all right. Emma was trying to spread jelly on a piece of toast. Sarah was standing on her head, her feet up against the living room wall. Hannah was in her room doing homework.

Missy called Laverne Ott, the assistant 4-H leader, and asked her to go ahead and start the meeting without her. She had something to attend to.

The girls hadn't eaten, so she found some ground beef in the fridge and a can of peas in the cupboard. She looked in the freezer and pulled out a bag of French fries.

"Burgers and fries?" she asked, and that was enough to get Sarah to stop standing on her head and Emma to jump up and down and Hannah to come out of her room. "And peas," Missy said.

"No peas," said Sarah. "Peas make me gag."

"If you want fries, you've got to eat your peas." Missy tapped her finger on Sarah's nose. "Just pretend they're candy, and you'll do fine."

After supper was done, and Missy was drying the last of the dishes, she heard the front door open, and there was Brandi. The girls were in their rooms doing their homework.

Missy came right to the point. "Do you know what he's done? Ronnie? How can you be with him?" She'd never said the word before, but she said it now. "A murderer. How can you think he'd be a good father to these girls?"

"None of this is your business," Brandi said.

But Missy wouldn't stop. She told Brandi about Shooter's claim that Ronnie had started the fire. She said Angel had told her about finding his knife in the snow.

Brandi couldn't bear to hear it. She couldn't stand to think that he was capable of what people were saying he'd done.

"I don't want to hear that." Her voice was trembling. She saw Missy's coat draped over the arm of the couch. She picked it up and threw it at her. "You've got it in for Ronnie and me. That's plain. Get out of my house. I don't want you here."

Missy was calm. She put her on coat and took the time to button it. At the front door, she turned back to Brandi. "I'm going to Sheriff Biggs with this," she said. "You tell Ronnie he better get a lawyer."

When she left Brandi's house, Missy drove to Lois and Wayne's, and there in the dimly lit living room she told Lois that, as much as it broke her heart to say it, facts were pointing to the possibility that all the rumors were true: Ronnie had started that fire.

"I don't think the girls should be in that house with him," she said. "Who knows what else he might do."

"Oh, Lord," said Lois. "My grandbabies. It's just about all I can do to look after Wayne now."

Wayne was in bed, sick again with the spins, but he could hear Missy and Lois talking in the living room. He said, "I don't want to lose them to foster care. Missy, come back here."

The bedroom was dark except for the dim glow of a nightlight plugged into the wall. Lois took Missy's hand and led her to the side of the bed, where Wayne lay flat on his back, his eyes closed.

Then he opened them to look at her. "Della always thought you'd done well for yourself. Truth is, she envied you more than a little, though I shouldn't tell you that about her. I know she asked God to forgive her for that, and surely He did." Wayne closed his eyes, and Missy imagined he was trying to make the room stop spinning. He didn't open them again. He said, "I'm old, Missy. I'm old and sick. Too old to be raising up those girls, as much as I love them. Della always said you had the nicest home, and she always thought the world of Pat. She always said it was a shame you having no kids of your own, because she could see how much love you had in you. That's why she wanted you and Pat to be godparents to her kids. I know she wouldn't want her girls with Ronnie and Brandi. I think you know what I'm trying to say. I think Della would want it. That is, if you're willing. I expect I speak for Lois, too."

"She told me to go on," Missy said to Pat, when she was finally home and relating the story. "Lois. She told me we had their blessing."

All of this happened after Ronnie picked up the phone from the bar at the Kozy Kiln and was surprised to find Brandi on the other end of the line.

"How'd you know I was here?" he asked her.

"I remembered you and I were there once. I figured you might have gone to Brick Chapel to see about that job, and then I just started adding things up."

Her voice was tight and flat, not the baby-sweet-baby voice he was used to hearing from her.

"That job's gone," he said. "You heard about the fire marshal's report?"

"I heard." That same flat voice, like he was a stranger to her. "That was no call for you to forget about Emma and Sarah this afternoon. No excuse for you to be there in that bar, making me hunt you down."

He was ashamed of that fact. He'd been so caught up in his own misery and trouble he'd forgotten how to be a father.

"Baby, I'm sorry."

A long silence stretched out between them, as if she were on the other side of the world instead of only thirty miles away.

Then finally she said, "Ronnie, you better come home," and it was clear to him from the way she said it that she wasn't really sure she wanted him to.

"I'll be there," he said. "I love you, Brandi."

He waited for her to say she loved him too, but there was no response, and finally he figured out that she'd already hung up the phone.

21

Before Brandi made that call, she talked to Angel. They sat together on the side of Brandi's bed, and Angel wished more than anything that she could be with Missy. She kept her head bowed and listened to Brandi talk to her in low tones so Hannah and Sarah and Emma wouldn't hear from the living room.

"You know this is very serious." Brandi hadn't even taken off her coat, a black pea coat with a double row of big buttons. "Angel, do you hear me? Are you telling the truth about finding your father's knife behind the trailer?"

Angel kept thinking about that knife, *his* pocketknife, and she'd given him a chance to say it didn't mean anything, and he wouldn't say that, *couldn't* say it, because the truth was he'd been behind their trailer the night it burned. Somehow he'd dropped that knife in the snow, and though he wasn't willing to tell her what he'd been up to, he'd left enough room for her to believe that the rumors were true. He'd come to do her and her mother and her brother and her sisters harm.

"I showed him the knife." Angel looked up at Brandi and tried to keep her voice level. "He didn't deny anything. He was there that night."

"That doesn't mean he did anything."

"Then why was he there? Mr. Rowe saw him. He was there right before the trailer caught on fire."

Later, Brandi would wonder who she'd been trying to protect—the girls? Ronnie? Herself? She'd scold herself for not being more sympathetic. She'd try to think back to that moment when she understood what was about to happen, and she'd try to determine whether even the smallest part of her could imagine that Ronnie had started that fire. What she knew for sure, even as she spoke to Angel, was that this family that she and Ronnie were trying to keep together would never be the same. Maybe, she'd think, it had been her and the dream she'd always had of having a man to love her and a family to take care of that she'd been trying to save above anything or anyone else.

"This will change us," she said to Angel. "No matter what turns out to be the truth."

When Angel didn't answer, when she just hung her head and kicked her heels against the bed frame, Brandi left her there. She walked out of the bedroom and went to the computer to look up the phone number of the bar in Brick Chapel, where she thought Ronnie might be. She'd driven around Goldengate and Phillipsport before it had hit her—Brick Chapel—and she'd hurried home to make this call, but Missy was there and she said she needed to tell her something.

Now Brandi had no idea how long it would be before everything got sorted out, and she didn't know what would happen to her and Ronnie and the girls because of it. She laid her hand on her stomach as she settled down into the chair at the library table, and for the first time she felt her baby kick. Once, twice. Enough to thrill her for just an instant. Her first thought was, *I can't wait to tell Ronnie.* Then she remembered what else she would have to tell him, and the wave of sorrow that swept over her was greater than any she'd ever felt. Already, just because Angel had said what she had, he seemed different to her. Even though it might not be true—it *couldn't*, could it?—just the thought and the fact that they'd have to talk about it was enough to make everything seem strange. Brandi knew that the story would continue to spread. People were already talking, and that notion would always be there even if it got proved a lie.

And if it turned out to be true? She couldn't bring herself to think about that. She found the number of the Kozy Kiln and she picked up the phone.

Ronnie drove out of Brick Chapel, not knowing what was waiting for him at home. He was worried. He'd told Brandi he was sorry for not picking up Sarah and Emma from school, and she'd said that fumble had better be the least of his sins. He wondered what she knew.

He picked up Route 50 to Goldengate, and though he'd had a few beers—how many exactly, he couldn't have said—he pushed the Firebird up to seventy-five and hurried on through the dark.

Soon he crossed the river, and there on the flat bottom land, the lights of Phillipsport twinkled in the distance ahead of him.

Just outside the city limits, where the highway curved past the Wabash Sand and Gravel yard before straightening out for the last clear shot into town, he let his foot off the gas and brought the Firebird back to the speed limit. He eased into the curve, and when he came out of it and glanced up to his rearview mirror, he was surprised to see red lights flashing behind him. As much as he wanted to keep going—to be home with Brandi—he knew he had no choice but to pull off the road into the parking lot of WPLP to see why someone wanted to talk to him.

It was Biggs. He got out of his sheriff's car and made his way to the Firebird. Ronnie didn't give him the chance to get in the first word.

"Was I speeding?"

"I couldn't say."

"Why'd you stop me, then?"

"Taillight's out." Biggs had his hands on the door frame, leaning in through the open window. "Where you been, Ronnie?"

"Brick Chapel. Seeing after that job you cost me."

"Now how did I do that?"

"All that nonsense this afternoon."

Biggs leaned in closer. "Get that taillight seen to," he said, and Ronnie told him he would.

He pulled the Firebird back onto the highway and followed it, just under the speed limit, on into Phillipsport and then the eight miles to Goldengate where Brandi's house was full of light. To Ronnie, at the end of this winter day when so much had gone wrong, it was tempting to believe that something festive was waiting for him inside those brightly lit rooms.

The first thing he noticed when he came through the front door was that Brandi had on her coat, and that gave him a strange feeling. To see her standing there with her coat on as if any second she might walk out the door, which, stunned as he was, he didn't bother to close. He'd taken the old storm door down a while back, meaning to replace it with a new one, but he hadn't gotten around to it yet, so there was nothing to block the cold air rushing into the house.

"Brandi?" he said.

She had her arms crossed, resting on her stomach. The girls were nowhere to be seen, and to Ronnie's dismay there was no sign of them living in that house. No toys or dolls scattered on the floor as usual. None of their snow boots or gloves or coats tossed willy-nilly. Someone had picked up everything and put it away. The house was quiet. No television. No video games. No music. No squealing laughter. Just Ronnie and Brandi facing each other across the tidy living room. Just the two of them, the way it'd been before the fire.

Then, with a suddenness that startled him, she said, "Did you burn up that trailer? Is that why you went out driving that night?"

Ronnie felt all the air leave him. Here he was in that place he'd never wanted to be, that place where he had to start answering questions, and he knew it was because Angel had found his pocketknife and had apparently started to tell the story.

"Oh," he said. That was all. Like he'd been punched in the stomach and couldn't get his breath. "Oh," he said again. "I wish Angel hadn't told you about that."

He'd never seen a look on Brandi's face like the one that came to it now, not even on the night Pat Wade came to tell them about the fire. It was like something gave way inside her, and he could see the fear in her quivering chin, and the disbelief in her slack jaw and the distress in her watery eyes. It hit him with a force that almost brought him to his knees, because for a moment he had the eerie sensation that he was looking at Della's face, the way it surely was countless times after he left her heartbroken and fearful of what the future might hold, or, worse yet, the way she looked the night of the fire at the moment she lost hope and knew she wasn't going to get everyone out of the trailer.

Such a thought froze him, and even though he knew he should say something more, should explain it all—he could only stand there, dumb and looking guilty as sin.

Brandi was shaking her head. She was pointing to the door. "Get out."

"But, baby—"

"I mean it. Now."

"But my girls." He looked around the room again, eager for some sign of them, something that would tell him all of this was a bad dream and any second he'd wake from it and find his family welcoming him home. "What's happened to my girls?"

Brandi was on him now, her hands balled into fists, beating against his face, his arms, his chest. He could smell her perfume,

Love's Musky Jasmine—he'd given it to her for Christmas. She wouldn't stop hitting him, and, finally, stumbling backward to the front door, he thought to take out his pocketknife. If he could show her that knife, maybe he could start to explain.

He wasn't aware that he'd opened the blade. Just a matter of habit, but Brandi had no way of knowing what he intended. She was screaming now. She made one more rush at him and he let her come. She shoved him backward through the open door and he stumbled over the threshold strip and fell. Just before the door closed, he saw Angel in the hallway, her arms folded over her chest. He called out to her. He got to his feet and pounded on the door. He pounded and pounded. "Brandi," he said. "Brandi, let me in." But there was no answer, and then, one by one, the lights went off inside the house.

22

While all of this was happening, Shooter and Captain were going over their story of what had taken place the night of the fire. They'd had an argument over Della and her goats, and Captain had gone off to his bedroom in a snit. Shooter turned on a John Wayne movie and fell asleep. When he woke, the movie was over, and the house was very still. He got up and went to check the front door lock. He looked out the window and saw Ronnie's Firebird. He stood there long enough to see Ronnie come out from behind the trailer, get into his car, and drive toward town. This much he'd told Pat and Missy—he'd even told them that Ronnie was toting something—but Shooter hadn't told them everything.

He hadn't told them how he'd gone down the hallway to Captain's bedroom that night.

The door was open, but Captain was nowhere to be seen. Shooter could see that his bed was still made. He went into the kitchen and grabbed his coat off the peg hook by the door. Then he opened the door and stepped out into the cold night.

"What did you do first?" Shooter asked Captain now. "I mean, when you first went outside that night."

Captain was sitting at the kitchen table looking at a *Hot Rod* magazine. He turned the pages slowly, studying the pictures of cars: a 1933 Ford Coupe, a 1955 Buick Roadmaster, a 1966 Ford Mustang, a 1981 Chevrolet Malibu. He had on plaid flannel pajamas—green and black—and his hair smelled fresh from his shower. It was getting too long, the blond bangs hanging down over his eyes, and Shooter, who was pacing back and forth alongside the table, knew he'd have to remember to take him into Goldengate soon for a haircut.

"What night?" Captain wanted to know.

"The night of the fire. Now listen to me. What did you do first?"

"I went to see the goats." Captain turned another page. "Della's goats. They got out that afternoon."

"That's right. They got out, and we herded them back in and we patched the fence, right?"

"And you were mad."

Shooter stopped pacing. He said, "I wasn't mad. What was I mad about?"

"The goats," Captain said. "Della. You were mad."

Shooter reached over and closed the magazine. Outside, the wind had come up, and the arborvitae shrubs at the corner of the house were scraping the siding and making a noise that put him on edge.

"What did you do after you saw the goats were all right?"

"I don't remember."

Captain was looking down at the cover of the magazine. *Hot Rod Drag Week—2010,* the cover said across a picture of a white Chevelle, smoke coming off its rear tires. Shooter reached down and cupped Captain's chin. He lifted his face, made him look him in the eyes.

"The sheriff might ask you questions." They'd heard the news about the fire marshal's report on WPLP at supper, and ever since, Shooter had been thinking about everything that might happen. He was thinking that it might be time for him to have a talk with Biggs. "You're going to have to know what you're going to tell him," he said to Captain.

Shooter had meant to tell the fire marshal's deputy when he'd been by earlier to question him that he'd seen Ronnie come from behind the trailer the night of the fire. Then Shooter started thinking about Biggs asking questions, as he surely would, and how sooner or later he'd want to talk to Captain, and Shooter had put off going to the authorities a day at a time because he couldn't bear the thought of Captain being in the spotlight. Hadn't there been enough wrong-headed stories and out-and-out lies about him? Sure, Shooter had heard them, rumors boys spread about Captain having done this and that. Malicious gossip about deviant sexual practices, devil worship, anything the boys could make up to give themselves a thrill. Any right-thinking person would know those stories to be lies as soon as they heard them, but there were the idiotic and the cruel who wanted them to be true so they could feel justified in what they'd always thought but perhaps had been hesitant to say: that Wesley Rowe— that Captain—needed to be put somewhere for those of his kind, somewhere he couldn't hurt anyone. Shooter had sworn he'd protect him, but now that the fire marshal had ruled the fire suspicious, he knew he couldn't wait much longer. He'd have to start talking, and so would Captain. Shooter didn't want him to appear to be dumb when he made his answers. It was important that he offer up the facts with honesty and clarity so no one would be able to doubt him.

Shooter squeezed Captain's jaw, and Captain said, "I went to Della's to check on the goats."

"And that's when you saw Ronnie."

Captain nodded. "He was behind the trailer."

"That's right." Shooter let go of Captain's jaw. "He was behind the trailer, and what was he doing?"

"He was—I think—" Captain stumbled along. "He was behind the trailer, and—"

"What did he have with him?" Captain squinted as if maybe that would help him see the answer. He chewed on his lip. "A can of gas," Shooter finally said.

Captain's face relaxed. His eyes opened wide. "He had a can of gas."

"Yes."

"Behind the trailer."

"Good."

"He had a can of gas behind the trailer."

"And did he see you?"

"No, he didn't see me."

"Right as rain." Shooter ran his hand through Captain's bangs. He petted his head. This boy. His boy. "You tell the sheriff that."

23

The news about Brandi turning Ronnie out of her house broke when Anna Spillman admitted that he'd spent the night with her. "It wasn't like what you might think," she said. "He just showed up, said Brandi locked the door on him, and he needed a place to sleep. Didn't say anything more than that, and I never in the world would have thought—well, I mean, I just wouldn't have thought it of him, would you?"

By this time, late afternoon the next day, the word was out. Missy Wade had called Sheriff Biggs that morning, who in turn had called Laverne Ott at Children and Family Services to express concern for the safety of Ronnie Black's daughters, and Laverne, when she heard the story that Missy had told Biggs, knew she'd have to look into the matter.

It was just before noon when Laverne walked into the Wabash Savings and Loan and said to Brandi, who was about to take her lunch break, "There's something we need to discuss."

Brandi was putting on her coat. "I've got an hour for lunch."

"Why don't we just get that lunch together?" She handed Brandi a business card with her cell phone number on it. "So you can get in touch with me whenever you need to," she said.

It was the waitress at the Mi Casita, Maxine New, who let it slip that Brandi and Laverne Ott had been talking in hushed tones and that Brandi seemed upset. Meanwhile, in Goldengate, Willie

Wheeler was at the Real McCoy Café telling Pastor Quick that there seemed like there'd been trouble at Brandi's last night. He'd heard Ronnie pounding on the front door and begging to be let in. Bit by bit, the word made its way around Phillipsport and Goldengate: something was out of kilter with Ronnie and Brandi, and now Laverne Ott from Children and Family Services was involved. It wasn't long after the noon hour when Pastor Quick, who was pumping gas at Casey's convenience store, looked across the pump and saw Missy Wade on the other side, filling up her van.

"Missy," he said. "I'm worried about what's going on with Brandi Tate and Ronnie Black. Seems she threw him out last night. What's that mean for his girls?"

"So she threw him out." Missy took the nozzle out of her tank and returned it to the pump. "Good."

"They say Laverne Ott is involved. Do you know anything about it?"

"I called the sheriff." Missy screwed her gas cap back in place. She opened the door of her van and got in. Before she closed the door, she said, "I had to. I've got to take care of those girls."

All of this was happening while Brandi and Laverne talked at a back table in Mi Casita.

"We really ought to be talking about this in my office," Laverne said. "Or at your home. Somewhere more private."

"I don't mind." Brandi stirred a little sugar into her tea. They were in the corner along the back wall where the restrooms were, and no one else was sitting at the tables around them. "It's not an easy thing to talk about no matter where we are."

Laverne knew that was true. She'd seen it time and time again: a woman coming to her, ashamed, afraid to say what she suspected might be the ugly truth about a husband or a boyfriend—something not on the up and up, but the woman not wanting to believe it.

As soon as that woman said what she feared—said it to Miss Ott—she knew it became something to be investigated; she knew her life was about to change. For that reason alone it took more than one woman a while to work up the nerve. She had too much to lose—the man himself, maybe, and the way she'd always thought of him. The money from his paycheck, sometimes even the house where they'd all lived. Some women tried to talk themselves out of it, tried to convince themselves that the facts didn't add up and the allegations were just that: talk.

Laverne had to coax the story out of so many of the women, but that wasn't the case with Brandi. She looked Laverne straight in the eye. She said, "What Missy told you is true. I was just waiting for my lunch break to tell you myself. I'm starting to believe that Ronnie burned up that trailer. I confronted him last night, and he didn't deny it."

"He said he did it?"

Brandi swirled her straw around in her tea. "He was out there that night. Shooter Rowe saw him, and Angel found Ronnie's knife behind the trailer. At first, I didn't want to believe it, but now I know too much. He was there and he was behind the trailer and then it burned."

"You heard the fire marshal has said it was arson?" Laverne could tell how hard this was for Brandi. "You know there's been talk about Ronnie?"

"He pulled a knife on me. The knife Angel found and then gave back to him." It was at this point that Brandi got shy. She bowed her head and moved her silverware about, lining up the knife and fork just so. She put her hand on her stomach. "I'm having Ronnie's baby. I've been taking care of his girls. I thought I had everything right where I wanted it."

Maxine New arrived with their lunches. She set the steaming plates on the table.

Brandi was dabbing at her eyes with her napkin. "I swear," she said. "I thought we were going to have a wonderful life."

Now Laverne had questions of her own. Chief among them: where was Ronnie?

Brandi didn't know. She'd locked him out of the house the night before and hadn't heard from him since.

At that exact moment he was pounding on Missy's door. She looked out the window and saw the Firebird. She took a deep breath and thought about just standing there and doing nothing. Maybe he'd get tired of pounding and head on back up the blacktop.

"Missy," he said. "I know you're in there."

He'd awakened at Anna Spillman's house, and she'd told him he could stay there as long as he wanted. Then she'd gone off to work. Late in the morning, it came to him that if he were headed toward trouble—and the question Brandi had asked him about whether he set the trailer on fire, on top of the suspicion that Biggs held, indicated that he might very well be doing just that—he'd need a lawyer, and to hire one would take money.

Missy pulled the door back a crack so she could see Ronnie, but she wouldn't open the storm door.

"You told me you wouldn't let my girls go without." He tried the storm door, but it was locked. "You said any time they needed something, just to ask. I want a thousand dollars."

"Better get out of here, Ronnie. I've already talked to the sheriff."

"Damn it. I need that money. I know you've got it in the account, and I want it so I can do right by my girls."

That was too much for her, his claim that he was looking after the girls. "So you can make a run for it?" she said. "I don't think so. I know that Angel found your knife behind the trailer. I know what you did, and all I can say is God save you, Ronnie. God take mercy on your soul."

Missy closed the door, and Ronnie felt a tremendous rage filling him. How dare she turn down his request for money and then sit in judgment of him? He tromped on back down the driveway and got into his Firebird. His hands were trembling. He backed out of Missy's drive, dropped the Firebird into first gear, stomped the accelerator, and tore up the blacktop to town.

But he didn't stop in Goldengate. He slowed enough to get him through there without calling attention to himself, and then he went on to Phillipsport.

Brandi was with a customer at the counter when he stomped into the Wabash Savings and Loan.

DeMova Dugger was finally getting around to taking down the last of the twinkle lights they'd put around the window for Christmas, and when she saw him, she said, "Hey, Ronnie. Brandi's with a customer right now." The customer, Henry Greathouse, was renewing a certificate of deposit. He was a bachelor farmer, tall and gaunt in his bib overalls, his barn coat riding up in the back due to his stooped shoulders. "Haven't seen you in a while," DeMova said. Her big glasses had slipped down and were resting on her cheekbones. She had that cheery grin on her face like she always did and a new frosted hairdo that she was happy with, so she was in a good mood when she went ahead and said to Ronnie, "How's life treating you?"

She had no idea what that would do to him, but what it did was toss him even further into his rage because, of course, life wasn't treating him well at all and hadn't been for some time.

He stopped for just an instant and gave DeMova what she would later call "a look to kill." Then he went on toward the counter, where he crowded in next to Henry Greathouse and said to Brandi, "How in the world can you think I'd ever do a thing like that?"

"Ronnie, I'm working," Brandi said. She tried to keep her voice even. "I'm helping Mr. Greathouse."

Henry Greathouse took a step to the side and studied Ronnie the way he must have a hundred or more bulls in his life when he was trying to herd them and could tell they were getting chancy.

To Ronnie's credit, he calmed down enough to apologize to Henry. "I'm sorry, Mr. Greathouse. I'm not looking to cause a scene here."

"You need to take it easy, son." Henry's voice was steady. "That's what you need to do."

Ronnie was tired of people trying to tell him what to do—Brandi telling him not to press charges against Wayne after he clocked him with that tire iron, Missy telling him what could and couldn't be done with the money for the girls, and now Henry Greathouse, a man he didn't much know, telling him to take it easy.

"Damn it, Brandi." Ronnie slapped the counter with his open hands. "You believe all this talk?"

"I'm working, Ronnie." This time Brandi's voice had an edge to it. "We can't talk about this now."

"Did you tell all this to Laverne Ott?" Ronnie's voice was rising as if he and Brandi were the only ones in the Savings and Loan. "Did you tell her you thought maybe I—"

"I talked to her." Brandi cut him off before he could finish his sentence. "I told her you were at the trailer that night, and I told her you pulled that knife on me."

"My knife? I was just trying to show it to you. I was just trying to explain."

"I can't have you being like that around the girls. What else did you expect me to do but to talk to Laverne? Especially if it's true that you did what it looks like you did." Tears welled up in her eyes and her voice shook a little. "Good God, Ronnie."

"You're not going to cost me my girls." Ronnie swept his arm across the counter, scattering the documents Henry Greathouse had been resting there. "I mean it, Brandi. I won't let that happen."

DeMova Dugger said later that she was afraid he might come after her as he was on his way out. He had that kind of look on his face. He was mad, mad, mad.

Said Henry Greathouse, "That boy was out of his head."

Brandi asked DeMova if she could please finish up Mr. Greathouse's business, and then she slipped back into the break room, found the card Laverne Ott had given her at lunch, and called her cell phone to let her know what had just gone on.

"I've never seen him so mad." Brandi was still trembling. "I'm afraid he might go after the girls."

"Don't let him get Sarah and Emma after school," Laverne told her. "Can you get off early? I'll be waiting for you at the grade school. I'll call for the sheriff if need be. Don't worry, Brandi. I won't let him harm those girls."

As soon as Brandi got permission from Mr. Samms to leave work early, she called Missy.

"It's Brandi," she said. "Please don't hang up. I know I treated you bad last night, but now I'm in trouble."

For a long time, Missy didn't say anything, and Brandi was afraid to go on—afraid even that Missy had already hung up the phone.

Brandi couldn't know that Missy was standing in her house looking out the front window, distracted by the sight of Shooter Rowe in the field across the road. He was leading one of Della's goats by a rope around its neck. He was leading the goat toward the woods at the back edge of the field, and Missy couldn't keep from wondering why he felt compelled to do such a thing, and why he had a shotgun cradled through the loop he made with his free hand stuck into his coat pocket.

Finally, she found her voice. "He was here this afternoon. Ronnie. He wanted money."

Brandi wondered whether he might be thinking about running, maybe taking the girls and hitting the road, or worse—and she could barely bring herself to believe this—maybe he was about to do something more horrible than that. Maybe the girls were in danger. If he'd set that trailer on fire, then who knew what else he might do, especially now when he was so mad.

"I've talked to Laverne Ott," Brandi said. "We're worried about what Ronnie might try to do. I'm leaving work early to meet Laverne at the grade school in Goldengate. We want to make sure Ronnie doesn't try to get Emma and Sarah. Do you think he wanted money so he could run off?"

It was at this moment in the conversation when Missy saw Shooter stop a moment at the far end of the field. He got down on one knee, resting the shotgun barrel across his leg so it wouldn't droop to the snow-covered ground. With his hand, he scratched the goat's head, leaned in close and rubbed his face against his neck.

"That's what it seemed like to me," Missy said.

Shooter got back to his feet, tugged on the rope, and continued leading the goat across the snowy field.

Mr. Samms came out from his office and began sorting through some papers on DeMova Dugger's desk. He was a tall man with narrow shoulders and a long, slender neck. From time to time, he raised his head and gave Brandi a disapproving look.

"Missy, I can't be there for the girls every day after school." It hurt her to have to say this, tore her up to know what she was about to ask. "I know we've never been friends, but I don't know what else to do."

Shooter slipped into the woods with the goat. Missy watched them though the bare trees. They climbed a hill and then went down the other side and disappeared from her view. Crows called from somewhere across the field. She heard the anguish in Brandi's voice, and though she knew she'd always hold her to account for Ronnie walking out on Della, Missy couldn't help but feel a little sorry for the mess that Brandi was in the middle of now.

"I've talked it over with Lois and Wayne," Missy said. "They know I can give the girls a good home, a good life. That's what Lois and Wayne want. Brandi, Pat and I are godparents to the girls. In the eyes of the State of Illinois, that makes us relatives. That makes us someone who could get custody."

For a good while, Brandi didn't say anything. Then in a quiet voice—she could barely bring herself to form the words—she said, "I expect that would be best, at least for now."

Missy heard a noise from the woods, a percussive blast she felt in her chest. Crows lifted up from the trees. She put the phone down and pressed her hands to the window glass.

"Thank you," Brandi said. She had no way of knowing that Missy was no longer listening. She was staring out the window, waiting for Shooter to come out of those woods. "Can you come to the school?" Brandi asked. "Can you meet Laverne and me there?"

Brandi waited for a response, and when none came—and when Mr. Samms gave her one more stern look—she did the only thing she could. She put the handset back in its cradle and glanced at the clock. Two-thirty. She needed to leave for Goldengate and whatever might be waiting for her there.

At a quarter till three, she pulled her Mustang to the curb in front of the grade school. Ronnie's Firebird was already there, parked across the street. The driver's door was open and a Prairie Farms milk truck rumbling by had to move to the left to safely pass. She didn't know where Ronnie might be, but she didn't like the sight of that car door open out into the street. When he'd gotten out of the Firebird, he'd still been mad. He hadn't even stopped to shut the door. She feared that he might already be inside the school, waiting to grab up Emma and Sarah. Maybe he'd make his way to the house and tell Hannah to come with them—maybe he'd force Angel to do the same—and then he'd take off, even if he didn't have much money. A crazy stunt like that. Brandi had no idea what he might try to do, but none of the thoughts that came to her were good ones. She remembered the knife he'd pulled when she'd thrown him out of the house last night, and a shiver went up her neck.

She got out of her Mustang and looked up and down the street. No sign of Ronnie. No sign of Laverne. The wind had picked up, and it hit Brandi in the face as she turned to the north. The chain-link fence around the school playground shook and rattled. The snap hooks clanged against the flagpole with a banging that set her heart to pounding. Such an insistent sound, one that told her to move.

First, she slung her purse strap over her shoulder and crossed the street to Ronnie's Firebird. She'd seen the way the driver of that Prairie Farms truck, a little man with clip-on sunglasses flipped up now that the light had weakened, had shaken his bald head in disgust as he'd swerved to the left to avoid that open door. Brandi couldn't bear to look at it, knowing it was a sign to anyone who saw it that the life she'd thought she was making with Ronnie was coming apart. She wanted it shut.

She started to close the door, and then she saw something inside the Firebird that caught her attention. Poking out from underneath the passenger seat was one of Ronnie's T-shirts, his favorite T-shirt, one he'd found in the Goodwill in Phillipsport. A black shirt with the Sun Records logo on the chest, that yellow disc of music notes and inside the circle at the top the word SUN in big black letters, shaded with yellow and an arc of what Brandi supposed was to be sun rays, though she could turn them into piano keys if she took a notion. A crowing rooster stood atop a yellow bar beneath that arc. The bar said RECORD COMPANY, and below that, in yellow letters, were the words, THE LEGENDARY SUN STUDIO and its address on Union Avenue in Memphis, Tennessee.

Ronnie was thrilled to death to find that shirt in the Goodwill. He rattled off all the big stars that had started at Sun—Johnny Cash, Jerry Lee Lewis, Carl Perkins, Elvis. "What a deal," he said to Brandi. "Cool." That shirt was such a treasure to him, it struck Brandi funny now to see it wadded up and stuck under the car seat. She leaned in and pulled it out, meaning to fold it neatly—just force of habit, she guessed—and that's when she noticed something that puzzled her.

The shirt, along the bottom, had been ripped. Not just a little tear. It was clear from the jagged cloth that someone—Ronnie, she assumed—had torn a strip all the way around the bottom of the shirt. A strip needed for a purpose, and though she didn't know what that purpose might have been, she knew Ronnie would have had to have been in dire need of that cloth to ruin his favorite shirt.

She held it up in front of her to get a closer look at its now jagged edge, and that's when she caught the scent of gasoline. She pressed the shirt to her face and breathed in through her nose. Just the faintest smell of gas.

She'd run out of gas on her way to work the morning of the fire, and Ronnie had carried some to her in a can. Could he have sloshed some on his shirt? She didn't know. Toward bedtime that night he went out for a drive—just a little jaunt to help him work out the heebie-jeebies. Just needed to unwind a little, he said. At the time, she'd believed him. Driving did that for him, especially when he could get the Firebird out on a straight stretch of country road like the blacktop and let it go. That was all right with her. She was cozy in bed where it was warm. She was reading her baby books.

When he came back—she wasn't sure how much time had passed; she'd been so caught up in what she was reading—he called to her from the hallway and then went into the bathroom and took a shower. He was naked except for his boxers, and he slipped into bed beside her. In the midst of all the upset after the fire, she'd had no reason to notice that Ronnie had stopped wearing that Sun shirt, and she'd never stopped to think that it wasn't showing up in the weekly laundry. She hadn't given it a thought until now. Nor had she given much thought to the fact that Ronnie said he made a call to Della the night of the fire, a call that wasn't answered.

"Brandi." She heard her name and, without turning around, she knew it was Laverne calling to her. "Brandi, have you seen Ronnie?"

She shoved the Sun T-shirt into her purse, snapped it closed, and spun around to see Laverne coming down the sidewalk in front of the school. Her long wool coat was unbuttoned, billowing out behind her in the strong wind.

Brandi held her own coat closed and hurried across the street as best she could to meet her.

"His car was there when I pulled up." Brandi was talking fast. "His car door was open. A truck almost hit it. I went over to close it. Now what are we going to do?"

Just then, bells in the school started ringing, signaling the end of the day. Laverne glanced over her shoulder at the front door. Soon there would be students streaming out, book bags drooping from their shoulders, the coats the teachers and aides had zipped already undone, the mittens tugged on now stuffed into pockets.

"We're going in there to get Sarah and Emma," she said. "Come on."

At that moment, out in the country, Missy was still watching out her window, praying that any moment now she'd see Shooter come out of those woods, and it would be even better if he had that goat with him. She knew that what she'd heard had been a shotgun going off, and she waited and waited and waited. At one point, she realized that she'd put down the phone while Brandi had still been talking to her. How long ago had that been? She glanced at the anniversary clock on the fireplace mantle. Ten minutes till three. Missy picked up the phone, and even though she knew it was ridiculous—she'd been talking to Brandi nearly twenty minutes ago—she said, "Hello?" She said it in a timid voice, and it startled her to hear it in her quiet house. "Hello?" she said again, but there was no one on the other end of the line to hear her.

Brandi and Laverne stepped into the main hallway of the school, and there at the other end, crouched down to tie Emma's shoe, was Ronnie. He was taking his time, making neat bows with the laces. Sarah was behind him, frantically searching through her book bag.

When he finished with Emma's shoes, he put his arms around her and pressed her to him.

Brandi called out, not giving a thought to the children now filling the hallway and the teachers coming out of classrooms to see their students off.

"Ronnie," she said.

He stood up and looked at her. Then he took Emma's hand with his right and Sarah's with his left, and they came down the hall to where Brandi and Laverne were standing.

"Hello, Brandi," he said. "Hello, Miss Ott."

"Ronnie, what are you doing?" Brandi asked.

He seemed perplexed by the question. "Doing?" He cocked his head to the side and squinted his eyes at her. "I'm picking up the girls. The way I do every day. You know that."

Emma was tugging on Ronnie's hand. "Let's go, Daddy. Let's go."

With her free hand, Sarah was searching her coat pockets—still looking, Brandi supposed, for whatever she'd misplaced.

Ronnie let go of Sarah's hand. He put his arm around her and gave her a hug. "We'll find it later, sweetheart," he said. "Don't worry."

The hall was emptying out, the children's voices growing faint as they ran out into the cold day. Soon it was just Ronnie and the girls and Brandi and Laverne in the hallway, and when Laverne spoke, she did so in a hushed tone as if she were soft-talking a skittish horse so he wouldn't bolt.

"Ronnie—" she said.

"I know why you're here."

"I'm going to have to talk to you, ask you some questions. You know that, too, don't you?"

He nodded.

A clock in the hallway clacked as the second hand marked off another minute. The classroom door nearest them creaked on its hinges, and Sarah's teacher, Cynda Stout—Tommy's mother—came out into the hall carrying a plastic cup full of watercolor brushes. Brandi saw the way she hesitated, surprised to find her and Laverne there with Ronnie and the girls. Then she said, "Oh, Sarah. Good. You're still here." She reached into the front pocket of her purple smock and pulled out a pink pompom hair scrunchie. "You left this on the art table. I bet you've been looking for it."

Sarah took the scrunchie, a sheepish smile on her face.

"Better put it on your hair, baby," Ronnie said. She let him have the scrunchie and he bent over and gathered her fine hair into his hand and then deftly spread the scrunchie with his fingers and crisscrossed it around Sarah's hair so when he was done it held her ponytail. "There you go," he said. "That looks good, baby."

Brandi wasn't sure what she should feel watching Ronnie. He was so tender with Sarah. He stroked her ponytail, fluffing out the fuzzy scrunchie. How could this be the same man who had been so angry with her, the man who had pulled that knife, the man everyone thought set a house trailer on fire with his wife and children inside, asleep? Brandi caught herself feeling sorry for him—this man she thought she loved—but then she drew herself up short, steeled herself for what was to come. Like Laverne said, he had questions to answer.

She stepped up to him now. Laverne Ott. Brandi imagined she must have done this countless times, not only in her job with Children and Family Services, but in all the years she'd taught school. Again and again, she must have done what she was doing now with Ronnie, talking to him in that soft voice that was still firm, making it plain that hers was the voice that mattered here.

"Ronnie, I want you to let Emma and Sarah go with Brandi. She'll take them home. Then you and I will find a room here where we can be alone, and we'll have the talk we need to have. Cynda here will help us find that room, I believe. Do you understand?"

He nodded his head. Then he looked right at Brandi, and she felt her heart go the way it had that first time in Fat Daddy's when she'd danced with him. He had that look of being lost, of wanting someone to hold onto him.

"Brandi, do you really think—"

He couldn't go on. He swallowed hard and squeezed his eyes shut.

Laverne nodded to her, and Brandi took Emma and Sarah by their hands.

"What's wrong with Daddy?" Emma asked.

Ronnie opened his eyes and forced a smile. "Nothing, doodlebug," he said. "Not a thing in the world. You go on with Brandi now. I'll see you later."

Brandi said, "I bet we can find you some cookies. And Hannah and Angel will be home soon. How about that?"

"I'll save a cookie for you, Daddy," Emma said.

Brandi had wanted a family so badly. She'd wanted it with Ronnie. She was carrying his baby, and she didn't have any idea what was going to happen.

Missy knew exactly what she was going to do. She couldn't stand there at the window a second longer, waiting for some sign of Shooter. She'd heard that shot and she had to know what it meant. Pat, she knew, would tell her to mind her own business, but he wasn't there. She was all alone. She was going to put on her boots and coat. She was going to step out into the cold. She was going to walk across that field into those woods and see what there was to find.

24

Crunch of snow underfoot. Tangles of corn stubble poking through. The ridges uneven beneath her feet. Missy tried her best to stay between the rows where the ground was more level. Her breath made little clouds in the cold air. It was some hundred yards across the field, and by the time she got to the end where the woods began she could feel the cold in her toes, and her cheeks and nose stung from the wind lashing her face.

She took her first steps into the woods, where the land began to roll, and she stopped to rest before trudging to the crest of the hill.

At first she thought she was hearing the wind as it rose and fell and then rose again with an eerie noise of breath and complaint. Then she came to understand that what she heard coming from somewhere deeper in the woods was a noise from a living thing—a grunting, snuffling sound that froze her and made her strain to listen more closely, trying to determine if what she heard came from a person or an animal.

She was afraid to find out, but she knew she couldn't just walk away. She moved on, feeling the strain in her calves and hamstrings as she climbed the hill.

Once Brandi had gone, and it was just Laverne Ott and Ronnie in the hallway of the school, Cynda Stout went to fetch the principal and then excused herself to slip into the bathroom to clean up those watercolor brushes.

The principal, Mrs. Piper, was a woman Laverne knew from the days when she'd taught Ronnie and Della and Missy and so many others at Victory School out in the country. A two-room schoolhouse, before all the country schools consolidated and the kids rode the bus into Goldengate.

Irene Piper had taught in those country schools too, before becoming the principal at Goldengate. She was a woman from Laverne's generation—a tall, white-haired woman in a navy blue suit and an ivory blouse with a ruffled bodice.

"Laverne," she said, "is there something I can do for you?"

"I need a room," Laverne said. "Somewhere I can have a private conversation."

Irene nodded. "You can use my office." She smiled. "By this time of day, I'm sick of it anyway."

"I shouldn't be long. Then maybe you and I can have a chat?"

"Take your time. I'm not going anywhere. It's the fourth-grade class play tonight. I'll be eating a sandwich for supper."

"My daughter is in that play." Ronnie's voice was hoarse with emotion. Laverne could imagine the day he'd had. "Sarah Black. She's the bridge. I'd forgotten the play was tonight."

Irene touched him lightly on his arm. "She's a good girl, your Sarah."

"Forgetful," he said. "Good thing her head's attached."

"Well," said Irene. "Most kids her age are a little scatterbrained." She nodded down the hallway to the open door of her office. "Go on," she said to Laverne. "Have your talk. I'll be down in the cafeteria. Just come look for me when you're done."

"She's been working on her part," Ronnie said, his voice growing louder now. "Sarah. I've heard her around the house."

"I'm sure she'll do fine," Irene said. She glanced at Laverne and lifted her eyebrows in concern.

"Yes," said Laverne, putting her hand on Ronnie's shoulder as if to nudge him down the hallway. "Sarah will make us all proud."

"I love her," Ronnie said, and his lip was trembling now. "I love all my girls. I wouldn't do a thing to hurt them. Really, Miss Ott, I swear."

From the crest of the hill, Missy looked down to the bottom of the slope. A gully cut through the floor of the woods, and there at the lip of that gully, where the land gave out and fell away, Shooter Rowe was on his knees. His back was to Missy, and she could see his shoulders convulsing with his sobs.

The goat—it was the old billy goat, Methuselah—was on the ground a few feet from Shooter, looking as if it had lain down for a sleep, but Missy could see the blood on his chest and blood on the snow, and she knew he was dead.

Shooter's back straightened, and he got to his feet. That's when Missy saw that he still held the shotgun. He had the butt end resting on the ground, and he used it for a crutch as he pushed himself up. Then, with a cry that came from somewhere deep in his chest, a cry barely human, he threw the shotgun down into the gully.

The wind had suddenly died down, and the crows were back, coming to perch on the bare limbs of the trees. Their calls split the air.

Shooter turned to the goat, and though Missy knew she'd happened upon something so private she should have turned away and left Shooter Rowe to finish what he'd come into the woods to do, she couldn't. She called out his name. She let him know she was there, watching.

Laverne and Ronnie sat in the chairs in front of Irene Piper's desk, the chairs students took when teachers sent them to the principal's office, or parents who came to have a chat about their children. Laverne purposely chose not to sit behind the desk with Ronnie across from her because she didn't want that space between them. She wanted to put him at ease so she could talk to him about the night of the fire and whether he'd meant to threaten Brandi with that knife. She meant to ask him what dark thoughts might be in his heart, and she wanted him to feel comfortable enough to tell her the truth.

"Ronnie, I've known you a good long while. Ever since you were a boy in my class."

"Yes, ma'am. That's right."

He'd always been a polite boy. Always a little bit smaller than the other boys, a little slower with his lessons, just a few ticks behind his whole life. Maybe that's why he always seemed to be barreling ahead—whether running on the playground, or later driving fast in his Firebird, or walking out on Della for a life with Brandi Tate—like he knew he had to catch up, so intent on getting somewhere that he failed to see that he was about to crash into something.

Now there was this business about the fire and what he might have done, and what more he might be capable of doing. "I understand there's a matter of this knife," she said. "Your pocketknife."

Ronnie sat, bent over with his elbows on his legs and his hands, fingers and thumbs pressed together as if in prayer, pointing down to the floor. It seemed so long ago to Laverne that he was her student and also a member of her Sunday School class, and she taught him how to do "Here's the church, here's the steeple" with his fingers. So long, and not so long at the same time. She could tell he was afraid, the way he'd been all those years ago when she'd had to give him a talking to about something or the other. She could see that little boy inside his man's body, but now she had to ask him these questions.

"I never meant any harm to Brandi." He lifted his face to look at Laverne Ott, his mouth twisted into a grimace, his eyes narrowed. "I know Angel told you about finding my knife out at the trailer. I know Brandi's talked to you, too."

On the wall behind Ronnie was a poster of a quote from Dr. Seuss. Laverne remembered that it came from *Horton Hears a Who*. White letters on a pale blue background: "A person's a person, no matter how small." She had to keep asking Ronnie questions. She had to determine whether he was a threat to his children, whether there was cause to remove them from his care.

"Ronnie, I'm going to ask you straight out. Were you at the trailer the night it burned?"

He answered right away, his voice a whisper. "I'm not denying that."

"Why were you out there?"

Her tone changed then to the severe voice she'd always used with students when she wanted to make sure they understood that they needed to tell the truth.

"Miss Ott, don't you know me well enough?"

She wouldn't answer because it was her job to get the facts straight. Her opinion of what kind of man someone was didn't matter. One thing she'd learned over the years was that all sorts of people, no matter how upright they seemed, were capable of all sorts of things.

"You walked out on Della and took up with Brandi." Laverne couldn't stop herself from saying it even though she knew she shouldn't. "I never thought you'd do that either."

"Are you saying you think I started that fire?"

She shook her head. "I'm saying I can't rule anything out. I'm sorry." She meant it as she always did when she investigated a case: sorry that circumstances were such that they required her attention, sorry for what people's lives could come to. "I have to look at everything, Ronnie." She paused a moment and then asked him again. "Did you put that trailer on fire?"

He wouldn't answer. He just kept rocking back and forth in his chair. "You just have to trust me," he finally said.

"Ronnie, I want you to understand something." Laverne was patient. She explained to him that it was her job to make sure the girls were safe. She let the silence settle around them. Then she said, "If the court thinks your girls are in danger, I'll have to take them out of your and Brandi's house and put them in foster care."

"I don't want my girls in foster care. I know what that's like, and you should know too. If you want my girls safe, you won't do that to them."

Laverne knew that he'd moved in and out of foster homes after his mother died and his father wouldn't keep him. She also knew that, hard as Children and Family Services tried, they couldn't always ensure that each foster home was ideal.

"I'll do my best by your girls," she said. "And you should know I'll get to the truth. I was your teacher, Ronnie."

"Yes, ma'am."

"You can't hide from the truth. No matter what you choose to say or not say." Laverne waited for her words to sink in. She hoped that Ronnie would say something, anything that might save him, but when enough time had passed to make it clear he wasn't going to let her know anything else, she said, "The truth always finds us. I taught you that in Sunday School." She stood up from her chair, eager to find Irene Piper to tell her she was finished with her office, anxious to get to Brandi's house to talk to the girls. But first she had a last word for Ronnie. "I'm disappointed that you don't seem to remember what you learned from me."

Then she left him to think about that.

———

Shooter lifted his head, looking up the long slope to where Missy stood, feeling her heart in her chest. She didn't know what to say, didn't know how to explain why she'd come looking for him. It was something about everything she felt, the miscarriages, the trailer fire. All the sadness, all somehow contained in the sight of Shooter leading that goat across the field and into the woods.

"I saw you," she finally said, meaning of course that she'd seen him from the house.

"That goat was sick." He shouted up to her. He waved his arms about, his open barn coat flapping at his sides. "Foot and mouth disease. There's no cure, you know, and it spreads fast. What choice did I have? I had to put him down."

"I know it was a hard thing." Missy was struggling to find the words that would say all she felt. "I know how Captain loves those goats."

Shooter nodded. He wiped his sleeve across his face. "I don't know how I'm going to tell him." He bent over and put his hands on his knees. Then he straightened and said to her, "Methuselah was his favorite. It's going to break his heart."

"Did you come out here so Captain wouldn't see?"

"Sometimes when something's sick like that, all you can do is put it down."

He went to the goat and before Missy knew he was going to do it, he stooped and pushed against the goat's stomach, shoving it toward the lip of the gulley.

She couldn't watch anymore. She'd already turned to start back toward home when she heard the snapping of branches, the thump of the body, dead weight falling.

Laverne hoped that Ronnie wouldn't follow her to Brandi's house. She'd call for the sheriff if he tried to make trouble. Not that she thought he would. He'd been devastated when he'd left the school. He'd been pulling away from the curb in his Firebird when she came out from saying goodbye and thank you to Irene Piper. Not in his usual rambunctious way, foot heavy on the accelerator, but slow and easy. She watched his brake lights come on at the stop sign where Cedar intersected with Main, and she held her breath as he sat there and sat there though there was no traffic coming, before finally making a left-hand turn. It was like he was thinking about what his next move should be, and that was enough to worry her.

Brandi was alone with the girls when Laverne got to her house. It was dark now, nearly five o'clock, and Brandi was getting supper on the table.

"Sarah's school play," she said, when she let Laverne in the door. "With so much going on, I forgot all about it."

Laverne thought for a moment how it could have been an ordinary evening, and this, an ordinary family—Brandi dishing up food so the kids could eat, Ronnie about to walk in any minute, saying he was sorry he was late, couldn't be helped. Then everyone eating as quickly as they could so they could get to the school because Sarah was the voice of the bridge in *The Three Billy Goats Gruff.*

"Ronnie said he never meant to hurt you with that knife," Laverne said to Brandi. The girls were in the kitchen helping with supper, and Laverne and Brandi were standing just inside the front door. Laverne kept her voice down so the girls wouldn't hear. "Do you think he meant to come at you with it?"

Brandi had on a red bib apron, and her stomach swelled beneath it. "Come in here with me." Brandi's eyes were wide open, urgent. She took Laverne by her elbow. "I've got something to show you."

Laverne followed Brandi back to her and Ronnie's bedroom. A stack of baby books teetered on the bedside table, clumps of used Kleenex scattered over it. A pair of house shoes with the faces of sock monkeys on them peeked out from under the bed. A yellow bathrobe with red hearts on it had fallen onto the floor. The bed hadn't been made that morning. The top sheet and a purple blanket were twisted into a wad. The flowered comforter spilled over the end. It was the bed of a woman who'd had a night of trouble.

Brandi's purse was on the dresser. She opened it and took out a black T-shirt. "Look at this," she said to Laverne. She showed her where a strip of the shirt had been torn away. "Smell it." Brandi held the shirt up to Laverne's face. "Go on. What's it smell like?"

"I'm not sure," Laverne said.

"Take another sniff." Brandi offered the shirt again. "Gasoline?"

"I'd say so. Yes. Is this Ronnie's?"

Brandi nodded. "I found it in his car right before you got to the school. What do you think it means?"

So they'd come to this: everything meant something. Laverne knew that was the point where living stopped seeming natural and everything became a struggle. That's where Brandi and Ronnie were now—that place where each little thing was suspect.

"I don't know what it means," Laverne said, and it was true. She didn't. "But I think Sheriff Biggs should know about it."

Brandi put her hands on her swollen stomach. "Here I am less than five months away from my delivery." She put her hand to her mouth and choked down a sob. "This was supposed to be such a happy time for Ronnie and me."

"Don't give up on happiness yet." Laverne patted Brandi's arm. "This story isn't over."

"But I talked to Missy. She wants the girls. I told her I thought that would be best. I can't be home to take care of them. She can."

Laverne knew that Missy's heart was good. She loved those girls and wanted to do right by them, and now the threat that Ronnie seemed to present had given her the chance to step in.

Brandi shook her head. "And now that Wayne's in poor health, there's no chance that Lois can take on more." She chuckled. "And she and Wayne sure as heck aren't in my fan club. They think the world of Missy. They're happy for her to have the girls." Brandi dabbed at her eyes with the heels of her palms. "I just hope I'm doing the right thing."

"How can it ever be wrong when someone tries to get at the truth?"

"I don't know. I just feel everything coming apart."

"We'll get it right," Laverne said. "Trust me."

When she got back from Shooter's woods and stepped into her house, Missy picked up the phone meaning to call Brandi at home, but just then the phone rang, startling her.

It was Pat. He said, "I've been thinking about Ronnie's girls." He went silent for a few seconds, and Missy waited, wondering whether he'd give her his approval. She'd made it clear last night that it didn't matter. She'd go ahead with or without his support. "I want you to know," he said, "that I'm with you. I love those girls. We'll make a good home for them. I've been trying to call you to let you know."

She felt the tears coming. This was what it had been like the times she'd been pregnant, the two of them excited about having a baby.

Laverne Ott had already made plain what would have to happen to put the girls in her and Pat's custody. First, Laverne would have to determine that it was unsafe for them to stay with Ronnie. Then, once Lois and Wayne confirmed that they couldn't care for the girls, Missy and Pat would have to pass medical checks, and the State and the FBI would have to run criminal background checks on them. Then, within forty-eight hours, a sheltered care hearing in the local court would determine custody. The good news was that the State of

Illinois recognized godparents as relatives, and Children's Protective Services always wanted to try for placement with family if at all possible. Missy and Pat, now that Wayne's health made it difficult for Lois to take the girls, were a more preferable option than licensed foster care parents, according to Laverne.

Missy knew that if she and Pat got the girls, they'd come with all the hurt they carried after the fire. She knew everything wouldn't be smooth sailing at first, but she'd win them over with love. She'd give them all the love she'd saved up for the babies she'd lost.

"I was out in the woods," she said to Pat.

"What in the heck were you doing out there?"

She told him about Shooter and the goat and how she heard the shot and had to go see what had happened. "I stood and watched for as long as I could stand it."

"Why did he put that goat down?"

"He said it had foot and mouth."

For a good while, Pat didn't say a word. Then, finally, he said in a very quiet voice, as if he were afraid of what he was saying, "Missy, there hasn't been any foot and mouth in this country for nearly eighty years."

25

Inside Shooter's house, as dark settled around the open countryside, he was explaining to Captain, as gently as he could, why he'd had to put down Methuselah.

"That goat was sick," he said. "We'll be lucky if he hasn't made the others sick too."

Captain had his pocketknife open, that Case Hammerhead, the one he'd said he'd lost. Now he was using the point of the blade to dig at the soles of his Big Horn Wolverine boots. Size elevens, just like the ones that Ronnie wore. Captain had come in from feeding the other goats, and he was sitting at the kitchen table, head down, as if he weren't listening to Shooter at all. He just kept digging at those boots, gouging out pieces of the rubber soles until finally Shooter noticed the blood stains on the blade.

He was drying a pot with a dishtowel now, and he dropped the pot into the sink. The clanking sound caused Captain to jerk up his head. Shooter was standing over him with his hand out, palm up, and he was saying, "I thought you lost that knife." Captain didn't answer. He just kept digging at his boot soles. "Give it to me." Shooter's voice was harsher now. "Wesley, I mean it. I won't stand for you lying to me."

Captain closed the blade and started to stuff the knife back into his jeans pocket, but Shooter wasn't about to let him off easy. He grabbed his arm and narrowed his eyes at Captain. "I'm not playing," he said. "I want that knife."

Finally, Captain let him have it.

Shooter snapped it closed and slipped the knife into his own pocket.

"That goat was sick," he said. "We didn't have any choice but to put him down. Right?"

After a time, Captain nodded. Shooter put his hand on his back, rubbing a slow circle.

"That's right," Shooter said. "That's one thing we know for sure."

Ronnie, at that very moment, was on the river. He'd parked his Firebird at the fishing camp, three miles out of Phillipsport, where one of his foster fathers had kept an old Airstream trailer. Ronnie had gotten out of the Firebird and walked a hundred yards or so down to the water.

The river was iced over, frozen thick enough for him to walk out onto it, all the way to the center—the deepest part—where for a moment, he tipped back his head and looked up at the sky. The stars were out and a crescent moon, just enough light to let him see the snow-dusted ice. Wind moved through the bare limbs of the syca-mores and red oaks and hackberry trees that lined each bank. The smaller branches clicked together.

He liked being out there in the cold night, gazing up at the sky, imagining a heaven where Della knew the truth of what he'd done. Maybe in that heaven she'd even forgive him.

At any rate, she'd be the only one—at least it was so in Ronnie's mind—who'd bear witness to what he was about to do, and she'd be the only one he'd feel inclined to tell why he had to do it.

"I'm sorry," he whispered to the sky. He got down on his knees. "I'm so sorry."

Then he took his pocketknife, the one Angel had found in the snow behind the trailer, and he opened the blade.

26

All through Sarah's class play, Brandi couldn't stop thinking about that moment in the kitchen when Laverne said it was time to talk to Sheriff Biggs. It was then that Brandi felt the two storylines begin to merge—her story with Ronnie and the girls, and the story of what had happened the night of the fire.

The youngest Billy Goat Gruff, a boy wearing a white sweat suit on which his mother had dyed brown spots, was trying to cross the wooden footbridge set up on the stage. The boy wore whiskers that were supposed to look like a billy goat's beard and a set of droopy ears. A brown tail hung down from the seat of his sweatpants.

Sarah's voice rang out, "Trip, trap, trip, trap."

Hearing Sarah, her voice so full of confidence, made Brandi remember all the evenings at the house when she'd helped her practice her part. She thought of how the girls had been shy around her at first and how Emma had finally asked her to read her a story and then Sarah had stood by her one evening when she was on the computer, nestling in close, inviting a hug. Hannah had made her the friendship bracelet she still wore, and there had been times when even Angel had asked if she could put her hand on her stomach and see if the baby would kick.

Laverne was standing along the wall. Brandi could see her profile in the shadows cast by the stage lights. She'd left her house less than two hours ago with a promise to talk to Sheriff Biggs.

Missy and Pat were sitting a few rows in front of Brandi, to her right, and Brandi could see the way Missy was positively beaming as she watched the play unfold.

"Who is that walking on my bridge?" the troll in the play said. He was a scrawny boy who stood all hunched over. Someone had put wrinkles on his face and warts on his nose.

"It's only me, Little Billy Goat Gruff."

Brandi knew the story, remembered it from when she was a girl and her mother read it to her from a Little Golden Book. It was a fable of greed and trickery, the troll persuaded to let the two smallest goats pass over the bridge in favor of making a meal of the largest goat who would soon come his way. But the largest of the three goats knocked the troll off the bridge, and there you had it. "Snip, snap, snout," it said in the book. "This tale's told out."

In Sarah's play, the narrator merely said this: "Big Billy Goat Gruff ran across the bridge. He ate the green, green grass and apples. That mean, ugly old troll never came back to the bridge. He learned that being mean never pays."

Brandi leaned forward and glanced down the row at Hannah, who was sitting with her hands folded neatly in her lap, and little Emma, who was bouncing up and down on the edge of her seat, and then Angel, who was clapping. Brandi wanted to find a way to keep them. That is, if they wanted to stay. She had no idea, though, what would happen to her and Ronnie. She had no idea where he was or what might happen when Sheriff Biggs found him.

After the play, Brandi sat through the curtain call, the actors executing their curtsys and bows. Then she and the girls went to gather up Sarah.

"Was I good?" Sarah grabbed on to Brandi's hand. "Did I do everything right?"

Brandi gave her a hug. She bent over and whispered in her ear. "You were the best."

Then it was out to the lobby for cookies and punch, and parents cooing over their children, and the kids hopping about and laughing their squealing laughs. And it was all the most wonderful music to Brandi.

Then Laverne found her. She said, "I talked to Sheriff Biggs. He's out looking for Ronnie right now."

For a moment, Brandi wondered if she'd done the right thing by showing Laverne that T-shirt. As much as she still didn't know what she felt about Ronnie, she could imagine him out there somewhere thinking the world was against him, and that tore at her as much as the disgust she felt, imagining that it might be true that he'd started that fire.

But what if it wasn't? Everything was mixed up in Brandi's heart. She wasn't sure what was right anymore, but something about the thought of the sheriff looking for Ronnie unsettled her. When she'd set out to win him, she'd never imagined anything like this.

"It cuts me," she said to Laverne. "All this about Ronnie and what might be true."

Laverne slipped her arm across Brandi's shoulders. "I know this isn't easy. Let's hope Sheriff Biggs can find him soon, before—" She hesitated, letting her voice trail off, and Brandi knew that what she'd been about to say until she realized it wasn't a thing for Sarah to hear was, *before he hurts someone.*

That was enough to make up her mind to do the right thing, to make sure the girls were safe.

"Laverne," she said, "can the girls go to Pat and Missy's tonight?"

"I think it would be best, don't you?"

Brandi nodded. She couldn't find any voice left to say, yes, yes she did.

So it went from there. Laverne gathered the girls and put them in her car. It killed Brandi that she wouldn't let them ride with her to the house, as if she might try to run away with them. Their welfare, Laverne said, was a concern of the State now, and she needed to make sure that this transfer to Missy's care went smoothly.

Missy and Pat followed in their van. They at least had the decency to sit out in the van with the engine running while Brandi packed a few things for the girls and Laverne supervised.

"Brandi," she said at one point, "I know this is hard for you, but for now it's the best thing. You'll see. You should know that if Sheriff Biggs arrests Ronnie, there'll most certainly be a sheltered care hearing, and that'll sort things out for good as far as who gets the girls."

Emma was tired and cranky. Sarah was still excited about the success of the play and kept tromping around the house saying, "Trip, trap. Trip, trap. Trip, trap."

Hannah was uncharacteristically sullen, moving about mechanically as she gathered her things.

Angel got packed quickly. She had her earbuds in, listening to the iPod Missy had given her.

Laverne asked Brandi if she had someplace to stay. They'd found themselves alone for a few moments in Angel and Hannah's bedroom. At least for the night, Laverne said. At least until the sheriff found Ronnie.

Brandi said she didn't think Ronnie would hurt her, and if she weren't home, how would he have a place to stay.

"He stayed somewhere last night," Laverne said as gently as she could. "Brandi, you need to look after yourself. You can stay with me if you don't have anywhere else to go."

Brandi shook her head. "I'll be all right. Thank you."

"He has that knife." Laverne raised her eyebrows, inviting Brandi to give that some thought. "You remember how he threatened you with it last night?"

"Did you see how he helped Sarah with her hair at the school this afternoon?" Brandi was recalling it all in her mind—how gentle he'd been, how lost he'd seemed. "He looked like he was all alone in the world."

"What about that T-shirt you showed me? What about him being at the trailer the night it burned?" Laverne took Brandi's hand and squeezed it. "What about the knife Angel found? All of that will speak volumes in a courtroom."

In the van, the heater spread hot air across Missy's feet and legs. She watched out the window, keeping an eye on the comings and goings inside Brandi's house, feeling her heart spark and leap each time she saw one of the girls pass by the windows. Soon she'd have them all tucked in at her house and things would be the way they were in those days after the fire when she'd kept them. Only this time their sorrow would have diminished some. That's what happened as the days passed. The grief lessened, got covered over with the business of lives moving forward. Missy knew as much from the babies she'd lost. Time kept moving, and though the grief never really disappeared, it could be covered over with what the world still had to offer, and that's what she hoped would happen with her and the girls.

Pat tapped his fingers on the steering wheel. The van smelled of his aftershave, which he'd applied too liberally while getting ready for the school play. It was the Black Suede from Avon that Missy had given him for Christmas. She loved the scents of leather and deep woods. Sitting there in the van with the heater running, she felt cocooned and protected. She looked over at Pat, and she lifted a hand and rubbed the back of it tenderly over his cheek. He took her hand and kissed it.

Finally, the girls came out of the house—first Angel and then Sarah and then Hannah helping little Emma along. They were bundled up in coats and hats and boots, and they carried their duffle bags. Laverne Ott followed them.

Missy got out of the van and opened the sliding side door so they could all pile in. Sarah was still saying, "Trip, trap," and Missy could hear the buzz of music leaking out of the earbuds of Angel's iPod. Emma was sleepy, and Hannah was quiet, a stunned look on her face.

"It's going to be okay," Missy said to her, and gave her a hug.

In the midst of getting the girls into the van and settled, Pat checked to make sure everyone was in, and as he turned he barely registered the fact that a few yards up Locust to the east a pair of headlights went out. Someone coming in for the night.

"Everyone buckled in?" Missy called out with great cheer. "All right then. Let's go home."

Brandi stood at the window and watched the van pull away. She watched until it was gone. Then she drew her curtains closed. She turned to face the rooms of her house. Already they felt so empty. The silence settled around her.

Laverne got into her car and breathed a sigh of relief. She started the engine and was glad to be finally heading toward her own house at the end of a very long day.

Neither she nor anyone else took note of the fact that the headlights that Pat had seen go out belonged to Ronnie's Firebird. Not even Mr. Wheeler, who kept tabs on everything that happened in the neighborhood, would be able to say later that he saw the Firebird parked maybe fifty yards up Locust in the shadows between two streetlights.

No one was there to bear witness to the fact that shortly after Pat and Missy left with the girls and Brandi closed her curtains and Laverne made her way to her own home, the Firebird's headlights came back on and the car eased away from the curb. It crept along, as if the driver already knew exactly where he was going, and, therefore, found no need to hurry.

27

Pat was a few miles up the blacktop, still nearly five miles from home, when he saw a set of headlights on high beams coming closer behind him. Soon they filled the van with their glare.

"Jeez, someone's trying to blind me," he said, and then he slowed down so the car would have to pass.

But it didn't. It stayed right on his bumper, the lights so bright Missy had to shade her eyes with her hand.

"Some idiot," she said. "A real bozo. Doesn't he know how dangerous this is?"

Pat couldn't pull off onto the shoulder because the little strip of pavement and grass before the road slanted off into a deep ditch was covered with a bank of snow from where the plow on the salt truck had pushed it. He put his window down and stuck his arm out to wave the car around him.

The cold air rushed into the van, and Missy shivered. Still the car stayed where it was.

Finally, Hannah's quiet voice came from the back. "It's Dad," she said, merely stating that fact.

Pat put up the window and tightened his hands on the steering wheel. "Hang on," he said. He tapped his brakes, and Ronnie's Firebird braked hard and fell back a tad. Pat looked into the rearview mirror. "Maybe that'll do the trick."

But soon the headlights were close again and this time Missy could hear the roar of the Firebird's engine.

"Here he comes," Pat said, and he eased off the accelerator, letting the van coast along at forty miles per hour, hoping Ronnie would press on and soon he'd be around them and his taillights would be growing dimmer in the distance.

The Firebird, though, swung out into the left lane, and after all that brightness the van seemed so dark to Missy. She could look across Pat and see the Firebird pull even with the van.

Then Ronnie started to edge the Firebird across the center line. Pat steered as far to his right as he could, but the Firebird edged closer until its front fender scraped up against the van, and Missy felt it rock a little.

"Dear God," she said.

And it was as if Ronnie had somehow heard her prayer. He slowed the Firebird. He steered it back to the left of center.

Pat saw his chance, and he pressed down on the van's accelerator. He shot ahead, his headlight beams stretching out down the blacktop.

The Firebird fell back, and soon its headlights disappeared. It was dark again inside the van, and though Missy was trembling, she steeled herself and she told the girls everything was all right. That they were almost home, and everything was fine.

Ronnie watched the van pull away from him. He slowed to forty and then thirty-five, and finally he was creeping along at twenty miles per hour, watching the taillights of Pat's van crest a hill. Ronnie kept his eyes on those taillights until the van went down the slope of the hill, and then he couldn't see them anymore. His girls were in that van, and he understood now the danger he'd put them in when he'd bumped it.

He hadn't meant to do it. At least he didn't think he had. He'd only wanted the van to stop. He'd wanted to gather his girls into the Firebird and take them someplace where no one would ever be able to find them, and little by little all the bad things swirling around them would stop, and they'd be a family, happy forever. He feared he'd ruined any chance at that, but still he had to try.

At the next crossroads, he slowed and turned the Firebird around. He started back up the blacktop toward Goldengate. It was time to start facing facts, time to tell his own story, time to say exactly what was what.

28

Ronnie didn't bother to knock. He just opened the door and walked in. Brandi was sitting on the couch, facing the front door, every light in the house turned on as if she were waiting for him.

She didn't even move when she saw him. "Where have you been?"

Her voice was all flattened out, not soft and sweet the way it was the night she came into the bedroom and told him Pat Wade was there and he'd better come out to hear what he had to say. Ronnie remembered the way her fingers trembled when she buttoned his shirt for him and how later, once Pat had told him about the fire—once Ronnie understood that Della and Emily and Gracie and the baby were gone and he knew he needed to get to the ones who were left—Brandi said she'd be there waiting for him. She'd made it plain she wasn't going anywhere. Her heart was tied up with his. Then, now, forever.

"I've been driving," he said

He couldn't bring himself to tell her that he'd gone to the river, walked out on the ice, got down on his knees, and looked up at the stars and the crescent moon. He couldn't tell her about opening the blade of his knife and thinking long and hard about what he might do with it before giving up on that idea. Most of all, he couldn't tell her what he'd just done out there on the blacktop. He couldn't say that he'd been so angry about Missy and Pat taking his girls, he'd been a crazy man. He'd tried to chase them down. He'd bumped their van, and if they'd been driving any faster, or if Pat hadn't been on the lookout—well, Ronnie didn't like to think about what might have happened. He couldn't get the picture out of his head, the one he'd manufactured, of that van leaving the blacktop and going airborne, turning over and over, his daughters—the people who mattered most to him in this world—at the mercy of another one of his hotheaded decisions.

His life was out of control, but all he could offer Brandi was this: "That night," he said. "The night the trailer burned." He got down on his knees in front of her, and he gathered her up, his arms easing in between her back and the couch. He lay his head on her swollen stomach. He listened for the baby moving about. Then he said the rest. "I didn't go out for a drive because I was antsy. I knew I was going out there to the trailer."

He closed his eyes and held onto her. He needed to know what she'd say next, but he was afraid to hear it.

"Ronnie," she finally said in a shaky voice. "Did you—"

He wouldn't let her say the words. He'd save her from that. "Please," he said before she had to finish her question. "Baby, please don't think that of me."

She let the minutes stretch on, willing to do that, wishing that she and Ronnie could stay where they were for a good long while. Just the two of them in the brightly lit house, his head on her stomach, her hand stroking his hair again. She'd feared when Laverne had gone and Missy and Pat had driven away with the girls that she'd turned a corner into a dark room and she'd never be able to see her way out of it. Then Ronnie came back. Here he was, holding onto her, and she'd asked the question she'd had to ask. Had he set that trailer on fire? He'd asked her to please not think that of him, and she was trying. She was doing her best to believe he was innocent. She let that belief build from the way his hands fit into the small of her back and cradled her, the way he lay against her now, his eyes closed as if there on his knees he was giving himself to her. Broken down as he was, he was still hers. She'd loved him long and hard and she couldn't bear the thought of losing him and then being alone when their baby came.

"That knife," she finally said, though really she didn't want to say anything at all. She just wanted the closeness of him with no need for words. She wanted this story that they were in the midst of to stop and for there to only be the story of their love. But there were still questions that needed answers, and she forced herself forward. "Your pocketknife. When I was pushing you out the door last night, you looked like you wanted to hurt me with it."

"No, baby. Not for a minute." He opened his eyes and raised his head. "Oh, baby. I'd never hurt you like that."

It was then that Brandi told him that Laverne Ott had gone to Sheriff Biggs and the sheriff was looking for him. She scooted to the edge of the couch and tried to get to her feet. He got up from his knees, and he took her hands and helped her.

"Wait here," she said.

He did as she asked. He watched her go down the hall and turn left into their bedroom. He heard a dresser drawer open, the drawer that screeched on its runners every time he opened it. The bottom drawer, which was his.

As soon as she came back into the hallway, he knew what she had: his Sun Records T-shirt. He didn't know how she'd found it in his car, but she had, and now he knew she'd have another question and it wouldn't be one he'd want to answer.

"How'd your shirt get ripped?" She held it up and showed him where the cloth had been stripped away. "Ronnie, it smells like gas. Why? Did you spill some on you when you poured it into my car that morning?"

"I can't get that smell out of my nose."

"So you did? You spilled some?" When he didn't answer, she remembered again that he'd called Della that night and she hadn't answered. Brandi said, "Ronnie, why did you go out to the trailer that night if you thought no one was there?"

He waited, barely able to look her in the eyes. "You're not going to want to hear everything there is to say."

"Maybe not." She took a deep breath and let it out. "But it's too late for secrets now. Tell me."

So first there was the telling, and then before Brandi could decide what she believed and what she didn't, she heard footsteps on the porch and a sharp knock on the front door.

Ronnie squeezed her hand—he'd held it the whole time he told his story—and she had to tug hard to get free from it.

She opened the door, and there was Biggs and two deputies. Biggs didn't say a word, didn't acknowledge her at all. He just stepped into her house and said to Ronnie, "I've got enough evidence to arrest you, and we're going to search this property."

Ronnie said, "Then do it."

"Ma'am," the tall deputy said to Brandi. He had a long neck, and there was static electricity in his thin hair, making it stand on end. "We've come with a warrant."

The shorter deputy handed it to her. He was red in the face from the cold. He moved his feet about on the front porch.

"What's this mean?" she said.

"Means we're here to search the premises," said the tall deputy. "We're here to remove any items that might serve as evidence in the matter of the arson at Della Black's trailer on the night of January tenth."

She looked at them, still not quite understanding.

"Ma'am," said the shorter deputy, "you really don't have any choice."

She understood that. She stepped aside and let them in.

29

By noon the next day word was running around town. Ronnie Black was in custody. Maybe all that gossip? That gossip about him having something to do with that trailer fire? Well, maybe it wasn't gossip at all. Maybe it was gospel.

"You wouldn't think it'd be possible," Roe Carl kept saying to folks who came through her checkout line at Read's IGA. "But, lordy, these are strange times."

Certain facts had come to light, and now folks were passing them around tables at the Real McCoy. Anna Spillman listened in as she served lunch platters and refilled coffee cups and iced tea glasses. The investigators from the State Fire Marshal's Office had found footprints in the muddy ground where the fire had melted the snow cover and thawed the frozen earth. A man's footprints. The ridged tread of work boots. Those prints were frozen into the ground now, just under the fresh snow. You could drive out the blacktop and see them if you took a notion. They'd be there until the thaw came in the spring. The investigators had made plaster casts of those prints, and Sheriff Biggs had them in his office now. That was as true as true could be.

It was also true that Della's furnace had been acting up, but her daddy had it running fine the day of the fire. Wayne Best had told the investigators as much, and sure enough, when they gave it a look-see, they could tell it hadn't malfunctioned that night. Nor had the Franklin stove, which Wayne said Della was using, been to blame.

But one fact stood out as a cruel irony. Overlooked at first by investigators, a cardboard box containing wood ash, surely from the Franklin stove, finally got noticed behind the trailer.

When the fire erupted, the points of ignition had been along the back of the trailer, far from the front corner where the stove was—multiple points of ignition near the back door off the kitchen.

Ronnie had filled up a five-gallon gas can at Casey's the morning of the fire. Taylor Jack reminded everyone about that. He'd been the one to take Ronnie's money. "You running something?" Taylor asked, and Ronnie said that Brandi had run out of gas on her way to work, and he was carrying some to her. That all made sense, Taylor said later, but how come Ronnie came back the night of the fire to buy five gallons more?

The diner went quiet when Taylor Jack told that part of the story, and even Anna Spillman, who'd always felt sorry for Ronnie and even let him stay with her, had to admit that the unthinkable was possible: Ronnie Black might have burned that trailer, not caring a snap who was inside.

Laverne Ott and the State of Illinois were moving forward. Missy and Pat passed their medical exams and their criminal background checks. Lois and Wayne confirmed that they weren't in a position to care for the girls and that their wish was that Missy and Pat be granted custody.

On the day of the sheltered care hearing, the judge considered the evidence: a father under investigation for the arson that had killed his wife and three of their children, the story of how that father had tried to run a van off the road knowing that his daughters were inside.

Laverne was there to answer questions concerning her inquiry, and as much as it pained her to say so, she recommended that the girls be allowed to stay in the custody of Pat and Missy Wade.

"I can personally vouch for their character," she said. "I've known them since they were children in my class."

The judge said, "Everything considered then, I'm awarding custody of these girls to Mr. and Mrs. Wade."

And like that it was done.

When Missy and Pat got home after the sheltered care hearing, they heard a chainsaw running out in Shooter Rowe's woods.

"I wonder what he's up to now?" Pat said.

"I don't know, but I don't like that noise." Missy felt the cold air on her neck. She wrapped her arms around her chest and shivered. "It gets on my last nerve. Come on. Let's get in the house."

Pat changed his clothes and got ready to drive out to the job site, a new house out on Highway 50, a few miles west of Goldengate near the Crest Haven cemetery. The framing crew was finishing today and he needed to get out there and see how things were going.

"I might be late this evening," he told Missy. "Can you handle getting the girls?"

"Angel's coming on the bus," she said. "I'll gather up Hannah and Sarah and Emma."

"All right." Pat zipped up his Carhartt coveralls. "Call me if you need anything."

He leaned in and kissed her on the cheek, and she clung to him a little longer than she usually would, putting her arms around him and pressing her face into his chest. She loved the solid feel of him, and she understood that through all their trouble—through all the miscarriages and the numbing sense of loss—she'd depended on him to be there for her no matter how many times she'd disappointed him.

"We're doing the right thing, aren't we?" she asked.

He kissed the top of her head. "It's what you've wanted, isn't it?"

She pulled back from him and looked up into his eyes. They were hard-set as if he were squinting into a bright sun. "Haven't you always wanted a family?" she said. "You love those girls."

"I do love them. There's no doubt about that. I just hope we're not leaving ourselves open to trouble. You saw how crazy Ronnie was when he tried to run us off the road."

She nodded. "It'll be all right." She took Pat's hand and squeezed it. "I know it will."

"I hope so," he said.

He was thinking of the night of the fire and how he'd run up the road to find Della trying to save everyone from the flames. He'd done what he could. He'd wanted to do more. Then the trailer caved in and he knew there was nothing that he or anyone else could do for Della or the kids who were still inside. All that he and Shooter and Captain and the girls who had made it out could do was watch that trailer burn, backing away from the heat, lifting their heads at the first sound of the sirens coming from Goldengate.

Later, once Biggs had started to sort things out, Pat volunteered to drive into town to tell Ronnie what had happened. And like that, their long strange journey began.

Now it was getting close to an end. Pat could sense that. Questions were going to be answered, and his life and Missy's and the lives of those sweet girls, who deserved none of this upset, were going to move on.

"I'll be back when I can," he told Missy.

She grinned and gave a little shrug of her shoulders as if to say of course he would. Everything was going to be fine. It was going to be easy-breezy. "I'll be here," she said.

———

At the courthouse, Biggs had Ronnie in an interrogation room. Biggs sat at a foldout table. He allowed Ronnie to wander over to the window, where he stood looking out at State Street. A fine snow, half rain, was falling. Ronnie watched a man come out of the J.C. Penney store, a blue scarf wrapped around his face.

"You better start talking," Biggs said.

For a good while, Ronnie didn't speak. He just stayed there at that window, his head bowed. Then he turned to face Biggs. He lifted his head, drew his shoulders back.

"All right," he said. "Now listen." His voice started to quaver, then, and he had to bite his lip and look down at his feet to get control of himself. "I'm not what people say I am."

Biggs said, "No one's condemned you yet."

Ronnie let out a little puff of breath. He gave Biggs a weak grin. "If you ask me," he said, "that's exactly what this town's done."

It was Willie Wheeler who finally came into the Real McCoy that afternoon and told Anna Spillman in a voice loud enough for everyone in the restaurant to hear that he'd seen a deputy carrying what looked to be a man's T-shirt in a big ziplock plastic bag out of Brandi's house. Another deputy had a bag that held Ronnie's work boots. The deputies spent some time going through the storage shed in the backyard, and they carried out a five-gallon Marathon gas can, the kind with that logo of the nearly naked man running with his arm in the air and the red block letters that spelled out MARATHON.

Willie didn't know that at one point the taller deputy went back into Brandi's house and told her, "We found a gas can in your shed."

Brandi said, "It's the can Ronnie used the morning when I ran out of gas before I got to work. He carried five gallons to me in Phillipsport."

"Did he put it all in your car?"

She nodded. "Every drop."

For a while, the deputy didn't say anything. He took out a small pocket notebook and a pen, and he wrote something down. Then he said to Brandi, "That can in your shed? Ma'am, it still had about a gallon of gas in it."

Missy was making a shopping list—things she needed now that the girls were there—when she heard a racket outside. She got up from the kitchen table, went to the living room window, and peeked outside.

Shooter Rowe was sitting on his Bobcat tractor in her driveway, looking toward the house. He lifted his arm and pointed a finger at her.

What else could she do but go outside to see what he wanted.

He had a scoop shovel on the front of the Bobcat, and she could see the chain saw riding inside. The scoop was stained with fresh mud, speckled with dead leaves and sticks.

"You got those girls with you now." He shouted over the idling tractor engine. "I saw you all leave this morning."

She was in no mood for chitchat. "What is it you want?"

He sat on his tractor. "It's a good thing you're doing, taking those girls."

"You said that goat had hoof and mouth." The words were out before she could even think about where they would lead. "Pat said we haven't had hoof and mouth in this country for almost eighty years."

Shooter shut off the tractor and, after the noisy idling, the silence was unnerving. "That goat was sick." His voice was low and pointed. Missy knew he was telling her to pay attention, warning her that she was going somewhere she really didn't want to go. She felt certain that he'd been in the woods cutting trees and bulldozing them into the gully to cover the body of the goat. He'd been filling in that grave. "He was sick," Shooter said, "and I had to put him down."

"But Pat said—" She heard the weakness in her own voice, and she stopped to gather herself.

Then Shooter said this last thing: "You've got what you want, Missy. You've got those girls. You wouldn't want anything to get in the way of your happy-ever-after, would you?"

She didn't know what to say.

He held her eye a moment longer, and when she still didn't say anything, he said, "That's right. You keep to your business, and I'll keep to mine."

With that, he put the Bobcat into gear and backed out of the driveway. She watched him go, and then she took out her cell phone and called Pat.

"It's Shooter," she told him. "He's up to something." Then she related the story of what had just happened. "He threatened me, Pat."

"Threatened you? How?"

"He told me to keep to my business and let him keep to his. Pat, I've got this feeling. This very bad feeling."

"Do you want me to come home? I'll leave right now. I'll be there as soon as I can."

"No, I'm on my way into town. I've got to get some things for the girls. I'll stay and pick them up from school. They get out earlier than Angel. Maybe we'll all drive over to Phillipsport to the high school and pick her up so she doesn't have to ride the bus. I want to make sure everyone stays safe tonight."

"Try not to worry too much about Shooter. He's mostly full of bluff."

"Still," she said, "just to be on the safe side."

"All right, Missy. You know best. Call if you need me."

———

Missy moved through her day trying to convince herself that nothing was unusual. It was the first day of what was going to be her life for a good while to come, the life of a mother. She stopped at Read's IGA and ticked off the items on her list: breakfast cereal, orange juice, bread, milk, apples, bananas, canned soups, lunch meat, ham salad, ground beef, frozen pizzas, pasta, and tomato sauce. It was so cold outside the perishables would be fine in the very back of the van. It wouldn't take her long to gather up Hannah and Sarah and Emma and then drive over to Phillipsport for Angel. They'd all ride home together, a family, and she'd ask the girls to help her put the groceries away.

By the time she got to the checkout line, Missy's cart was heaped full.

"Got a load there," Roe Carl said.

"Cooking for five now," Missy said.

"I heard you got Ronnie Black's girls."

Missy nodded. "The sheltered care hearing was this morning."

"Good luck to you."

"Thank you," said Missy, feeling her breath catch.

She knew Roe didn't mean to give her any alarm, but something about that wish for good luck made Missy afraid of everything she'd soon know about the night of the fire. Here she was dreaming about the future, all the good parts of it, not stopping to think what it would do to the girls if they found out that indeed Ronnie had set fire to the trailer.

As Missy loaded her groceries into the back of the van and made ready to drive to the grade school, she thought back to the day that ended up being the last one of Della's life. She'd been making plans too, not knowing she was about to run out of time.

At the high school in Phillipsport, Angel slouched at her desk behind Tommy Stout's in algebra class and kept kicking her foot against his chair back. The teacher, Mrs. Ferenbacher, was writing equations on the board. She was about a million years old, and she kept a handkerchief balled up in her left hand, and sometimes she had a coughing spell and she spit phlegm into her hanky. When Tommy turned in his seat, Angel rolled her eyes, letting him know how bored she was, and he laughed a little, but not enough for Mrs. F. to hear. The chalk kept on squeaking, and Mrs. F. coughed a little, and Angel stuck her finger in her mouth like she was gagging, and that sent Tommy into a laughing fit he couldn't control. Mrs. F. turned on her heel and surveyed the class. "Tommy Stout," she said. "Would you mind telling us what's tickled your funny bone?"

In Goldengate, Hannah was dressing for P.E. class. They were square dancing with the boys today, so all she had to do was put on gym shoes and then hope that she didn't get stuck with someone like Kyle Dehner, who always put his hand too low on his partner's back, sneaking a feel of a hip. He'd been kept back twice and was almost old enough to drive a car. His brown hair hung over his eyes in bangs, and his breath smelled like bread and sour milk. All things considered, Hannah should have thought him disgusting but she couldn't quite manage it. He was her secret crush, though she couldn't figure out why she felt the way she did. She was afraid to dance with him. She didn't want to say something stupid. She didn't want him to feel her hip and find her too skinny for his taste. She didn't want to think of him making fun of her later with his friends.

At the grade school, Sarah was passing notes back and forth with Amy Cessna, whose desk was across the aisle from hers. Amy had played one of the Billy Goats Gruff in the class play, and she and Sarah were reviewing the highlights of the performance and giggling behind their hands when their teacher, Mrs. Stout, leaned over to search through a drawer in her desk. "Where is my stapler?" she asked. "Has anyone seen my stapler?" For some reason, Sarah and

Amy thought this was the funniest thing they'd ever heard, and they covered their mouths and snorted.

Down the hall, in the first-grade classroom, Emma was doing a reading lesson on the computer. She was learning the sound a short "a" made by reading a story about Zac the Rat. *Zac is a rat. Zac sat on a can. The ants ran to the jam.* The cartoon that went with the story was funny. She had on a purple sweater with fuzzy sleeves, and she liked the way the sweater felt when she folded her arms on the desk and put her chin on one of those sleeves. The fuzz tickled. It made her l-a-u-g-h.

Sarah and Emma weren't thinking much at all about what it meant that they'd had to pack their things and go back to Missy's. They understood that it had something to do with the fire and with their daddy, but they didn't know what that something was. Since the fire they'd gotten used to going where people told them to go. So they went to Missy's and they understood that for the time being they didn't live with their daddy and Brandi. They lived with Missy and Pat, who were kind to them, and the girls imagined, with the trusting natures that disaster had forced onto them, that everything would eventually work out. They knew it was their job to keep their attention on what they were responsible for: a class play, a friend named Amy, fuzzy sweater sleeves, Zac the Rat.

Hannah, though, was old enough to worry, and worry she did. She missed Brandi. She knew that her father might be in trouble. She wanted things to quiet down. She wanted all the talk to stop. The talk about her father and what he'd maybe done. She wanted to sit somewhere by herself for a very long time and not have to give any thought to what was happening and what might happen and what it all meant for her and her family. But the square dancing music was starting, and boys were choosing partners, and here came Kyle Dehner.

Angel thought she was right where she wanted to be: back with Missy, who bought her nice things and cooked her favorite foods and loved on her with hugs and kisses. She'd let Missy be her mother. She wouldn't argue with that at all. Given the choice between Brandi and Missy, she'd choose Missy anytime, which she had, and now everything was working out the way she'd always dreamed. Mrs. F. was waiting for an answer from Tommy Stout. Exactly *what* had tickled his funny bone? "You're in trouble now, buddy," Angel whispered to Tommy. "You should've kept your mouth shut."

The girls were quiet after school as Missy drove to Phillipsport, even Sarah and Emma who were usually such chatterboxes. Now, away from school, they somehow understood—though Missy had certainly never said as much to them—that they might not see their father for quite some time.

Finally, Hannah said to Sarah, "Where's your hair scrunchie? Did you lose it?"

Missy glanced up at the rearview mirror and saw Sarah pat her head and run her fingers through her hair. She finally shrugged her shoulders. "Yeppers," she said.

At the high school, Missy parked along the street right behind the bus that was waiting for the final bell and the students who would tromp up its steps and flop down onto its seats. What a lucky stroke, she thought, to find this place from which she could watch for Angel and honk the horn at her before she could get onto the bus. Missy took it as a sign that everything was going to work out just fine.

"We picking up Angel?" Emma asked, and Missy couldn't resist the lighthearted feeling that had suddenly filled her.

"Yeppers," she said, and Emma and Sarah began to giggle.

"She said, 'Yeppers,'" Emma said. "Didn't she?"

"Yeppers," said Sarah, and that started them giggling again.

Then Angel was coming down the school steps, her book bag slung over her shoulder, the wind blowing her hair across her face.

Missy honked the horn, and Angel saw her. The other girls were in the second row of seats, so the front was empty. Missy leaned over and opened the door, and Angel started to get in.

Then someone called her name. Missy turned around to look for who it was, and that's when she saw Brandi coming up the sidewalk.

"Angel," Brandi called. "Angel, wait."

Missy didn't know why Brandi had come or what it might mean, but she saw how worn down she was. How washed out her face looked with only the slightest tint of pale pink lipstick to adorn it, how burdened and overwhelmed she was, how unlike the sassy woman who had stolen Ronnie from Della. She hadn't taken time to fix her hair—it had tangles in it—and she was wearing sweatpants and a sweatshirt, an old quilted coat thrown on. It was her voice that caught Missy by surprise. So tender it was, so sad.

"Angel," Brandi said again, taking her by the arm, and though part of Missy resented the intimate tone—one earned from the days Brandi had tried to do the right thing by the girls after the fire—she also felt herself drawn to it, wishing that could be the way she'd speak to Angel all the rest of her days. "Sugar," Brandi said. "Oh, sugar," she said again. "There's something you need to know."

So there were stories. After weeks of speculation and gossip, people who claimed they knew things—the real, true things—were starting to talk.

Shooter Rowe came into the sheriff's office and told the deputy at the desk that he had something to say, and he was sure Sheriff Biggs would be very interested to hear it.

Captain was in shop class at the high school. He was staining a gun cabinet he'd built, but his mind was somewhere else. With each stroke of his brush he whispered the chain of words that had become a chant inside his head: *gas can, pocket, match.*

Brandi was still talking to Angel by Missy's van at the high school, talking in a whisper. "Sugar, you know the sheriff's got your daddy."

"Is he going to go to prison?" Angel's own voice was calm.

"Oh, sugar, he might."

Missy couldn't stop herself. "Maybe that's just where he needs to be," she said, and she could barely stand the look that Angel gave her, a hard, hurt look, as if suddenly she'd realized how serious everything was and how awful it was for Missy to have said what she did.

Biggs had questions for Ronnie.

"Ask 'em," Ronnie said. He'd waived his right to have an attorney present. He folded his hands on top of the table. Biggs sat across from him, and the questions began.

Why had he bought all that gas at Casey's? Brandi's boss, Mr. Samms, had verified that Ronnie brought five gallons to put in Brandi's car the morning of the fire, but what about the five gallons more that he bought that night? Why did the T-shirt he was wearing then now smell like gasoline? Why had a strip of that shirt been cut away? Why were there footprints behind that trailer that matched the size and tread of his boots?

All Ronnie said was, "Everyone in town's been talking about me. What I might have done. Guess there's no reason for me to say anything. Folks have already made up their minds."

The door opened, and a deputy, his bushy brows arched with urgency, stuck his head inside. "You need to come out here," he said to Biggs.

"It better be important," Biggs said.

"Shooter Rowe's wanting to talk to you. Says he knows exactly what happened the night of the fire."

Biggs nodded his head toward Ronnie. "See what you can get out of him."

The deputy stepped into the room. Biggs went down the hall to see what Shooter Rowe had to say.

Brandi rubbed her thumb over the back of Angel's hand, making that one gentle motion to let her know that things could turn out just fine. "I know you've gone through a lot," Brandi said. "More than any girl your age ought to have put upon her, but there are people who love you, Angel. *I* love you, and your sisters love you, and so does your father."

Angel wouldn't look at Brandi. "But he left us. You took him away, and look what happened."

Brandi didn't know what to say to that. It was a fact she couldn't deny. "Sometimes people are lonely," she finally said. "So lonely they'll do practically anything to feel happy again. Does that make it right? No, I suppose it doesn't. I'm just telling you the way it was. I was lonely, and your father was lonely, and there we were."

"Why was he lonely? He had us, my mother and all us kids. Why weren't we enough? We all loved him."

"Sugar, that's something you're going to have to ask him." Brandi made herself count to ten. She took a deep breath and let it out. "But you should know what he told me before the sheriff came."

At that moment, Brandi felt a sharp, stabbing pain in her abdomen. She held onto Angel and waited for the pain to pass. The sun had come out and the light splintering off the snow-covered ground was too much for her. She felt sick to her stomach. Everything started to spin. Then she could feel the light dimming. She was slipping away. It was like a curtain was being drawn slowly over her eyes, and she felt like she was ducking under a thick pile of quilts.

Angel, she tried to say. *Listen, sugar.* But she wasn't sure any words were coming out of her mouth.

Then she heard Angel say, "Missy, help. What are we going to do?"

"It was like this," Shooter said. "Ronnie Black ran out from behind the trailer that night. He was a man in a hurry, and it's no wonder, seeing what he'd just done."

Biggs had taken Shooter into his office. They were standing just inside the door behind the frosted glass with the word SHERIFF stenciled across it. Two men. One, Biggs, barrel-chested and broad-shouldered; the other, worn down by too much, his back starting to hump with the strain of it all.

"What exactly did he do?" Biggs asked.

Shooter couldn't get the words out of his mouth fast enough. He'd kept them there so long. He'd thought of this moment over and over the past few weeks, and now it was here.

"He burned down that trailer is what he did." Shooter realized his voice was too loud. He feared he was coming across like a lunatic. He tried to get himself calmed down, and then he tried to say it all again, this time in as steady a voice as he could manage. "He slopped gasoline all over it. He struck a match and lit it up. Then he ran."

Biggs studied Shooter for a while. "Anyone else see him? Anyone who can corroborate your story?"

Shooter cleared his throat. He swallowed hard. Then he nodded. "My son," he finally said. "He saw it too."

Biggs didn't waste any time. He told Shooter to wait in his office, and then he went back to the room where the deputy had been interrogating Ronnie.

"Well?" Biggs asked.

The deputy shook his head. "Nothing we don't already know."

"I'll tell you who *is* talking." Biggs pulled up a chair next to Ronnie. He leaned in close, but Ronnie didn't try to move away. He met Biggs's stare. "Shooter Rowe, that's who. He just told me a very interesting story. Claims he and his boy saw you sloshing gasoline on that trailer and then lighting it up. Looks to me like if you didn't do that, you might want to take this chance to say so."

A space heater was running in the corner of the room, and for a while the only noise was the hum of its fan, that and the deputy tapping a pencil against the edge of the table.

Finally Ronnie shifted his weight in his chair, and the deputy put the pencil down. Ronnie cleared his throat.

"Go ahead, Biggs. You chase that story around and see where it takes you."

Missy called 911 and soon the ambulance arrived, and the EMTs took Brandi away on a gurney. Angel's fingers were trembling, and she tucked her hands up into her armpits to hide them.

She wanted to ride in the ambulance with Brandi, but Missy said, "You wouldn't want to be in the way of the EMTs, would you?"

"But who'll be there for her?" Angel said. "She shouldn't have to be alone."

"Honey," said Missy. "I'm sure she'll be all right."

Missy tried to pet Angel's hair, but Angel pulled away from her.

"You said my dad should be in prison."

"I shouldn't have said that. It was wrong of me. I just get mad sometimes."

Angel could understand that. It was how she'd felt for a good while on both sides of the night of the fire. Before and after. Just mad, mad, mad. Hearing Missy admit that she sometimes felt the same caused something to let go inside her; that anger came unknotted. She let her hands drop to her sides, and she felt a great calm pass through her, the first time she could remember not being on edge, as if strands of barbed wire were tangled up inside her since the night of the fire. Ever since her father had walked out and taken up with Brandi she'd been mad. Just mad at everyone, even herself. Mad at her mother sometimes for not being able to keep her father there. Mad at him for leaving. Mad at Brandi for taking him away. Mad at herself for not being a better person the night of the fire.

Now Brandi was in trouble—and what about her baby?—and Angel was tired of being mad, tired of people's messed-up lives.

"I want to go to the hospital," she said. "I want to be there for Brandi. She's been trying her best with me."

It was then that Missy realized she was holding Brandi's purse. It had slipped from her arm when she'd fainted, and somewhere in the bustle of the EMTs, Missy had seen it on the ground and picked it up so it wouldn't be in the way. She'd been clutching it to her chest.

"Get in the van," Missy said, and in an instant, though she didn't yet know this would be true, she got a picture of Pat and her going on into old age alone. As much as that thought saddened her, she felt a light and airy space somewhere deep inside. Something was opening in her heart—some little part of her she'd kept locked ever since her missed chances to have a child of her own. Angel and her sisters—they'd be all their children now. Brandi's and Laverne Ott's and Lois and Wayne's, and every person in Goldengate and on out the blacktop who loved them and wanted them to have a good and happy life. Missy knew that was what she wanted most of all. "Come on," she said to Angel. "We'll go to the hospital."

Biggs told Shooter to go home. "I'll come by this evening," he said. "I'll have a talk with your boy."

"He'll tell you," Shooter said. "Count on it. He'll tell you exactly what I did."

Then he left the courthouse and drove straight home. Captain was in the barn with the goats.

"Come on," Shooter said to him. "Let's go for a ride."

"What for?"

"No reason. Let's just go."

In the emergency room, Missy went to the front desk to ask about Brandi.

"Are you family?" the woman at the desk asked.

Missy put her hands on Angel's shoulders and nudged her forward a bit. "This is her daughter," she said.

Angel reached up and laid her right hand on top of Missy's left, and then Missy let her go. Angel followed the woman to a set of double doors, and as the doors opened Missy got a glimpse of nurses bustling past in scrubs. She saw an empty gurney against the wall, a row of cubicles with curtains drawn closed. For a moment Angel hesitated, looking back at Missy, who smiled at her and motioned with her hand for her to go on. Angel mouthed the words *Thank you*, and then she was gone.

Shooter just drove. He had Captain in the truck, and he didn't know where he was going. He only knew that for the time he didn't want to be at home, didn't want to think about that evening when Biggs, if he were true to his word, would come to talk to Captain.

For now, Shooter only knew he wanted to keep moving. He didn't want to sit still and have time to think. So he drove into Phillipsport and then out of it, letting State Street become Route 50. Soon he was driving past Wabash Sand and Gravel and WPLP, and then he was crossing the river, driving over the bridge that would take him into Indiana.

He slowed down and took a look at the river. The swirls of gray and white and blue in the ice made him think of clouds, puffy white against a blue sky, and it was easy from the height of the bridge to imagine a heaven. There were times like this when he could believe in an afterlife, when he could convince himself that someday he'd see Merlene again.

What would he tell her about Captain? Would he be able to say he'd done his best by him?

"Where we going?" Captain asked.

Shooter glanced at him. "Nowhere in particular. We're just driving. You in a hurry?"

Captain looked down at his hands. He rubbed at some brown streaks of oak stain on his fingers. "I'm making a gun cabinet in shop."

"Looks like you made a mess." Shooter tried a little laugh, as if he'd been cracking a joke, but he could tell that Captain was hurt. He pulled his coat sleeves down over his hands. "I thought I got rid of that coat." Shooter had buried it down deep in a cedar chest that had been Merlene's. The chest was in the basement now, full of the clothes of hers that Shooter hadn't been able to bring himself to get rid of. Apparently Captain had found the coat and dug it out sometime that morning when Shooter was out to the barn getting the Bobcat tractor ready to go. He hadn't even seen Captain get on the bus wearing that coat.

"I like it," Captain said.

"It's ratty." Shooter reached over and pinched the coat sleeve in his fingers. "You didn't have any business snooping around and snatching this up."

The coat was a fake leather bomber jacket that Captain had always favored since Merlene bought it for him from Walmart. The sort with vinyl made to look like leather. Shooter raised Captain's arm and made him look at the patch as big as a pancake where the vinyl was missing. The quilted lining beneath was dappled, light brown in some places and black in others.

"Mom bought it for me." Captain yanked his arm away from Shooter's grip. "She said it was a bomber jacket fit for a Captain."

They were over the bridge now, coasting down onto the flat plain of the river bottoms. Shooter pulled off onto the shoulder and they sat there while the wind swept across the barren fields, not enough of a treeline anywhere to stop it. The truck shook a little when a gust came up, and out across the fields a fine powder of snow swirled.

"Stay here," Shooter said.

Then he got out of the truck and tromped through the snow and the corn stubble, fifty feet or so, until he was confident that he was far enough away so Captain wouldn't be able to see him very well. He listened to the wind howling around him, felt its sting on his face, let it bring tears to his eyes. He forced himself not to look back, not wanting to see Captain's face looking out the window of the truck.

He reached into the pocket of his barn coat and closed his hand around Captain's Case Hammerhead lockback knife. He dug out a spot in the snow with the toe of his boot until he could see the frozen ground of the furrow. Then he dropped the knife into that hole and covered it with snow. If luck would have it, he thought, no one would find that knife and spring would come, and the farmer who worked this field would plow the knife under.

It took everything he had to turn around and walk back across the field to the truck where Captain was waiting. He wanted to lie down in the snow and let the cold have him. He wanted to close his eyes and think of Merlene. He wanted to just slip away from the living and not have to answer for anything.

But Captain was waiting. He could feel him watching. Captain, who was his to take care of. No one else's. He'd promised Merlene that he'd do that much.

"What were you doing?" Captain asked him when he came back to the truck.

"Had to take a leak," Shooter said. "Let's go home. It's getting late."

"Almost time for supper," Captain said, and Shooter told him, yes, it was, and after supper the sheriff, Ray Biggs, was going to stop by to ask Captain some questions.

For a long time, Captain didn't say anything. He rubbed at the stains on his hands some more. Then he said, "About the fire?"

"That's right," said Shooter. "You remember what you're going to say?"

Captain nodded. "I remember."

"All right then," Shooter said, and then he pressed down on the gas pedal, hurrying now toward home.

Missy watched the doors close behind Angel. Then she turned to find a seat in the waiting area, where Hannah was keeping Sarah and Emma entertained at a table that had puzzles and games on it.

To Missy's surprise, she saw Lois Best occupying a chair back in the corner, nearly hidden by a half wall. She'd nodded off with her pocketbook on her lap, her hands resting on top of it, and with her head down like that, Missy nor the girls had taken any notice of her.

Missy wasn't sure whether to wake her, but she could only assume that Lois was there because of Wayne, and it would certainly be rude not to inquire. So she took the seat next to Lois, hoping that the motion would make her open her eyes.

But it didn't. Missy reached over and touched her on the arm. "Lois," she said. "It's me. Missy."

Lois snapped up her head and opened her eyes. She blinked a few times as she studied Missy, and Missy knew she was coming back to the living with reluctance.

"Oh, honey," she finally said. "It's Wayne. He's not a bit good."

Missy asked her what the trouble was, and Lois explained that he'd gotten out of bed that morning and fallen, striking his head against the corner of the dresser.

"Opened up a big old gash." Lois felt her own scalp. "It just bled and bled. I knew I had to call for the ambulance. They're sewing him up now but honey, I'm not sure he even knows where he is or what happened. That's how out of it he is."

Lois reached out her hand, and Missy took it. She felt the dry skin, cracked from the cold, and she put her free hand on Lois's back and rubbed slow, gentle circles to give her some comfort.

"I'll sit right here with you," Missy said. "I won't leave you alone. Did you ride in the ambulance with Wayne?"

Lois nodded.

"Then I'll wait right here, and when it's time, I'll give you a ride home."

"You've always been good to me, Missy. And you were good to Della, too." Lois pressed her finger to her lips, shushing herself. "Oh, just listen to me going on about myself. Shame on me. Is it one of your own that's brought you here? Don't tell me something happened to Pat?"

"No, it's not Pat." Missy hesitated, not sure whether what she was about to say would upset Lois. "It's Brandi. She fainted."

"And you were with her?"

Missy nodded. "At the high school. She was talking to Angel."

"About Ronnie?"

"She was about to tell the story that Ronnie told her just before Biggs arrested him. Then she passed out. Angel's back there with her now."

Lois crooked her neck to peek around Missy at the double doors. "My poor grandbaby. She's been through a world of hurt. I hope there's no more on down the road for her, but it looks like Ronnie's going to have something to answer for come the judgment."

Biggs was waiting in the driveway when Shooter and Captain got home. His patrol car was idling, a cloud of steam roiling out from the tailpipe.

Shooter pulled alongside him and turned off the truck. "Go on in the house," he said to Captain. "Get out of your school clothes. Go on."

By this time, it was close to five o'clock. Only a few minutes of daylight left. Shooter got out of the truck and watched Captain hurry by the patrol car and on up to the front door. He had a key, and he used it to let himself in.

A pair of Canada geese flew overhead, honking as they came to settle in the barren cornfield that ran along the side of the house toward the woods. Shooter knew that those geese mated for life and they were protective of each other. If one was hurt or sick, the other would guard it, not leaving until the mate got well or else died. It was a beautiful thing, Shooter thought. A very beautiful thing.

Biggs was out of his patrol car, unfolding to his full height. Shooter said, "I thought you were coming after suppertime."

"This can't wait." Biggs hunched his shoulders against the cold. "I need to get your boy's story right now."

He slammed the patrol car door shut, the noise echoing across the fallow fields. The car door startled the Canada geese, and they lifted into the air, the gander trumpeting the alarm call. Soon they were flying over the woods.

Shooter watched them go. He stood there in the open country, his head tilted up to the sky, and he thought how easy it must be for God to look down and see everything there was to see.

"Wild geese," Shooter said. "Just looking out for each other. Just trying to get by."

———

The doctors found out that Brandi had passed out because her blood pressure was high.

"They say I've got toxemia," she said to Angel, who had come to sit beside her gurney while she waited to see if she'd be discharged or admitted.

"What's that?" Angel asked.

"Sometimes pregnancy causes the mother's blood pressure to go up. Pregnancy-induced hypertension. It can happen with first-time moms like me."

"Will the baby be okay?"

Brandi closed her eyes a moment as she said a silent prayer. Then she explained to Angel how the placenta might not get enough blood and how if that happened the baby wouldn't get enough oxygen and food and would have a low birth weight.

"But that might not happen," she said. "Now that we know what's what, there are things I can do to make sure I deliver a healthy baby."

Those things turned out to be eating less salt, drinking eight glasses of water a day, and bed rest. The doctor told her she could go home, but he wanted her in bed most of the time, lying on her left side to take the weight of the baby off her major blood vessels.

"Who's going to take care of things around the house?" Brandi said after she'd listened to the doctor and tried to imagine everything she'd have to do. "Who'll take care of me?" she said, not knowing whether Ronnie would be back anytime soon, if ever, and there were the girls living with Missy and Pat. Brandi closed her eyes and thought about what might happen with Ronnie, wondered whether anyone would ever believe the story he'd told her. Then she said, "My family all lives in California. I don't want to go all the way out there."

"I don't want anything to happen to the baby," Angel said. Then a nurse came in to take out Brandi's IV and Angel stepped out through the curtain so she'd be out of the nurse's way and so she'd have a chance to find Missy to tell her she was worried about what was going to happen to Brandi.

Shooter and Biggs went into the house, and to Shooter's dismay, Captain was just standing there, as if he'd been watching out the window, still in his school clothes. He hadn't even taken off his coat. That ratty-assed bomber's jacket—Shooter knew he should have thrown it out, but it was one of the last gifts Merlene had given Captain, and Shooter couldn't bring himself to get rid of it. But now here was Biggs, eager for Captain's story.

"You ought to get out of those school clothes," Shooter said. He glanced at Biggs and lifted his eyebrows. "You know how boys are. Always ruining their good things. Go on and change, Wesley. We'll wait."

Captain headed toward the hallway, his head down, but as he tried to get past Biggs, Biggs reached out and grabbed him by his coat sleeve.

"This won't take long," he said. "I need to ask some questions and then get back to the courthouse." He said to Shooter, "You understand."

"Well, at least let the boy take off his coat."

Biggs let go of Captain's sleeve and said, "Sure. No harm in that. Go on, son. Make yourself comfortable."

Captain lifted his head and found Shooter's gaze upon him. Captain opened his eyes wide, asking his father what he should do, and Shooter gave him an almost imperceptible nod, but it was enough to tell Captain to go ahead and take off his coat. He slipped his arms out of the sleeves and then folded the jacket across his arm, bunched it up into a wad that he hugged to his stomach.

"You got a belly ache?" Biggs asked him.

Captain shook his head no, and then he sat down on the couch, the coat still clutched to him.

"Wesley." Shooter sat down beside him and put a hand on his back. "Tell the sheriff what you saw the night Della's trailer burned. That's what he's come to hear."

At the courthouse, the deputy said to Ronnie, "You know what it looks like, don't you?"

"Looks like what you all want it to look like," said Ronnie.

"Bought a can of gasoline the morning of the day the trailer burned and another can that night. We found that can in Brandi's shed, almost a gallon still in it, and she said you used it all up in her car that morning. Looks to me like you used that can again later." The deputy listed all the evidence that seemed to be adding up to Ronnie's guilt. "Footprints that match yours found behind the trailer. A T-shirt smelling of gas. Shooter Rowe's story. And now this? Ronnie, do you know what'll happen if a jury finds you guilty?"

"Lock me up, I expect."

The deputy nodded. "For a good long while. Forever, if the State's Attorney can prove premeditation. And, Ronnie, if you ask me, that won't be hard to do. I doubt you'll ever see the outside again."

It was then that the deputy noticed the first sign of emotion from Ronnie. His lip quivered, and his eyes got wet, and he tipped his head back, his nostrils flaring, as if he were fighting as hard as he could to keep whatever he'd held secret all those weeks balled up inside him.

The deputy said, "Your kids? They'll come to see you in prison sometimes if they can bring themselves to forgive you for what you did, and if they can manage for someone to drive them down to Menard, which is where you'll end up. Or maybe they'll never come and it'll just be you and those walls and all that time to know the way you ruined them by killing their mother and their sisters and their baby brother. You think they'll ever be able to get the picture out of their heads of how those kids clung to Della in the flames and the smoke, or what their charred bodies looked like when all was said and done?"

That's when Ronnie covered his face with his hands. "I didn't do it," he said. "I swear."

"All right then," the deputy said. "Tell me why we should believe you."

He was outside that night, Captain said, because he was worried about the goats. "We tried to patch the fence for Della, but they kept busting out."

He kept his eyes down, focusing on the boots Biggs was wearing. The toes were stained with road salt. Biggs stood in front of the couch, listening to the story.

"So you were outside and you went back behind the trailer to check on the goats?"

Captain nodded.

Biggs said, "Tell me everything you saw."

"He saw Ronnie's car," Shooter said, but Biggs wouldn't let him go on.

"I want to hear the boy tell it. Let him say what he's got to say."

"Ronnie drives a Firebird," Captain said. "It was parked along the road. That car can go fast. I helped him work on it when he still lived with Della. He said I was his right-hand man. You know what kind of carb that car has? A Barry Grant Six Shooter with a three-deuce setup. Sugar tits! Now that's something."

Captain was getting worked up, and Shooter rubbed his back and said, "Wesley, just tell the story. Tell it plain and simple for the sheriff."

"Ronnie was behind the trailer," Captain said. "He had a five-gallon gas can. He was sloshing gas all along the back of the trailer. And he reached into his pocket and jerked out a book of matches." Captain looked up at Biggs for the first time. "He had a book of matches. He lit one up." Captain was rocking back and forth a little. "He had a gas can and a book of matches. The whole trailer went whoosh. That's what I remember. That big whoosh. And Ronnie ran away."

Biggs was quiet for a while. Then he squatted down in front of Captain so the boy would have to look him in the eye.

"You felt pretty close to Ronnie, didn't you, son? Like you said, you were his right-hand man."

"I like Ronnie," said Captain. "He always treated me good."

"You wouldn't want to see him get in trouble if he didn't do anything wrong, would you?"

Captain squeezed his eyes shut and shook his head from side to side until, finally, Shooter had to take him by his shoulders and tell him to stop.

"He had a gas can and a book of matches," Captain said again. "He lit one up and everything went whoosh. That's what I know."

Shooter stood up from the couch. "You got what you need?" he asked Biggs. "Captain always thought the world of Ronnie. This hasn't been easy for him."

The words came from Captain's mouth in chunks, like they were made of steel and hard to bite off. "I always—thought the world—of Ronnie—sugar tits."

"Wesley, don't talk like that," Shooter said. "It's not proper."

Biggs said to Shooter, "Why'd you wait so long to tell me your story?"

"I was thinking about Wesley. Things have never been easy for him. And this?" Shooter couldn't go on. He laid his hand on Captain's head and stroked the blond hair with a tenderness that almost made Biggs uncomfortable to see it, this moment that should have been private. "But I know what's right and what's wrong," Shooter said, "and I know I have to teach Wesley as much. So what I'm telling you is the right thing to do. I know that for sure now, no matter how this ends up."

Angel was surprised to see her grandmother in the emergency room waiting area. "Grams?" she said.

"Oh, honey." Lois got to her feet and put her arms around Angel, gathering her in. "It's your gramps. He fell and hit his head." She let go of Angel just enough to hold her at arm's length so she could get a good look at her. "Honey, are you all right?"

Angel nodded. "I'm fine, Grams. Is Gramps going to be okay?"

"I'm waiting to hear, honey. Missy's been sitting with me. She just now went out to call Pat. Guess she wanted some privacy."

Angel saw her then, Missy. She was standing outside the glass doors to the emergency room with her back turned. She had her head down, and Angel could see her nodding as if she were agreeing with what Pat was saying in response to what she'd called to tell him. Then she dropped her cell phone down in her purse.

Angel told her grandma she'd be right back. Then she went out through the doors to where Missy was standing, and she told her everything that Brandi had told her about the high blood pressure and the baby and bed rest.

"We have to take care of her," Angel said. "She doesn't have anyone else. Her family is all the way out in California."

She'd already made up her mind. She wouldn't be like her father—she'd stay where she was needed.

"But who's going to take care of you and your sisters?" Missy said.

"We'll take care of one another."

"You're all in my custody now."

Angel said, "We're going to stay with Brandi tonight."

And with that, Angel turned and went back into the hospital. Missy had no choice but to follow.

A doctor was there to talk to Lois, and he was saying that Wayne was going to be all right. He had some stitches in his head, and he was still a little confused, but his vital signs were good, and she could see him now. They'd admitted him and wanted to keep him at least overnight to make sure that he was strong enough to go home.

Missy said she'd wait as long as Lois needed her to.

Angel went back to check on Brandi, and in a few minutes she was back. "They're releasing her," she said, and Missy told her she'd drive Brandi home too, and she'd stay that night to help take care of her if that's what she wanted. She'd drive Lois home first, and then she'd go to her own house and carry in the groceries—who knew if the milk and frozen things would be any good now—and she'd tell Pat what was going to happen.

"Pat can do for himself." Missy bit her lip and looked away. Then she took a deep breath and turned back to Angel, a tremulous smile on her lips. She waved her hand in the air as if she were swatting away an annoying fly. "He won't even know I'm gone," she said. "He's used to a quiet house."

After Biggs left, Shooter let Captain sit there on the couch, rocking back and forth, his bomber jacket still clutched to his stomach.

The furnace clicked off and then enough time went by for it to come on again. The hem of the curtains by the front window—the long curtains Merlene had sewed—danced a little in the air from the floor vent.

Finally, when the quiet had become too much for him, Shooter walked across the room to where Captain was sitting and he reached down and took hold of the bomber jacket. For a few seconds, Captain held onto it. Then he let his grip go slack, and Shooter pulled the coat away from him.

"Change out of your school clothes," Shooter said in a tired voice. "I'm going to take care of the trash. Then we'll think about supper."

Captain got up from the couch and went into his room. He tried not to think about anything. *Don't think about the fire,* he told himself. *Don't think about the goats. Don't think about Della or Emily or Gracie or the baby. Don't think about Mother.* She'd bought him that bomber jacket. *Don't think about that. Don't think about Ronnie. Don't think about the sheriff and the questions he asked. Don't think about anything.*

Captain heard the back door open and close. He went to his window and peeled back the curtain. He watched his father walking down the path he'd cleared through the snow so he could get to the burn barrel. He had a paper grocery bag full of trash in his left hand, the bomber jacket in his right. He put it all in the barrel.

Then he set it on fire. He stood there, his head bowed toward the flames, and Captain knew he was praying.

Captain turned away from the window, no longer wanting to see the flames rising above the top of the burn barrel. Even in the closed house, he could hear his father coughing. He could smell the same bad odor the air held the night Della's trailer burned, but now he knew the stink was coming from the vinyl on his bomber jacket.

He opened his closet, and stepped inside. He closed the door and crouched down on the floor in the dark.

Della was his friend. More than that, she loved him. He knew that, and when he was with her, he remembered how it was when his mother was still alive. That's what Della gave him—that mother's love—and when he finally crossed the road that night, he only meant to help her. Her car wasn't in the lane. His father had noticed that just before their argument over the goats had started, pointing out that it was so cold that Della and the kids had gone to spend the night somewhere else, probably with Lois and Wayne. Captain thought it was the exact right time to do a good turn for Della.

The deputy sat across from Ronnie. He said, "You went back out there that night, didn't you?"

Ronnie nodded. "I was in a state when I left there that afternoon. I won't deny that. It was over between Della and me—she'd made that plain—and I guess it caught me by surprise even if I'd thought that's what I wanted. Pissed me off, is what it did. A crazy idea came to me. You have to understand I wasn't thinking right. I stewed about it all evening, and then finally I made up my mind I'd do it."

"Do what, Ronnie?"

"I'd call and see if Della and the kids were in the trailer or if they'd gone to her folks. I'd buy five gallons of gas, and if no one answered the phone, I'd go out there and burn the place. If she was going to push me, then I was going to push back. I'd put her in a mess. I'd make her sorry."

"So you told Brandi you were going out for a drive?"

Ronnie nodded. "I pulled on my boots. I'd made up my mind."

"But you never told Brandi that?"

"I stopped at Casey's and called Della. No one answered. I bought that gas and drove on out the blacktop. When I got to the trailer, it was dark, and Della's car wasn't in the lane. She always left it in the lane, and it wasn't there. So I felt certain she'd taken the kids and gone to Lois and Wayne's. I parked a ways down the road. The neighbors had enough to gossip about. People like Missy Wade. I didn't want her seeing my car pulled in the lane and wondering what was what."

Just as he got the gas can out of his car, he said, he heard a door slam shut across the road at the Rowe house, and that was enough to spook him. "That's when I hauled that gas can through the ditch and angled through the front yard." He tromped through the snow and got in behind the trailer where he thought no one would see him. "I just stood there a while, catching my breath, listening, just letting things calm down."

So, yes, Ronnie was there that night, out there behind the trailer. Brandi was retelling the story—the one he'd told her—to Angel and Missy, but she wouldn't tell it all. No, there were parts of it she wouldn't want the girls to ever know, parts that shamed Ronnie, parts that Brandi didn't want to think about ever again. Angel sat on the edge of the bed. Missy stood just inside the door. Lois hadn't said a word all the way from Phillipsport to Goldengate, and she'd refused to come inside, preferring instead to wait in the van until Missy came out to drive her home. It was then that Lois would say to Missy, "I don't know how you can be a friend to her. Not after what she did to Della."

How would Missy ever be able to explain what rose in her as she watched Angel help Brandi with her pajamas, and then, once she was in bed, pull the covers over her with such care? How strongly Missy felt Brandi's need, and in that moment she let sorrow have every bit of her until it could have no more. She grieved for Della and her children, for Angel and the girlhood she was leaving behind too soon.

Standing there, looking at Angel and Brandi in the lamplight, listening to Brandi's soft voice, watching Angel reach out and brush a few strands of wayward hair from Brandi's face, Missy understood in a way she never quite had that life—everyone's life—came down to this. The chance to do something good, to let people know they weren't alone. To do it with no thought of what advantage or reward might come to you. To do it because you knew everyone was sometimes stupid, deceitful, selfish, weak. To do it because you knew you were one of those people, no matter how spotless your life. Sooner or later, trouble would find you, either of your own device or a matter of circumstances. Love was sacrifice and forgiveness. She'd heard it in church, read it in her Bible, listened to it from her parents, but somewhere along the line— somewhere in the midst of losing the babies she thought she was meant to have—she'd forgotten it all. She'd become bitter, and this business with Ronnie leaving Della for Brandi had brought out all her anger. She'd been determined to save Angel and her sisters. She'd had no way of knowing that all along it was Angel who was saving her, bringing her back to being a better person than she'd been in too long, bringing her—the thought startled her at first, but then she settled into its comfort—as close as she would ever be to feeling like a mother.

"He went out there that night," Brandi said to Angel, "because he loved you. He knew the furnace in the trailer was acting up, and he wanted to know you were all right. All of you. All you kids and, yes, even your mom. He wanted to make sure nothing was wrong."

It wasn't true—though there was at least a bit of truth in it—but Brandi convinced herself that God would forgive her this one lie, all for the sake of the future.

It was cold, and the wind was coming in gusts, and Ronnie was shivering from the thought of what he was about to do. He noticed a cardboard box on the back steps, a box of ashes.

"The wind had caught some embers," he said, "and from time to time a shower of sparks sprayed up into the air. I didn't care. I knew what I'd come to do, and that box of ashes didn't mean anything to me."

He unscrewed the cap off the gas can spout and got at it. The old upholstered chair he'd dragged out behind the trailer in the fall just before he'd found out that Della had lied to him and wasn't taking her birth control pills was still there. He doused it with gasoline, knowing it would soak into the foam and burn hot and quick when he finally lit it. He went down the length of the trailer, slinging gas up onto the hardboard siding, pouring it along the bare ground where the roof's overhang had kept snow from collecting. The tall grass was dry and brittle. He heard his breath and the noise the can made as it emptied, popping every once in a while as its volume decreased. He smelled the gas, and he felt the wind burning his bare ears. He didn't have on any gloves, but it wouldn't be until later that he'd feel the sting in his hands.

"I stopped to rest." He looked away from the deputy and closed his eyes, playing it all out again in his head. "I still had about half of that can left. I set it down, and I put my hands on my knees. That's when I saw it."

A hole in the siding of the trailer, down low, just before the concrete slab. A ragged hole as big as a boot heel right where he knew the wall furnace was. A hole, he assumed, one of the goats had made at some time or the other.

"It was the most amazing thing," he said. "Like it was a sign to me, an invitation to do something other than what I'd come to do."

He crouched down and put his finger into the hole. It went all the way through the siding and the insulation and the drywall. He could feel the back of the furnace. It was hot when he touched it, and he knew that meant it was still running. Why, then, had Della taken the kids to her folks, as he assumed from the fact that she hadn't answered the phone when he called?

"I got to thinking what would happen if a gust of wind came through that hole and blew out the pilot light. I wondered what it meant that right then, when I'd been determined to burn the place down, I was thinking about that pilot light. It came to me, then: *Here's a chance to do something good, and if you do this one good thing, maybe then you can do another and then another, and before long you'll have your life back on track.* That hole was my chance to save myself. I was so close, you see, to doing something I'd never be able to live down. Burn that trailer and then walk away. But now I had this chance to do something different, patch that hole. Then I'd be able to go home and think better about myself."

That's when he put the cap back on the gas can. He took out his pocketknife. He opened up his coat and grabbed the bottom of his T-shirt with his hand. It was his Sun Records T-shirt, the one that Brandi had found for him at the Goodwill, and yet he didn't think about how much it pleased him, nor how much he loved Brandi. He thought only of needing something to stuff into that hole.

He pressed the point of his knife into the T-shirt, down around the bottom, just enough to make a place where he could grab the cloth and rip it. Working with his hand and the knife, he managed to tear away a strip that was sufficient for the task. He wadded it up and stuck it into the hole.

"My fingers were stiff with the cold," he told the deputy, "and I fumbled my knife and it fell to the ground. I'd just started to feel around for it when I heard a noise. It was Shooter Rowe's boy, Wesley, the one they call Captain. He was coming around the end of the trailer, headed for the goat pen. I stood dead still and hoped he wouldn't see me."

Ronnie watched Captain open the gate to the pen and step inside. The goats were bleating, and Ronnie could hear Captain moving about, his boots whisking through the loose straw on the ground. Once, he cursed. Said, "Goddamn it." Then, after a time, he came out with one of the nannies, something tied around her neck. He was leading it with a length of something, and he had a kid up under his other arm.

"By this time, I'd gotten over behind the back steps, and I crouched down," Ronnie said. "I was afraid for him to see me. I didn't know what I'd say about why I was there."

Captain went around the other side of the trailer, and Ronnie couldn't make up his mind whether to go or stay. He wanted to go—wanted to get as far away from there as he could—but he was afraid that if he made a move, Captain would spot him. It was hard for Ronnie to tell where he was. And, too, he was curious about why Captain had come for those goats.

It wasn't long before he was back, and he led out the other nanny. Again, he had her kid under his arm.

"I thought it was curious," Ronnie said. "Like he'd come to steal those goats. I thought, *What in the world?*"

The deputy said, "So it was you and the boy out there?"

Ronnie opened his eyes. "Yes," he said. "It was the two of us. I was just waiting to see what would happen next."

Captain remembered what his father had said when they'd patched Della's fence that afternoon: *Sometimes it's best to start over. Put a match to that fence.*

All evening, he'd thought about that, how if that pen and shed were gone, then he and his father could build a better shed, a better pen, and then the goats wouldn't get out. Della would have that one less thing to worry about, and Captain felt good knowing he could give her that. It was only right after she'd been so kind to him.

His plan was to lead the goats one by one across the road to his father's barn and leave them there while he got down to work. He had a box of Diamond matches, the ones he used when he burned the trash. He knew there was straw in the shed behind the goat pen. Dry enough even on a cold night to catch and burn. The wood planks of that shed and pen were dry too. It'd be a snap. It'd all go up so quick.

He knew his father was asleep in front of the television, and wouldn't he be surprised when he found out what he'd done?

Della would be surprised too, and so would Ronnie.

When Captain slipped out of the house that night, he remembered to put on his bomber jacket, and he grabbed his sock hat and his gloves. He spotted Ronnie's Firebird pulled off alongside the blacktop. He didn't know what to make of that, and he really didn't have time to think on it. He had to keep his mind on what he was going to do.

Half of the shed was a lean-to, open to the east, facing the blacktop. A doorway cut into the interior wall of the lean-to led to the closed part of the shed, and that's where the goats had gone to lie down in the straw, where they could be away from the brunt of the wind.

Captain realized he needed something to use for a lead. Otherwise, how would he get those goats across the road to his father's barn?

That's what he was wondering as he stood in the pen's shed.

Then he thought of the bales of straw. Just enough light from the snow cover outside coming in through the doorway helped him find the bales, and in an instant it all clicked inside his head, and he knew what he'd do. A great happiness spread through him. The light from the snow cover, the straw bales—it all meant that someone was helping him to do the thing he'd come to do. It meant that what he intended was right.

He couldn't get at his knife with his gloves on, so he slipped his hands out and stuffed the gloves into his jacket pockets. He opened the blade of the knife and felt it lock into place. Then he bent over and grabbed one of the strands of twine that held the bale together.

Just as he was ready to cut it—he'd use it for a lead—the billy goat, Methuselah, butted his head against him and the blade slipped and gashed the hock of his left thumb. He felt the cold air sting the flayed skin, and he knew right away he was bleeding.

"Goddamn it," he said.

Then he went back to work. He cut the twine and then made a slip knot around the neck of the first goat. He'd save the cantankerous one, Methuselah, for last.

The other four were agreeable. The two nannies let him lead them across the road to his father's barn with little complaint. He was able to carry one of the kids on each trip.

He put his gloves back on, blood soaking into the left one. When it came time to loop the twine around Methuselah's neck, the goat balked, jerking his head this way and that, filling the shed with his bleats. Captain kept at it, finally getting the job done, and Methuselah let him lead him a few steps before he dug in and refused to go any farther. Captain tugged hard on the lead. That's when the twine snapped. He went stumbling backwards, falling on his butt on the frozen ground.

That made him mad. First the cut on his hand and now this. He could feel time ticking away, and he still had so much to do.

Methuselah kicked up straw with his hind hooves. Captain decided to leave him alone. He needed to get back to work.

Then Methuselah charged him, and Captain turned and ran out of the shed, out of the pen, ran through the snow toward the trailer.

Methuselah stopped. He went quiet. Captain turned and watched him to make sure he was calm enough not to cause trouble. The goat went closer to the trailer, right up to the back steps, and there he got something in his mouth and started chewing on it. A spray of sparks danced in the air, and that startled the goat, and he stepped away from what Captain could now see was a cardboard box.

He thought that shower of sparks was a beautiful thing, something he, like Methuselah, didn't expect. It reminded him of fireworks on the Fourth of July, which had always been his mother's favorite holiday. He could remember sitting on a blanket at the State Park with his father and her. He lay on his back with his head in her lap, and he watched the fireworks burst into sprays and showers in the night sky above the lake. "Look at that one," his mother said. "Oh, and that one. How pretty they are."

He liked to imagine that the fireworks were the wings of angels, painting the sky red and blue and silver and gold as they streaked down to Earth to see to this or that.

His mother had something she liked to say to him when she told him goodnight. It came from a poem she learned in school when she was a girl:

> *Silently, one by one, in the infinite meadows of heaven,*
> *Blossomed the lovely stars, the forget-me-nots of the angels.*

He wasn't sure he could say exactly what that meant, but he'd never forgotten the sound of her voice when she said those words—hushed and dreamy—and he knew, without her having to say as much, she was telling him that he was one of those lovely stars. He was one of the forget-me-nots of the angels, and no matter where he found himself, he could count on them to keep him from harm.

Methuselah was coming back to the box now. *Well, just let him*, Captain thought. He realized then that there was a man behind the trailer, and he knew that man was Ronnie.

"That's when he saw me," Ronnie told the deputy. "I knew I was caught, so I stood up. Methuselah stopped in his tracks, stopped bleating, just nosed at the snow. Captain turned back to watch him, and then, after a while, he came up to me, and he said, 'You come back for good?'"

The wind was really howling now, and Ronnie had to get up close to Captain to make himself heard. He leaned in toward the boy's ear. He said, "No, not for good. I came out to check on Della and the kids."

"They're gone," Captain said. "Car's nowhere to be seen."

Ronnie nodded. "Good thing I came, though." He pointed down toward the other end of the trailer. About two-thirds of the way down, his Marathon can sat in the snow. "Hole in the siding there. Wind could've blown out the pilot light on the furnace. I patched it up."

Captain looked down at the Marathon can and then back at Ronnie. Captain's nose wrinkled up, and Ronnie knew he smelled the gas. He waited for Captain to ask him about it, and when he didn't, Ronnie knew he was afraid to ask him what he was doing with a can of gas back there because he was up to something himself that he didn't want to have to explain.

"So you're not back for good?" Captain finally said.

He was clearly disappointed, and Ronnie, who couldn't work a miracle and make that gas jump back into the can, felt ashamed to be standing there in his presence.

"No, Captain," he said. "It's too late for that."

"Your daddy would never hurt you," Brandi told Angel. "You know that, don't you? You know he loves you, and I love you."

Angel's bottom lip quivered. "It's all been so hard," she said.

Brandi gripped her hand. "It's going to be all right. Everything. You'll see."

She was thinking of the night that Ronnie told her he was going for a drive, that he was feeling antsy. She was reading one of her baby books, and when he came back, she couldn't have said how long he'd been gone. He came in and went right into the shower. She wouldn't know until he told her later that on his way back to town, he smelled gasoline and recalled that earlier in the day, when he'd brought the gas for Brandi's Mustang, the cap on the can's spout had been difficult and he'd crouched down and used the tail of his T-shirt to get a better grip so he could twist it off and get about the business of pouring gas into the Mustang's tank. All day, he'd thought he was catching the faint scent of gasoline, and finally that night as he sped up the blacktop, he imagined that not even the strip of the shirt that he'd cut away while he was behind the trailer was enough to get rid of that smell—a smell that seemed dangerous to him now on account of what he'd just done.

At the city limits, he pulled off into the parking lot of the Dairy Dee, closed for the winter, and there he slipped off his coat and pulled the T-shirt over his head. He wadded it up and stuffed it under the passenger seat. Then he put his coat back on and zipped it up. He went on to Brandi's, and he went straight into the bathroom and undressed and got into the shower.

When he came out, he was ready for bed. She heard the siren at the fire station but barely gave it a thought. Then she reached up and turned off the lamp, and the two of them drifted off to sleep.

When Shooter woke and couldn't find Captain in the house, he put on his barn coat and went out the back door to look for him.

The pole light in the barnyard was enough for him to spot the footprints in the snow. He recognized the corrugated tread of Captain's Big Horn Wolverine boots, and the hoof prints the goats had left. Shooter followed the prints to the barn door. Inside, he found four of Della's goats, bleating their dismay over whatever had happened to move them there. The lights were on in the feedway. Dust motes and chaff hovered around the bare bulbs.

"Wesley," Shooter shouted, but there was no answer.

In her bedroom, Della thought she heard voices, but she was so far down in sleep she convinced herself it was only the wind.

The baby was asleep. The twins were asleep, and Gracie, and Sarah, and Hannah, and Angel. They were snuggled down in their dreams. The furnace was working fine, and they were cozy in their beds on this cold winter night.

Shooter stepped out of the barn and heard the back door of the house go shut. He hurried inside, and there he found Captain at the bathroom sink, letting the water run over his hand. The only light in the room was a nightlight plugged into the wall below the mirror, that and the light from the snow cover coming in through the little window in the wall facing the road. It was enough light for Shooter to see Captain's sock hat and his bloody glove on the vanity top.

"You're cut." Shooter grabbed the hand and looked at the slice across the hock of Captain's thumb. "How'd that happen?"

"Knife slipped," said Captain.

"Knife? Your pocketknife? What were you using it for?"

"To cut baling twine. I found a bale of straw. I didn't want the goats to get hurt."

"How were they going to get hurt, Wesley?"

Captain wouldn't answer. He hung his head and wouldn't look at his father. Shooter reached over and turned off the faucet. "Wesley, I asked you a question."

"I meant to start over." Captain's voice was flat. "Just like you told me. Put a match to that fence."

Shooter remembered then what he'd said in passing that afternoon when he and Captain had been mending the fence over at Della's.

"Oh, good Christ," he said. "That was just something to say. Something because I was mad. Why would you ever think I was serious?"

Captain shrugged his shoulders. "I just wanted to help Della."

Shooter looked down at the sock hat and the glove on the vanity. The glove had blood on it.

"Where's your jacket?" he asked him. "Did you have it on? Where's your knife?"

"My jacket's behind the trailer," Captain said. "It fell off. I don't know what happened to my knife. I must have dropped it."

Shooter didn't know that he was lying about the knife, that he still had it in his jeans pocket, the blade stained with his blood. Shooter was about to tell him to go get his coat and to look for that knife, but then—it was almost imperceptible—the light grew brighter in the room, just enough of a change for Shooter to register. He turned his head toward the window, and he saw light waver behind the curtains. He drew one of the panels back and looked out across the road.

He stood there longer than he should have because he thought Della and her kids weren't home. He stood there, watching the flames licking through the roof of the trailer, thinking, if he had to be honest, that even though he was stunned to see the fire, a small part of him thought he'd found a convenient answer to his problem with the goats. If the trailer burned, Della and the kids would have to find somewhere else to live, and they'd take the goats with them or else sell them, and spring would come, and he wouldn't have to worry about them getting loose and eating up his garden. He stood there watching until he saw the first girls, Angel and Hannah, come running from the flames and out into the cold night.

Then he caught a whiff of gasoline, and he knew it was coming from Captain. "My god." He spun around to look at his son. "Surely you didn't tote a can of gas over there."

Captain bowed his head. He didn't say a word, and Shooter's mind raced ahead, convinced that his assumption was true.

"Oh, Wesley," he said. "What in the world have you done?"

30

Biggs had just backed out of Shooter's drive when he saw Pat Wade up the road at his place waving his arms in the air, motioning for him to come down there.

"There's something you ought to know," Pat said, when Biggs pulled his patrol car into the driveway and got out to see what Pat wanted. "He put that goat down," Pat said. "Shooter. He killed that billy goat, one of Della's goats. Shot it back there in his woods. Told Missy it had foot and mouth."

"Foot and mouth?" Biggs said. "Hasn't been foot and mouth in this country since before you and me."

"That's what I know."

"Missy see him shoot that goat?"

Pat shook his head. "She saw him push it down into a gully. Come inside and she'll tell you."

Missy was waiting just inside the front door. She'd left Hannah and Angel to heat up some soup and make cheese sandwiches for her and her sisters and Brandi, and then she'd left the girls there to drive Lois home and then to come and talk to Pat.

"He killed that goat." She started right in once Biggs and Pat were inside the house. "Then today he was back there with his Bobcat and his chainsaw. Filling in that gully, I expect. Burying what he put there."

"Seems odd that he'd tell you it had foot and mouth," Biggs said.

"He threatened me," she said. "Today. He told me I had what I wanted and not to do anything to ruin my happy-ever-after."

"Della's girls," Pat said.

"I want to know why Shooter killed that goat." Missy crossed her arms over her chest and tipped her head back a little so her chin pointed out. "And I want to know what brought him to lie about why."

"I'm going to find out," said Biggs, and he told Pat and Missy goodnight.

Once he was gone, there wasn't much for them to say. They stood awhile just inside the front door, though they didn't speak until the patrol car left their drive and started back up the blacktop toward Shooter's.

Then Pat said, "Missy?"

His voice was strained, and it was clear he wanted to say more—wanted to know what it meant that she'd left the girls with Brandi—but he didn't know how.

"That's done," Missy said.

She'd unloaded the groceries from the van and put the perishables away. She still had canned goods to stack in the pantry. Then she had the rest of the night, and the ones after that, to get through.

Pat nodded. The quiet of the house and all the sadness it held choked him. "All right," he managed to say, but by that time, Missy was gone.

Biggs drove back to Shooter's and said he had more questions. He could tell that Shooter was surprised to see him again, but he let him into the house, and he answered his question about the goats.

Yes, he had Della's goats, he said.

"I've been keeping them as a favor to Wayne Best." He knew Wayne and Lois weren't up to seeing to them, and he didn't mind footing the feed bill for a while since the goats gave Captain so much pleasure. "My boy loves taking care of them," he said.

Biggs said, "Where is your boy?"

The house was quiet. Night had fallen and stretched on past the supper hour, and there was no sign of Captain. From where Biggs stood in the living room, he could see through the archway into the kitchen, and he noticed there were no signs of a supper having been prepared and eaten—no frying pans on the stove, no dishes in the sink or in the drainer, no pots or pans left to soak, no sign at all that Shooter and the boy had seen to their supper after Biggs left their house earlier. A light above the sink was on. That was the only sign that someone had at least passed through that kitchen long enough to switch it on. Biggs couldn't have said why he found that tidy, quiet kitchen unsettling, but he did. Something about it told him that Shooter and his boy had been too busy to even think of supper.

"He's at a 4-H meeting," Shooter said.

"Isn't Missy Wade the 4-H leader?"

"One of them."

"How come she's home if there's a meeting tonight?" Biggs waited for that to sink in. Then he said, "I just came from there. I had a talk with Missy and Pat."

Shooter clapped his hands together and the noise was loud in the quiet house. "How the hell would I know that? I'm not Missy Wade's keeper."

Biggs took a step closer to Shooter. He liked to do that when he knew someone wasn't telling him the whole truth. He liked to get into their personal space just to see what they'd do.

Shooter took a step back and bumped into the coffee table.

"Why'd you kill that billy goat?" Biggs asked.

"He was sick." Shooter turned around and started straightening a stack of magazines on the coffee table—*Popular Mechanics, Car and Driver, Reader's Digest.* "Nothing the vet could cure. I had to do it. Didn't have any other choice." Shooter was quiet for a while, and Biggs let the silence build. He knew that in cases like this, when someone had something they didn't want to say, as he suspected was true about Shooter, the longer the silence went on the more likely they were to fill it, which eventually Shooter did. "I guess Missy told you all about it." Still Biggs waited, not saying a word. "Guess she thinks it's her business—everything that goes on around here. Sick goat. That's the whole story." He turned back to Biggs. "Now was there something else you wanted?"

Biggs asked the question that had been going through his mind since he'd left Shooter's house earlier. He hadn't been able to forget something he'd noticed as he was leaving. The boy was sitting on the couch, his jacket wadded up in his lap. A sleeve of the jacket had come loose and was trailing down to the floor. For some reason, the image of that jacket sleeve kept coming to Biggs after he talked to Missy and Pat. Something about that sleeve that wouldn't let him go.

Finally, as he stood here with Shooter, he knew what it was that was troubling him. That sleeve. A patch of the vinyl was missing and the lining beneath it was ratty with holes. Biggs swore that when he recalled those holes he could see charred edges, as if they'd been burned into the material.

"Where's your boy's jacket?" he asked Shooter now. "The one he had with him when I was here before. I want to look at it."

"That jacket?" Shooter said. "Well, that jacket was old."

"He can't show it to you." Captain's voice startled Biggs. The boy had come down the hallway that led from the living room to the bedrooms. How long he'd been standing there, listening, Biggs didn't know. "He burned it," Captain said. "He put it in the burn barrel and set it on fire."

"Like I said." Shooter's voice all of a sudden got too bright and cheery. "It was old."

"I'm tired of lying." Captain stepped out of the hall and fully into the light of the living room. "I want to tell the truth."

So it was Captain who told Biggs the story of what happened the night of the fire. He stood in his own house, his father no longer able to keep him quiet, and he said all of it, starting with what his father had said about that goat pen and how it would be best to put a match to it and start over.

"I got worried about the goats that night," Captain said, "and I went outside to check on them. I remembered what my dad said, and I thought I could help Della."

He took his time. Biggs could tell that the boy had thought about this moment when he'd go against his father's wishes and confess everything, had steeled himself for it and was now reciting the facts with little show of emotion. He told Biggs about leading the goats over to his father's barn. It was just the billy, Methuselah, he said, that wouldn't go.

"He charged at me, but, finally, he settled down. He saw Ronnie there, and he just stopped."

"So Ronnie was behind the trailer?" Biggs said. "Just like you told me earlier? You're sticking by that?"

For a long time Captain didn't say a word. He looked down at his feet. Then he raised his head. His lip trembled. "Yes," he finally said, "Ronnie was there."

Captain was talking fast now, telling Biggs how Methuselah got stirred up again and came charging at him, butted him in the stomach and sent him sprawling backwards into the snow. Then Captain was back on his feet and trying to get away from the goat, running, spinning in circles, dodging this way and that. He unzipped his jacket and slipped his arms out of the sleeves. He stood still and let Methuselah come at him. Then, when the goat was close enough, he threw his jacket over his face and stepped to the side.

But Biggs wanted to know what Ronnie was doing when Captain saw him.

"He wasn't doing anything," Captain said.

"Was there gasoline?" Biggs kept his voice low and as gentle as he could manage, coaxing Captain. "Son, listen to me now. Did you see Ronnie pour gasoline on that trailer?"

Captain said, "No, I didn't see him do that."

"But you told me you did. Said he slopped it all over that trailer and lit it up. Son, were you lying?"

"Wesley." Shooter's voice was flat and worn out, as if he were giving in to what he knew he couldn't stop. "Tell him the rest."

At the courthouse, Ronnie told the deputy that when he drove back to town that night, the smell of gas was too much for him. He had the Marathon can resting on the floor in front of the passenger seat, and he couldn't bear to hear the gas that was left in it sloshing around.

"I was disgusted with myself," he said. "So I pulled over to the side of the road, and I got that can out, and I poured what was left into my car, as much as it'd hold anyway."

The deputy said, "There was about a gallon left in it when we found it in Brandi's shed."

"That sounds about right," said Ronnie. "That was all I could do. So I went back into town, and I put that can in the shed and then went in to go to bed."

Captain said, "We were in the bathroom when we first saw the fire. My dad went to the phone to call 911, and I ran out the front door and across the road. Angel and Hannah were outside. I ran around the end of the trailer to see if I could get in the back door. People think I'm stupid, but I knew what was happening. That trailer was on fire, and Della and the other kids were inside, and they needed help."

The whole back side of the trailer was in flames—flames leaping up to the windows, the siding already curling and melting, the back door wreathed with fire.

For the first time since he'd begun to tell his story, Captain's voice quavered. He bit his lip. He closed his eyes, squeezed them shut so tightly his face pinched up in a grimace. "There wasn't anything I could do," he finally said in a shaky whisper.

Shooter kept quiet. He let Captain tell his story.

"Then I saw Methuselah," he said.

The goat, calm now, had Captain's bomber jacket in his mouth. The sleeve of that jacket had gotten wrapped around one of his forelegs.

"It was on fire," Captain said. "My jacket sleeve. It was burning."

So was Methuselah, the vinyl of the burning sleeve melting into his hair and the skin beneath it. Captain ran to him.

"I threw my arms around him," he said, "and I wrestled him down. I hoped the snow would put out the fire."

Which it did. Captain got the bomber jacket free from Methuselah. Then he let the goat up and watched it run, disappearing into the night—into the place where the darkness held, black and deep, in spite of the fire.

When Captain got back around front, his father was there, and soon Pat Wade came running from his house, and Della was handing one of the twins out to Shooter. Captain stepped up and took her in his arms, tears running down his cheeks now because he knew.

"I knew exactly what had happened," he said. "I didn't want to know it, but I did."

For a good while, no one said a word. The clock ticked. The refrigerator hummed. The furnace clicked on.

Biggs waited for Captain to tell the rest of his story, but it was Shooter who spoke next. He said, "That vinyl from Captain's coat melted into that goat's leg, and I couldn't get it out. When the fire marshal's deputies started coming around, I was afraid they'd see it, and I didn't want them to know that Captain had been anywhere near that fire. That's why I put that goat down. I couldn't take the chance."

Biggs could see the guilt that must have wracked Shooter all those weeks. He could see it deep in his eyes—the pain he'd never be able to rid himself of, not even now that the story had been told. The telling only made it worse. The telling made it true.

"I had to protect Wesley," Shooter said.

His Adam's apple slid up and down his throat as he swallowed words he could hardly make himself say. Finally, though, he said them, and, when he did, Biggs felt his heart catch. He was a father, too.

"You're telling me your boy started that fire," Biggs said.

"I was afraid you'd take him away from me if the truth got out. Put him in a juvenile home. Or worse, try him as an adult and lock him up. I promised his mother I'd always look out for him."

Biggs said to Captain, "Son, you need to tell me everything. If you started that fire, I need you to tell me exactly how you did it."

It was a trick that Ronnie had showed him, a trick Captain had tried and tried to master and finally had.

That night behind the trailer, he said to Ronnie, "I won't tell anyone."

Ronnie knew he was saying he wouldn't let it out that he'd been there, wouldn't say a word about the gasoline. Captain was telling him he'd keep it all a secret. There was still time then to believe that such a thing was possible, that they could go their separate ways, step back into their lives and no one would be the wiser.

"You're a good friend," Ronnie said. "You're better than a million of me."

He knew he didn't deserve such goodness. He'd come out in the night to do a bad thing, but he'd spotted that hole in the trailer's siding, and then Captain was there, and now as much as Ronnie was relieved, he was humbled and ashamed to be standing before this simple boy who, no matter what he was up to with those goats, was good of heart enough to know there were things a man should ignore, things too ugly to let out into the air. Captain was doing him that favor, leaving him to go back into town and to do his best to face the truth about himself. He was the kind of man who could burn out his wife and kids, and Captain was passing no judgment on him for that, was telling him that would be his and his alone to live with.

"You always treated me good," Captain said. "You let me be your right-hand man."

Ronnie couldn't stop himself. He asked Captain why he'd come for the goats. "Why'd you take them?"

Captain's voice, when he finally spoke, was tinged with just the slightest air of disbelief, as if he couldn't imagine how Ronnie didn't know. "They need a better place," Captain said. "It's a cold, cold night. They need a warmer place to be."

That was enough to break Ronnie, the fact that Captain had come to do this favor. The wind was sweeping across the open fields. Overhead, the stars were brilliant in the clear sky. He wanted to put his arms around Captain. He wanted to thank him for being there on this night when he'd come to do harm. He wanted to press the boy to him and believe that people, even him, could be good.

But instead he said, "Guess we both need to get inside where it's warm."

Then he gathered up the Marathon can and made his way to his car. He was moving into the wind now, and he couldn't hear Captain calling his name. He didn't know that the boy had taken the box of Diamond matches from his jeans pocket, didn't know that he'd pressed the head of a match against the strike strip, didn't know that he'd flicked it with his finger—at that moment, the wind died down, and Ronnie felt the eerie calm after all the ruckus—didn't see that match, perfectly lit, twirling in the dark.

"Look what I can do," Captain said. "Look what you taught me."

But Ronnie couldn't make out the words. He was too far away.

Captain heard the Firebird come to life, not with a revving of the engine like Ronnie usually gave it, but with a low rumble of the exhaust pipes. The Firebird's tires cracked through the thin ice at the shoulder of the blacktop as the car eased forward. Captain went to the end of the trailer in enough time to see Ronnie creeping up the blacktop, no headlights on, the white of the snow cover on each side of the road enough to guide him before he felt it was safe to turn on his headlights and make his way back into town.

"Ronnie," Captain said, and he felt something warm his chest, something he had no words for—he only knew it had something to do with the way his mother had always made him believe that he was special, the Captain of the Universe. He only knew it had something to do with his father and Ronnie and Della and all the kids and Missy and Pat and, yes, even with Brandi Tate. Even the goats. All of them on this cold night.

Captain held that feeling inside him. He let it lead him home. He didn't know that his legs had brushed through the dry grass or that his boots had tracked through the gas that had pooled up on the frozen ground. He didn't think a thing about the match he'd lit and sent twirling toward the trailer. He didn't know that the match had fallen onto the old chair, but later he'd know—the kind of knowing you know in your knower, nary a need for proof—that the lit match had twirled and dropped through the suddenly still night and fallen in a place where the first flame, such a small thing it must have been, caught hold, took in fuel and air and before long became something headstrong and wild, nothing anyone could hope to stop.

Biggs listened to the story of the match. Then he said, "Son, where did that gas come from?"

"There was a can sitting on the ground behind the trailer."

"You didn't tote it from your place like your daddy thought?"

"No, it was just there."

Shooter said, "But you gave me cause to believe—"

Biggs interrupted him. He was growing impatient. "So you poured the gasoline around the trailer?"

Captain wouldn't answer. He got interested in the scab on his hand, picking at the crust. Biggs knew he wouldn't answer because he hadn't thought his story all the way through. He didn't have an answer because he hadn't been the one to spread that gasoline.

"Son, if there was a can of gas back there," Biggs said, "what happened to it?"

Shooter answered for him, "I guess it burned up in the fire."

"Fire marshal deputies went through everything left over there." Biggs shook his head. "No gas can. You know why, son?" Biggs waited for Captain to look at him, but he wouldn't. "Because Ronnie took that can away with him, didn't he? He was the one who poured that gas. Isn't that so, son? He poured it, and then, if what you're telling me is the truth, you lit it up."

Captain's voice was barely a whisper. "I didn't mean to. I just wanted to show Ronnie what I could do with that match."

"I didn't know any of that," Shooter said, his voice getting softer now. "I thought Wesley—you know—I thought—well, I wasn't too far off from what I thought to be true. I couldn't take a chance that you'd find out."

"So you made up that story about Ronnie," Biggs said, "and it turned out to be near enough true."

Shooter's voice was fierce now, pleading with Biggs. "Wouldn't you have done it too? Tell me, wouldn't you have done whatever it took to save your son?"

Biggs couldn't say what he would have done had he stood in Shooter's place, nor did he have an answer to the next question that Shooter asked.

"So tell me, Biggs, who's to hold to account? My boy or Ronnie Black?"

31

That was the question that haunted the folks in Phillipsport and Goldengate all through the rest of winter. It was a question, really, that wouldn't go away, not as long as there were folks alive who knew the story of Ronnie Black and his wife, Della, and how she and three of their children died late one night when their trailer caught on fire.

Caught on fire because a simpleminded boy loved a man who may have loved him back, but who, in the end, had no right to his devotion. Because the man made the boy feel special, and as a result the boy wanted to impress him with the trick he'd learned. Because the man went as far as to pour out that gasoline. Because the wind died down at the moment that lit match was twirling through the air. A trailer burned and four people died, and some said, *well what do you expect from a boy like that,* and some said, *that poor boy, no mother and now this.*

Laverne Ott said, "Wesley Rowe is God's child. He may not always think the way you and I do, but I'll tell you this, he knows what it is to love someone."

Of course, there was the matter of what to do now that the facts were clear: a pissed-off man sloshing gasoline on a trailer with the intent of setting it on fire and then coming to his senses and walking away; a boy who meant no harm striking the match that started the blaze.

Spilled gasoline, a fancy match trick, a cold winter night.

"I never meant to hurt anyone," Captain told Biggs. "Della was always good to me. I wanted to do something nice for her."

In the swirl of all the talk that followed Captain's confession, that was the one indisputable fact—he hadn't intended to set that trailer on fire.

"I didn't know anyone was in there," Shooter said again and again when he told his story. "I thought Della had taken the kids to her folks' house."

After Ray Biggs had Captain's story, he went back to the court-house, and one more time he sat across the table from Ronnie in the interrogation room, and he questioned him again about the events of the night the trailer burned.

"Tell it to me again, Ronnie," Biggs said. "Take your time."

So Ronnie went through it all—the gas can, Wesley Rowe, the goats, patching the hole in the siding with a strip from his T-shirt, the trip back to town, taking off the T-shirt and stuffing it under the pas-senger seat before going on to Brandi's house and getting into bed.

"I didn't want her to see that shirt, torn up like that. I was afraid if she saw it and asked what happened, I'd tell her everything. I didn't know how to tell her I'd gone to Della's meaning to burn the trailer." He bowed his head and didn't say a word for a good while. Then in a voice he was straining to hold steady, he said, "Then Pat Wade came with the news. He came to tell me—"

He couldn't go on, and Biggs took pity on him. "It was the boy." He told Ronnie about Captain and the lit match. "He wouldn't say that you poured that gas. Guess he was trying to keep that a secret. But we know you did, now don't we?"

Ronnie nodded, choking back the thickness in his throat that came to him when he thought of how Captain had done his best to protect him. He thought how there were two kinds of people in the world. There were people like Captain, and then there were people like him. There were people who were faithful, and there were people who weren't. "I patched that hole in the siding." Ronnie's eyes were wet. "I could do that much for my family, and that's what I did."

"You know that boy's not to blame for this," Biggs said. "But you? Even though you didn't do what you went out there to do, you still had the intent, a criminal intent, and you poured that gas, and then you walked away." He let Ronnie think about that a while. "You understand what I'm saying? Four people are dead because you did what you did. That's reckless homicide, Ronnie. That's exactly what that is."

"I'd go back and change it if I could."

The next day, Biggs carried the story to Lois and Wayne Best, and when Lois had heard all there was to hear, she asked Biggs if he could drive her over to the Rowes'. She had things she needed to say.

Biggs brought her to Shooter's house in his patrol car. She walked into that house, her back bent from her years of trying to move forward through the world, her worn-out knee balky but her head lifted and her eyes set straight ahead.

She didn't bother to take off her coat or to accept Shooter's offer of a chair.

"Ma'am," he finally said. He hadn't shaved—had barely slept, Biggs would wager—and now he looked wrung out and ready to pin to the line. "My boy, he didn't mean any harm."

Lois drew herself up as straight as she could. "I know what it is to have a child. Della knew that too. She did everything to make sure her kids were loved and safe. Put up with Ronnie's mess, cleaned other people's houses nearly every day of her life. We all did what we could for those kids."

Shooter rubbed his hand over his face. He looked so scared and lost. "I keep worrying over what's going to happen to Wesley. You know how some of the kids make fun of him."

"Where is he?" Lois asked. "Is he here?"

"Yes, ma'am," Shooter said. "I kept him out of school today. I figured the talk would be making its way around. He's back there in his room."

"I want to see him, please." Lois pointed down the hall. "This way?"

"First door on your left."

Shooter took a few steps ahead of her before Lois stopped him by grabbing onto his arm. "I'd like to be alone with him, please. Just the two of us. Just him and me."

"Well—" Shooter glanced at Biggs, looking for a sign of what he should do, and Biggs gave him a nod. "I guess that'd be all right." He stepped aside so Lois could move past him. "Yes, ma'am."

She tapped on the closed door with her knuckles. "Honey?" she said. "It's just Lois. You know me. I want to make sure you're all right."

When no answer came, she turned the knob and opened the door a crack. "I'm going to come in, honey. Is that all right?"

Captain's voice seemed to come from somewhere very far away, just a mumble, saying, "You won't yell at me?"

"Oh, honey. Don't you worry now."

He was sitting up in bed, a quilt over his legs, and Lois recognized that quilt right away. She knew it was one his mother had made after she got sick, working on it little by little as she felt up to it. It was a pattern called *Heart after Heart*—five rows of four hearts each, all pieced and appliquéd. "I want to do this for Wesley," she told Lois once when she came to visit. "I want him to know that I might be gone, but my heart will always be part of his."

Looking at it now, Lois knew the patience Merlene needed to do the hearts in all different shades of red and then frame them with a reddish-brown border. Lois could imagine her hoping that time would hold out until she finished, knowing she'd done everything she could for Wesley and now there was only this—this quilt to remind him of all the love they'd shared. Maybe in some small way, whenever he felt sad or afraid or alone, he'd be able to look at that quilt and think of her.

He was rubbing his hand gently over one of the hearts now.

"You miss your mother, don't you?" Lois said to him.

"She wouldn't like what I did."

Lois sat down on the edge of the bed. "No, she probably wouldn't, but she'd forgive you. I have absolutely no doubt about that."

Captain looked at her. "She would?"

"Yes, she would. She loved you for you. No matter what, you were her son." Lois scooted closer to him and held her arms open. "Come on," she said. "Let me hug you."

She sat there a good while, letting him press his face into her neck, patting his back while he sobbed, telling him over and over, "Hush, now. Hush. Everything's going to be all right."

Finally, once Captain had cried himself out, Lois asked him if he'd eaten anything.

"Not since lunch yesterday."

"Lordy, you must be starving. Get dressed. I'm going to make something for you." He looked at her, hesitating. "There's only one thing to do when trouble comes," she said. "I know it for a fact. Get out of bed every morning. Keep moving ahead."

She went back to the living room, where Biggs and Shooter were still standing. Shooter was leaning against the wall, his head bowed. He was rubbing the back of his neck. Biggs had his hat in his hand, turning it around by its brim.

Lois said to Biggs in a soft voice, as if it were only the two of them in the room, "Our baby's gone, and her babies, too, and nothing's going to change that. Wesley Rowe? He's still alive. I don't want any hurt to come to him."

Not everyone was willing to overlook Captain's part in the fire. Even though it was generally known that Ronnie had gone to the trailer with the intent to burn it, had spread that gas before having a change of heart and driving away, there were still folks who couldn't get beyond the fact that if Captain, a boy who wasn't right from the get-go, had been home in his bed as he should have been that night and not out there striking matches, Della and her three children would still be alive. Too many people had invested too much in the suspicion that Ronnie set the fire, and even though he was the one who'd pay the price, they couldn't help but spread the blame to Captain as well.

Boys at school made goat noises sometimes when he was near. They flicked lit matches at him and called him Scarecrow after the character in *The Wizard of Oz*.

Whether it was those boys who night after night came driving by the Rowe house, their car and truck horns blasting, or else adults who'd forgotten how to be civil, no one could say.

Then someone went too far. Someone came one night when Shooter and Captain were in Phillipsport doing their grocery shopping, and they went to work on the side of the barn with a red spray paint can. It was the side people could see from the road. They could drive by and see the gigantic red letters spelling out KILLER.

That was too much for Missy. She knocked on Shooter's door and told him she was sorry for his trouble.

"I don't approve of the way you handled things," she said, "but you and Captain don't deserve this."

"Yes, I do," he said, and then he closed the door.

———

Ronnie told Angel he was sorry. He should have told her everything the night she showed him his pocketknife, hoping that he'd have some explanation. He did, but he didn't know how to say the right words to her then, so he kept quiet, and in his silence, a horrible possibility took life.

"You know it all now," he told Angel. "You know I got mad at your mother, and I started to do something bad." Even though he'd never wanted his girls to know that he'd had thoughts about burning the trailer, had gone as far as spreading some gasoline, it was out in the open now, and he had no choice but to own up to it. "But I stopped myself. I got back to a better way of thinking. I patched the hole in the trailer to keep the pilot light on the furnace from going out. I had no idea you were all inside. I wish I'd knocked on your door. Maybe your mother would have asked me to come inside, and then who knows what might have happened." His voice got so shaky then he could barely make the words he knew he had to say. "After it happened—after the fire—I was afraid you'd never want me. I didn't know how to tell you I'd been there that night. I was there, but not when I needed to be. Not when I might have made a difference. I'll know that the rest of my life."

Angel said, "Brandi lied to me when she was in the hospital and she told me the story of that night."

"She didn't want you to think bad of me," Ronnie said, "and right now I'm scared to death that you'll never forgive me."

Angel threw herself into his arms. She held him tight. She told him how she'd seen sparks outside her bedroom window just before the fire, but she hadn't thought to get out of bed and move the ash box to the compost the way she was supposed to have done earlier that evening. She told him about how her mother had awakened her that night and told her the trailer was on fire.

"She told me to wake the others and help them to get out." Here she paused, her breath coming hard, reliving it all in her mind. "I didn't do it. Hannah was awake, and I told her to run. I ran with her. If I'd only tried to help."

"Shh." Ronnie rocked her in his arms. "Shh, now, baby. Shh. You didn't do anything wrong."

Ronnie waited while the State went through the process of discovering all the facts. In Illinois, his attorney told him, reckless homicide was a Class 3 felony, punishable by two to five years in prison, but probation was a possibility—a strong possibility, the attorney said, given the tragic circumstances and the fact that there were four daughters who needed their father.

Ronnie was able to hire his attorney because Missy Wade turned over the account at the bank to him.

When he called to thank her, she said, "I don't imagine I'll ever get over any of this." Then she told him the story of the day in the bank when her silence started the rumor that he'd had something to do with the fire. "Even though you did what you did, it wasn't right of me to let that gossip spread, and I've got no right now to keep watch on that money."

The State decided not to prosecute. Even though Ronnie had gone to the trailer that night, he'd done so on the assumption that Della and the kids were at Lois and Wayne's. Yes, he'd meant to set the trailer on fire, but in the end he'd come to his senses. He'd held his temper in check. He'd never meant for anyone to come to harm.

And now there were his girls to see to, those girls who had suffered enough.

The court put Ronnie on probation and left the question of custody of the children to another hearing.

Missy testified. She spoke of Ronnie's love for the girls.

"He made mistakes," she said. "We all made mistakes. But at the end of the day it's clear to me that he loves those girls. I had no business to try to take them from him, and I wouldn't want to now. He's their father. I don't believe he means them any harm, never meant to hurt them at all."

Laverne Ott said the options were few. Lois and Wayne were in poor health, and if Missy and Pat, the godparents, were saying they trusted Ronnie, and if the court wanted to avoid a foster home situation, as Laverne believed they did as long as a biological parent was capable and willing, then the proper thing to do would be to entrust the girls' care to Ronnie.

Finally, the judge asked Laverne to bring each of the girls individually to his chambers.

He asked them, one by one, where they wanted to live.

Angel was direct. "Brandi needs us. We want to be a family."

Hannah was earnest. "I love my father."

Sarah had a puzzled look on her face. "Aren't kids supposed to live with their parents?"

Emma simply said, "Daddy and Brandi."

"You want to live with your daddy?" the judge asked.

"Yeppers," Emma said.

Then the judge asked to speak to Ronnie and Laverne.

"Mr. Black, I can't say I'm pleased with you."

"No, sir," Ronnie said.

"You can see why this is a difficult decision."

"Yes, sir, I can. I've not always been an upright man, but this has changed me. I've owned up to everything. I'm just hoping for a chance to keep my girls."

The judge tapped the end of a pencil on his desk and studied Ronnie a good long while.

"Children's Protective Services will have a sharp eye on you. Isn't that right, Miss Ott?"

"You can count on it," Laverne said.

"And this court will be watching you. Mr. Black, I feel you've lost enough. Make sure you make good on this second chance."

Brandi and Ronnie gave the story of Captain a good deal of thought on those evenings when Ronnie sat with her while she was lying in bed as her doctor had commanded. Brandi had already thought hard about what she knew about Ronnie. He'd gone out to the trailer that night meaning to burn it. He spread that gasoline. Then he saw a hole in the siding and got his senses back. He tried to do a good thing. He patched that hole and then he came back to town and got into bed beside her. He was still there. After everything they'd gone through, he was still there. The baby was coming, and she wasn't alone. She told Ronnie to forgive himself for what he almost did that night. She told him to believe in love.

Her due date at the first of July seemed far in the distance, but neither she nor Ronnie complained. Time seemed to slow down for them, and that's exactly what they needed. Too much had been happening too quickly. Now they had the drowsy evenings of winter. They had time to talk.

They played board games with the girls. Then once Ronnie had them off to bed, he and Brandi lay close together, and he rubbed his hand gently over her stomach and felt the baby kick, and the joy of those moments was so pure and good there was no need for either of them to say a word.

In the moonlight slanting through the window and falling across their faces, they began to talk.

Brandi said, "I bet you're sorry you ever ended up with me."

No, Ronnie told her. He wasn't sorry. "We're going to have a baby," he said.

"Sometimes I still have trouble with what you did." She reached over and took his hand. "I won't lie about that."

They lay together awhile, not speaking. Then Ronnie said, "It could have been true. All of it. I was that close to setting that trailer to burn."

"What I've decided is maybe we're all that close to doing things we'd regret. The right chain of circumstances, and there we are."

"I know, but still."

"We both have to let it go. Your girls need us. This baby needs us. Day by day, we'll go on."

Ronnie knew in his heart that Captain hadn't meant for that match to catch the gas on fire. At night, he and Brandi talked it over.

Sure, maybe Captain didn't have any business taking it upon himself to even think about burning down the goat pen and shed— and on a windy night like that, no less—but Ronnie knew, from all the time he'd spent with Captain while he worked on the Firebird, the boy was always eager to please. Ronnie knew how close he felt to Della, especially after his mother died.

"He didn't mean for any of this to happen," Ronnie said to Brandi. "Shooter should have been better with him, but who am I to say that? I guess I'm not exactly the Father of the Year."

"I imagine it's been hard for him to raise a boy like Captain by himself," Brandi said.

Ronnie agreed. "I'm sorry now to see the way some folks are treating them. So much of that is my fault."

That's when Brandi had the idea of taking out ads in the Goldengate and Phillipsport newspapers.

"Why would anyone listen to me?" Ronnie asked. "They're ready to run me out of town."

"You'll see," said Brandi, and then she told him how she thought it might work.

When the ad came out in the papers, it was the talk of Phillipsport and Goldengate. Mr. Samms and DeMova Dugger at the Wabash Savings and Loan saw it when Mr. Samms stepped out of the office that afternoon to appraise a property and came back with the *Messenger*.

"Good for him," Mr. Samms said after he'd showed the ad to DeMova. "He said it just right, and I hope people listen. And he had the courage to put his name to it."

"It was a horrible accident," DeMova said. "That's what it was. That poor boy didn't mean to burn that trailer."

In Goldengate, the ad came out that same day in the *Weekly Press*. Anna Spillman sat at the counter at the Real McCoy and leafed through a copy on her afternoon break. When she saw the ad, she recalled how Ronnie spent that night with her when Brandi put him out. He was lost that night, all scraped out. "What am I going to do?" he asked her. "Other folks know trouble," she told him. "You just keep remembering you're not alone."

When she saw the words he'd put in the paper, she felt her breath catch. "Oh, my," she said, and Herbert Quick came around the counter to see what she was reading.

"That's the truth." He tapped his finger on the ad. "You have to admire a man for saying the truth, no matter what you might happen to think of him."

Not everyone agreed. Taylor Jack read the ad and thought to himself, *Who in the hell does he think he is, saying something like that?*

"And in the newspaper, no less," said Roe Carl the next day at the IGA. "Leave it alone, if you ask me."

Missy read the paper before bed, and the ad nearly took her breath away. When she got down on her knees to pray that night, she asked God to forgive her for whatever mistakes she'd made all because she'd been so eager to have children of her own.

Shooter Rowe saw the ad when he sat down with the paper after supper. "Come in here," he said to Captain, who was finishing drying the dishes. "Come look what Ronnie's done."

Captain looked over his father's shoulder as he read the ad aloud.

"In spite of everything." Shooter's voice was strong and clear in the quiet house. "I still believe that people are really good at heart." That part of the ad was in quotation marks, and Shooter knew it came from the diary Anne Frank kept while in hiding from the Nazis. He knew this because the book of that diary had been one of Merlene's favorites. She'd written out that quote in her beautiful handwriting and kept it in her Bible. In the ad, Ronnie's words came after the quotation, and Shooter read them aloud, too. "I can't change what's done. Neither can you. We all have lives to live. We need to help one another. We need to forgive. That's what I aim to do. In my heart of hearts, I hope you'll do the same."

For a good while, neither of them spoke. Then Captain said, "He's talking about me."

Shooter let the paper settle down onto his lap. "He's talking about all of us, Wesley. He's saying we ought to know we're all doing the best we can."

Brandi had read *The Diary of Anne Frank* while she'd been on bed rest, and the part about believing that people were good stuck with her. After she'd written that down for the ad, she told Ronnie to just speak from his heart.

"What do you want to say to folks?" she asked.

He thought for a minute. "I want to tell them we all mess up and do things wrong. Things happen and we can't go back and change them. All we can do is try to be better. Something like that."

"Keep talking," Brandi said. "We've got all night. I'll help you say it just the way you want."

At that moment, when she lifted the pen from the paper, the frayed friendship bracelet that Hannah had woven for her fell from her wrist.

"Looks like I get my wish," she said.

"What did you wish for?"

"This. All of this right now. You and me and the girls."

They were alive to him now more so than they'd ever been. Everyone who mattered to him was more alive—the girls and Brandi and Pat and Missy Wade and Shooter and Captain, and, yes, Wayne and Lois, even the woman Della had been in his last days with her, the woman who loved having a baby in the house. They were more alive to him because of the part of the story he swore he'd never tell, the part that left him knowing in a way he never had how scared they all were, how broken.

He hadn't told Ray Biggs and his deputy everything about the night the trailer burned. He hadn't told it all to Brandi. He wished he could. He especially wished he could say it to Captain, the one who most needed to hear it.

Ronnie wanted to tell him that when he first pulled away from the trailer that night, he glanced up to his rearview mirror, and he saw Captain standing at the edge of the trailer looking after him as if he expected him to change his mind and come back.

Just a shadowy figure out there in the cold, but it was enough to remind Ronnie of how he'd felt all the times he'd been the new boy at a foster home, how all of the other foster kids knew one another, and he was too shy to try to be their friend. How he waited for them to come to him, to treat him with kindness, but that rarely happened. More often than not, they thought him standoffish and weird, and they left him to the misery he nursed in his heart.

"If you'd just smile more," a helpful boy said to him once, "maybe people would like you."

He'd been that boy, the one who wouldn't smile.

When Ronnie saw Captain standing there in the moonlight, he almost stopped the Firebird, almost threw it in reverse and went back to the trailer, but he couldn't imagine what he'd say to explain why he'd returned. He had no words for what he wanted, no words at all. He only knew that deep down he wanted to stand there again with Captain, who refused to judge him, who knew from experience that people were mostly just who they were and all you could do was try to love them for that. But as much as Ronnie wanted to give himself over to Captain's goodness, he was too ashamed to admit that he needed it. He was too ashamed to admit that he'd needed it all along, that Captain, a boy he'd only thought he was humoring with his attention, had mattered to him much more than he'd known, had been the one who could have saved him.

So he kept his foot on the gas pedal. He put his eyes on the dark road stretching out ahead of him.

He glanced back only once, and, when he did, Captain was gone.

Ronnie went a good ways up the blacktop before he turned on his headlights, and when he did, a quick picture came into his head and he wondered whether just before he'd looked away from Captain in his rearview mirror, he'd seen a spark of light flash behind the trailer. He slowed down. He almost turned around. Then he told himself, no, he was only imagining things. He was only afraid of what he'd almost done. He was afraid of himself.

That's when he punched the Firebird, worked it through its gears, gave it full throttle, in a hurry now to make his way back to town.

That was the moment that would haunt him forever, the moment in which he almost knew there was danger, when he almost went back. The fire wouldn't have been raging just yet. He could have done something to stop it, and even if he hadn't been able to do that, he would have been there when it became clear that his family was inside, and he would have gotten them out.

He wanted to tell Captain that there was that moment when he convinced himself nothing was wrong, that moment when, eager to escape his own shame, he drove up the blacktop, choosing to be ignorant. Captain wasn't the stupid one. He was.

Remember that, he wished he could say to Captain. *Your father was right. He was right all along. I was the stupid one. I was selfish and stupid, and now here I am, too much of a coward to tell you any of this.*

Brandi tapped her pen on the paper, and Ronnie remembered he was supposed to be telling her what he wanted to say in the newspaper.

"Keep talking," she told him.

His voice was soft, but in their rooms, Angel and Hannah and Sarah and Emma almost came up from sleep. He never spoke loudly enough to completely rouse them, but the murmur of his voice was something they felt just at the edge of waking. In that twilight, they listened long enough to know they were hearing their father, a fact that brought them comfort as they sank back into sleep on this cold winter night. They were all there in the house. They were warm beneath their covers. They had tomorrow waiting on them and the day after that. A baby was coming, and they were all doing what they could to help Brandi make her way to July.

"Do you want me to write it like this?" she asked Ronnie.

She wrote another line and then let him read it.

"Yes," he said.

People were asleep in Goldengate and Phillipsport, and out the blacktop into the country. Snow was falling—a steady snow that would cover the fields, settle over the roofs of the houses where Wayne and Lois Best slept, where Shooter and Captain slept, where Missy and Pat Wade slept. A snow that would blanket the graves behind the

Bethlehem Church. An all-night snow coming down on what was left of the trailer after the fire. Coming down to cover, at least for a while, the charred scraps of furniture and bedding and dishes and toys and clothing and photographs and everything that had once made the trailer a home. The last big snow of winter, but Ronnie and Brandi took no notice.

"Go on," she told him, and he did.

Acknowledgments

This book wouldn't exist without the faith and effort of my agent, Allison Cohen. I'm forever grateful for her encouragement, support, and her sharp editorial eye. Guy Intoci made this book better, and I'm indebted to him and everyone at Dzanc Books for welcoming me into the fold. There were people who knew things that I didn't, and they generously shared their expertise with me. Thank you, Philip Grandinetti, Dale Perdue, and Ruth Ann Zwilling. Thanks, too, to the Ohio State University for their continued support. Above all, thank you to Cathy Hensley for the love she gives me every step along the journey's way.